Keeping Her

By Allie Everhart

Keeping Her
By Allie Everhart

Copyright © 2015 Allie Everhart
All rights reserved.
Published by Waltham Publishing, LLC
Cover Design by Okay Creations
ISBN: 978-1-942781-03-5

CHAPTER ONE

PEARCE

Rachel and I just returned from Las Vegas. Royce flew us there on his private jet but we took a commercial flight home. We probably shouldn't have taken Royce's jet to Vegas. Nobody knew Rachel was on it, but if my father or one of the members ever found out, people would know Royce helped me elope and he'd be punished. I can't let that happen, which is why I played it safe and Rachel and I flew back on a regular plane.

I need to keep Royce out of this. He came up with this plan and helped me execute it, and I don't want him to be harmed because of it. I don't want anyone suspecting he had any involvement in it. The story will be that Royce thought he and I were just having a guys' weekend in Vegas, but that I invited Rachel to meet me there without telling him.

I've never liked Royce, but he actually did something nice for once and I need to protect him from any fallout. I'm sure he'll make me repay him someday and that's fine. After he helped me out like this, I owe him.

"It feels like we've been gone for more than a few days," Rachel says.

We landed in New Haven and are now on our way to Rachel's apartment. I had to hire someone to bring my car to the airport so I'd have it.

"I wish we could've stayed longer," I say.

"Me too."

I glance over and see her smiling at me. She hasn't stopped smiling since the wedding. I love seeing her so happy. I wish her happiness could continue, but I know it won't. The next few weeks, or months, will be bad. My family. My so-called friends. Everyone I know will try to ruin this for us, and they'll do so by attacking Rachel. They'll berate her. Tell her she doesn't fit in my world. Try to turn her against me so she'll leave me.

I'll do my best to shield Rachel from these things, but I can only do so much. It'll be pure hell for a while, for both of us. I've tried to warn her, but she won't truly understand what I mean until she's actually living it. Until she's actually experienced that side of my life that she hasn't yet been exposed to.

Part of me wants to take her away from all that. Start somewhere new. Begin an entirely new life with her and leave my past life behind.

I know I can't do that. The organization would never let me. They'd track me down and drag me back here and punish me for trying to leave. They own me. They own my life, or at least the part of it Rachel doesn't know about.

And then there's my father. I don't even want to think what his punishment would be if I ran off with Rachel. The punishment for marrying her will be bad enough. I have no idea what he's going to do to me. I'm sure he's heard the news by now. He doesn't watch TV but I'm sure someone's told him.

I feel Rachel squeeze my hand. "Pearce. Are you awake over there?"

"Yes." I smile at her, then focus back on the road. "I'm just tired from the trip. It was a long flight."

"I think our lack of sleep the last couple nights might've had something to do with why you're so tired."

"I think you're right." My mood lifts for a moment as I think back to last weekend. Rachel and I never left the hotel room. And she's correct when she said we didn't sleep much. Our time was spent in bed, but not sleeping.

It was pure heaven. And now we're heading to hell.

2

"I can't believe that's the first time you've ever flown commercial," she says.

I merge into the turn lane. "We've always had the jet, so there was no need for me to fly commercial. Besides, my father wouldn't be caught dead on a regular plane. He thinks it's beneath him."

"Has your mother ever been on one?"

"Yes. Before they were married, my mother travelled a lot. Her family also had a jet, but if it wasn't available she'd fly commercial. First class, of course."

"First class was incredible," Rachel says with a happy sigh. "I never thought I'd fly first class."

"Well, that's all you'll be flying now. Or we'll take the private jet."

"I don't know, Pearce. I don't feel safe on those tiny planes. You saw how nervous I was on Royce's plane."

I rub her hand. "I thought you were nervous because of the wedding, not the plane."

She shifts in her seat, turning toward me. "I wasn't nervous at all about the wedding. I was surprised by your proposal, but once the shock wore off and you explained why we needed to elope, I was all in."

"So you don't regret it?"

"Pearce." I look over and see her smile is gone. "Of course I don't regret it. Don't even say that. I love you, and I'm ready to start our life together." She pauses. "Are *you* having regrets?"

"Absolutely not." I bring her hand to my mouth and kiss it. "Marrying you is the best decision I've ever made."

Her smile returns. "Mine was calling your number."

"My number?" I turn onto her street, stopping as the light at the intersection turns red. "What do you mean?"

"Back in September, after you gave me your business card, I almost didn't call you."

I glance at her. "After a week had passed, I assumed you never would."

"You were waiting for me to call?"

3

"Waiting and hoping. I barely got any work done that week. I couldn't stop thinking about you. I wanted to see you again, but I didn't have your phone number." The light turns green and I continue toward Rachel's apartment building. "So what made you decide to call?"

"Shelby talked me into it. I didn't think you'd ever agree to go out with me, but she said I should at least ask. And good thing she did or I may have never called you."

It's ironic that Shelby is the one who talked Rachel into calling me, given how much Shelby tried to keep me away from her. But if Shelby had known it was *me* Rachel was calling, she would've told Rachel not to do it. She would've talked her out of it.

We're parked now and Rachel takes her seat belt off. "It's strange that I'm not going to live here anymore."

"It's not strange. It's good," I say, just as two men walk by on the sidewalk. They look like they just got out of prison. "You'll finally be out of this neighborhood."

I step out of the car and the two men turn back, eyeing my Mercedes. I stare at them, and when they notice me doing so, they glance away. I go around and open Rachel's door and help her out.

"I'll hire movers to get the rest of your things," I tell Rachel as I take her hand and we walk to her building. "I don't want you coming back here." I keep my eyes on those two men, who keep glancing back at my car.

"I don't need movers." She unlocks the door to her building and we go inside. "I don't have much stuff. It won't take me long to pack everything and load it into my car. And I'm not packing everything yet. I'll still be coming back here during the day between classes."

We're walking up the stairs and I stop her. "Rachel, if you need a place to go between classes, I'll get you a different place. A safer place."

She laughs. "Pearce, you're being crazy. I'm not renting a place for a month just so I can use it for a few hours."

We continue up the stairs. "Did you see those two men out there? I don't trust them and I don't want you around them."

"What men? I don't know who you're talking about."

"They walked by when we got here. They kept looking back at us. They looked like criminals."

"You shouldn't make judgments about people based on how they look. And you usually don't, which is one of the many reasons I love you." She stops briefly to kiss me.

Her refusal to see people for what they are is extremely frustrating. She only wants to see the good in people, refusing to believe that anyone is truly bad. She thinks bad people just need to be given a chance and they'll suddenly turn good. She doesn't realize that some people are just plain bad and always will be. There's no hope for them. They have no desire to change. I know this because I know people who truly are bad. My father, for one.

When we get to the door of Rachel's apartment, Shelby's door swings open and she bursts into the hall. "Rachel, where have you been? I haven't seen you for days and I was getting worried."

"I was with Pearce." She motions to me with her left hand.

Shelby grabs Rachel's hand, looking at her ring. "Oh my God! Did you get engaged?"

Rachel pauses like she forgot the fake story for a moment. But then she remembers and smiles. "Yes! Pearce and I are engaged."

"Congratulations!" Shelby hugs her, and as she does, she scowls at me and mouths the words 'What the fuck?'

I knew she'd be angry. But I told Shelby I wanted a future with Rachel so she shouldn't be surprised. And Shelby knows how much Rachel and I love each other, so she needs to stop interfering and focus on her own life.

When the two of them break apart, Shelby extends her hand to me. "Congratulations, Pearce."

I shake her hand. "Thank you."

This is awkward. It's the first time the three of us have been together since Rachel found out I slept with Shelby.

Rachel glances between Shelby and me. I step closer to Rachel and put my arm around her and kiss the top of her head. I don't

5

want Rachel even thinking I have any kind of feelings for Shelby. Maybe she isn't thinking that, but even so, I want to make it very clear to Rachel that she is the only woman for me.

Rachel looks up at me and smiles, then looks back at Shelby. "So how's your dad?"

"He's doing better. I mean, he's not *getting* better. He's still terminal, but this new medication he's on is helping with the pain."

"So that doctor was able to help? What was his name again?"

"Logan," she says. "Well, Dr. Cunningham. I call him Logan." She blushes a little. Why is she blushing? "Anyway, he's really smart and seems to know what he's doing."

"Is he still in town?" I ask her.

"No, but he's coming back in a few days to check on my dad. He said he'll probably come check on him twice a week."

Twice a week? I assumed Logan would just give her father some pills and that would be it. I didn't think he'd continue to make home visits.

"You'll have to let me know when he's here again," I say. "I'd like to meet him for coffee and catch up. I haven't seen him in years."

"You could come by the house next time he's here."

"I don't want to disturb your family. Your father needs his rest."

"Actually, my dad was wondering if you'd stop by so he could thank you for introducing us to Logan. I mean, Dr. Cunningham."

I can't be going to Shelby's house. That would be overstepping boundaries. We can't have outside contact with the associates, although I've already broken that rule several times.

"Tell your father it's not necessary. There's no need to thank me. I was happy to help."

"He really wants to meet you," Shelby says. "My mom does too."

"You should go," Rachel says to me. "I'll go with you." She looks at Shelby. "If that's okay."

"Yeah, that'd be great. My mom keeps saying she wants to meet you. I told her I have this weird friend who hugs everyone she meets." Shelby smiles. "Maybe you guys could stop by next weekend, after all the holiday stuff is over. By the way, what are you doing for Thanksgiving?"

Rachel looks at me. "We're going to my parents' house."

"I bet you've never been to Indiana," Shelby says to me.

"No. I never have." I smile at Rachel. "I'm looking forward to it."

I told Rachel I'd go to Indiana with her for Thanksgiving, but I'm not sure if I can. I need to deal with my parents first. They'll be furious when they find out I got married, so I may have to stay here and deal with the fallout rather than go to Indiana with Rachel. But for now, I'm planning on going.

Shelby looks at us both. "Did you guys go out of town? Is that why you haven't been around?"

"We were in Las Vegas for—" Rachel stops before she says any more.

We weren't going to tell people we went to Vegas because if we did, they'd assume we got married, and that needs to remain a secret, at least to people like Shelby. We'll tell our families, and when we do, my father will tell the organization, but other people can't know.

"We just went for the weekend." Rachel opens her door. "I need to use the bathroom. I'll be right back."

She goes in her apartment, and when the door shuts, Shelby glares at me and whispers, "You MARRIED her?"

"We're not married," I say casually. "We're engaged."

"Don't lie to me, Pearce." She's still whispering. "I know you married her. Why else would you go to Vegas?"

"There was no other way," I say quietly. "You know the rules."

"Are you saying they can't do anything now that you two are married?"

"I don't know, but you need to stay the hell out of it. You need to go along with the engagement story and you need to act happy about it. If you don't, she'll assume your negative attitude means there's something going on between us. She's still upset about finding your earring. She says she's over it, but I know she's not. So you need to stop being so angry and be happy for us."

Shelby glances at Rachel's door, then back at me. "You love her, right?"

"More than anything."

"And you'll protect her?"

"With my life."

"You'll make her happy?"

"I'll spend the rest of my days trying."

She sighs and rolls her eyes. "Fine. Then I guess you kinda, sorta have my blessing. Not completely, but maybe if you give her a baby someday, I'll give you the rest of it. If she can't have one, then adopt one. She really wants a baby."

I half smile. "I'll see what I can do."

The baby issue is one Rachel and I haven't yet discussed, but Shelby's right. More than anything, Rachel wants a child someday. But she's been told she can't have one. And I don't want children. I would make a terrible father, and if I ever had children, they'd be forced into my world. They'd be part of the organization and I won't let that happen.

I thought Shelby knew this, but apparently she doesn't, or she doesn't fully understand the rules, because if she did, she wouldn't be telling me to have a child with Rachel.

Rachel appears again. "Pearce, we should probably start packing."

"You're moving?" Shelby asks her.

"Now that we're engaged, I decided to move into Pearce's loft."

"It'll be easier that way," I say, giving Shelby a look, reminding her not to interfere.

She gets my look and smiles at Rachel. "I'll miss you, but I totally understand. You need to be with your fiancé."

Rachel hugs her. "We'll still be friends. I'll call you every day, and we'll meet for lunch or go out for coffee, okay?"

"Yeah." Shelby opens her door. "I need to go, but I'll talk to guys later. If I don't see you again this week, have a nice Thanksgiving."

"You too," Rachel says.

Shelby goes into her apartment and Rachel and I go into hers. As she's walking to the kitchen, I grab her from behind and wrap my arms around her.

"Pearce." She's laughing. "What are you doing?"

"I was stuck on that plane for hours." I trail kisses down her neck. "I finally have you alone."

She turns around, smiling. "We don't have time for that. I have to pack and then I need to study."

"You can do that later," I say, kissing her. Just the feel of her lips immediately turns me on. We spent the past two days doing it, but somehow it wasn't enough. I press myself against her. "I want to be with my wife."

She smiles even more. "Okay, but we have to be quick."

"Don't rush me," I say, my lips brushing against her ear. "I don't like being rushed." I place my hands around her waist and slowly lift her sweater up and over her head. It's a light blue cashmere sweater that my personal shopper picked out. Rachel would have a fit if she knew how much it cost, but she needs to get over it. She needs to get used to the fact that money is no longer a concern.

Even if my father disowns me, I still have my trust fund, and it contains more money than we'll ever need. When I turned 21, I was given full access to it. The money is officially mine and my father can't touch it. And now it's Rachel's money as well and she can spend it as she chooses.

I reach around and unzip her skirt, another purchase I made. Before we left for Vegas, I bought Rachel a suitcase and filled it with new clothes. All designer. All very expensive. And worth every penny. She looks gorgeous in them. Then again, she looks gorgeous in anything.

"Pearce," she breathes out, her eyes closed, her head tipped back as I kiss the delicate skin over her throat. I tug on her skirt until it falls to the floor. I'm left with her standing there in the lingerie I bought her; a champagne-colored silk and lace bra with matching panties.

Looking at her like this has me so aroused that it's straining the fabric of my pants. Rachel reaches down and unzips them, relieving some of the pressure, but then she touches me and I ache to be inside her.

I scoop her up into my arms and take her to the bedroom, setting her down on the bed. I shove my pants and boxers down and rip my shirt over my head. I told her I wasn't going to hurry, but now I can't slow down. And she can't either. She already has her bra off, so I quickly slip off her panties and put myself inside her. And then I slow down, kissing her cheek and then her lips.

"I love you," I whisper.

"I love you too," she says.

I open my eyes and see her looking at me. Her face always conveys so much emotion. She never tries to hide it. And right now, it conveys an overwhelming love. For me. I don't understand why she loves me, and maybe I never will, but I know she does. I can feel it.

Our eyes remain on each other as I move in and out in a slow, steady rhythm. I'd never looked at a woman while having sex until I did so with Rachel. She asked me to open my eyes, so I did. At first, it was too intimate for me and I had to close them. But the next time we did it, as uncomfortable as it was, I kept them open. I felt exposed, because I know my eyes express what I'm feeling. I can mask the emotion on my face, but my eyes can't hide it. And Rachel always knows what my eyes are saying. So I let her see them, and we reached a level of closeness I've never had with anyone else. She saw me at my most vulnerable. It was the most intimate experience I've ever shared with someone. And now, I crave that intimacy with her. I crave the closeness and the emotions shared between us when we're together like this. Sex is no longer just physical for me. It's so much more. More than I ever thought sex could be.

Rachel's hands go down my back, holding onto me as I thrust harder and quicken my pace. She's signaling me to keep going, so I do, and she matches my movements and we continue until we both go over the edge, her first and then me.

I lie on my back and she hugs my chest, her head on my shoulder, a blissful smile on her face. I kiss her forehead and take a moment to gaze at her.

She's so incredibly beautiful. Her body is perfect. All those years of competitive swimming have given her lean shapely muscles, but she still has womanly curves and soft, full breasts. As I look at her, I can't believe she's my wife. How is it possible I convinced the most beautiful woman on earth to marry me? And to marry me for *me*? And not my money?

Truthfully, she didn't marry the real me. She only married the man she knows. I've hidden my dark side and only allowed her to see the good. If she knew all of me, she wouldn't be here right now. Even though she's someone who always sees the good in people, if she really knew me, I don't think she could look past what I've done. Or what I'll have to do in the future.

The thought of that makes my muscles tense and Rachel notices.

She lifts her head up slightly. "Pearce, is everything okay?"

"It's more than okay." I kiss her forehead. "It'd been far too long since we'd done that."

She laughs. "We did it this morning before we left."

"That was hours ago." I check the clock. "I suppose we should get going."

She moves off me and sits up. "I'll start packing my clothes. I'm just going to leave all my other stuff here for now since I'll be here between classes."

"Rachel. I told you, I don't want you coming back here."

"It's just during the day. I'll be at your place at night."

I sit up, leaning against the wall. "It's OUR place now. This isn't your place anymore. You don't need to come back here. Go to a coffee shop between classes. Or go to the library."

She turns to me. "Why are you being like this? I lived here just last week and you were fine with it."

"I was never fine with it. And I told you that, several times. But now you're my wife and I can't have you staying at a place like this. Not even during the day."

"Why?"

I didn't want to get into this now, but I guess I can't put it off any longer.

"What is it, Pearce?"

"Now that our relationship is public, things will need to change. Even though people think we're only engaged, and not married, it still changes things."

"Like what?"

"Where you live. How you dress. What car you drive."

"What are you saying? I can't drive my car? You just had it repaired. It's completely safe to drive. It's like brand new."

"It's not brand new. It's twelve years old. And although it's safe, it's not the type of car Pearce Kensington's fiancé should be driving. You need to be seen in something new. Something expensive."

"That's ridiculous. Who's going to notice or care what car I'm driving?"

"The people I associate with, for one. But also people in the media. Reporters. Magazine editors. Now that the media has been told about us, they'll want to find out as much as they can about you. And if they see you staying in a place like this and driving an old car, they'll start making up stories to explain why someone with my kind of money would let his fiancé live in such a dangerous neighborhood or drive an old car."

"It's none of their business where I live or what car I drive."

"I agree, but unfortunately my private life isn't always private. And with this announcement of our engagement, we've just made our relationship very public." I see the worry in her face. She's all new to this and it's going to be a huge change for her. "Rachel, as I've told you before, this isn't going to be easy. Being in my life means people will always be talking about you. Making

12

assumptions. Making up lies about you, and about us. Judging your clothes. Your hair. The way you speak. The words you use. And they'll twist those words to have whatever meaning they want them to have. Up until now, I've lived a fairly private life. Aside from the publicity surrounding my previous marriage, I've tried to be very discreet in my personal life so people will leave me alone. But now that we've put ourselves out there for the world to see, things are going to change."

"I think you're exaggerating. Nobody cares that much about us. It's not like we're celebrities."

"Let's get dressed. I need to show you something."

Rachel hasn't watched TV since before we left for Vegas. I turned the TV on at the hotel when she was in the bathroom, but I didn't let her see it. She hasn't seen the papers either, but I bought one at the airport. Actually, I bought several so I could see how they spun the story.

I didn't show them to Rachel because I wanted her to remain calm and relaxed until we got home. But now we're back. And it's time for Rachel to see what she's in for.

CHAPTER TWO

RACHEL

Pearce went out to the car and returned with a stack of folded-up newspapers. He hands them to me.

"Why are you giving me these?" I ask.

"Look at the front page." He points to it.

It's a Los Angeles newspaper, and on the front page of the lifestyle section is a photo of Pearce with the headline, 'Billionaire Pearce Kensington Off the Market.' There's a short story underneath it, saying how Pearce and I are engaged.

I skim the article again. "Why would people in LA care about this?"

"My last wedding received a lot of media attention. People are interested in the lives of billionaires, especially younger ones, so I knew when I sent out that announcement that it would make the papers."

He shows me the next newspaper, this time a financial one. There's a photo of Pearce along with news of his engagement. Again, it's just a few lines, but it's still there in a national newspaper.

There's another newspaper under it, also a financial one. It's folded back to the third page and reads, 'Holton Kensington's Son Engaged Again.'

I set the papers down on the table. "When you told me you were sending out an announcement, I never thought it would get national attention. It's just news of our engagement. It's not actual news."

Pearce takes my hand. "Rachel, I told you that announcement would get the media's attention. I'm from a well-known family. People know my name. They know who I am. Something like this will make the news. Even if I hadn't sent out that announcement, eventually the news would've got back to the press. But I'd rather have it come from us than someone else, which is why I alerted the media."

"I guess I just didn't believe you. I thought maybe the papers on the East Coast would mention it but not a newspaper in LA."

"It was also on TV."

"It was on the news?" I start to panic, my heart racing.

"Yes, but the financial news, not the regular news. It was announced on one of the financial news channels. My father and our company are regularly talked about on those channels, so it's not surprising they would mention this."

"Do you think it was on any other channels?"

"I don't know. The announcement was sent to all the major news outlets so it's possible it was mentioned elsewhere."

"What if my parents saw it? I wanted to tell them myself." I race over to my answering machine and see five new messages. On Friday, I called my mom and told her that Pearce and I were spending the weekend together and that I couldn't call her until today. But seeing all those messages, I'm certain she heard the news. She's probably crying in every message, saying how she can't believe I told the media before I told my own mother.

"Pearce, we shouldn't have done this." I see the sadness in his eyes and quickly correct myself. "Not the wedding. I meant we shouldn't have sent out that announcement."

Pearce comes over to me. "We had to. If we hadn't, my parents would've done everything in their power to stop us from getting married."

"We're already married. That's why we eloped. So your parents wouldn't interfere. But we could've waited to send out the announcement."

"We couldn't wait. If we had, my parents would still try to interfere. They'd try to force me to get an annulment."

15

"They can't force you to do that. You're an adult."

"You don't understand my family. My father is obsessed with appearances. Making sure our family always presents itself the way he sees fit. That includes being seen with the right people, and marrying the right person. And as far as my parents are concerned, that person is not you. I don't like admitting that to you, but it's the truth."

"Pearce, you can't let this continue. You need to stop letting your father have all the control."

He nods. "I did. When I sent out that announcement, I took away his control. Now that our engagement is public, he'll have to accept our marriage."

"Why would that make a difference?"

"Because he doesn't want me being seen as irresponsible. I'm next in line to take over the company. I need to appear to be stable and mature. Someone who can be trusted. If people think I'm not, then we risk losing our clients, and my father would never allow that to happen. Right now, we're trying to grow the company, and as much as he tries to deny it, my father knows I'm key to the company's future growth and success. I'm his only son and everyone in the business world knows I'll be taking over the company, which is why they're closely watching me and have a vested interest in my personal life."

"And breaking off an engagement makes people think you're irresponsible," I confirm.

"Yes. Especially since I was married for such a short time before. Back then, people blamed *me* for the divorce, saying I wasn't mature enough to be married. So if I break off my engagement, it'll appear that I'm still immature. That I'm unable to make a decision and stick with it. This wouldn't have been an issue if we'd only told a few people about our engagement, but making it public changes everything. I can't back out of this now. It would reflect poorly on me, which would in turn reflect poorly on my family and the company, and that's the last thing my father wants."

"Isn't marrying someone like me going to reflect poorly on you?" I ask, annoyed that his family follows these ridiculous, antiquated societal rules.

He holds my shoulders, his eyes on mine. "To my father, and people like him, yes. But their opinions don't matter to me. They can say what they like, and I know that they will, but we don't have to listen to them, and we're not going to." He sighs. "Rachel, I know I've told you this before, but I need to say it again. The next few months are going to be very difficult for us. Once I bring you into the side of my world that I've kept you out of until now, you'll see what I mean. People will treat you poorly. They'll say horrible things. They'll make up lies. They'll gossip about you, and us. Or they'll pretend to be nice, only so that you'll tell them information that they can later use against you."

"Everyone can't be that bad, Pearce. There must be some decent people you know."

"There are very few. But even those few, I wouldn't trust."

He waits for me to respond but I don't know what to say. He told me some of this last Friday, but I was on such a high from the proposal that I wasn't really taking it all in. But now, the reality of that part of his life is finally hitting me and making me uneasy and a little scared of what's to come.

Pearce must sense my worry because he brings me into his arms. "I'm sorry things have to be this way. I wish I could somehow make this easier on you. I promise you I'll try, but there's only so much I can do."

"It's fine. Let them say what they want about me. Like you said, I don't have to listen to them." I pull back to see his face. "Pearce, I know your life is complicated and I know it's going to be an adjustment for me. For both of us. But we'll get through it."

He smiles. "I don't know how you stay so positive."

I smile back. "Being in love helps." I give him a quick kiss. "Now are you going to let me pack? It's getting late."

"Yes. Go ahead." He lets me go and I return to the bedroom. I hear him in the kitchen. "I'm going to order us some dinner. What would you like?"

17

"Anything's fine. I don't care."

As I'm taking some clothes from my closet, the phone rings. I freeze, then drop the clothes on the floor and run to the kitchen where the phone is. Pearce is standing in front of the fridge.

"I bet it's my mom," I say to him. "Should I answer it?"

"Yes." He closes the fridge and kisses my cheek. "You need to talk to her. I'll go get us some dinner so you can have privacy."

I nod nervously. "Okay, bye."

I answer the phone as he goes out the door. "Hello?"

"Rachel, it's Dad."

My body relaxes just slightly. I can handle my dad better than my mom. "Hi, Dad. Is Mom there too?"

"No. She had to run to the store. She'll be back in a few minutes."

That's strange. My dad never calls without my mom around.

"Is something wrong?" I ask.

"I'm not sure. That's why I'm calling. Your mother and I heard some news today about you and Pearce." He pauses. "Your mother was watching one of those financial news shows and they said you and Pearce were engaged. Is that true?"

I hesitate. "Yes."

"I see. That's very, um, sudden."

"I know. And I'm really sorry I didn't call and tell you guys about the engagement. Pearce and I were out of town last weekend. I told Mom I'd call when I got back but we just got back like an hour ago." I pause and squeeze my eyes shut. "Is she mad? Or...are *you* mad?"

"No, honey. We're not mad."

I open my eyes. "Really?"

"You're an adult now and you have to do what you think is right. And if this man makes you happy, then we're happy for you."

I breathe out a sigh of relief. "Thanks, Dad. And again, I'm really sorry you had to find out that way."

"So why was it on the news?"

"It's complicated." I can't tell him all the reasons Pearce gave me for why we had to announce our engagement. Doing so would only worry my dad, especially the part about Pearce's parents disapproving of me. But I can at least tell my dad part of the truth. "When you're rich and somewhat well-known, like Pearce is, it's a common practice to announce your engagement to the world. I don't really get it, but Pearce said it's done all the time with people like him."

"This is going to be a big change for you, being married to him."

"I know, but I'm ready for it. We've talked about it."

"Rachel, before your mother gets home, I need to tell you that she was upset when she heard the news, but only because you didn't call and tell her yourself."

"I know." I feel tears forming. I feel terrible hurting my mom. "I should've called her."

"She's fine now, but I did want to ask you to include her in the wedding plans. I know you like being independent and doing things on your own, but being her only daughter, it would mean a lot to your mother if you'd let her be part of it, even if it's just helping you pick out your dress."

Now I really feel bad. I was just about to tell my dad that Pearce and I were already married and that the wedding is just for show, but now I can't. My mom would be crushed if she found out she wasn't there for her only daughter's wedding. I need to keep it a secret and let her think the wedding isn't until this spring.

"Yes. I'll definitely ask Mom for help. I'm going to need it. I've never planned a wedding."

"Your mother hasn't either." He chuckles. "We got married in her parents' back yard and had the reception in the barn. She didn't plan anything. She didn't have time to."

I laugh. "Is that why you married her ten days after you proposed? Because you didn't want her planning a big fancy wedding?"

"Actually, I offered her a big fancy wedding." He pauses, like he's remembering it. "But she didn't want it. She didn't care about the wedding. She just wanted to be married to me. She didn't want to wait. I didn't either. I loved her too much to wait. I loved her from the first moment I saw her."

I smile as he says it, because his words and his tone express how much he loves my mom. I'm grateful to have parents that love each other the way they do. I feel like Pearce and I have that same kind of love. That's one reason why I agreed to marry him last weekend. Like my mom, I didn't care about a big fancy wedding. I just wanted to be married to him. I was ready to start our life together.

I hear noise on the other end of the phone and then I hear my dad again. "Rachel, your mother's home so I'm going to hand over the phone. But before I do, I need to say congratulations."

"Thanks, Dad."

"I love you, honey."

"I love you too."

He hands my mom the phone and I hear her voice. "Congratulations, honey! We heard the news. That's great!"

She's trying to sound excited for me, and I think she really is, but I can also hear the hurt in her voice.

"Mom, I'm really sorry I didn't call and tell you myself."

"It's okay. I'm sure you two had a lot going on and I know you were out of town. Where did you end up going? You never said."

I was going to say Las Vegas, but that was when I was going to confess I was already married. Now I'm not going to tell her, so I can't say Pearce and I went to Vegas or she might assume we got married.

"We went to Manhattan," I say. "We saw a show. Ate at some great restaurants. Stayed in a nice hotel."

"That sounds fun."

She's reacting much better than I thought she would. It doesn't make sense. She's always so protective of me and now I tell her I'm engaged and she's not mad? Maybe she is, but she's saving her anger for a later discussion. I'd rather just have her get mad at me now and not wait.

"Mom, if you're mad about this, just tell me. I know it's sudden and—"

"Rachel, your father and I had a long talk about this yesterday after we heard the news. I admit I was upset, but your father reminded me that he and I didn't exactly make our parents happy when we got married so soon after we met. But it all worked out in the end, despite our parents' objections. Sometimes you just have to trust that your child knows what's best. I know I have a hard time doing that, but I'm trying to get better at it. But I still worry about you. I always will."

"I know, but you don't have to worry about this. I love Pearce and I don't have any doubts about marrying him."

"That's good, honey. I'm glad you're happy. So why was your engagement on the news?"

I explain it all again, the same story I told my dad, except my mom seems to get it more than my dad did. She follows celebrity news and at least has an idea of what Pearce's world is like. He's not a celebrity, but from what I've told her about him, she knows his life isn't always private.

"Mom, I know you're not going to be happy about this, but I'm moving in with Pearce."

"I assumed you would."

"You did? But we're not married yet."

"Rachel, this isn't the 1950s. I know couples live together before they get married. And honestly, I'm relieved you'll finally be out of that dangerous neighborhood. From what you've said, it sounds like Pearce lives in a very nice place."

"Yes, it's really nice, and you have to go through a security gate to get into his building. It's very safe and in a great neighborhood."

Just as I say that, the door opens and Pearce walks in, carrying a big paper sack.

"Mom, Pearce just got back with dinner so I should probably go. But I'll call you tomorrow."

"Could I talk to him?"

"Who?"

She laughs a little. "You're fiancé. My future son-in-law."

"Oh. Yes. Of course. I guess you've never spoken to him, have you? For some reason I thought that you had."

"No. We never have, but I'm looking forward to meeting him in a few days. You're still coming for Thanksgiving, right?"

"Yes. We'll be there." I motion Pearce to the phone. "My mom wants to say hi."

He nods and takes the phone from me. "Hello, Mrs. Evans. This is Pearce Kensington. It's nice to finally speak with you."

He's using his formal tone. I told her he's kind of formal, but it's hard to know what that means until she hears it herself. She'll like that about him. It makes him sound mature and respectful, which he is.

As he listens to her, he puts his arm around my waist and pulls me into his side. "I'm sorry it's taken so long. Your daughter has been remiss in her duties to introduce me to you and Mr. Evans."

I look up and see Pearce smiling at me. I can hear my mom's voice, but I can't hear what she's saying.

"Yes, we're looking forward to it," Pearce says, then he listens again. "Very good. We'll see you then. Before you hang up, is Mr. Evans close by? I'd like to speak with him." Pearce lets me go and walks into the living room. "Mr. Evans. Pearce Kensington." He listens. "Yes, it's nice to meet you as well. Mr. Evans, I would like to apologize for not asking for your daughter's hand in marriage. It was inappropriate of me and I didn't mean to disrespect you in any way."

Pearce has his back to me but I'm watching him as he talks. I never expected Pearce to ask my dad for his blessing and I don't think my dad expected him to. But I think it's kind of sweet. And romantic. Pearce listens again, and I'm wondering what my dad is saying.

"It may not be necessary," Pearce says, "but it's what I've been taught to do. So when Rachel and I are at your home later this week, I will ask you in person, once you've had a chance to get to know me. Hopefully you'll give us your blessing. I love your daughter very much and I promise to take good care of her." He nods. "Yes, you as well. Goodnight, Mr. Evans."

Pearce walks back into the kitchen and hangs up the phone. "So for dinner, I ended up getting—"

"Pearce." I go up to him. "Thank you for talking to my parents."

He smiles. "Why would you thank me for that?"

"I don't know. I guess I just wanted to thank you for being so polite and for saying that stuff to my dad. You didn't have to do that, by the way. Ask for my hand? It's kind of old-fashioned."

He leans down and kisses me. "It's not old-fashioned. It's the right thing to do. I'm just sorry I wasn't able to do it before we got married. That's probably why he acted so strange when I mentioned it."

"That's not why. He was just surprised you asked." I reach up and unzip Pearce's coat because he never took it off. "My parents don't know that we're married."

"You didn't tell them?"

I shake my head. "I couldn't do it. My mom heard about our engagement on TV. My dad said she was upset that I didn't call and tell her, and then he said how much it would mean to her if I let her help plan the wedding. So I couldn't tell them. I just couldn't do it."

"That's fine, but I'm still going to tell *my* parents."

"I know. But tell them not to say anything to mine."

"I will, but they never listen to me."

I sigh and hug him. "You're right, Pearce."

"About what?"

"Hiding this from people. It's going to be really hard."

CHAPTER THREE

PEARCE

We're back at my loft now. After we had dinner at Rachel's apartment we packed both our cars with her clothes and a few other items, then drove here separately so she'll have her car to take to class tomorrow. I need to get her a new car, and soon. I live in a very expensive building and my fellow tenants will complain about having such an old, run-down car in the parking garage. I know it sounds ridiculous, but that's just how it is. Besides, even though I had her car fixed, I'd still feel better having her drive a newer, safer car.

When we arrived at my loft, I expected to have someone there waiting for me. My father. My mother. Jack. I was sure at least one person would be there waiting to yell at me. So when I didn't see anyone, I was both surprised and worried. I know my father's furious, so why the hell isn't here? And why hasn't he called me? I checked my messages, but the only ones I had were from Jack. I couldn't make out all that he was saying, but there was a lot of profanity and he sounded extremely angry. I'll deal with him later. For now, I need to deal with my father.

"Rachel, I need to go." I lean down and kiss her.

She's sitting on the couch, going over her notes for a test she has next week. She missed class today because we were traveling, but she wasn't too worried about it. A lot of her classmates have already left to go home for the holiday, so her professors didn't plan to go over any new material.

"Pearce, it's late. Why don't you wait and talk to them tomorrow?"

"I can't wait." I go to the closet and get my coat. "I need to get this over with."

She meets me by the elevator. "How long do you think you'll be gone?"

"I have no idea." I put on my coat. "But if I'm not back by morning, I think it's safe to assume my father's killed me."

"Don't even joke about that." She hugs me. "Just relax. Everything will be fine."

"You don't know my father. I wasn't joking when I said my father might kill me. I'm basically heading to my execution."

It's true, but I don't know why I'm telling her this. I guess because I know she doesn't believe me. She can't imagine a father killing his own son, but I have no doubt he'd kill me if he didn't need me to take over the company someday.

"If he's going to be that upset, then don't go."

I kiss her. "I need to talk to him and find out if I'm supposed to show up at the office tomorrow." I step onto the elevator.

"You think he'll fire you?"

The elevator closes before I can answer. But the answer is that I'm hoping he will. I'd love to have him fire me. If he did, I'd be free to start my own company. Be my own boss. Pursue a dream I never thought was even possible.

Unfortunately, my father knows about that dream, which means the chances of him firing me are slim to none. He wants me to be miserable, and I will be if I keep working at Kensington Chemical with him as my boss.

My parents' mansion is a half hour away. It's ten o'clock but my parents usually stay up until eleven. My father's usually up even later than that, reading or doing work in his office.

When I get there, I don't bother announcing my arrival to the guard. Instead, I punch the security code into the large iron entrance gate, and when it opens, I drive down the long winding road to their estate.

The estate includes their mansion, which is 22,000 square feet, as well as a large guest house, and a smaller house for the hired help. They have several acres of land, surrounded by trees, giving them the privacy they desire.

My father doesn't like people, even rich people. He doesn't like talking to them or being around them or having them anywhere near him. If he could, he'd live in total solitude, but he's forced to interact with people both as a business owner and to fulfill his obligations as a member of high society.

My mother is more social, which reflects well on my father. People see them as a couple rather than individuals, so my father benefits from my mother's active social life. When they see him with her, they assume he wants to be at all the charity auctions, dinner parties, and other social activities she forces him to go to, when in fact, he despises those events.

Over the years, my father has learned to put on a fake smile and engage in conversation, so people think he's much more personable than he really is. And being seen at these social events helps his image, and the image of the company, which has helped us get new business. My father should thank my mother for that, but he never will. He thinks his success is all his. He'd never give any credit to my mother.

I go up to the front door and ring the bell. I grew up here, but now that I don't live here, my parents wouldn't approve of me just walking in. It's bad enough I didn't call before coming over or announce myself at the gate. But I didn't, because I wanted to take them by surprise. Otherwise, my father would probably be waiting at the door with his gun. I shouldn't be thinking that, and yet part of me really is worried about it. I should've brought my *own* gun, just in case.

"Mr. Kensington." The maid answers the door, nodding at me. Actually, it's more like a bow. My father thinks he's a king, which is why he expects his hired help to practically bow down to him when they greet him. And since I'm his son and look just like him, the help always treats me like they treat my father. I don't like it. It makes me feel guilty, like I'm forcing them to act this way because I'm rich and think I'm better than them. I know they're just doing what my father tells them to do, but I still don't like it when they greet me that way.

"Are my parents still awake?" I ask as I step inside the house.

"Yes, sir." The maid helps me with my coat. Again, I don't like it. I grew up surrounded by hired help taking care of my every need, but as I got older, I grew tired of it. I'm a grown man. I can take off my own damn coat. And I don't like being called 'sir.' It's not necessary.

I hear my mother coming down the hall toward the foyer. "Kelsa, who's at the door?"

"It's your son, ma'am."

My mother stops abruptly when she sees me. "Pearce."

She only said my name, but I could hear the anger in her voice and I can see it in her face.

"Mother."

She says nothing.

And so the standoff begins.

She waves her hand at the maid. "Kelsa. Go make some tea."

The maid scurries off.

"I'm not here to have tea, Mother."

"I didn't say it was for you." She folds her arms over her chest.

She's wearing a black pants suit. I've never seen her wear it before. Perhaps she bought it for the funeral she's planning to have for me after my father kills me, which given the way she's acting, seems more and more like a possibility.

If my mother's this angry, then how angry is my father? My mother is usually the reasonable one. In the past, when I've done something my parents disapproved of, my mother would try to make excuses for my behavior in an attempt to get my father to back down and lessen the punishment I would receive. She'd say I was still learning to be a man, still making mistakes, and that I shouldn't be harshly punished for simply being young and naive.

That excuse has worked in the past because my mother is basically telling my father I'm stupid, careless, and irresponsible,

27

and although my father looks down on those traits, having my mother describe me that way makes my father feel superior. It makes him think he's smarter than me and still has things to teach me. It makes him feel powerful. My mother knows all this, so she uses it to my advantage to convince my father to lessen my punishment. But I get the feeling that won't be the case this time.

"Why are you here, Pearce?"

"I'm here to talk to you and Father."

My heart's beating out of my chest, but on the outside I remain calm. I don't want them getting the upper hand here. I need to appear strong.

"We've already heard your news," she says. "It's late. You should leave."

"I need to speak with Father."

"Your father is in his office, working. You shouldn't disturb him. You'll have to speak with him later. Call his secretary and make an appointment."

"Are you saying I'm no longer employed at the company?"

"I don't know what his plans are for your employment. You'll need to discuss that with him."

I step closer to her and lower my voice. "Just tell me what he said. How is he going to punish me?"

"He hasn't said much, so I really don't know."

I drop my head and squeeze the bridge of my nose, trying to relieve the pounding headache that formed as soon as I left my loft.

"Pearce. You need to leave."

I look up at my mother again. "I'm not done talking to you."

"There's nothing more to say. We already know what you've done."

"You only know part of it." I pause. "When Royce and I were in Las Vegas last weekend, I asked Rachel to meet me there."

My mother's arms drop to her sides. "Please tell me you didn't."

I nod. "I married her. We got married last Saturday."

"Shit." She whispers it as she looks down the hall toward my father's office. My mother never swears, so I know this is bad. He's definitely going to kill me. She grasps my arm. "Why would you do this, Pearce?"

"Because if I didn't, I couldn't be with her. They're voting in a week. They're making it a rule that you have to marry whoever they choose. And I couldn't do it, Mother. I couldn't get married again to someone I didn't love. I know you don't approve of her, but I love Rachel. I can't live my life without her. I know, deep-down, you want me to be happy. So why can't you accept this and just be happy for me?"

She takes a step back and folds her arms over her chest again. "Your father's right. You're a fool, Pearce! A complete and utter fool! It doesn't matter if there isn't an official rule in place. You know how it works. You know they make the decision."

"You said I could have a say in the matter. When you tried to set me up with Sydney—"

"Sydney was on the approved list! I was trying to help you! Give you a woman you might actually enjoy being with. Someone you could someday come to love."

"I already love Rachel. I love her more than I could ever love any other woman."

"Then you're an idiot for getting involved with her in the first place. We taught you better than that. Were you not listening to us all those years? Did you really think you could marry this girl without any consequences?"

"I know there will be consequences and I will take whatever punishment they impose upon me. But I will not give up Rachel."

"You may not have a choice," she says, glancing down the hall at my father's office. "Your ignorance and careless actions are going to cause you harm, Pearce. And this time, I can't protect you."

She storms off, leaving me alone in the foyer.

I slowly make my way to my father's office. The hallway is long and narrow and dark, and I really do feel like I'm walking to

29

my execution. My throat is dry, my heart is pounding, and my muscles are aching from being clenched so tightly.

I hate that I'm reacting this way. It's completely insane. At my age, I should be able to marry who I please and my parents should accept that and be happy about it. But instead, I have to get married in secret and then live in fear of what will happen next.

"Father." I skip knocking and just open the door. He's sitting behind his long mahogany desk, his head down, a pen in his hand and a stack of papers in front of him. The office is dark, except for the small amount of light coming from his desk lamp. The light shines down directly onto his papers, so from where I'm standing, my father just looks like an outlined shadow of a man in a suit.

He lifts his head slightly. "Pearce."

I check to make sure I can see both his hands. It doesn't really matter. I know he keeps a gun in his desk drawer and I know he keeps it loaded. If he wanted to kill me, he could, and I wouldn't be able to stop him. I know he needs to keep me around to take over the company, but if his rage takes over, he won't be thinking about that. He'll only be thinking about how to get rid of me so he never has to see me again.

I slowly walk into the room. "I spoke with Mother and she said you heard the news regarding my engagement."

He sets his pen down. "That's correct."

I stop, not sure what to say next. I was expecting him to do all the talking while I just stood here, letting him tell me what a horrible son I am.

"Sit down, Pearce." He motions to the chair across from him.

I cautiously step forward and lower myself into the wooden chair. I feel like I'm a child again. I've sat in this chair many times, for as long as I can remember. I've received many punishments while sitting here. I've also been criticized in this chair. Yelled at. Been told I'm useless. A disappointment. Not good enough. Not smart enough.

This chair has bad memories, which I'm certain is why he told me to sit in it.

"Go ahead, Father." I want to get this over with. This is already taking way too long.

"I didn't invite you here, Pearce. You came here to see *me*. Did you have a purpose, or were you just stopping by to say hello? You should know it's inappropriate to show up unannounced, especially at this late hour."

"I'm aware of that, Father."

"You didn't answer my question. What is the purpose of your visit?"

I take a breath, but I don't get much air in. The walls of my chest are closing in fast, crushing my lungs and making it impossible to breathe.

"I know you don't approve of her, but I am in a relationship with Rachel."

"The girl your mother and I found at your apartment."

"Yes. That's her."

"You said she was nothing more than a sex toy. Someone to mix things up from the associates."

I clench my fists, trying to hold in my rage at hearing him call Rachel a 'sex toy.'

"I never said that about her. Jack is the one who told you that."

"So Jack was lying to me?"

Shit. What do I say? I have to protect Jack. He protected me and I have to repay him for that.

"Jack wasn't lying. I told Jack I was only involved in a physical relationship with Rachel so that he'd leave us alone. If Jack had known I was seeing her for real, he would've forbid it. He would've put an end to it and reported it to the members. He made that clear, several times. He warned me repeatedly to stay away from her."

"He still should've ended it." My father picks up his pen and taps it on the table. "If he had, we wouldn't be having this conversation."

31

"He wasn't aware it had gone on for so long. He thought I had just started seeing her."

"I hired Jack to do surveillance on you last September while I was in Europe. I had him follow your every move until I returned in November. He never mentioned this girl until I asked him about her that night I found her in your apartment. So he's either incompetent in his surveillance work or he was lying to me. And given that he's an expert in surveillance, that would lead me to surmise that he was lying."

Dammit. I didn't expect Jack to be drawn into this. My father already hates Jack and I don't want their ongoing feud becoming even worse because of my actions. And I don't want my father reporting Jack to the organization, accusing him of being involved in this.

"He wasn't lying, Father. I kept Rachel hidden. We always stayed in. I never took her out."

"Getting back to your reason for coming here. Since you seem unable to explain yourself, I will take an educated guess." He pauses. "You're here to tell me you're engaged to the girl, in the off chance that I would not have heard about it by now, despite the fact that it was announced on all the financial news outlets as well as several major newspapers."

"I assumed you would've heard by now, so no, that's not why I'm here."

He holds his hand up in the air. "Let me take another guess. You wanted to rub my face in the fact that you went behind my back and did something you knew would embarrass the family and harm our family name and the future of our company."

"That was not at all my intention. This announcement will not harm the company in any way. And as for our family, my marriage to Rachel is not a detriment to us. She's a very intelligent woman who comes from a good family. She'll graduate with her masters degree in a few weeks, which makes her more educated than my last wife."

My father says nothing. He just stares at me, tapping his pen on his desk is a slow, steady rhythm.

I can't take the silence. "What is it, Father?"

He's still silent, then finally says, "You can't possibly think you are actually going to marry this girl."

"Our engagement has been announced. The marriage has to occur. If it didn't, then as you said earlier, it would embarrass the family and could be a detriment to the company. Breaking off an engagement would only show people that I'm not the mature, responsible man that you expect me to be. And that our clients expect me to be, as the future CEO of Kensington Chemical."

He sits up straighter. "Are you really that ignorant, Pearce?"

I clench my fists. "Explain yourself, Father."

"The biggest embarrassment to our family is not the engagement itself, but the person you are engaged to." He leans forward, his arms on the desk, his eyes narrowed. "YOU, my son, have now announced to the world that a Kensington is fucking some low-life degenerate hick from God-knows-where Indiana."

I lean forward as well. "Do NOT refer to her that way EVER again. And I did NOT announce to the world that I am fucking her. I announced that I am MARRYING her."

He bursts up from his chair and slams his fist on the desk. "You are NOT marrying her! We will find a way to minimize the damage you have caused with this engagement and you will be punished for doing so in the first place. And you will be punished by the organization as well for not following the rules."

I stand up so that we're face to face. "There is no rule in place forbidding me from marrying her."

"There is going to be within a matter of days."

"Yes. But as of now, there isn't."

My lips turn up just the slightest bit and he notices. I see the movement of his chest and hear him breathing hard.

"What are you saying, Pearce?" he asks through gritted teeth.

"I'm saying." I stand up straighter and look him directly in the eye. "I already married her."

He straightens up as well, his eyes not leaving mine. He's silent. Too angry to speak. Too angry to hide what he's feeling. His face, which never tells me anything, is now giving him away.

He's not just angry. He's also confused. Confused as to how this could've happened. Shocked that it did.

For once in my life, I feel like I beat him. He looks like he's trapped in a corner and can't find a way out. Seeing him like this makes me feel an overwhelming sense of power. A sense of control.

I should relish it and keep quiet. But I can't. I need to finish this.

"Rachel and I got married in Las Vegas last weekend. It's a shame you and mother couldn't be there. But I'm hoping you'll be able to attend the wedding in March. The invitations will be sent out shortly. Be sure you and mother RSVP. It's inappropriate to show up unannounced," I say, throwing his words back at him. "Goodnight, Father."

I turn and walk out of the room, not looking back. I said what I came here to say and I'm leaving before he can stop me. For once, I'm getting the last word.

That look on his face just now is one I'll never forget. It was one of pure shock. He's trying to figure out what just happened. Unable to believe I would challenge his authority. Unable to believe I would even dare to try to have my own life. A life without him controlling me. A life in which I'm happy.

This is just the beginning of a long battle between us. But tonight? I feel like I won the first round.

CHAPTER FOUR

PEARCE

As I'm driving back to my loft, the thrill of excitement I felt over telling off my father is quickly replaced by regret. I never should've done that. I know better than to talk to my father that way. As good as it felt to say those things to him, I just provoked him. Whatever punishment he had planned for me just became a million times worse. I knew he'd be furious about the marriage, but then I boasted about the fact that I went behind his back. It was the worse thing I could've done.

When I arrive back at the loft, the lights are off, except for one small lamp on a side table. Rachel must've gone to sleep. It's late and I know she's tired from our trip.

I hang up my coat and go to the bedroom and see her sound asleep. The sight of her there in my bed, here in my loft, allows me to breathe again. I was completely stressed just moments ago, but then I see her and I start to relax. She's my safe haven. My comfort. My home.

I take off my suit jacket and set it on the chair in the corner. I wore a suit to my parents' house because it's the only attire that's acceptable to them. It used to be all I wore, but now Rachel has me dressing in jeans and casual shirts and I'm starting to like it. I undo my tie and my dress shirt and continue undressing until I'm down to my boxers.

I slide into bed, trying not to disturb her. She's on her side with her back to me. I slip my hand around her waist and press my body against hers and just breathe, letting her presence calm me.

"Pearce?" I hear her whisper.

"I'm sorry I woke you," I whisper back.

"It's okay." She turns to face me. "How'd it go?"

I brush my fingers over her soft cheek. "Let's not talk about it. We need to sleep."

"Are you going to work tomorrow?"

"I don't know."

It's true. I don't know if I should go there or not. I don't want to fight with my father at the office. It would be completely unprofessional and something our employees shouldn't witness. But I do have meetings tomorrow and people are counting on me to show up.

"You seem really tense." She lays her head on my chest and hugs me. "I'm guessing it didn't go well. What did your parents say?"

"I don't want to talk about this right now. We'll talk later."

She reaches up and kisses me. "Pearce. I'm sorry."

"You have nothing to be sorry for. My parents just aren't good people. And I can't change them."

Her head lies back on my chest. "I love you."

"I love you too." I keep my arms around her and hear her breathing change as she drifts back to sleep. I lie there awake for the next hour, then finally fall asleep myself.

The next morning my alarm goes off at five, as it usually does. I turn it off, seeing no use in getting to the office this early. If I'm going into work, I'm not going in at six, when my father's the only one there. I need to wait until the other employees arrive, giving me somewhat of a barrier between him and me.

I go back to sleep and wake up again at seven, unable to sleep any longer. This day will be hell, and the sooner it starts, the sooner it'll be over. I'm going to call Jack today and see if we can meet. It's another conversation I've been dreading and need to get over with.

"I have to get to class," Rachel says, flipping over on her side.

36

She's facing me so I lean in and kiss her. "Your class isn't until ten. It's only seven."

"I know, but I have to get ready and it's a half hour drive and I wanted to spend some time at the library before class."

I reach around her waist and draw her into me. "You're going to leave me here in bed all alone?"

She smiles. "You're already late for work."

"I'm on my honeymoon."

"I think with everything going on, we'll have to skip the honeymoon."

"We are most definitely not skipping the honeymoon. I'm taking you somewhere." I leave kisses along her neck. "Some place we can be alone and spend all day in bed if we choose."

"Pearce, we can't go anywhere. People think we're engaged, not married. We can't go on a honeymoon until after the second wedding."

"We can still go on a trip. People don't have to know it's a honeymoon." I slip my hand under the silk nightgown I bought her. It's short and has thin straps on top. I wasn't sure if she'd wear it once we got back from Vegas because she normally wears cotton pajamas to bed. But I hope she continues to wear it at least some of the time because it's incredibly sexy on her.

She puts her hand behind my neck, gently massaging it. "Where would you like to go?"

"Where would YOU like to go?" I kiss her. "I'll take you anywhere."

"I haven't been to many places, so I'm not really sure."

"How about Italy?"

Her eyes widen and she smiles. "Are you serious? Italy?"

I smile back. "From your response, I take it you've always wanted to go to Italy."

"I would love to go there."

"Then that's where we'll go. We'll leave in a few weeks, right after your graduation."

"But we'll miss Christmas."

"Yes, I forgot about that. Are you wanting to go back to Indiana at Christmas?"

"I don't know. I was thinking we should spend Christmas with *your* parents since we're spending Thanksgiving with mine."

"I can tell you right now that we will not be attending Christmas at the Kensington estate."

"Do you think they'll still be mad at you in a month?"

"Don't worry about them. Just tell me when you'd like to leave and I'll get to work on the travel arrangements."

"Let me talk to my mom. Maybe I could miss Christmas this year. I'd really love to get away for a while. I could tell my parents it's a graduation gift. They know how hard I've worked this past year and if I told them I was going to Italy, I don't think they'd mind if I missed Christmas."

"I wish my parents were as understanding as yours."

"Believe me, I didn't think my parents would be this understanding. I think the only reason they are is because they can tell how happy I am with you. I know my parents don't agree with a lot of my decisions, but in the end they just want me to be happy."

I kiss her. "So you're happy?"

"Extremely."

I kiss her again and that's all it takes to make us forget about work and school and focus on each other. I slip off her nightgown and we start the day on a high, first in bed, then in the shower.

Then she heads to New Haven and I head to the office. When I get to my desk, I'm surprised to see that nothing has changed. The stacks of paperwork that were there last Friday are still there, and there's a folder on one of them that contains spreadsheets printed out just this morning. So I guess I'm still working here.

"Pearce, the meeting is in 1A instead of 1B." I look up and see Marshall, one of the marketing guys, standing at my door. "We had to change rooms because your father is using the other room."

I nod. "Thank you. I'll be there shortly."

I tensed up when he mentioned my father. Part of me wondered if he'd even show up here today. I thought he might be home, plotting his revenge.

My meeting starts in a few minutes so I gather what I need, but as I'm heading out of my office, my cell phone rings. It's the organization calling. I have a sick feeling this is about me. I step back in my office and shut the door.

I answer the phone, and instead of hearing a recording like I usually do, I hear someone speaking. It's a deep voice and he asks for my member number. After I give it to him, he says, "The ruling council is currently reviewing details of your involvement with Rachel Evans."

Just hearing him say her name sends a chill through me. I don't want her involved with them in any way. I don't even want them knowing she exists. Obviously I know they do, but up until now, I've told myself they'll leave her alone. That this is all about me, and that I'll handle it and keep her out of it. But I need to face the facts, and the cold hard facts are that Rachel is part of this now. She doesn't know it, and probably never will, but she's still part of it.

Guilt and panic fill me as I realize what I've done. I brought Rachel into this. What the hell was I thinking? How could I be so selfish? I was so focused on making her part of my life, thinking I could keep her hidden away in only the good part. Thinking she'd never be exposed to the bad. But she's exposed to it just by being married to me. Before, she was just a regular girl, going to college and living her life. But now, she's my wife, and the organization knows about her. And I have no idea what they'll do.

The deep voice speaks again. "Pearce. Are you still there?"

"Yes. Continue."

"This Sunday, there will be a meeting to discuss how we will deal with your relationship with Ms. Evans. The meeting will be at location 182 and will commence at noon. An end time has not been given. This concludes the message."

The phone goes dead. I toss it on my desk. "Shit!" I rub my forehead, but it doesn't relieve the intense throbbing behind my eyes.

Someone knocks on my door. "Pearce?"

"Yes. Come in."

It's Marshall again. "Just letting you know we're ready to start the meeting. We didn't want to start without you."

"Go ahead. I'll be there in a minute."

I grab my phone and shove it in my suit jacket, then try to compose myself for this meeting. I don't even know why I'm going. Right now I need to be spending my time figuring out how to protect Rachel. But I'm not sure how to do that because I don't know what they're planning.

I need to talk to Jack. I call his secretary. She says he's in a meeting but she puts me through to him anyway, saying he's been awaiting my call.

"Pearce, where the fuck have you been?" He's angry, as I knew he would be.

"Hello to you too, Jack."

"Today at noon. My house. Be there, or I'll kill you before your father does." And then he slams the phone down.

This morning is going downhill fast. And I'm sure it's only going to get worse.

I go to the meeting, hoping it'll let my mind rest for a moment. It's a marketing meeting and I'm really just here to listen rather than participate. Marshall is going over things with the sales team and it's things I've already heard before, but he wanted me here to back him up on some decisions we made since the sales team can be rather stubborn and unreasonable.

The meeting ends an hour later, and although I know I said a few things, I don't even remember what I said. My mind is far too distracted to be here today. I return to my office and my phone rings. The office phone this time.

I pick it up. "This is Pearce."

"Pearce, this is your mother. I need to know what time you'll be here on Thursday."

40

This must be some kind of joke. She can't possibly think I would show up at her house for Thanksgiving.

"Pearce. Answer me. I don't have all day."

"Mother, given what has transpired the past few days, and more specifically last night, I assumed you knew I would not be there on Thursday."

"It's Thanksgiving. Despite what's going on, our family must be together for Thanksgiving dinner."

"And Father is okay with this?"

"Your Father has no say in it. You know he has no interest in holidays, which is why he puts me in charge of them, and that includes making the guest list."

"And does this guest list include Rachel?"

"The guest list is the same as it was last year and the year before." By that, she means her, my father, and me. Nobody else. "Now what time will you be here?"

"I'm sorry, Mother, but I already made plans. I will be unable to attend this year."

"Pearce! You will NOT miss Thanksgiving."

"Yes, Mother, I will. And I will likely miss Christmas as well. But I hope both you and Father enjoy the holidays. Goodbye, Mother."

She hangs up without saying goodbye. I tried to politely decline her offer, but it was difficult to do when she excluded Rachel like that. So I did my best to stay calm and get off the phone before our conversation escalated into a full blown fight.

I scan the paperwork on my desk. I can't concentrate long enough to work on any of it. I might as well leave and go home and start packing for the trip tomorrow. But before I go, I need to tell my father I'll be gone. I could just not tell him, but why make things worse than they already are?

His office door is closed so I knock, which I normally don't do.

"Father, may I come in?"

I think I heard a 'yes' so I go in, closing the door behind me. He's sitting at his desk. I take the seat across from him.

41

"What do you need?" He's displaying his power pose, in which he rests his elbows on the table and clasps his hands together forming a pyramid shape. He lowers his head slightly, so that it's just above his locked hands, and peers across the desk at me.

"I wanted to let you know that I'm leaving early today and will not be in the office the rest of the week."

"Is that so?" He's much calmer than last night. But it's not a good calm. It's a frightening calm because it's not normal. He shouldn't be this calm.

"I'm going out of town for the holiday," I tell him.

"There's a meeting on Sunday."

"Yes. I'm aware of the meeting and I will be there." I clear my throat. "Have you been given any indication of what might happen at this meeting?"

"No." His lips curl up. "But I must say, I'm looking forward to it."

He's looking forward to my punishment? Of course he is. He hates me.

"I assume they'll harm me in some way, but as for Rachel, they'll leave her alone, correct?" I don't know why I asked that. Probably because I know my father has inside information he isn't sharing, but I know he would never tell me anything so I shouldn't have asked.

"They typically don't harm a member's wife."

"They know that I got married? Did you tell them?"

"I had no choice. As members, we're required to report any and all information we learn about our fellow members. Did Jack not teach you that?"

"I'm aware of the rule. And I assumed you would tell them."

I wanted the organization to know I got married, so this isn't a problem. But I find it disturbing how quickly my father reported me. He has no desire to protect his son. He wants me to be punished as severely as possible.

"So you're saying they won't harm her?" I ask, going back to my earlier question.

"This isn't a typical situation. I don't know if they would harm the girl."

I look him in the eye. "Would YOU?"

He chuckles. "Pearce. Do you honestly think I would kill your wife?"

I never said the word 'kill' so the fact that he came up with that himself is concerning. But I know he wouldn't do that. Although just hours ago I was worried he'd kill ME, his own son, when I thought about it later I realized I was overreacting. I was in such a state of panic having to tell my parents the news that I wasn't thinking straight.

"Despite what you may think, I'm not a monster, Pearce." He grins, but just slightly.

His words and the way he's looking at me is making me uneasy and anxious. I need to get out of this room. I rise from my chair. "I have to go. I'll see you at the meeting on Sunday."

"After the meeting, you need to come into the office. You're way behind on your work and I expect you to be caught up by next week."

"So you still want me working here?"

"Why wouldn't I?"

"I thought perhaps you'd fire me, given you're disapproval of my decision to marry Rachel."

"I know how much you enjoy working here, son. I wouldn't take that away from you." The grin appears on his face again. "As I said, I'm not a monster. I'm your father. I only want what's best for you."

I nod. "Yes. Well, goodbye."

I hurry out of there. I stop by my office to get my coat, then head back to my loft. What the hell was that? Why was he acting that way? He didn't yell or scream or even punish me.

He does this to me all the time and I hate it. He plays these mind games with me, leaving me wondering what he's up to. It's psychological warfare and he's an expert at it. As my father, he knows everything about me. My strengths. My weaknesses. And he uses that knowledge against me. I know he's not going to just let me get away with marrying Rachel. So what is he planning to do to get back at me?

When I arrive home, I take out my suitcase and start packing some clothes. I pack my jeans and casual shirts because I'm sure people don't wear suits on a farm. But I do pack a suit for dinner on Thursday.

As I'm packing my shoes, I hear someone on the intercom. It's George, the man who works at the security gate. "Mr. Kensington?"

"Yes, George."

"There's a Mr. Sinclair here to see you. Can I let him through?"

"Yes. I'll meet him in the lobby."

Royce must be back from Vegas. He really shouldn't stop by like this. It's too soon. We need to keep our distance from each other until we're sure nobody suspects he had a part in my elopement.

When I get to the lobby, I find a different Sinclair. It's Arlin, Royce's father.

"Pearce." He shakes my hand. "I'm sorry to stop over here like this. I called your office and they said you were here, but I wasn't able to reach you."

"I must've missed your call. I just got home a few minutes ago. Come upstairs."

We take the elevator up, and when we get to the loft, I take his coat. "Would you like a drink?"

"No, thank you. I'm fine." He sits on the couch. "I came by to ask if you've heard anything from Royce."

I sit in the chair next to the couch. "Not since Sunday."

"Grace and I haven't heard from him either and we're starting to get worried."

Unlike my parents, Royce's parents actually care about him. Grace and Arlin have been friends with my parents for years, but they are not at all alike. Arlin owns and runs one of the world's largest pharmaceutical companies, but he's very down to earth. He doesn't look down on people without money the way my

44

parents do. And he's very supportive of his sons. His wife, Grace, is as well. Grace is one of those caring, nurturing types of mothers that I longed to have when I was a child.

Royce doesn't realize how fortunate he is to have such good parents. He doesn't treat them well, which has always irritated me. Back when we were in college, his parents would come visit him on a weekend and he'd spend it passed out in some girl's room, not even caring his parents were there to see him. Or they'd stop by during the week to take him to dinner and he'd be drunk when they arrived. Sometimes I'd go to dinner with Grace and Arlin if Royce was too drunk to go. One time I remember sitting at a restaurant with them, wishing I could trade places with Royce. I'd gladly give him my parents in exchange for his.

"Royce is probably still in Vegas," I say to Arlin.

"He is, but I don't know where. I received a call late last night from a woman who I believe is a prostitute, saying that Royce owed her money. If that's true, he could be in serious trouble."

Vegas is not a place you want to owe people money. This prostitute likely has a boss, and that boss could be connected to the mob or some other crime ring. And you don't want to mess with those people.

"I'm sorry, Arlin, but I don't know what to tell you. I haven't seen Royce since Saturday. I talked to him on Sunday, but just briefly."

He sighs and shakes his head. "I don't know what to do with that boy. His brother is such a responsible young man, and yet Royce is the complete opposite. Grace and I didn't raise the boys any differently, so I don't understand how Royce turned out the way he did. We were hoping you'd rub off on him when you two went to college together."

"Arlin, I was no saint in college."

"Nobody is. And we didn't expect Royce to be either. We just wanted him to grow up a little. To put some effort in so that he'd have a good future. Look at you, Pearce. You're a hard worker. Very mature and responsible. Extremely intelligent."

Right there is an example of how Arlin is different than my father. My father would rather be burned alive than give me a compliment, yet Arlin just gave me several.

He continues. "If Holton retired today, you could step in as CEO and succeed at the job. If *I* retired, Royce would have no clue how to run the company, despite having a business degree from an Ivy League college. I'm not trying to put down my son. I'm just concerned that he'll destroy his future if he continues to live like this."

"Are you saying they might change their mind about making him a senator?"

"No, that's still the plan. Although Grace and I are against it. The last thing Royce needs is to live the life of a politician. All that money and power. It's what he craves, but it's the opposite of what he needs. It's the wrong path for him. It will only make him continue the behaviors Grace and I are trying to get him to stop. The drinking. The drugs. The women. It all needs to end or he's going to destroy himself."

"Maybe when he gets married, he'll settle down."

"I have a feeling Victoria will only make it worse. She sees Royce as her ticket to fame and she'll do whatever it takes to get him to the top. There couldn't be a worse match than the two of them. They'll feed off each other's need for power and end up in a very bad place." He stands up. "I should go. I'm going to have to fly to Vegas and deal with this myself."

As he says it, his cell phone rings. His regular phone, not the phone from the organization. He answers it, and as he listens, his expression turns dark. "Yes. I'll take care of it. Thank you."

He ends the call and puts his phone away. "That was the hospital in Las Vegas. Royce was found passed out in a hotel room on the strip. They said he had a cocktail of drugs in his system."

"Is he okay?"

"Yes. I'll fly out there and make sure he gets home." He sighs. "His mother's been worried sick and this will upset her even more. Royce could've killed himself."

46

"Arlin, I'm sorry. I should've insisted Royce come back with me. I shouldn't have left him there."

"It's not your responsibility to take care of him." He smiles. "By the way, I should've congratulated you. I hear you're a newlywed."

"Yes."

He notices the worry in my tone and puts his hand on my shoulder. "You didn't break any rules, Pearce."

"My father would disagree. And so would the other members."

"You obviously really love this girl if you're willing to put yourself at risk like this."

"I do. She means everything to me."

"Then fight for her. Fight for your marriage. Don't let them intimidate you."

"They're going to punish me. There's a meeting on Sunday."

"Yes. I received the notice."

"They're going to ask me questions. Make me explain why I did this. I don't know what to say that will make them back down and leave Rachel and me alone."

"You'll figure something out." He squeezes my shoulder. "You're smart, Pearce. Much smarter than them. Use that to your advantage." He walks over and takes his coat from the chair where I left it. "I'll see you on Sunday."

"Yes. Goodbye, Arlin."

He waits for the elevator to open, and when it does, Rachel is there.

"Oh, hello." She smiles at him as she steps off the elevator.

"Hello." Arlin shakes her hand. "You must be Rachel."

"Yes. And you are?"

"Arlin Sinclair."

"Sinclair. Are you related to Royce?"

He nods. "Yes. I'm his father."

"Well, it's a pleasure meeting you."

"You as well." He looks at me. "Goodbye, Pearce." He gives me a wink, signaling his approval of Rachel.

If only Arlin were my father. He'd support me and my marriage to Rachel and do everything in his power to limit my punishment from the other members. Royce has no idea how lucky he is. If it were me in a hospital room in Vegas, my father would never come get me. He'd leave me there, then punish me later for being so irresponsible.

When Arlin is gone, Rachel hugs me. "What are you doing home?"

"I decided to take the rest of the day off, although I do have to go in for a meeting at noon."

"So your father didn't fire you." She kisses me. "I knew he wouldn't. He's not going to fire his own son."

"He *would*, and he still might."

"Did you talk to him?" She takes me to the couch to sit down.

"Yes. And he demanded I come into the office on Sunday and catch up on work. I told him I would since I'm taking the rest of this week off. I'm going to change my return flight and come home Saturday night. But I want you to stay in Indiana. You don't need to come back early."

"Are you sure? I feel like we should fly back together."

"If you're not going home for Christmas, then you should spend time with your parents."

"Yeah, you're right." She gets up and goes into the kitchen. "The museum decided to close at noon today so I won't be going into work later. But I do have class at two."

"I'm surprised you came all the way back here. I thought you were going to go to your apartment between classes."

"I was, but..."

I turn and see her pouring herself some water. "What is it, Rachel?"

"Promise you won't overreact?"

I go to the kitchen and stand next to her. "Tell me."

"I went to my apartment and when I got out of my car, these two men came up to me and started taking photos. They got really close and it scared me so I got back in the car and drove here."

48

"Shit." I pull her into my arms. "Did they hurt you?"

"No. I just banged my elbow when I was trying to get in the car."

"Which arm?"

"The right one, but Pearce it's fine."

I take her arm and check her elbow and see a small bruise there. "You're hurt."

She takes her arm back. "It's just a bruise."

"Have you seen these men before?"

"No. They were probably in their mid-thirties, dressed in jeans and sweatshirts, and they both had very expensive cameras. Why would they be taking pictures of me?"

I sigh. "Someone from a magazine or newspaper sent them to get photos of you. Either that, or those men are paparazzi who know they can get a lot of money for the photos. We need to get professional photos taken of you and send them to the media. Actually, we should get one of the two of us. An engagement photo."

"Pearce, this is getting out of hand. It was just supposed to be an engagement announcement. Nothing more."

"It's going to be a lot more than that."

"How do you know?"

"I just have a feeling that it will be. That announcement is generating more press than I thought it would."

I knew the fallout from our elopement would be bad, but not this bad. Now we not only have my father to deal with, and the organization, but we also have the media. I assumed the media would be interested in us, but I didn't think photographers would be following Rachel around.

I've put Rachel in danger. Danger from the organization, and now the media.

What the hell have I done?

CHAPTER FIVE

PEARCE

At noon, I arrive at Jack's house, preparing for yet another lecture. It starts as soon as he opens the door.

"Well, well, look who's here. It's Mr. Fly Off to Vegas and Do Whatever the Fuck I Want." He turns and walks off. "Good to see you again."

I come inside and shut the door. "Are you going to wait for me?"

He doesn't answer. He just keeps walking down the hall. He's barefoot and wearing baggy white pants that are rolled up to his knees. His top half is covered in a loose white shirt with the sleeves rolled up. The shirt hangs long and drapes over his hips. And he has a piece of white fabric tied around his forehead. As usual, I have no idea what he's up to.

I follow him into a room I've never been in before. The lights are off, but there are candles lit all around it. The burning flames make me cough.

"Quiet!" a voice says. I look to my side and see a man sitting on the floor. He's dressed just like Jack. "This is a room of silence!"

I find it ironic he's saying that and yelling at me at the same time.

There are thin mats on the floor. Jack sits on one of them and tries to cross his legs but can't. "Fuck it," he says, and extends his legs out in front of him, leaning back on his arms. "No one's that damn flexible."

"Mr. Ellit," the other man says. "Room of silence."

"Fuck that room of silence shit! It's my own damn house! If I want to make noise, I'll make fucking noise."

The man mumbles something to himself.

"Who's that?" I ask Jack, keeping my voice down.

"Some meditation guru. My therapist said I needed to meditate to reduce my stress. This guy's supposed to be one of the best. He's from Hollywood. Works with a lot of celebrities." Jack glares at the man, who's sitting up very straight with his eyes closed. "I hate him. He's just making me *more* stressed."

"Breathe," the man says, as he takes a deep breath.

"I'm not paying you a thousand dollars an hour for you to tell me to fucking breathe! I've been breathing on my own just fine for the past fifty-eight years."

The man clears his throat. "That's what meditation is, Mr. Ellit. You clear your mind and breathe."

"That's it? We're just going to sit here and breathe?" Jack turns onto his hands and knees and pushes himself up to standing. "We're done here. Clean this place up, then get the hell out of here. Pearce, follow me."

I glance over at the guru and hear him swearing under his breath. I don't think he'll be coming back here.

Jack takes me to the hidden room he took me to before. I take a seat at the poker table while he heads to the bar.

"You know why I had to suffer through that just now?"

"Because you're trying to reduce stress."

"Yes, but also because I knew you were coming over and I'm trying to calm myself down so I don't kill you."

"Jack, I know you're upset but I was running out of time."

He pours some whiskey into a glass and drinks it all at once. "Can you believe that?"

"Believe what?"

He fills his glass with more whiskey. "That people actually pay to have someone tell you to goddamn breathe! That's the last time I listen to my therapist."

"I didn't know you had a therapist."

"She's not really my therapist. She's more like a friend with benefits. But she *is* a certified therapist, so sometimes she feels the need to toss out some advice after one of our..." He smiles. "Private sessions." He swigs his drink, then closes his eyes as the liquor goes down his throat. "Now *that's* how you relax."

I'm trying not to look at his bare feet because it's not a pleasant sight. It's also unpleasant to look at the chest hair sticking out of his shirt, which is unbuttoned way too far. I glance away.

"Anyway, Jack, as I was saying, I was running out of time. They're getting ready to vote on the rule that would forbid me from being with Rachel."

"I've told you this before, Pearce. There doesn't need to be a goddamn rule." He walks over to the poker table. "You marry who they tell you to marry, and if you don't...well, I don't know what's going to happen. Guess we'll find out on Sunday." He takes a seat across from me. "What the hell were you thinking marrying her like that without even telling me? I said I'd help you, but once again, you didn't listen."

"I hadn't heard anything from you in weeks. I couldn't keep waiting."

"I run an international corporation, Pearce. I also had an assignment to complete. So forgive me for not making time to focus on your love life."

"I'm just saying that I had to figure something out. I couldn't wait."

"Who the hell came up with that asinine plan, anyway?"

"I did."

"No, you didn't." He rips the piece of fabric off his head and tosses it aside. "Running off to Vegas? That doesn't sound like you. Someone else came up with that. It was that idiot Royce Sinclair, wasn't it?"

"Royce had nothing to do with it. I just had him go with me to throw people off track."

"You're lying. You still need to work on your body language and facial expressions. You give too much away." He unbuttons more of his shirt. "God, it's hot in here. Are you hot?"

"No, I'm fine." I focus on the wall behind him. His chest hair was disgusting enough, but now he's exposed his old man skin, wrinkled up from years in the sun.

"Why would you listen to an idiot like Royce?"

Jack knows the truth, so there's no need to continue denying it. "It was a good plan. He actually helped me out for once."

"I can't believe they're considering him for president."

"Who?"

"Who the fuck are we talking about here? Royce Sinclair! Pay attention, Pearce." He gets up and goes back to the bar.

"I thought they were making him a senator, not president. They're seriously considering Royce for president?"

"It won't be for a long time, but yes, they're considering him. And if they want him for the job, they need to start training him soon." Jack belches. "Pardon me."

"Why would they choose Royce?"

"Because he's the best damn liar anyone's ever seen. The man could lie his way out of hell. Even the devil would believe him." He waves his hand at me. "You know, you should take some lessons from Royce. Or maybe he can't teach you. Maybe it's just a natural talent. But you should at least ask. He might be able to give you some pointers."

"So going back to Rachel and me, what do you think's going to happen?"

He exhales a long breath as he reclines back in the chair. "You'll be punished, but I don't know what the punishment will be. What did Holton say? Or is he no longer speaking to you?"

"We spoke last night and this morning. He said he doesn't know what will happen."

"How did he act? Angry or quiet?"

"Both. He was angry last night and quiet this morning."

He nods. "That's bad."

Jack's thinking the same thing I am. My father's outburst last night was good, because it meant he had no other way to deal with what I've done. But now his anger has been replaced by an eerie calmness, which means he's found a way to deal with me. He feels in control again.

"He's planning something," I say to Jack.

He nods again. "Something big. Something fucking huge." He takes a drink.

I point to his glass. "I think I need one of those."

"Help yourself."

I make my way to the bar and pour myself some bourbon.

"He's going to try to harm her," I say, taking a drink.

"That would be my guess. An unfortunate accident."

"I meant he'll try to scare her. He wouldn't kill her, Jack."

He spins his chair around to face me. "Are you sure about that?"

"Of course I am. He wouldn't take it that far."

"He wouldn't do it himself. He'd hire someone, making sure he—"

"Stop it!" I slam my glass down on the bar. "My father would NOT do something like that! Not to an innocent woman, who is also my wife. And his daughter-in-law."

Jack shrugs. "Okay."

I go over to him. "Don't be so damn condescending. I'm not naive. I know what my father is capable of, but he would NOT do that."

"Does Holton think I'm involved?"

"I don't think so. But he thinks you lied about Rachel and me. He thinks you knew I'd been dating her for months. By the way, why didn't you tell me my father hired you to spy on me?"

"What's the point? You already knew I was spying on you."

"Did you tell him anything?"

"Bits and pieces, just so he'd know I was actually doing my job." Jack leans back and clasps his hands behind his head. "So what are you planning to do about this fucked-up mess you got yourself into?"

"All I did was get married. People do it all the time. It shouldn't be a fucked-up mess. I should be allowed to continue on with my life without their interference."

"And I should be able to go an entire night without having to get up and pee fifty times, but we don't live in a fantasy world, Pearce. It is what it is and now you have to deal with it."

I pace the floor, the drink in my hand. "She needs protection. I don't trust the other members."

"So you're going to surround her with bodyguards? And how are you going to explain that to her?"

"Not that type of protection. I need something bigger."

"Would you stop pacing? You're making me dizzy." He shuts his eyes for a moment, then opens them. "This is what you're going to do. That idiot friend of yours, Royce, has already set this is in motion, so you might as well keep it going."

"Keep what going?"

"The media circus surrounding this wedding of yours. You need to keep it going. Make it an even bigger story than when you married that lesbian. You got a ton of press from that wedding. So do it again, but don't wait. Start right now. Make people fall in love with you two, and more importantly, make them fall in love with Rachel. Do interviews, photo shoots, whatever it takes. The organization won't harm a celebrity. It's too high profile. Too easy for them to get caught."

"Rachel doesn't like the spotlight."

"Well, she needs to get the hell over it. The media will eat this up. Midwest farm girl marries the billionaire bachelor. That's a fairytale story, and everyone loves a fairytale."

"How long would we need to keep it going?"

"At least until the wedding. Maybe longer. I'll keep my ears open and let you know if I hear anything from the other members. As of now, they haven't even mentioned the girl."

"How do you know that?"

"I have inside sources, Pearce."

"Then you know what my punishment will be."

"No. They haven't decided yet." He yawns and stretches his arms out. "I need to get back to work. I'm supposed to be at a meeting that started ten minutes ago." He stands up. "Drink what you want from the bar, then see yourself out."

He disappears out the door.

That went better than expected. At least he didn't spend the entire time lecturing me. But he didn't really help me, other than his idea to make my relationship with Rachel even more public. It's probably a good idea, but I don't think she'll go for it.

The next day Rachel and I leave for Indiana, not arriving there until late afternoon. I've flown over the Midwest many times, but never actually been there. From the air, it looks like a lot of wide open space, with houses few and far between.

When we get off the plane, Rachel's parents are waiting for us.

"Mom! Dad!" She runs up and hugs them both.

Her mother is tall, like Rachel, and has short brown hair. They look similar, but Rachel's eyes look like her dad's. He has the same bright blue eyes. He's almost as tall as me, and has a rugged look, like someone who works outside a lot. His dark brown hair is thinning on top and he's got deep wrinkles around his eyes from the sun. When he smiles, more wrinkles crease around his mouth. Rachel also has his smile. I noticed the similarity right away.

"Mr. Evans, it's nice to finally meet you." I extend my hand and he shakes it, but then pulls me in for a hug.

"You're my future son-in-law." He laughs. "I need more than a handshake." He steps back. "And call me Henry. No need to call me Mr. Evans."

"And call me Beth," Rachel's mother says as she gives me a hug.

Now I know why Rachel hugs everyone. Her parents do the same thing. My parents wouldn't hug someone if you paid them to. My father has never hugged me, not even as a child. He tried to avoid even touching me, which he didn't have to because he had nannies take care of me. And the few hugs my mother has given me have always been distant hugs, with just our shoulders briefly coming together.

Beth stands back and looks at Rachel and me. "You two make a beautiful couple." She winks at Rachel. "You didn't tell me Pearce was so handsome."

Rachel laughs and kisses me on the cheek. "Yes, he's very handsome."

"Let me see the ring." Her mother picks up Rachel's hand. "Oh, my. That's the biggest diamond I've ever seen."

"Yes, he spent too much," Rachel says to me.

I lean down and kiss her. "It was worth every penny."

"He also bought me diamond earrings and a diamond necklace," Rachel tells her mother. "They're so expensive I'm almost afraid to wear them."

Rachel tends to forget how much money I have. If something happened to her jewelry, I'd just buy her more. But she has trouble spending money. She's so used to not having it that it'll take her some time to adjust to being wealthy.

"Should we go?" Henry waves us toward the baggage area. "I'm starving. We need to eat."

Beth shakes her head and says to me, "The man never stops eating. And yet he never gains a pound."

Henry has a lean frame and seems to be in good shape for a man his age. I don't know what farmers do all day, but I'm sure it's a workout, more so than sitting at a desk all day.

Rachel's hometown is a half hour from the airport, and on the drive to her house her parents ask me a million questions. I expected they would since they've never met me, but I didn't think I'd get quizzed the second I arrived. But it's fine. I'm sure if I had a daughter I'd be doing the same thing. I can tell how much they love Rachel and I can already see some of her mother's overprotectiveness. She brought Rachel some gloves and a scarf to wear home from the airport, just in case Rachel forgot to bring them. It's not that cold outside, but Rachel wore them anyway just to appease her mother.

We drive past miles and miles of farmland and finally arrive at the house. It's a simple two-story house that is plenty big enough to live in, but still smaller than my parents' guest house. The inside is very basic and functional with a living room on one side, a dining room on the other, and a kitchen in the back. Three bedrooms are upstairs; Rachel's room, the master for her parents, and a guest room.

"This is where you'll be staying," Beth says as she shows me to the guest room. It has a double bed and a dresser off to the side. "Let us know if you need anything. The bathroom is down the hall. Go ahead and get settled. I need to check on the roast." Her mother goes back down the stairs.

I smile at Rachel. "Separate rooms?"

She smiles back. "They're old-fashioned. And remember, we're not married yet."

I draw her into me. "I don't know if I can go a whole night without you."

"Then don't," she whispers.

I kiss her neck, right by her ear. "I don't think your parents would approve of me sneaking in your bed at night."

"We'll be quiet. And you're not staying the whole night."

My lips move to her mouth and I talk softly over them. "I thought you were a good girl, Miss Evans."

"You thought wrong. And it's Mrs. Kensington."

I kiss her, and keep kissing her, because I haven't done so all day. We've been stuck on a plane, and then in the car with her parents, and I can't wait any longer. I need to kiss her. I need to do more than that but I can't right now, so I back away.

"What time do your parents go to bed?" I ask.

"Usually ten-thirty. But they might want to stay up later tonight so they can talk to you."

"I'll tell them I'm tired and have to get to bed."

"Don't you want to talk to them?" she teases.

"I do, but there's something else I want to do even more." I kiss her again. "Let's go downstairs. I think your parents have a couple thousand more questions to ask me."

She laughs. "They're just making sure you're a good guy. They don't want me marrying just anyone."

"It's fine. I understand."

As we're coming down the stairs, Henry walks in from outside. "Pearce. Would you mind helping me with the firewood?"

Rachel nudges me, signaling me to agree to it.

"Sure," I say. "Just let me grab my coat."

"I have one in the barn you can borrow. That coat of yours is a little too fancy for farm work."

I brought a black wool dress coat. It's the one I always wear, but apparently it's not appropriate for gathering firewood.

Henry takes me out to the barn. Inside it are large pieces of farm machinery and equipment and tools.

"Take that one." He points to a dark green coat hanging on a hook. "It's big on me so should fit you just fine."

I go over and put it on, then follow him outside again. "So how do you like farming?"

"I like it. Then again, it's all I know. I grew up here and worked the land with my father and he did the same with his father." He smiles. "You want a farm, Pearce?"

I don't know what he's asking, so I keep quiet.

He pats my back. "I'm just kidding. Part of me hoped Rachel would marry someone who wanted to take over the farm."

I laugh. "That's definitely not me. I don't know the first thing about farming."

"Not many people your age do, even around here. A lot of these farms are being bought out by corporations. I'm sure that's what'll happen to this one." He stops next to a woodpile, which is between the house and the barn. In front of the woodpile are a couple adirondack chairs that face the fields.

"Do you want to sit for a minute?" He lowers himself into one of the chairs.

I take a seat, although I'd rather go inside. It's cold out here, and dark, the only light being the light coming from the porch.

"So you wanted to ask me a question?" Henry's smiling, and I know what he's referring to.

"I assumed you'd want to get to know me better before I asked."

He shakes his head. "No. Go ahead."

"Well, I would just like to say that, although I haven't known your daughter for very long, I do love her very much and I promise to take care of her and do everything possible to give her a good life."

"And what's a good life to you, Pearce?"

That's a tough question. I take a moment to think about it.

"I suppose everyone defines that differently. And before meeting your daughter, I'm not sure I could've given you an answer. My life used to be all about work and nothing else. But after meeting Rachel, I realized there's so much more to life. Rachel has introduced me to a side of myself I didn't even know was there. And now, I can't imagine my life without her. So I guess in response to your question, I'd say a good life is spending it with the person you love."

He nods. "Good answer. I know Rachel would agree. I can tell you two love each other. But I must admit, I do worry about her being with you."

"Why is that?"

"She's never been around people with a lot of money. I don't really know how your world works, and maybe Rachel will adjust without a problem, but I still worry about her."

"I don't think you need to. Your daughter is very capable of handling herself. She isn't easily intimidated. If she were, she never would've gone out with me." I smile. "I can be a little intimidating sometimes."

"She's never been afraid of a challenge." He laughs. "I remember the first time we took the girls to a pool. Rachel went up to the water and jumped right in. She was only two and she just jumped in. No fear. Her sister, on the other hand, was scared to death of the water." He shakes his head. "Those girls were quite a pair. So similar and yet so different."

He gets quiet, and although I don't know him that well, I get a feeling I know what he's thinking.

"Henry, I can't imagine what a huge loss it was to lose your daughter, but I can assure you, you aren't losing Rachel. Marrying me and living in Connecticut won't change her. Living in my world, she's not going to become someone else. She always tells me what great parents you and your wife are, and how grateful she is for what you've taught her. She's the way she is now because of how you raised her, and nothing can change that. I know you miss her, and I'll make sure she comes back here as much as possible. I'm not trying to take her from you. I want her to still have a close relationship with her family. That's important to both of us."

He stands up and holds his hand out. I stand up as well and shake his hand.

"You have my blessing, Pearce." He points behind me. "But you still have to earn your keep. Grab some logs."

I go over and take some from the pile.

"Have you ever made a fire?" he asks.

"No. My loft has a gas fireplace. You just flip a switch."

"Well, there's no flipping switches here." He takes two of the logs I picked out. "You have to get a mix of sizes. Some large ones and then some smaller ones for kindling." He picks up another log. "This one's too big. I should've made it smaller." He looks at me. "I'm gonna guess you've never chopped a log?"

I smile. "That would be correct."

He takes the ax that's lying next to the woodpile. "Follow me. And bring those two logs."

I follow him to an area just in front of the house. There's more light here than by the woodpile, so at least I can see what I'm doing.

Henry points to a large tree stump. "Set the log there."

I do as he says, setting it upright.

"Okay, here's what you do. I'll show you, and then you try." He lifts the ax up, then swings it down on the log, splitting it into perfect halves. He makes it look easy, but I'm sure it's not.

He sets the other log on the stump and hands me the ax. I'm not sure he should be trusting me with an ax, given that I've never even held one before.

"Get a good stance going," he says. "Legs apart. Make sure you're stable. Then bring the ax down in one controlled movement, making sure to keep your eye on the log."

It's odd to get instruction like this. Whenever my father wanted to teach me something, he'd make me do it without telling me how, so that he could criticize me after the fact. It was less of a teaching experience and more of an opportunity for him to put me down and make me feel worthless, thus making himself feel powerful.

I follow Henry's instructions, but I hit the log at the wrong spot and just splinter it and it rolls off the stump.

"I guess I'm not good at it." I offer him the ax but he doesn't take it.

"You did fine. You at least hit the log. A lot of first timers miss it." He sets the log back on the stump. "Try again, and this time, aim for that dark line in the center."

I take another swing at it, doing as he said, and this time I split it, but only halfway.

"You just have to hit it harder," Henry says. "You have to do it a few times to get a feel for it. You want to try another one?"

"Sure."

He goes back to the woodpile. This is another new experience for me. And I don't just mean the wood chopping. I mean the fact that I'm being taught something without being yelled at or scolded or criticized. Henry is actually being helpful and wants me to learn.

For a moment there, he felt more like a father than my own.

CHAPTER SIX

RACHEL

"I can't believe how handsome he is," my mom says as I get some glasses from the cupboard.

I laugh. "Yeah, I know, Mom. You've said that like three times now."

"He's much more handsome than Adam. It's not even fair to compare them."

I go around her to get the iced tea from the fridge. "Aside from Pearce's good looks, do you like him?"

"Honey, I just met him, but I can tell you two are in love and I can see how happy you are with him, so that earns him some points. And he doesn't seem snobby at all."

"Not everyone with money is a snob."

"Does he act differently when he's around his friends?"

"We haven't spent much time around his friends. I met this guy, Royce, that Pearce went to college with, but that's about it. Pearce works so much that he doesn't have a lot of time to socialize."

"Do you think he'll keep working all those hours after you're married?"

"I hope not, but I really don't know."

"What are you going to do for a job?"

"I'm not sure yet. It depends on where we live. There aren't any jobs for me in the town where he lives now."

"Is he willing to move?"

"I don't know."

"Rachel, you and Pearce need to discuss these things. You shouldn't get married until you do."

"Mom, don't worry about it. Pearce and I will figure it out." I take some napkins from the drawer. "Are we ready? Should I call the guys in?"

"Yes, everything's ready."

Leave it to my mom to bring my mood down. I know Pearce and I have a lot to talk about and a lot of decisions to make, but I don't need my mom worrying about that stuff. I already worry enough about it, especially my job. I graduate in a couple weeks, and then what? What am I going to do for work?

When I get outside, I smile when I see my handsome husband swinging an ax over his head. Good old Dad. Putting Pearce to work. I watch as he hits the log. It splits right in half. He's good for someone who I'm sure has never done it before.

Pearce and my dad are laughing about something, so they must be getting along. It doesn't surprise me. My dad gets along with everyone. He makes friends everywhere he goes. And he loves teaching people stuff, which is why he's teaching my husband how to chop wood. If my dad wasn't a farmer, I'm sure he would've been a teacher.

"Dad." I walk up to him. "What are you doing? Pearce just got here and you're already making him chop firewood?"

My dad's arm goes around me and he squeezes me into his side, making me trip on my feet. It's his goofy dad hug. He always did it when I was a kid. He yanks me into his side so fast my feet can't catch up.

"I told him he has to earn his keep," my dad says, letting me go.

I smile at Pearce. "Did he earn it yet? Because it's time for dinner."

My dad inspects the logs on the ground. "I suppose that's good enough for now. But you'll have to do some more tomorrow, Pearce. I've got a whole pile that needs to be chopped."

"Dad! Tomorrow is Thanksgiving. He's not chopping wood on Thanksgiving."

"Chores still need to be done, honey."

"I don't mind," Pearce says, setting the ax down. "It's good exercise."

I take his hand. "I hope you worked up an appetite because my mom made a big dinner. And two pies for dessert."

We go inside to the dining room table. My mom has everything set out; roast, mashed potatoes, glazed carrots, a salad, rolls, and a few other side dishes.

"I wasn't sure what you liked," my mom says to Pearce, "so I made a few extra things to make sure you had plenty to eat."

"That's very kind of you," he says. "But you didn't have to go to all that work. I eat most anything."

Pearce is so polite. My ex-fiancé, Adam, never was. He pretended to be, but it always came off as fake. I hope I don't run into him this weekend.

After dinner, we all hang out in the living room and talk. Poor Pearce. My parents have made him talk about himself since the second he arrived. They've asked him so many questions that even *I* learned stuff I didn't know about him. Like the fact that he was valedictorian at his high school. He went to a very elite prep school. I'm sure he had tough competition from his classmates and yet he ended up the valedictorian. And he graduated at the top of his class at both Harvard and Yale. So how can his father not be proud of him? I don't understand it.

We stay up talking until eleven, then go to bed. My parents' bedroom is down the hall from mine with a bathroom in between, so they shouldn't hear Pearce sneaking into my room. But by eleven-thirty, he still hasn't shown up, so I sneak down to the guest room.

"Hey." I climb into bed with him. "I thought you were you going to come visit me."

"I wanted to make sure your parents were asleep."

I snuggle up to his warm body. "So what did you think of them?"

"They're very nice. Very hospitable. A lot better than my parents."

I don't disagree.

"I can tell they really like you." I kiss his cheek. "I'm sure by the time we leave here my dad will give you his blessing to marry his daughter."

"He already did. We had a discussion about it when you and your mother were preparing dinner."

"What did he say?"

"He said we had his blessing."

"Wow. You must've really won him over. He barely knows you and he already approves of you."

"Rachel, are you sure you don't want to tell them we're married? I don't feel right lying to them like this."

"I don't either, but it'd be worse if my mom found out she'd missed my wedding. She's all excited about helping plan it. Where do you think we should get married? We need to get a place fast if we're really doing this in March."

"Reserving a place won't be a problem. When we tell them who we are, they'll make sure to accommodate us." He hesitates. "Rachel, I want you and your mother to be included in the plans, but we're going to need to hire a team of wedding coordinators. You can give them direction, but it might be best if you just let them take care of everything."

"I can't plan my own wedding?"

"With something this public, people will be dissecting every decision that's made, from the flowers to the cake to the place cards at the reception. If it's not completely perfect, you'll be criticized by the media, and I don't want them doing that to you."

"Pearce, I want this wedding to be how *we* want it, not someone else."

"I'm not saying you can't be involved in the decisions, but I think you should let the professionals handle the details."

It's another part of Pearce's world I'm not used to. As someone who's fairly well-known, everything he does is judged, and like he said, if it doesn't appear perfect it reflects poorly on him. I know this wedding is just for show, but I was hoping I could plan it as if it were real. But that may not be possible.

"Maybe we should do this tomorrow night," I say, referring to why I came in here. "I'm really tired from the trip."

"I'm not tired." He brings me in for a kiss. "I have more than enough energy."

I pull back. "Let's just do it tomorrow."

"Is something wrong?"

"No. I'm just tired." I give him a kiss as I get out of bed. "I love you."

"I love you too."

I go back to my room and lie there, staring up at the ceiling. I can't sleep. Between what Pearce said and what my mom said, I'm feeling anxious about my future. Is this what it'll be like? Will I have to hire professionals to make decisions for me so I don't screw up? Pearce's mom has a stylist who picks out her clothes. Will I have to have a stylist too? Will Pearce and I be able to choose where we live, and what kind of house we have, and how it's decorated? Or will someone do all that for us?

That anxious feeling gets even worse as I think about that. I was finally living this independent life where I could make my own decisions, but now I feel like I'm heading backwards, no longer able to decide things for myself.

I hear the door open and see Pearce walking in.

"Pearce, what are you doing in here?"

He joins me in bed, turning on his side to face me. "I didn't like the way you left just now. Something's wrong. What is it?"

"Nothing."

"Rachel." He pulls me into his arms. "You need to tell me."

"I just...I'm panicking a little."

"About the wedding?"

"About everything." I hug his chest and breathe in his scent. That, and the feel of his arms around me, calms me.

"What do you mean by 'everything'?"

"Your world, and how everything has to be so perfect all the time. I'm not perfect. And I never will be."

He lifts my face up to his. "I never said you had to be perfect. I don't expect you to be."

"But the people around you do."

"To some extent, yes."

"I don't know what that means."

"It means that sometimes you have to put on an elegant dress, appear at events, and suffer through mind-numbing conversations with very wealthy people who like to drone on about the yacht they just purchased. But doing those things doesn't mean you have to change who you are."

"Will someone have to pick out my clothes?"

"If it's for a public event where there will be photographers, then yes, it would be easier if you let a stylist help you. But as for your day-to-day life, you can wear whatever you'd like."

"Does your mother always dress like she did that night we had dinner?"

"Yes. But the last thing I want is to have you dress like my mother. She's old, for one. You're far too young to be seen in those suits she wears."

"She looked nice when I saw her."

"Perhaps so, but that's not your style. I want you to wear whatever clothes you feel comfortable in. But I'm guessing you could use some new ones."

"Yeah, mine are pretty old. The past few years, I haven't had much of a budget for clothes."

"You do now, so go shopping when we get back. Buy whatever you'd like."

I smile at him. "Maybe *you* should do it. I liked the clothes you bought me for Las Vegas."

"I had some help with that. If you'd like me to set you up with the woman who picked out those clothes, I'm happy to do so."

"That might be a good idea. I'm not very good with fashion, especially high-end fashion."

"I'll call her on Friday and set something up. So what else are you panicking about?"

"I'm not anymore." I yawn. "I feel better now that you're here."

"Do you want me to stay?"

"Maybe until I fall asleep." I nestle into his arms.

He kisses my head. "Goodnight, Rachel."

When I wake up, he's gone and light is peeking through the drapes. The clock by my bed says it's just after seven. I hear some noise downstairs. My mom must be getting the turkey ready. I get up and pull my robe on and go down to the kitchen. My mom is there, also in her robe. Pearce is there too, but he's dressed in jeans and the sweater I picked out for him a week ago.

"Rachel, you're up early," my mom says. "Want some coffee?"

"Sure." I sit next to Pearce at the kitchen table. "What are you doing up?"

"Keeping your mother company." He sips his coffee.

"He's good company." She smiles at him. "And very helpful. He helped me stuff the turkey."

"You did?" I ask, trying to imagine him stuffing a turkey.

He shrugs. "I'd never done it before. I thought I should try it. I was telling your mother how you've made me try all these new things."

He puts his arm around my shoulder and leans over to kiss my cheek. My mom notices and smiles.

"And you chopped wood yesterday, so that was new." I scoot my chair over so I'm closer to him. "I'll have to come up with something else new for you to do." I stop to think. "I know. Have you ever been to a country bar?"

He laughs. "No. I can definitely say that I have not done that."

"Then we'll go there tomorrow night. We'll probably run into some of my friends from high school. A lot of them moved away, but some are still here. I can show you off."

"You should stop by and see Lisa while you're here," my mom says as she hands me a mug of coffee. "She had her baby a few weeks ago. A boy. I saw him at church last week. He's darling."

She turns to Pearce. "Rachel and Lisa were on the swim team together."

Pearce looks at me. "Your mother was saying how you were the best swimmer in your high school."

"She still holds the record for most wins," my mom says.

"You need to start swimming again," Pearce says.

"I don't have time." I sip my coffee.

"You will after you graduate. There's a gym just down the street from the loft. They have an Olympic-size pool. I'll get you a membership."

"Really?" I set my mug down. "I would love that. That could be my Christmas gift."

He pulls me into his side and kisses my head. "It's not a gift. It's a necessity. You need to be swimming again."

My mom brings the coffee pot over and refills Pearce's cup. "Speaking of Christmas, what are your plans?"

She directs the question to both of us.

I glance at Pearce. "We were thinking of taking a trip. Pearce offered to take me to Italy as a graduation gift."

Dammit. I shouldn't have said that. Now she's going to cry on Thanksgiving.

But surprisingly, instead of crying, she smiles. "That sounds wonderful. You should do it."

"You won't be upset if I miss Christmas?"

"You've worked hard this year, honey. I think it'd be good for you to get away. Besides, you're here now, and we'll see you in a couple weeks for graduation, so at least we've had some time together. And maybe I'll come out there in January to help with the wedding."

"What's everyone doing up?" My dad walks in, wearing jeans and his jacket. He must've been out working in the barn. He goes over to my mom and gives her a kiss. "Did you wake up the kids with your pots and pans?"

I see Pearce smiling at the 'kids' comment. Basically anyone under 30 is a kid, according to my parents.

"Pearce was up with me at six," my mom says.

"So you're an early riser, huh?" My dad pours himself some coffee.

"I'm usually at work by six," Pearce says. "So getting *up* at six is like sleeping in."

"He works too much," I tell my dad.

"Rachel, would you help me with breakfast?" my mom asks.

"Sure." I get up, taking my coffee with me.

"Do you want to learn how to get a fire going, Pearce?" my dad asks. "We'll use the logs you cut yesterday."

Pearce agrees to it and the two of them go outside to get the logs.

I'm surprised how well Pearce fits into my family. I was worried he wouldn't, but he does, which makes me really happy. I'm also happy that my parents seem to love him.

In fact, as soon as my dad takes Pearce outside, my mom goes on and on about how great Pearce is. I guess his early morning chat with her really won her over.

After everyone has breakfast, I help my mom prepare Thanksgiving dinner, getting the side dishes ready and baking the pies while Pearce and my dad hang out in the living room, talking and watching TV.

We have dinner at two. The food is amazing as always. I consider myself a pretty good cook, but my mom is even better. Pearce kept complimenting her on the meal, which made her love him even more.

That night, after my parents go to sleep, I wait in my bedroom for Pearce. After a few minutes, he comes in and gets under the covers with me.

"I feel like I'm 15, sneaking in your room like this."

I laugh. "Sorry. My parents are just old-fashioned about this type of stuff."

"So they don't know we're living together?"

"They do, but it's different when I'm under their roof."

His lips find mine in the dark room and I feel his hand on my backside, pulling me closer. "I'm finding it incredibly difficult not having you next to me all night."

"It's just a few more nights."

"It's three more nights. That's too long."

I sigh. "I know."

He kisses me, his hand slipping under the hem of my t-shirt. I sit up enough for him to take it off. He takes his off too, then his mouth moves down to my breast as his strong hands caress my skin. I breathe out, trying to suppress the sounds I would normally make in response to what he's doing to me. He tugs at my pajama pants and I lift my hips so he can take them off. He skims his hand up my thigh, stopping between my legs at the place that's now aching to be touched.

I moan, unable to stop myself.

I feel his lips over mine. "Shhh. We have to be quiet."

His hand continues, bringing me close.

"I can't be quiet," I say, gripping the sheet.

He's laughing at me. "Yes, you can."

He brings me to the edge, then moves off me just long enough to strip the rest of himself. I feel his body cover mine as he enters me, slowly. "God, you feel good."

I reach around his hips and pull him into me.

"Shit," he breathes out. "I'm going to make noise if you keep doing that."

I wrap my legs around him, pushing him even deeper. "You mean *that*?"

"You're killing me." He gets his hips moving. "It's payback time."

He's not kidding. He thrusts harder as his hand goes between us, back to the spot he warmed up. Moments later I'm coming undone, gripping the sheet again, trying to be quiet, but finding it nearly impossible as the sensations overtake me.

As my body relaxes, Pearce finishes up, then remains over me, kissing my shoulder.

"I don't think we can do that again," I say, out of breath. "It's too hard to be quiet."

"We're doing it again. This was practice for tomorrow night. I think you've got the hang of it now. You barely made a sound."

"I didn't make *any* sounds. I was quiet the whole time."

He lifts up and smiles at me. "You were making noise towards the end there, but I'm sure they didn't hear."

"I was?" I smile back at him. "I guess I can't control what you do to me."

He kisses me. "I should go."

"Can you stay until I fall asleep, like last night?"

"I'd stay all night if you let me."

"I know you would. And I would love that, but we can't."

He rolls onto his back. "Are you sure you don't want to tell your parents we're married?"

"Yes. I'm sure."

I fall asleep in his arms, and once again, when I wake up, he's gone.

The next day, we all load into the car and my parents give Pearce a tour of the town. It was dark when we got off the plane, so he didn't get to see anything. There isn't much to see. Just a small downtown with some restaurants and shops. We have lunch at a diner, then go back to the house.

Pearce and my dad watch football while my mom and I talk about the wedding. I told her it was going to be huge and that I'd be hiring wedding coordinators to do most of the planning, but that didn't stop her from wanting to give me all her ideas. So I jotted them down and added my own. Even if we don't end up doing them, it was fun to talk about.

Since my mom didn't have much of a wedding herself, she's excited for mine. As for me, I'm not sure how I feel about the wedding. Now that I know other people are going to be taking it over, part of me wishes we could just skip it, but I know we can't. We have to put on a show and host a big party for all these people I have yet to meet.

At eight, I steal Pearce away from my dad so I can take him to the country bar. I'm already laughing imagining Pearce there. I'm sure he won't like it, but it's the place to be on Friday nights and it'll give him a real feel for the town.

I borrowed my dad's pickup because you have to show up with a pickup. Everyone does. I'm wearing tight jeans and a pink and white plaid shirt with the sleeves rolled up. My mom loaned me her cowboy boots, which she never wears.

Pearce has on jeans and a black button-up shirt. I've taken him shopping several times the past few months, slowly filling his wardrobe with more casual clothes.

He looks really hot in that black shirt. This is the first time he's worn it, but now that I see how good it looks on him, he's going to have to wear it a lot more. He didn't shave, so he's got a thick five o'clock shadow. And he's wearing the cologne that I love.

"You look really hot," I tell him as I'm driving into town.

He smiles. "So do you. You're like my hot little cowgirl."

"We might just have to do it in the back of the pickup before we go inside. I bet that would be another first for you."

He looks up, like he's thinking. "No, I've done it in a pickup. At least twice."

"What?" We're at a stoplight and I look at him. "When did this happen?"

He laughs. "It didn't. I was kidding. You should've seen the look on your face. It was a mix of shock and anger, with a hint of jealousy."

"I wasn't angry. And why would I be jealous?"

"Because you thought I'd already done it and you wanted to be my first." He reaches over and puts his hand on my leg. "Just admit it. You wanted to be my first fuck in a truck."

I burst out laughing. "Oh my God. I can't believe you just said that! Those words are the absolute last words I would ever think would come out of Pearce Kensington's mouth."

"Well, I have a few beers in me, thanks to your father."

"Still, that's just too funny. And yes, I admit I wanted to be your first…fuck in a truck. But since it's only forty degrees, we'll have to do it some other time."

I park the car, still laughing. We get out and Pearce meets me on the sidewalk. The bar is at the end of Main Street, but it's

74

already crowded so we had to park down a ways. As we're walking past the storefronts, I stop in front of the drugstore.

"You want to see where I spent all my allowance as a kid?"

He looks at the sign. "A drugstore?"

"They sell all kinds of stuff." I drag him inside and over to the soda fountain. It hasn't changed since I was a kid. There's a long counter lined with a row of stools that have red cushioned seats that swivel. "I'd either get ice cream or candy." I point to the jars that hold an assortment of candy.

He smiles. "So that's why you like ice cream so much."

"Probably, although they don't add the crushed cookies and you have to have crushed cookies with ice cream. So I usually just got candy."

Pearce steps back suddenly and I look down and see a little boy attached to his legs. He must have run right into Pearce and now he's holding on and won't let go, his big brown eyes gazing up at Pearce like he wants him to pick him up.

Pearce is staring at the little boy, unsure what to do. I don't think he's ever been around kids.

I laugh. "I think you made a new friend."

"My new friend won't let go of my leg."

I lean down to the boy. He looks familiar. "Where's your mommy?"

"Right here." I hear a voice behind me. "Sorry about that."

I turn around. "Lisa!" I give her a hug, but only a partial one because she's holding an infant.

"Rachel, I didn't know you were in town."

"Yeah, I'm back for Thanksgiving. Is this the new baby?" I fold back his blanket a little to see his face.

"That's him. Three weeks old. His name is Sam. And you've already met Nathan." She looks at him. "Nathan, let go of that man."

I laugh because Pearce is frozen in place, afraid to move with Nathan still attached to his leg.

"I'll get him." I crouch down so I'm level with him. "Hi, Nathan. Last time I saw you, you weren't even walking, and now look how big you are. I almost didn't recognize you. How old are you?"

He releases his hold on Pearce and holds up two fingers.

"You're two?"

He nods.

I hold my arms out. "Can I have a hug?"

He gives me one and I hug him back. He's so cute, dressed in tiny jeans and a big red jacket.

"She was always great with kids," I hear Lisa tell Pearce.

Nathan doesn't let me go so I pick him up. "He's adorable, Lisa."

"Not always," she says, laughing. "But at the moment he is." She motions to Pearce. "Do you two know each other? Or were you just saving an innocent stranger from my son?"

I smile. "I know him. This is Pearce. We're engaged."

"That's great! Congratulations! When's the wedding?"

"It's in March."

Pearce extends his hand to Lisa. "It's nice to meet you."

"You too. And again, I'm sorry about Nathan."

"It's fine. He has quite a grip. Maybe he'll play ball someday."

"Yeah, maybe." She smiles at me. "Rachel, I have to get these two to bed, but it was good seeing you."

"Yeah, we'll have to get together next time I'm in town." I set Nathan down. "Bye, Nathan."

He waves at me as they walk away, and then he waves at Pearce.

"He's so cute." I take Pearce's hand. His body is still stiff. "You okay? You seemed a little freaked out by Nathan."

"I'm just not used to children."

As we're leaving the drugstore, I think about Pearce's comment. I told him I couldn't have kids, but what if I could? Would he even want them? It's another thing we need to discuss. Because I want them more than anything. Even if I could just have one, I'd be happy.

CHAPTER SEVEN

PEARCE

Watching Rachel with that little boy reminded me how much she wants to be a mother someday. If she can't have a child of her own, she'll want to adopt, and I can't adopt. Any child I have has to be mine. Part of the Kensington bloodline. It's another rule of the organization. Membership is passed down through sons, but those sons can't be adopted. The same is true for daughters, who can't be members but are paired with members for an arranged marriage. An adopted child would be seen as an outsider, so adoption is not an option.

"Are you coming?" Rachel asks, holding open the door to the bar.

"Yes. Sorry, I wasn't paying attention."

We walk inside and country music surrounds us, drowning out the sounds of conversations being had by the clusters of people scattered throughout the open room. There are small round tables with stools and a few booths along the wall, but all of the seats are taken so I'm not sure where we're going to sit. The place is filled to capacity with women in short skirts and cowboy boots, and men wearing cowboy hats. I didn't know Indiana was so country, but maybe they're only dressed this way because it's a country bar.

I feel out of place. The only bars I've ever gone to are very high-end, exclusive bars, some of which are invitation only. And they all have very strict dress codes.

Rachel links her arm with mine. "Should we get a drink, or do you want to dance first?"

Dance? I glance over and see a small dance floor in the far back corner of the room. People are doing some kind of dance where they all do the same movements in a line.

The only dancing I've ever done is ballroom dancing, mainly the waltz, and I've only done that when I've been forced to do so. I don't like dancing. And I definitely don't want to do whatever it is those people are doing in that line. They seem to be having a good time, but that's probably because they're drunk.

"I don't dance." I say it loudly so Rachel can hear.

"Come on. It's fun. I'll show you." I let her drag me over there, but I have no intention of partaking in this.

"Rachel, I really don't feel like dancing," I say when she stops next to the dance floor. "You go ahead."

"Rachel!" A blond woman around Rachel's age runs up to her. "I haven't seen you in forever."

"Hey, Cassie." She hugs her. "You look great."

"Come dance with me." Cassie grabs her hand and pulls her onto the dance floor.

Rachel looks back at me, mouthing 'sorry.' I smile and nod at her to go ahead.

Cassie seems a little tipsy. She's stumbling as she walks, but maybe it's because of her shoes. She has on short black boots that are at least three inches high. She's wearing a red plaid flannel shirt that she's turned into a dress by adding a belt. The shirt hits about mid-thigh so it makes for a very short dress and she's unbuttoned it enough to show off a lot of cleavage.

I watch as Rachel finds a place in the line and repeats the steps that everyone else is doing. How does she know how to do this? I don't think she listens to much country music, so how did she learn to dance like this?

A new song begins and some other people recognize her and encourage her to stay on the dance floor. She does, but checks to make sure I'm still there. I motion her to continue.

I like standing here watching her. It's another side of my wife I haven't seen before. She seems to have a lot of friends here and they all seem to love her. Why wouldn't they? She's hard not to love.

I watch as she spins around and claps and sings along to whatever song they're playing. She has a huge smile on her face and it causes me to smile as well.

This is so completely different than anything Rachel will ever experience with me. I hope she'll be okay with that. I hope she'll adapt and won't be wishing she were going to places like this, instead of stuffy charity balls where she'll be surrounded by people twice our age and will have to wear a gown and dance to classical music.

Sometimes I worry Rachel won't be happy in my world. And I fear that if she's not, she won't tell me. I want her to be happy and I need to do everything I can to make sure that she is. Because seeing her happy, like she is right now, is the best feeling in the world.

I know she doesn't want to come back and live here in Indiana, but after having spent a few days here, I'm finding that it's not that bad of a place. It's peaceful and quiet and the people are real, not like the fake people I'm used to. Just looking around this room right now and seeing all the faces, I can tell how people are feeling. Happy. Tired. Bored. Excited. It all shows on their faces. There's not a fake smile to be seen.

Rachel's parents are the same way. They're real. Genuine. And extremely kind, welcoming me into their family with open arms. It's only been a few days, but in just that short time, I've grown to love Rachel's parents.

I've really enjoyed spending time with her father. Watching football. Talking with him while he works outside. Having him teach me things. He already acts as though I'm his son and he treats me much better than my own father does.

Henry is a good man. Hard-working. Dedicated to his family. Involved in his community. Willing to help anyone who needs it. He's the type of man I wish I could be. But I never will. No matter how many good things I do, it will never be enough to outweigh the bad things I've done, and will do in the future.

Rachel's mother is also a good person. She's caring and generous and very smart. She handles the business aspects of the farm, and when we were talking the other morning, she asked for my advice on investments. She has some money stashed away that she'd like to invest, and when I told her about my knowledge in finance, we started talking stocks and bonds. She already knows a lot, but I gave her some additional advice and told her I'd connect her with some investment advisors I work with. They'd normally only deal with people who have at least a million to invest, but if I asked them to, they'd make an exception for Rachel's parents.

Since being here, I've noticed how overprotective Beth is of Rachel, but it's only because she loves her so much. And I'm already seeing Beth start to change now that she's met me and knows I'll take good care of her daughter. I promised her and her husband I would, but doing so means getting the organization to back down and leave Rachel alone. I'm dreading having to face them on Sunday. I have no idea what they're going to tell me.

"Who's Mr. Tall, Dark, and Handsome?" A woman with long red hair wearing a black cowboy hat and a skimpy black dress appears beside me. "I haven't seen you here before." She slides her hand over my chest.

"I'm with someone." I back away, but there isn't anywhere to go. People are jammed up against me.

"Who are you with?" She looks up at me, standing so close I can smell her breath. It smells like beer and cinnamon-flavored mints, not a good combination.

"I'm with her." I point to Rachel on the dance floor, but it's hard to see her unless you're as tall as me.

The woman grabs hold of my shirt, holding on as she gets on her tip toes trying to see. "What's her name?"

This woman is very annoying and very persistent. I want to remove her hand from my shirt, but if I do, she'll likely fall down.

She's wearing high heels and isn't stable standing on her toes like that.

"Rachel," I say loudly to make sure the woman hears me.

"Rachel who?"

"Kens—" I stop before I say it. I need to remember to use her maiden name until after our wedding. "Evans. Rachel Evans."

The woman sighs and lowers herself back on her heels. She lets go of my shirt. "I should've known."

"Known what?"

"That you were with Rachel. She always gets the hot guys. It's not fair." She rolls her eyes. "I guess if you're as pretty as her it makes sense, but still."

"How do you know Rachel?"

"We went to high school together. She's a year younger than me. All the guys wanted to date her. She was homecoming queen. Star of the swim team. She even had some Olympic coach come here asking if he could train her."

"Really?" I put my eyes back on Rachel. "And she turned him down?"

The woman waves at Rachel, getting her attention. "Rachel!"

Rachel hurries over to us. "Jen! Good to see you!" She hugs her. "I see you met my fiancé."

"Fiancé?" Jen steps back, eyeing me up and down. "You're marrying this guy?"

"Yep." Rachel hugs me from the side and I lean down and kiss her.

"Does he have any brothers?"

Rachel laughs. "Sorry, but no."

"He's smoking hot," she says, not caring that I can hear her.

Rachel nods, smiling. "I know. Girls have been telling me that all night."

"You better get him out of this place before someone tries to take him."

"Nobody's taking me." I move behind Rachel and wrap her in my arms. "I'm all hers."

81

Jen puts her hands on her hips and looks at Rachel. "Okay, where did you find him? Because I want one."

Rachel laughs again. "I found him in Connecticut, but I think he's one of a kind."

She smiles. "Then I guess I'll have to settle for one of the losers here. I'll see you later."

She walks off, tripping on her heels and falling on a guy, who catches her and smiles. I think she tripped on purpose.

Rachel turns to me. "Are you having fun?"

"Sure."

She smooths her hand over my shirt. "I know you're not, but we don't have to stay long."

"Should I get us some drinks?"

"Yeah. I'll take a beer."

"I'll be right back." I make my way to the bar. There's only one bartender and he's backed up with orders. It takes several minutes before I finally get two bottles of beer. I take a drink because I'm dying of thirst. It's cold outside, but it's hot and stuffy in here.

When I get back to the dance floor, I can't find Rachel. I search left and right and check behind me and still can't find her. Maybe she went to the bathroom. I scan the bar again and spot Adam, Rachel's former fiancé, a few feet from where I'm standing. He's facing the wall, talking to someone. He moves slightly and I see that he's talking to Rachel. I push my way through the crowd until I reach her.

I hand her the beer. "Let's go to the dance floor." I put my hand on her lower back, keeping my eyes on Adam.

She tries to go past him, but he steps in her way. "Why are you still with this guy?"

"Adam, we're done talking about this. Just go back to your friends."

"I found out he's a billionaire. Is that why you're dating him? For his money? So you're a gold digger now?"

That's it. I'm not going to let him talk to Rachel that way. I don't like to fight, and I usually don't, but I know how to. I've been trained by the best.

I set my beer on the table next to us and get in Adam's face. "What did you say to her?"

Adam tries to back up but there are people behind him, so he goes around me, ending up with his back to the wall. "So now you're going to fight me?"

"It wouldn't be a fight. You'd be down before you even had a chance." I tower over him. He seems even smaller now than when I saw him at Rachel's apartment.

He's breathing fast, but he tries to appear unaffected. "You may be bigger than me, but a city boy like you can't take on someone from the country. We know how to fight. You don't."

"Is that so?" I step forward, backing him against the wall. "Should we test that theory outside?"

"Pearce, no," I hear Rachel say.

"I don't need to fight you," Adam says, trying to sound calm even though his forehead is sweating. "I don't want her back. You can have her." He looks behind me to where Rachel is standing. "Although I don't know why you'd want her. She can't even have kids."

I don't think she heard him, but even so, his comment and that smirk on his face is enough to set me off. I grab his shirt and lift him up with one hand and slam him against the wall.

There are people all around us but they do nothing to stop me, so either they want me to beat up Adam or they're used to people fighting in the bar.

I hear Rachel behind me, telling me to let him go, but I'm not done yet.

Adam is silent, afraid to speak, and I feel him shaking a little.

I look him right in the eye and lean in just enough so he can hear me. "When it comes to my enemies, I am not a nice man. You have no idea what I'm capable of. And if you'd rather not find out, then I'd suggest you leave this bar right now. You will never speak to Rachel again. If I hear otherwise, I will hunt you down and show you just how unpleasant I can be. Do you understand?"

His eyes move to the floor, and he nods.

I lower him back to standing, then wait for him to leave. People are watching us out of the corners of their eyes. Adam turns and squeezes past some people and keeps going.

I feel Rachel's hand on my arm. "What did you say to him?"

I watch Adam work his way to the front of the bar. He stops and says something to his friends, then walks out the door.

"Pearce, what did you say to him?"

I lean down and kiss her. "I told him to leave you alone."

"He looked scared to death."

"Did he?" I pick up my beer from the table. "I didn't notice."

She smiles and pulls me down to talk in my ear. "Thank you for dealing with him."

"My pleasure." I grin as I think of Adam's face just now. Rachel's right. He *was* scared to death.

We stay for another hour. Rachel dances some more while I watch. Then we head back to her house. I drive this time because I've never driven a pickup and wanted to try it out.

"Thanks for going with me," she says, leaning her head back on the seat. "I had fun seeing everyone again."

"That friend of yours...the redhead?"

"Jen. We weren't really friends. She's a year older than me."

"She was saying you got a visit from a coach wanting to train you for the Olympics."

"That's weird that she would tell you that. It was such a long time ago."

"So it's true?"

"Yeah. Freshman year, a man who trains a lot of Olympic hopefuls came here to see me. He'd seen me swim at state and said I had potential."

"But you weren't interested?"

"Well, yeah, I was interested, but it costs a lot of money. My parents aren't poor, but they're not rich either. I didn't want them going broke sending me to the training facility and hiring the coach. Because what if it didn't work out and I didn't make the team? Then my parents would be left with nothing. I couldn't do that to them."

I reach over and hold her hand. "You continue to amaze me."

"Why?"

"You just do." I smile at her from across the seat.

It's true. The more I learn about her, the more she amazes me. Tonight I learned she's great with children. That she was homecoming queen. That she can line dance, which she said is what they call that type of dancing. And I learned that if she wasn't so worried about spending her parents' money, she might've made it to the Olympics. Even more amazing is that she doesn't seem to think any of this is a big deal.

When we get back to the house, her parents are already in bed.

"May I walk you to your room?" I ask when we're in the upstairs hallway.

She pretends to ponder it. "I guess that would be okay."

I walk her down there, stopping at her door. I give her a quick, innocent kiss. "Goodnight."

I turn and head down to my room.

"That's it?" she whispers.

I turn back around. "You didn't invite me in."

"Get back here!" she whispers.

I was teasing her because I know she's been dying to be with me all night. For some reason she really likes seeing me in this shirt, and I think getting rid of Adam earned me some bonus points.

I return to her door and she pulls me inside her room. And I do what I've wanted to do all night. I make love to my hot, sexy, beautiful wife. Twice. Because tomorrow I can't. I'm leaving. Going back to Connecticut. Back to my other life. Back to the hell that awaits.

CHAPTER EIGHT

PEARCE

The four of us go out for breakfast on Saturday to a restaurant that serves different kinds of pancakes. Rachel loves pancakes and this was one of her favorite places growing up, so she insisted on taking me there. I've never had pancakes, so it was another first for me. I didn't care for the pancakes, but I didn't tell her that.

We spend the rest of the day back at the house. I watch more football with Henry while Rachel helps her mother put up the Christmas tree. It seems a little early for that, but Rachel told me they always put the tree up a day or two after Thanksgiving. Rachel loves holidays, especially Christmas.

I've never really cared for Christmas. This time of year always consists of going to parties I don't want to be at and talking to people I have no interest in talking to. Even as a child, I didn't care for Christmas, probably because my parents never got into it. My mother didn't play Christmas music or make Christmas cookies. She always hires people to decorate the house and every year it looks the same. The same big tree in the same spot with the same white lights. That's it. No other decorations.

But the Evans' house is full of lights and decorations. After Beth and Rachel put up the tree, they strung colored lights around the windows and along the fireplace. Then Henry brought down boxes from the attic filled with decorations and Rachel and her mother found places to display them throughout the house. I find all the Santa and reindeer figurines a bit much, but I do enjoy all the lights.

At four, we go to the airport. Rachel could've taken me, but her parents insisted on coming with us. Her mother even packed me a sandwich in case I get hungry on the plane. She's such a kind woman. Her and her husband truly are the nicest people I've ever met. It's no wonder they raised such a great daughter.

They hug me goodbye, then wait in the car while I say goodbye to Rachel.

She hugs me really tight. "I know it's only a day, but I'll miss you."

"I'll miss you too. I'll try to pick you up tomorrow, but if I can't get away I'll send a car."

"You really don't think your father will let you leave?"

"He scheduled a meeting the same time as your arrival, but I'm hoping I can leave early and come pick you up."

"Don't worry about it. I don't want you and your father fighting even more. I'll just take a cab."

"We'll figure it out tomorrow." I kiss her. "I love you."

"I love you too."

The next day I go to the Dunamis meeting. It's at a mansion in Stamford. The mansion belongs to one of our members and has an underground room.

Technically, this is a sentencing, not a meeting, so it should be fairly short. A sentencing is as it sounds; a handing down of a punishment, in this case, *my* punishment.

Sentencings are attended by a smaller group of members than would attend our usual meetings. They're led by the ruling council, which consists of ten members who have been chosen to make the final decision regarding a person's punishment. Members serve on the ruling council for six months and you never know who is on the council at any given time. It's a secret because the organization doesn't want people trying to sway the decision of the council. So to hide their identities, they wear black hooded robes to the sentencing and sit in the dark so you can't see their faces.

I've only been to one sentencing. It was a year ago. I didn't like it. I found it to be quite ominous. I hoped I wouldn't have to attend another sentencing for a very long time. But now here I am, and this time, *I'm* the one being punished.

When I get in the room, I'm led to the middle of the floor. I stand there, facing the ten hooded robes. Behind me are the other members who were invited to attend. I know my father and Jack are here, and Arlin Sinclair, but I don't know who else is behind me. The room is dark, except for the light shining down on me, the accused.

The man in the hooded robe, seated directly in front of me, pounds his gavel. "The sentencing will now begin."

Please let it involve me, and only me, I say in my head, over and over again. They can hurt me. Torture me. I don't care. But they can't hurt Rachel. I won't let them.

The man continues. "Today we are faced with a situation we have not encountered before. Pearce Kensington, the accused, has announced to the world that he is marrying Rachel Evans, an outsider. Following this announcement, we learned that he had already married this woman during a secret ceremony that took place in Las Vegas. Therefore, his engagement announcement to the press was merely an attempt to keep us from forcing him to get an annulment. We could still order him to get the annulment and call off the wedding, despite the fact that it will reflect poorly on him, thus adversely affecting Kensington Chemical, or we could let the marriage continue and punish him some other way. Given that this is such an unusual case, we are breaking protocol and opening this topic up for discussion. Would any member like to offer an opinion on this matter?" He nods at someone to speak.

I hear Jack's voice. "Although we all know Pearce was aware that a wife would be chosen for him, he is technically not in violation of any rules currently in place."

The hooded man nods. "Yes, which is why this is such an unusual situation. Although Pearce's actions did not violate an existing rule, his behavior does show a blatant disregard for both our traditions as well as the sanctity of our organization. Therefore, we feel punishment is warranted."

"What do we know about the girl?" I hear someone ask.

The hooded man answers. "The girl is Rachel Evans. She is a graduate student at Hirshfield College in New Haven. She comes from a small town in Indiana and her parents are—"

"Stop," I blurt out. You are never to interrupt the ruling council, but I didn't want him talking about Rachel. The room is silent so I continue. "I'm very sorry to have interrupted you, but I don't think information about the girl is relevant to this discussion."

"Of course it's relevant," I hear my father say. I'm not allowed to turn around so I can't see exactly where he is, but I think he's sitting directly behind me. "The girl is the whole reason we're here. If it weren't for her, there would be no need for a sentencing."

God, I hate him. I hate him so much. He knows how much I want to protect Rachel, so he's purposely trying to bring her into this. He wants to make sure this marriage ends, even though he knows how much Rachel means to me. He wants to destroy me. Take away everything I have that's good and replace it with whatever will make me most miserable. Taking over the company. Working a hundred hours a week. Marrying whoever he picks. That's the life he wants for me. A horrible, miserable life.

I take a calming breath. "I respectfully ask the council to leave the girl out of this and focus your punishment on *me*. The girl is not a member. Therefore, she is not aware of our rules or our traditions. She should not be punished for my actions."

"Is the girl aware of our existence?" Arlin Sinclair asked the question and I know why he did it. He's trying to help me out. He's trying to give them another reason why they should leave her alone.

"No," I answer. "She doesn't know we exist. She knows nothing about us."

"Are you willing and able to keep this a secret from her?" Arlin asks. "Even if doing so causes discord within your marriage?"

"Yes," I say. "Absolutely. She will never know."

There's mumbling among the ruling council and I can see their shadows leaning toward each other. After about a minute, the hooded man leading the sentencing says, "Escort Pearce out of the room so that we may have a private discussion."

A robed man appears next to me and leads me down a hall. He takes me to a small room with nothing in it. Not even a chair. Once I'm inside, the man closes the door and locks it.

I wait there, nervously pacing the floor, wondering what they're saying. I know my father is against me, but I think Arlin and Jack are on my side. I don't know who's in attendance so I'm not sure if there's anyone else there to support me. If Royce is there, I think he'd support me, but it's hard to tell with him. He has his own needs to protect, so he could pretend to be against me just to show his support of the organization and their disapproval of outsiders.

After what seems like the longest hour of my life, I'm finally escorted back to my spot in the middle of the room.

The hooded man leading the sentencing says, "We were unable to come to a consensus regarding your punishment. Therefore the decision will be elevated to a higher level."

Fuck. That's bad.

I don't know who the higher level members are because lower level members like myself aren't allowed to know. But I know it takes a long time to get to that level, which means the higher level members are likely old, probably in their seventies and eighties. People that age tend to be set in their ways and even stricter about rules and tradition than members my father's age.

"What about my marriage?" I ask, my heart pounding so hard I feel like it might break through my chest.

90

"Your marriage will continue and the wedding ceremony will take place as planned."

I breathe a sigh of relief. They must've decided they didn't want me to look bad by calling off the wedding. The members know I'm the only one who can take over Kensington Chemical someday, so their concern about my reputation must be based on that.

The man continues. "Your engagement announcement has already generated a great deal of press and we are certain the wedding will as well. Therefore, we will be taking over the wedding and using it as a networking and promotional event for our members and their companies. A committee will be assigned to make the guest list. The people who are invited will be those who can provide the most benefit to us, both as members and for our organization as a whole."

"Will Rachel and I be allowed to have any input on the wedding?" I ask.

"No. We will be hiring people."

"You can't expect a bride to have no input on her wedding." I cringe, realizing that might've sounded too harsh. "What I mean is that not including her in the plans will cause her to ask questions. Questions I can't answer."

"That's your problem to figure out. You'll have to find a way to explain it. But I suppose it would be problematic if the press questions her about the wedding plans and she's unable to answer them." He stops to think. "We will hire the wedding coordinators and they will provide the girl with regular updates regarding their plans."

"Will I have input on who is invited?"

"In order for this to look real, the girl's parents should be present, as should yours. The girl should also choose her bridesmaids. If a reporter decides to research who these girls are, they need to have a connection to her. Other than that, no, we will make the guest list."

"When will my punishment be decided?"

"That hasn't been determined. But when it is, you will not be told."

"Why wouldn't I be told?"

"When you married that girl, you went behind our backs and purposely deceived us. So now, we will do the same to you. You will be punished sometime in the future, but you will not know when or where or how."

"*How?* So I won't know what the punishment is? Then how will I know when it's over?"

"You won't. You'll have to live the rest of your life wondering." He pauses. "Perhaps now, you won't step out of line, Pearce." He pounds his gavel. "This concludes the sentencing. Pearce is dismissed. Please escort him out."

What does this mean? I'll never know my punishment? Never know when it's over? So they want to torture me for the rest of my life?

This had to be my father's idea. Making me wonder every day if something bad will happen? He would love that, so I know it was his idea. But I'm sure he's furious that they're letting my marriage continue.

Royce's plan worked. The engagement announcement generated enough press that the organization doesn't want me backing out of the wedding. But now they're taking it over, turning it into a networking event that will connect our members with key people they're trying to do business with.

To most people, it would seem odd that strangers would attend my wedding just to do business, but in my world it happens all the time. Wealthy people will go anywhere to connect with people who could make them even wealthier.

Now I have to tell Rachel that she can't plan the wedding. She knows we'll have wedding planners but I told her she could have input. Now she can't. She won't be happy about that, but I'll blame my parents. She knows how unreasonable they are, so maybe I can convince her that they insisted on taking over the plans and that it would be easier to just let them do it than try to fight them.

As for my punishment, I'll take whatever they want to do to me as long as it doesn't involve Rachel. I don't know why it would. If they're allowing me to stay married to her, and if they're making the wedding an even bigger, more publicized event, then they wouldn't want to harm her. We'll have the public's eye on us, and if something happens to either of us, reporters will start digging for answers.

So does that mean Rachel is safe? I can't say for sure because I don't trust them and never will. I'll always be watching over her and protecting her, and not just because of Dunamis, but because my family has enemies, and just being wealthy attracts bad people.

I check my watch. Rachel's flight arrives in an hour. I told my father I'd go into work, but I'm not going to. Instead I'm going to pick up my wife at the airport and take her home. Then I'll get the fireplace going, open a bottle of wine, and we'll have a nice relaxing dinner.

Rachel won't know it, but to me, tonight is a celebration. I'm able to keep her in my life.

This isn't the end for us. This is just the beginning.

I don't care what they do to me now or in the future. The only thing that matters is that I still have Rachel.

CHAPTER NINE

PEARCE

It feels like home again now that Rachel's back at my loft. *Our* loft. I need to remember to refer to this place as *ours*, not mine. I want her to consider this her home. Or maybe we should move to a new place. A place that we pick out together. Now that I know I have a future with her, I want to start planning our life, starting with where we'll live. I like this loft, but it feels like a bachelor pad and I know Rachel would like a house.

This morning, we both got up at six. I'm going into the office and she's going to campus to study. This is her last week of class and she has an exam to take today.

Rachel's graduation is a week from Saturday and then we'll leave for Italy. I already have my travel agent planning our itinerary for the two weeks we'll be gone. My father will be angry that I'm missing that much work, but he needs to get over it. I haven't taken a vacation since I started working for him. Besides, the holidays are the best time to take off because things always slow down at the end of the year.

I get to the office at seven. I keep my office locked, but when I use my key to open it, it doesn't work. The maintenance guy walks by as I try the key again.

"Jerry," I call after him. He's an older man, bald, with a large protruding stomach.

He stops and walks back to me. "Yes, Mr. Kensington."

"Could you try this key for me?" I hand it to him. "It doesn't seem to be working. I think there's something wrong with the lock."

He glances down at the key, rubbing his thumb over it. "Have you talked to your father?"

"No. Why?"

He hands the key back to me. "You should probably talk to him."

I walk to my father's office, my coat still on, the key in my hand. I open his door and go in. He's at his desk, writing something down.

I hold up the key. "Did you change the lock to my office?"

His eyes remain on the pad of paper he's writing on. "It's not your office anymore."

"I'm changing offices?"

"You don't have an office. You're fired. Get out."

"I'm fired? Are you joking?"

He finally looks up at me. "Do I appear to be joking?"

"Why are you firing me?"

"Your performance isn't up to par."

"You say that about everyone in the company." I don't know why I'm arguing with him about this. I should just leave and be happy I'm finally free of this place. But I remain where I am because I don't understand this. He knows I hate working here, so this is almost like a reward, and he doesn't give out rewards.

"I'm tired of your insubordinate behavior," he says. "I told you to come into work yesterday and you didn't show up."

"It was a Sunday and I had to pick up Rachel from the airport."

He sets his pen down and leans back in his chair. "I assume you and the girl went to whatever flyover state she's from."

"Her name is Rachel," I say, annoyed that he won't use her name. "And we went to Indiana."

"You met her family?"

"Yes. I met her parents. They were very nice."

"Nice." He huffs. "Nice is just another word for ignorant. No one ever got anywhere by being nice."

"Yes, well, I—"

"You upset your mother."

"What did I do *now*?"

"Your absence from Thanksgiving dinner upset her. I had to endure her sulking all weekend."

"I'm sure she wasn't sulking. She knew I would not be at dinner. And I will not be at Christmas either."

"Fine," he says casually, as he picks up his pen and writes something on his notepad.

"Are we done here?"

Why do I ask? Why don't I just leave?

"You are not to show up at the house again," he says, setting his pen in the metal holder.

"And why is that?"

He pushes his chair back and stands up, then goes around the desk to face me.

"You are no longer part of this family. Your mother and I no longer consider you to be our son. You are not welcome in our house, and if you show up there, you will be turned away. I have instructed the hired help that they are not to take your calls. Your mother and I have no interest in speaking to you."

"Mother agrees with this?"

"Goodbye, Pearce."

"You're disowning me? Because I married Rachel?"

He points to the door. "Get out. Now. Or I'll call security."

I turn and walk out of his office and down the series of halls that lead to the parking garage. What the hell just happened? He fires me and disowns me all in one day? Why did he wait until *now*? Why didn't he do it when I told him I married her? Is it because of the organization's decision to allow my marriage? It has to be. He was sure they'd forbid it, and when they didn't, he was furious. His son married someone he doesn't approve of. Someone he didn't pick. Someone he thinks will tarnish the family name. And the only way he can deal with that is to declare that I am no longer his son.

I drive away from the building. I should be happy. I'm free from this job. Free from my family. Free from all of it. So why don't I feel free? Why do I feel this heaviness, weighing me down, and this tightness in my chest, restricting my breathing?

It's because of him. My father. He's playing mind games with me. Making me think I'm free when I'm really not. So what is he up to?

Dammit! I can't live this way. Always waiting. Always wondering. Knowing something bad is coming but not knowing what it is. But I can't do anything about it. My father will never tell me what he's up to. So I'm just left waiting. Wondering.

I need to talk to someone and find out what was said at the sentencing when they made me leave. Jack is at work, and if I went there, he wouldn't talk about this at the office. He might not talk to me at all about this. He's odd that way. He talks openly about some things and keeps other things hidden, like the fact that my father hired him to spy on me.

Arlin Sinclair knows what happened, but he's also at work and he probably wouldn't tell me anything either. But his son would.

I turn around and head the other direction toward Royce's townhouse. I haven't talked to him since our trip to Vegas. I'm not sure if he's home. If he is, he's probably still asleep. He usually doesn't get up before ten, and it's only eight, so there's a good chance he won't let me past the gate.

When I get there, I wait as the security guard calls Royce. He must've agreed to see me because the guard nods and opens the gate.

Royce answers the door wearing a suit. "Pearce."

I walk in, giving him a strange look. "Are you going somewhere?"

"I have to meet with my mentor in an hour and be lectured about my behavior."

His mentor is Cecil Roth, the man my father went to Europe with a few weeks ago. Cecil is very much like my father. A disciplinarian. Always follows the rules. I assume that's why they paired him up with Royce. They think Cecil can keep Royce in line, but so far it's not working, probably because Cecil is never around. He's always away on business, so he only meets with Royce four or five times a year.

"How are you feeling?" I ask, taking a seat on a chair in the living room.

He unbuttons his suit jacket and sits across from me on the couch. "My father told you what happened?"

"He came to see me and asked if I knew where you were."

Royce rolls his eyes. "Stupid old man. He should mind his own business. I don't need him tracking me down."

"He was worried. And he had reason to be. You were in the damn hospital."

"I was fine. I could've made it home by myself. The jet was ready to leave as soon as I was discharged. I didn't need my father coming to get me."

It's another example of Royce not realizing how good he has it. His father cares enough to fly out there to make sure his son gets home safely and Royce shows no appreciation.

"So what happened out there?" I ask.

He puts his arm up along the back of the couch. "Well, after your wedding I had sex with that showgirl. Then I invited her friends over for a party later, which led to more sex."

"I wasn't referring to your sexual encounters. I was asking how you ended up overdosing. You usually stop before that happens."

"I did." He picks a piece of lint off his suit. "But I think one of the hookers I was with slipped something in my drink."

"Why would she do that?"

He shrugs. "She thought I got too rough with her. So after we did it, I think she slipped me something to knock me out so I wouldn't do it again to one of her friends."

"Royce, you need to stop this."

"I've already cut way back. I haven't touched drugs for two days."

"I'm not talking about the drugs. I'm talking about the girls. You can't abuse women like that, even prostitutes."

"Don't start lecturing me, Pearce. If you do, I'll arrange another date with your little friend, Sophia." He smirks.

"That's not funny. Don't you dare even think of doing that again."

"How do you know that girl anyway? Have you been cheating on Rachel?"

"No. Shel—I mean, Sophia, lives in Rachel's apartment building. They're neighbors."

"What a coincidence." He laughs. "So does Rachel know?"

"She knows Sophia and I have been together, but she doesn't know the circumstances." I give him a look of warning. "And it has to stay that way. You heard them at the meeting. She's never to know. About any of it."

"What meeting?" He yawns. "Fuck, I'm tired."

"The sentencing. You weren't there yesterday?"

"No. Why? Who was the sentencing for?"

"Me. For marrying Rachel."

"Shit, that was fast." He leans forward, his forearms on his knees. "So what are they going to do to you?" His eyes widen and he grins. A big, wide, overly enthusiastic grin.

"You do realize you appear psychotic when you act this excited about your so-called friend being punished."

He chuckles. "I've been called worse. So what's your punishment?"

"I don't know. That's why I came over here. I wanted to know what they talked about. They made me leave the room so they could discuss it, and when I came back they said they were going to make the higher level members decide."

"Then I wouldn't know even if I'd been there."

"Yes, but I'm sure various options were discussed and I need to know what those options were."

"Well, I can't help you. I wasn't there."

"Your father was there. Do you think he'd tell me anything?"

"No. He worries too much about following the rules. Why don't you ask your *own* father?" He laughs. "I'm sure he offered up plenty of ideas for your punishment."

I sigh. "You should not find this amusing in any way. They could have me killed."

He stands up and buttons his jacket. "They wouldn't do that. They need someone to run your chemical company if your father ever dies."

"I won't be running the company. He fired me."

He laughs again. "Okay, now THAT is amusing. Your own father fired you? Good old Holton. Always filled with surprises. So he fired you for marrying Rachel?"

"He didn't say that, but I'm assuming that's the reason."

"They're letting you stay with her?"

"Yes, but I had to agree to never tell her about the organization."

He adjusts his tie. "So my plan worked."

"It did. And thank you again for helping me."

"When will you find out your punishment?" He walks to the mirror that's hanging on the wall and checks his appearance.

"They're not going to tell me."

"What do you mean? They have to tell you."

"Part of my punishment is that I'm left wondering what they'll do to me and when it will be done. And I won't be told when it happens, so I'll never know if my punishment is over or if I'm still waiting for it."

He turns back to face me. "That has Holton Kensington written all over it. You know that was his idea."

"Unfortunately, that's probably true."

"Your father's the psychotic one. Not me."

"I'll let you finish getting ready." I get up and walk to the door.

Royce follows. "I was thinking the four of us should go out to dinner. You and Rachel with Victoria and me."

"No. Rachel and Victoria would not get along."

"Victoria doesn't get along with anyone. Come on. You can't hide Rachel forever. She'll have to go to social events with you, so eventually everyone will meet her."

"I'll talk to Rachel about it. Goodbye, Royce."

I drive back to the loft and when I go inside, Rachel's there. She runs up and gives me a hug. "I'm done with my test!"

"How did it go?"

"Good. It's such a great feeling to be done. And I turned in my papers early, so I'm officially done!"

"You're not going to the last few lectures?"

"Maybe. I haven't decided yet." She glances at the clock, then back at me. "What are you doing home? Did you forget something?"

"I was fired." I go over to the leather couch and sink into it, putting my feet up.

"Your father fired you?"

"And disowned me. All in one day. I will say, he's efficient."

I joke about it, but deep-down, part of me is hurt. The firing doesn't bother me, but being told my parents want nothing to do with me causes an uncomfortable twinge in my chest.

"Pearce." Rachel sits next to me, gently rubbing my arm. "I'm sorry."

"It's probably for the best. My father and I do nothing but fight. Now that won't be an issue since we're no longer speaking to each other."

"What about your mother? I know you still want to talk to her."

"She's upset with me. I'm sure she has no interest in making amends."

"Why is she upset? Because we got married?"

Now is my chance to bring up the wedding plans. I have to lie to her once again, but it has to be done.

"My mother is upset that she wasn't able to attend the wedding, given that I'm her only child. To make it up to her, she wants me to let her plan our March wedding. She lives for planning these types of events. She wants to hire the wedding coordinators and work with them as they plan the various details. It's a lot of work and very time-consuming, but my mother has been rather bored lately, which explains why she was so excited about this. But I told her that you will be the one working with the wedding coordinators and she is not to be involved."

Rachel's quiet, then says what I was hoping she'd say. "If it's that big a deal to her, maybe we should just let her plan it. But your mother would at least involve me in the plans, right?"

"You'll get regular updates from the wedding coordinators, but my mother would handle the day-to-day details. So would you be okay with that?"

"It's probably for the best. I was thinking about it, and I really don't have time to plan a wedding. It's just a few months away and I need to spend those months finding a job. Besides, we're already married. It's not a real wedding."

"It's still your wedding, so if this doesn't work for you, just tell me. But keep in mind that even if my mother isn't involved, most of the planning will still need to be done by the wedding coordinators. As I said before, this will be a large, highly publicized event and there's a lot to be done and very little time to do it."

"I know. So we might as well let your mother handle it. If we weren't already married, I'd feel differently, but now it just seems like a formality and I'm sure your mother will do a good job." Rachel sighs. "But my mom will be disappointed."

"Have her plan the bridal shower. I'll cover all the expenses. She just needs to plan it."

"Okay. I'll talk to her about it."

I bring her into my arms. "You're being very understanding about this."

"I want you to still have your family. So if this will help, then we'll do it."

I kiss the side of her head. "I love you."

"I love you too." She sits up. "Oh, I talked to Shelby and she was wondering if we could come over tonight to her parents' house so her dad could thank you for helping him. That doctor-friend of yours will be there too."

"What time do we need to be there?"

"She said anytime after five."

"So we have the whole day free?"

"Yeah." She bites her lower lip as she unbuttons my shirt. "What would you like to do?"

"I can think of a few things."

And that's how we spend the rest of the morning.

It's strange being home on a weekday, but I guess I should get used to it now that I'm unemployed.

In the evening we go to Shelby's parents' house, which is in New Haven. It's a small house in an older neighborhood. Shelby's car is in the driveway and behind it is a black Lexus, which I'm guessing is Logan's car.

Rachel goes up to the house and I follow behind.

Shelby greets us at the door. "Thanks for coming. My dad was sleeping but he just woke up. Logan's checking on him. But you can meet my mom. She's in the living room. Follow me."

We walk down a short hallway that leads to the living room. The furnishings are dated, but the house is neat and clean and there are family photos all over the walls. It seems like a nice, normal place to grow up so I don't know how Shelby ended up being an associate. I know her parents need money, but there are other ways to get money. And how does she explain to her parents where the money comes from? She can't tell them she's an associate.

"Mom, this is my friend, Rachel, and her fiancé, Pearce."

A middle-aged woman with dark blond hair comes up to us. "Welcome. I'm Linda." She shakes our hands.

Rachel smiles at her. "It's nice to meet you."

"Shelby talks about you all the time. You've been a good friend to her." Linda turns to me. "And Pearce, I can't thank you enough for introducing us to Logan."

I nod. "I'm glad he could help."

"We should go see Dad," Shelby says to her mom. "I don't want to keep these guys too long."

"Shelby, don't worry about it," Rachel says. "We're in no hurry."

"He's in his room." Linda motions us to follow her.

We go down the hall, passing a tiny room with a twin bed and posters on the wall. That must've been Shelby's room. The house only has two bedrooms. Linda takes us to the master at the end of the hall.

She walks over to the bed where Shelby's father is lying, covered with blankets.

"Bob, you have company." She waves us over. "This is Shelby's friend, Rachel. And that's Pearce, the man who got us the doctor."

He mumbles something, but I couldn't make out his words. It's difficult to hear him because he's breathing hard and hooked up to oxygen.

I've never seen someone this ill. He's wasting away, his face gaunt, his body nothing but sharp bony edges sticking through his clothes. He has dark circles under his eyes and his hair hasn't grown back from the chemo.

I'm not good in these types of situations. I just got here and I'm already very uncomfortable, not sure what to do or say.

His eyes fall shut, then slowly open again.

Rachel goes up to his bed and sits next to him. "Hello, Mr. Parks." She smiles at him and gently lifts his hand and holds it in hers, softly rubbing it with her other hand. He doesn't seem fully awake, but her touch seems to get his attention and he turns his head to her.

"I'm good friends with your daughter," Rachel says. "We've been neighbors these past few months so we've spent a lot of time together." She laughs a little. "And eaten way too much macaroni and cheese."

"And ice cream," Shelby adds, sitting across from her on the bed.

"She's my…" Bob tries to say the words to Rachel, but has to stop to breathe. "She's my…baby girl."

"Dad." Shelby immediately tears up, biting her lip to keep from crying.

Rachel keeps her eyes on Bob, still holding his hand, a soft smile on her face. "I'm sure you're very proud of her."

He nods weakly, his eyes fighting to stay open.

Shelby gets up and quickly leaves the room, tears running down her face.

"I'm going to go check on her," Linda says to me.

Bob slowly turns his head and notices me standing at the end of the bed. He raises the hand that's not linked with Rachel's and motions me closer.

I still have no idea what to say to him. And I'm having a hard time looking at him. I know that sounds harsh, but it's difficult to see someone this close to death. Now I feel even worse for Shelby. It's bad enough to see a stranger in his condition, but this is Shelby's father. A man she loves, who clearly thinks the world of her. It must be killing her to do what she does, selling her body, knowing how much it would hurt her father if he knew. It would hurt him even more if he knew she was only doing it for him.

I go around the bed and sit across from Rachel. "Hello, Mr. Parks."

"Thank you," he says in a hoarse whisper. He puts his hand on top of mine. His skin is icy cold, his fingers bony. I glance at Rachel and she gives me a look to just act normal. She can tell I'm uncomfortable.

I follow her lead and place my hand over his. "You're very welcome. I'm happy Dr. Cunningham was able to help."

If I'd known Shelby's father was in such bad shape, I would've tried to help him sooner. This poor man is already suffering, but a few weeks ago he was also in excruciating pain. It sounds like Logan has found a way to at least relieve some of that pain, making this man's last days somewhat more tolerable.

"It might snow tomorrow," Rachel says, turning Bob's attention back to her. I'm thankful she did, because I couldn't think of anything else to say to him. "I'm from Indiana and my mom said it snowed six inches yesterday."

Bob watches her, gazing at her face and looking peaceful and content as she continues to rub his hand and talk to him. Once again, I am completely amazed by Rachel. The way she can comfort this man, a man she just met, is amazing to me. It's like she knows just what to do. She's so gentle and caring and she has this positive energy that I know he can feel. Because I feel it too. When we first walked in you could feel the sadness in the room, but it feels a little lighter now as Rachel talks to Bob like he's just a regular man. Not a sick man or a dying man, but just a man.

Rachel tells Bob about our night at the country bar and how I refused to line dance. She's laughing and smiling. He can't take his eyes off her. For just this brief moment, he isn't thinking about his illness or his death. He has a weak smile on his face, like he's happy that someone is finally treating him like he's not sick. And that someone is Rachel. My sweet, beautiful, kind wife, who I just fell in love with all over again.

"Mr. Parks." I turn and see Logan behind me. "It's time for your medication."

Logan looks the same as he did in college, just slightly older. He's about six feet tall, average build, with light brown hair.

I stand up and face him. "Logan, it's good to see you again."

"Can you stay a few minutes?" he asks. "I need to give Mr. Parks his meds, then maybe we could talk before you leave."

"Of course. I'll wait out in the living room." I look over at Rachel.

She sets Bob's hand back down on the bed. "It was nice meeting you, Mr. Parks. Maybe I'll stop by again."

"Please do." He looks like he doesn't want her to leave, but then his focus returns to Logan as he picks up his wrist and checks his pulse.

Rachel and I go out in the living room. Linda and Shelby are on the couch but stand up as we walk in. Shelby's eyes are still red and teary.

"Shelby." Rachel goes up and hugs her. "I know this is hard. What can I do?"

"Just being here is enough," she says. "He really likes you. I could tell."

Rachel steps back, but holds Shelby's hand. "If you want, I'll come over again and just talk to him."

She nods, a tear going down her cheek. "I think he'd like that."

"He doesn't get many visitors," Linda says. "Thank you again for coming, and Pearce, thank you so much for helping us like this."

I nod. "You're very welcome."

"Are you guys leaving now?" Shelby asks Rachel.

"Not yet. Logan wanted to talk to Pearce for a few minutes."

"Logan and I are going to get something to eat. Do you want to come along?"

Rachel looks at me to answer.

"Sure. We could do that."

I'm surprised Logan is spending all this time with Shelby. Usually physicians don't socialize with a patient's family, but maybe he's just trying to help her get through this.

Logan appears and goes up to Linda. "He's resting now. He'll be asleep for a few hours. Give him another dose around midnight. And as usual, just call if you have any questions."

"I will. Thank you." Linda goes over to Shelby. "I'll see you later, honey. I'm going to go sit with your dad."

"Okay, bye, Mom." As she walks away, Shelby says to Logan, "Pearce and Rachel are going to dinner with us."

He smiles at us. "Good. It'll give us a chance to catch up."

"We haven't met. I'm Rachel." She extends her hand to him and they shake.

"I'm sorry," I say. "I should've introduced you. Rachel is my fiancé."

"Nice to meet you," Logan says to her. "I need to compliment you. You were very good with Mr. Parks just now. Talking to him like that helped him relax and eased his breathing. You must've done this before."

Rachel nods. "My sister died of cancer. My grandmother did as well, and she always liked it when I would sit and talk to her in the hospital."

Shelby puts her arm around Logan's. "Should we go? We could take them to that Italian place down the street."

"That sounds good," Rachel says. "We'll follow you."

We all go outside and Shelby gets in Logan's car as Rachel and I get into ours.

"Is Shelby dating Logan?" I ask Rachel as we're driving to the restaurant.

"She didn't say she was, but it sure seemed like it."

"Yes, I thought so too."

This is not good. It would be fine if Shelby were just a normal girl, but she's not a normal girl. She doesn't have a normal life. She's tied to the organization, which means she could never have a real relationship. No man is going to put up with her taking off late at night without explaining where she's going. And if she told him the truth, it would end the relationship.

Like me, Shelby doesn't want the organization controlling her life. She wants to be happy. She wants to find someone who loves her. Someone to have a life with. But unfortunately, that's not possible.

CHAPTER TEN

RACHEL

We just had dinner with Logan and Shelby, and after watching them interact, I've now confirmed that those two are definitely dating. How could she not tell me this? I've been bugging her to go out on a date for months, only to find out she's been dating someone in secret. And not just anyone. She's dating a doctor. A smart, successful doctor who graduated from Harvard.

Logan is cute, but not my type. I like a large, muscular guy, which is why I'm so attracted to Pearce. Logan's average height and doesn't seem to be very muscular. But he has a cute face, with blue eyes and a dimple in his left cheek. He's very serious, like Pearce, but Shelby was able to loosen him up a little at dinner, just like I'm able to loosen up Pearce. So maybe that's a sign that Shelby and Logan will end up working out.

While we're waiting for the check, Shelby and I make a trip to the restroom. We go there for girl talk, not for using the facilities.

"Why didn't you tell me?" I ask her as we stand in front of the mirrors.

She gets her lipstick out. "There's nothing to tell. We're just friends."

I point to the door. "What I just saw out there was not just a friendship. You two couldn't stop flirting with each other. And don't think I didn't notice the handholding under the table."

"Handholding." She laughs. "Yeah, that's what it was. You caught us."

"I'm not even going to ask what you mean by that," I say, also laughing. "So how long has this been going on?"

"Almost a month."

"A month? Shelby, that's a long time."

"I only see him when he's in town, so it's not that big a deal."

"Have you gone up to Boston to see him?"

"Not yet. But he's down here two or three times a week to check on my dad." She puts her lipstick on, then smacks her lips together.

"I think he comes down here to see *you* as well," I say, smiling.

"Rachel, you're reading too much into it. We're just dating. It's only temporary. A rich, successful doctor is not going to stick around with someone like me."

"Why wouldn't he? He obviously likes you or he wouldn't be dating you."

She drops her lipstick in her purse and zips it up. "Come on. Let's go."

"So is Logan heading back to Boston now?" I ask as we leave the restroom.

"No. He's going back in the morning."

I grab her sleeve, stopping her. "He's staying overnight with you?"

She laughs. "We're adults. We can have sex."

"I just mean that it sounds like you guys are serious."

She keeps walking. "We're not. We're just dating."

Despite what she says, I get the feeling she wants more than that. I think Logan wants more than that too. I could tell by the way he kept looking at Shelby during dinner, and the way he always made sure they were touching as they sat next to each other in the booth. Their hands, their shoulders, their arms. Their bodies were always connected, like they didn't want to be apart.

"Did she confirm that she's dating him?" Pearce asks as we're driving home. He knows Shelby and I had girl talk in the bathroom.

"Yes, and I think she really likes him. And he definitely likes her. I'm happy for her. I hope it works out." Pearce doesn't respond, his eyes on the road. "So what did you and Logan talk about while Shelby and I were in the bathroom?"

"We talked about his work."

"What exactly does he do? I know he works at a clinic, but what kind of clinic? He didn't really explain it at dinner."

"It's a private medical clinic that focuses on a more individualized approach to healthcare versus the traditional one-size-fits-all model of treatment. Their services aren't covered by insurance. If you go there, you just have to pay out of pocket. It's very expensive so most people can't afford it."

"Which is why you're covering the expenses for Shelby's dad." I rub his hand, which is wrapped around mine and resting in my lap. "That's really nice of you to do that for Shelby and her family."

"Unfortunately, it's not saving her father."

"I know, but he's in a lot less pain."

"Logan told me he's not going to hold out much longer. He may not even make it to Christmas."

"Oh, that's so sad. Shelby will be devastated."

It was hard seeing Shelby's father. I know how difficult it is to watch someone you love go through that. I wish Shelby would open up to me and let me help her, but she doesn't like to talk about it. I call her every day, but she never wants to talk about her dad. Maybe she talks about him with Logan. Maybe he can help her get through this. I hope those two keep dating. I think they'd be good together. I'm not even sure why. It's just a feeling I have. Then again, I'm kind of a hopeless romantic. I like seeing people fall in love and live happily ever after. Like Pearce and me.

The next day, I go to class even though I don't need to. I wanted to say goodbye to my professor and a few of my classmates. After class, I go to an appointment I scheduled with my advisor to talk about job opportunities in the area. The past few months, he's been giving me postings for jobs in New York, but now that I'm staying in Connecticut I need recommendations for where to start looking for jobs here in the area.

When I get to his office, he invites me in and I take the chair across from him at his desk. He's a middle-aged guy, thin, with gray and black hair. I've never liked him. He's not very friendly and he always talks to me in this condescending tone and has made a few sexist comments in the past.

I didn't want to meet with him but he runs the job placement program for my major so I didn't really have a choice. Right now, he's my only link to a job.

"I should start by saying congratulations," he says, reaching across the table to shake my hand.

"Thank you." His hand is cold and clammy. Gross. "It's good to finally be graduating."

"Oh, yes, that too. But I actually meant congratulations on your engagement."

He congratulates me on my engagement instead of getting my masters degree? He'd never say that to a male student.

"How did you hear about my engagement?" I ask.

"My wife watches those morning shows and said they announced that Pearce Kensington was marrying a girl who goes to Hirshfield and is in the history program. My wife told me because she assumed I knew you. So when's the wedding?"

"March." I sit up straighter and clear my throat. "Anyway, as I said on the phone, I wanted to talk to you about job opportunities in the area. For now, I'm living in Weston so it'd be great if I could find something around there, but I don't mind commuting to one of the surrounding towns."

"How many hours a week do you want to volunteer?"

"Volunteer? Are you referring to an unpaid internship? Because I'd be fine with that if you think it will help me eventually get a full-time job."

He leans back in his chair, his hands crossed over his middle, a grin on his face. "You're not seriously looking for an actual job, are you?"

I feel my blood pressure rising. He asked the question in a condescending tone and his grin is now a smirk.

I don't smile back. I remain very serious. "Of course I'm looking for a job. That's why I made this appointment with you."

He leans forward, placing his arms on the desk. "Sweetheart, you don't need a job."

Now I'm really angry. I want to reach over and strangle him with his tie, but instead I take a moment to calm myself, then say, "And why is that?"

"You're marrying Pearce Kensington. He's a billionaire. A billion is a lot of money."

Oh my God. Does he seriously think I don't know what a billion is? I'm starting to hate this guy and I don't hate anyone. Dislike? Yes. But hate? Usually never.

"Mr. Burmwall, I hope you're not implying that women should live off their husband's money rather than make their own."

He laughs. "You have no need to make money. Having a job would be a waste of time. Pearce probably makes more money on his investment portfolio in one day than you would make in an entire year working at some museum."

I clench my hands, trying to control my anger. "Maybe it's not just about the money. Maybe I want to use my skills and my education and not just sit at home all day."

"Which is why you should go be a volunteer. Museums always need volunteers."

"Yes, to stuff envelopes for fundraising drives. I did not go to school to stuff envelopes all day."

"I'm sure they do more than stuff envelopes," he says, sitting back again.

"Are you saying you're not going to help me find a job? You're not even going to tell me where to start looking?"

"I could, but it's pointless. They're not going to hire you, sweetheart."

I shoot up from my chair. "Stop calling me sweetheart. In fact, don't call any woman sweetheart who isn't your wife. And for the record, I can and will get a job. On my own. Since apparently you refuse to assist me."

"Rachel, calm down. I was just trying to be—"

"Goodbye, Mr. Burmwall." I storm out of the room. I can't stand being told to calm down, so his final words just shot my anger up even higher.

I go out to my car and just sit for a moment, taking some deep breaths to calm myself down. What an ass. I doubt he'd treat a man that way. If a *man* is wealthy, is he not supposed to work? Pearce works, or at least he used to, and he plans to work again. But he doesn't need to, so according to Mr. Burmwall, Pearce should sit at home all day and do nothing. Or go volunteer somewhere a few hours a week. But would Mr. Burmwall ever advise Pearce to do that? No! Of course not. Because he's a man, and men have to work. But not us women. We should spend our days shopping or getting our nails done or waiting for our husbands to come home.

My attempt to calm down doesn't work, so I start the car and drive back to the loft. It's two-thirty and Pearce is home since he no longer has a job. When I get off the elevator, I'm still fuming mad. Pearce is on the couch, reading a newspaper, but he gets up when he sees me.

I hang my coat up and feel him behind me, his arms around me. "Hello, sweetheart, how was class?"

I cringe. "Don't say that word."

"What word?"

"Sweetheart." I break free from his arms and walk to the kitchen. "Don't call me that."

"Um, okay." He sounds confused. He comes over to where I'm standing. "I didn't realize that word upset you."

I sigh, and turn to face him. "It doesn't. I mean, it doesn't upset me when *you* say it. Only when other people do." I hug him. "I'm sorry. I'm just angry and frustrated and I'm taking it out on you. I think I'll just lock myself in the bedroom until I've calmed down."

He lifts my chin. "What happened?"

I replay the conversation for him, including the sweetheart references. When I'm done, he brings me into his arms. "Rachel,

I'm sorry he treated you that way. That was extremely unprofessional, as well as rude and condescending. You should report him to someone higher up at the college."

"It wouldn't do any good. Besides, he's probably only talked that way to *me*. I'm sure I'm the only student he's ever had who ended up marrying a billionaire. He was somewhat helpful to me back when he thought I was just a regular graduate student. But now that I'm the wife, or soon-to-be wife, of Pearce Kensington, everything's changed." I look up at Pearce. "Do you think he's right? Do you think I won't be able to get a job because I'm married to you?"

"I really don't know. All the women I know who come from wealthy families have never tried to get a job, so I don't have any examples of it."

"Did these women go to college?"

"Yes. All of them did. My mother has a business degree but she's never had a job, and her friends haven't either."

"But they're from a different generation, when women stayed home. The younger women must want to work."

"They have college degrees, but they don't actually get jobs, at least not regular paying jobs. They usually do charity work, such as organizing fundraisers or planning charity auctions."

"What about your ex-wife? Did she try to find a job?"

"No, and she had no intention of ever getting one." He hesitates, as if he doesn't want to say what he's thinking.

"What is it, Pearce?"

"I was just going to say that doing charity work is not a bad thing. Some of those events are very large and entail a lot of work and specialized skills."

"What kind of skills?

"Marketing, budgeting, public relations, event coordination, advertising. It depends on the event. Even though my mother has never held an actual job, she puts a lot of time and effort into her charity work. She finds it very fulfilling. And she's been able to put her business degree to use over the years, planning these events."

"So you think if I can't find a job, I should just do charity work?"

"I think you should do what you want to do. I'm just saying that there's nothing wrong with volunteering for a charity. It doesn't mean you're not working. You're just not getting paid for your work. And if it's an organization you feel strongly about, you might find it very rewarding." He puts his hand on my shoulder. "Rachel, if you want a regular job, then go get one. I'm not stopping you. I want you to be happy, sweethea—" He stops before he says it.

I laugh. "It's okay. You can say it."

He smiles. "Would you like me to go beat up Mr. Burmwall now? I'm more than happy to do so."

"No. That's okay."

He checks the clock. "Actually, we need to get going. We have that photo shoot in an hour and we have to drive to the studio."

Pearce lined up a photographer to take photos of us to send to the media so we won't have people following us around and taking our picture and selling it.

Ever since we sent out that engagement announcement, Pearce has had people from the media calling him, asking for photos of us. They also asked if we'd do interviews. We haven't agreed to it yet, but Pearce thinks we should. He said it's better to put ourselves out there and control what's said about us rather than have gossip magazines make things up.

I don't like all this publicity. Pearce warned me many times that his personal life was often made public, so I need to accept that and get used to it, but it still bothers me.

When we get to the studio, I'm whisked off to a room where an older woman does my hair and makeup. She uses a lot of makeup, way more than I'd normally wear, but she assured me it'll look natural on camera.

She finishes up just as Pearce walks in.

"They sent me in here," Pearce says to the woman, "but if you're not ready, I can go back out there and wait."

She looks him up and down. "Wow. Aren't you a catch?" She winks at me. "You did well picking him."

I laugh. "I agree."

"I think I'm the one who lucked out," Pearce says.

"You definitely did." The woman nods in my direction. "She's gorgeous. When she first came in here I thought she was a professional model. You need to get that girl to an agency."

Pearce smiles at me. "What do you think, Rachel? Would you like to be a model?"

I shudder. "No. Absolutely not. I get nervous in front of the camera, which is why I just want to hurry and get this over with."

The woman leads Pearce to the chair next to me, facing the mirror.

"Relax," she says to me. "It's nothing. You just stand there and smile." She steps back and checks out Pearce and me in the mirror. "You two are *both* gorgeous. You might just be the best looking couple I've ever seen."

"Thank you," I say. "But I'm sure you say that to everyone."

She shakes her head. "Believe me, I don't. You too really are a beautiful couple."

Pearce reaches over and holds my hand and the woman gets to work on his hair. When she's done, we change into the clothes we brought and go on set and wait for direction.

The photographer takes photos of us alone, then together, posing us all different ways. Halfway through, a young woman dressed all in black comes into the studio and watches as the photographer snaps more photos.

When we're done the woman goes up to Pearce and me and says, "I'm an editor at Celebrity Weekly magazine. I'm here for a different shoot, but I recognized you when I walked in. I heard about your engagement, and if you don't mind, I'd love to get an interview and maybe use some of these photos. Our readers love wedding stories. And your photos are great. You two are a beautiful couple. You might even make the cover."

"What do you think?" Pearce asks me.

"Um, sure, okay."

"Can we do the interview right now?" she asks. "It won't take long."

We agree to it. The interview is short, maybe ten minutes. She says it'll be in one of the January issues.

By the time we get home and have dinner, I'm exhausted. It's been a long day.

We get in bed early, and as Pearce is pulling the covers over us, he says, "I forgot to turn the lights on."

He gets back out of bed and goes over to the miniature Christmas tree I put on the dresser and plugs in the lights. It's just a tiny string of colored lights, but they add a warm glow to the room so we like to leave them on all night.

I decorated the loft yesterday while Pearce was at the gym. I told him what I was planning before I did it because this place still feels more like his than mine, and I wasn't sure if he'd be okay with having lights everywhere. He told me months ago that he's not really into Christmas, which doesn't make sense to me. I mean, come on, who doesn't like Christmas? Anyway, he said I could decorate however I wanted, but I didn't go overboard. I bought a tree for the living room and put multicolored lights on it, then strung some lights around the windows and put a miniature tree in the bedroom.

When Pearce got home, I couldn't tell if he liked what I'd done. But when it got dark later and he could see all the lights, he got a big smile on his face. And as soon as we got home tonight, he immediately plugged in all the lights. I take that as a sign that he's starting to like Christmas. Eventually, I'm going to get him to love it.

"There." He gets back into bed. "How's that?"

"It's good." I wrap my arms and legs around him and hug his chest. "Do you think we should stay home for Christmas?"

"And not go to Italy? I thought you wanted to go."

"I do, and I'm really excited about it, but this is our first Christmas together so maybe we should be spending it here at home."

He kisses my forehead. "We'll spend the next one at home. We have plenty more Christmases ahead of us. And maybe next year we'll be in a house."

I sit up slightly. "You want to get a house?"

"Why do you act so surprised? We've talked about getting a house."

"Yes, but I thought you meant in a few years."

"We don't have to get one right away if you don't want to. I was just thinking that you might want to live in a place that we picked out together instead of living here. Just think about it and we can talk about it later."

I do want to get a house. I just haven't said anything to Pearce about it because where we live will depend on where we work, and right now, neither of us has a job. And talking about that is stressful, at least to me, because my job prospects aren't looking good. There are almost no job openings around here.

Pearce reaches into his nightstand and pulls something out. "I almost forgot. This is for you." He hands me a small box. "An early Christmas gift."

"The trip is my gift." I sit up and turn the light on next to the bed.

"The trip is our honeymoon. Now open it."

I open the box and inside is a small crystal ornament in the shape of a star. "Pearce, it's beautiful. I love it."

"I noticed we didn't have any ornaments. I'll get you some more, but I thought you might want to pick out the rest."

"Actually, I was thinking of continuing a tradition my family does where we collect ornaments over the years. Something that reminds us of something special that happened that year. Would you be okay with that?"

"Of course. Whatever you want."

I hold out the star. "So what does this say about this year?"

"That you're my bright shining star?" He laughs as he kisses me. "Or the star of your class? You're graduating with honors."

"I think it should symbolize a wish. You know how you wish upon a star? We should each make a wish for the thing we want most in our new life together. Not something that's a given, like love, but something that we really want but may not get. That way, when we see the star every year, we'll be reminded to keep working toward whatever it is that we hope to have someday."

"Are we telling each other these wishes?"

"No. So wish for whatever you want. Ready?" I hold up the star.

"We're doing this right now? You gave me no time to think."

"Oh. How much time do you need?"

"Never mind. I've got it. Go ahead."

I dangle the star between us. "Okay, make your wish."

I close my eyes and imagine my wish. It's a wish that's not likely to happen, but that's why it's a wish. It's something to hope for.

My wish is for Pearce and I to have a baby. I want that more than anything. So that will be my wish every year when I take this ornament out. A wish I'll make every year at Christmas. And maybe if I'm lucky, that wish will come true.

CHAPTER ELEVEN

PEARCE

It's nine in the morning and I'm heading over to Jack's house. I've been trying to reach him since the sentencing last Sunday but he hasn't returned my calls. He finally got back to me last night and told me to meet him at his house today, before he left for the office.

"Pearce," he says when I arrive. "Come on in."

Today he's wearing navy pinstripe suit pants and a white shirt, a much better look than his meditation outfit. At least now I'm not having to look at his bare feet and chest hair.

He takes me to his hidden room. "Have a seat. You want breakfast?" He sits down in front of a heaping plate of bacon and a Bloody Mary.

"I already ate."

"Well, I haven't, so you talk while I eat." He stuffs a slice of bacon in his mouth, then rolls his sleeves up.

"Do you always eat that much bacon?" I point to his plate. There must be at least a half pound of bacon there. Maybe more.

"Don't nag me about my diet. You sound like my damn wife." He wraps his greasy fingers around his Bloody Mary glass and takes a swig. "Now what do you want?"

"I want to know what happened when I left the room on Sunday. What did they talk about?"

"I can't tell you that." He stuffs a wad of bacon in his mouth.

"You're my mentor. You're supposed to look out for me."

"No," he says, talking with his mouth full. "I'm supposed to *teach* you things, not protect you. You have to protect *yourself*, Pearce. I've told you that many times. And I've provided you with the tools to do so."

"I can't protect myself when I don't know what I'm up against, or when it's going to happen. So tell me so I can prepare myself."

"I don't know what the hell's going to happen. You heard what they said. The higher level members are making the decision."

"Yes, but you could at least tell me what was discussed."

"I'm not allowed to do that."

I feel like I'm talking in circles here. And the fact that he's acting so casual about this is infuriating.

"Did they say anything about Rachel?" I lean forward, pleading with him. "Please. I need to know."

He glances to the side as he dabs his mouth with a white cloth napkin.

His silence is causing my heart to thump harder. "What is it, Jack? Are they planning to do something to Rachel?"

He doesn't answer. He goes to pick up a slice of bacon but I grab his wrist. "Dammit, Jack! Tell me! Are they going to hurt Rachel?"

He looks down at my hand on his wrist, then glares at me. "DON'T touch me when I'm eating. I'm like a dog. I'll attack."

I release him and sit back in my chair and wait for him to speak. But he remains silent as he finishes his bacon. I sit there, having to listen to his disgusting chewing sounds. It might even be worse than having to look at his bare feet. When he's finally done eating, he gulps down his Bloody Mary, then wipes his napkin over his mouth.

He sets the napkin down on the table. "Your father requested to have input on your punishment."

"He can't. He's not at that level."

"Which is why we discussed it while you were out of the room."

"And what was decided? Are they allowing it?"

"Yes. Holton will meet with the ruling council privately and express his thoughts on the matter, then the ruling council will share Holton's input with the upper level members."

"Dammit!" I slam my fist on the table. "Jack, why the hell didn't you put a stop to this? You know my father will make my punishment more severe."

"I'd already stood up for you enough in that meeting. I don't need a damn target on my back. Holton's already suspicious of me. Besides, just because they're allowing him to express his opinions doesn't mean they'll listen to him. The upper level members will make the final decision."

"Did my father indicate what he wants my punishment to be?"

"Of course not. He wouldn't risk one of us telling you what he said."

"Who else was there?"

"I can't tell you that."

It's so damn frustrating the way Jack picks and chooses what information to share.

"Then what exactly can you tell me, Jack?"

He leans back and folds his arms over his chest. "What do you want to know? Ask me and I'll see if I can answer."

I shoot up from the chair. "I'm not going to sit here and play guessing games all fucking day! Just tell me what they said!"

"Pearce," he says calmly. "Sit down."

I take a breath and lower myself back in the chair, rubbing my hand over my forehead. "Are they going to hurt Rachel? I need to know."

"I honestly don't know." He's serious now, and I feel like he might finally tell me something. "Now that the decision has been moved to a higher level, anything could happen. But I can tell you that when you weren't in the room, Rachel wasn't discussed. And the fact that they're allowing your marriage to continue is a good sign. Frankly, I'm still rather shocked that they did that."

"Do you think it's some kind of game they're playing? A ploy to make me think she's safe when she's really not?"

"It could be." He shoves his plate aside and puts his arms on the table, learning forward slightly. "I'm glad you're finally thinking that way, Pearce. You should always think that way. Never trust anyone. Never think you're safe. Because you're not. None of us are."

"So if they didn't talk about Rachel, what did they talk about when I left the room?" I know I've already asked him this, but I've found that sometimes I have to ask several times before I get an answer.

"They talked about what type of punishment would be appropriate for something like this, but no one could come up with anything since we've never had to deal with this before. Some of the younger members who were present said the punishment shouldn't be overly harsh, given that you simply married the girl. As long as she never knows our secrets and is able to adapt to your lifestyle, attending social events, etcetera, then they didn't find it to be that terrible of a crime. The older members, on the other hand, want a more severe punishment, mainly to use you as an example to the other members that this will not be tolerated. They don't want our men just going off and marrying whoever they please."

"And what did my father say?"

"He was quiet, except for his request to share his ideas with the higher-level members." Jack pauses, looking like he wants to say something.

"What is it, Jack? What else did my father say?"

He quickly shakes his head. "Nothing. That was it." He stands up. "I need to get to work."

"Speaking of work, my father fired me." It almost sounds comical when I say it. I guess I've accepted it now, to the point that it's rather humorous.

Jack smiles. "Lucky you. Did you go out and celebrate?"

"No, but I suppose I should, shouldn't I?"

"It's what you wanted. You're finally free of that place." He motions me to get up. "Come on. I'll walk you to the door."

As we're going down the hall, he glances at me and says, "So you want a job?"

"Why? Do you know of one?"

"I need a strategy guy for my new product line on the surveillance side of the business. You interested?"

I stop walking. "Are you serious?"

He stops as well and turns to face me. "You're smart and you have good ideas. And you're a hard worker. You're the type of person I like to hire. I know you want to start your own business, but maybe you'd like to do this in the meantime. It's better than sitting at home all day." He smiles. "And I guarantee you'd like your new boss a hell of a lot better than your old one."

"My father would be furious if I worked for you."

Jack smiles. "All the more reason to say yes."

I smile back. "I need to think about it, but thank you for offering. Could I get back to you later? Maybe in a few weeks? Rachel and I are going out of town and—"

"But you'll be at the meeting," he interrupts. "You can't miss the meeting, Pearce. It's the biggest one of the year."

"Yes, I know. I'll be there."

He's referring to the organization's end of the year meeting. It starts the Monday after Christmas, and lasts the entire week. Christmas is on a Saturday this year which means Rachel and I have to fly back Sunday so that I'm back in time for the meeting. I haven't told her what I'm doing that week because I haven't come up with an excuse yet. Coming up with these lies is exhausting.

"Let me know your decision by early January," he says.

We continue down the hallway to the open room that leads to the foyer. There's a staircase there and I hear a woman talking as she walks down the stairs.

"Hey, Jack-ass," she says kiddingly, as she meets Jack in the foyer.

"What do you want, woman?" he says, also in a kidding tone.

It's Jack's wife. She notices me and blushes. "Oh, sorry, I didn't realize you had company, Jack."

"Relax, Martha. It's just Pearce."

I've met his wife before. She's on the heavy side and has thick, dark brown hair that's cut to her chin. Martha doesn't really fit in with the other members' wives, who are stick-thin. She also swears a lot, which the other women never do, at least not in public. And when Martha drinks, she can be a little loud and say inappropriate things. The other women find her to be rather crude and improper. That's why Jack and Martha make a good pair. They're both outcasts.

"Jack-ass is her nickname for me," Jack says as he yanks her into his side and kisses her.

She laughs and says to me, "I'm sure you can guess how I came up with that." She sniffs her husband's shirt. "Jack, were you eating bacon again?"

"See?" he says to me. "You sound just like her." He kisses her again and smacks her rather large ass. "Love ya. See you tonight." He whispers something in her ear and she smiles and winks at him.

I don't know why these two cheat on each other. Almost all of the members do, but that's because they're stuck in loveless marriages. Jack and Martha seem to be in love, so I don't understand it.

Martha hands him his suit jacket. "You left this upstairs." She turns to me. "He'd forget his head if it wasn't attached."

I chuckle. "It's nice seeing you, Martha."

"You too, Pearce. Oh, and tell your wife I'd love to have her over sometime."

"That girl doesn't want to spend time with an old crazy bat like you," Jack kids as he puts his suit jacket on. "She's young enough to be your daughter."

I smile at Martha. "I'll be sure to tell her."

Jack and I leave, and as I'm driving home I think about what he told me. About how I should never assume I'm safe. Or that Rachel's safe. I keep telling myself she is because it's what I want to believe. I can't handle the thought of ever losing her. If something ever happened to her, it would destroy me. I wouldn't be able to live with myself, knowing I was the one who put her in danger.

Last night Rachel had us make a wish on that ornament I bought her. I wished that she would always be safe. That no harm would come to her. I don't believe in wishes so I never bother making them. But I did last night because I'll do everything possible to make sure Rachel is safe, even if that includes wishing on a crystal star.

As I sit at a stoplight, waiting for the light to turn, I consider Jack's job offer. I'm somewhat intrigued by it. Although I want my own company, I'm not ready to start it tomorrow. I need time to think and plan, and while I do that, it might be good to get some experience at a different company. One in which I'd actually get to voice my opinion and have people listen to my ideas.

My father would be furious if I took the job, but I don't really care. He already hates me and isn't speaking to me and I'm sure is on a personal mission to make my punishment as harsh as possible. So maybe I should go work for Jack. The problem is Rachel doesn't know I'm friends with Jack. She still thinks he's just some crazy old man who came to her apartment. So how do I explain to her who he really is and why I didn't tell her months ago when he showed up at her apartment?

Back at the loft I find Rachel on the couch, talking on the phone. Her eyes are red, like she's been crying.

"Mom, I know, but it's just better this way. And I don't have time to plan it even if I wanted to." She nods. "Yes. Okay." She pauses. "I love you too." She hangs up and lies back on the couch. "That didn't go well."

"What happened?" I lift her feet up and place them on my lap as I sit down.

"I told my mom that your mother is doing all the wedding planning and my mom got really upset. I told her the issues you're having with your parents, so she kind of understands, but she's still upset about it."

"Because she wanted to plan the wedding?"

"It's less about her and more about me. She's okay with your mom wanting to help with the wedding, but she doesn't know why I'm not allowed to have input. I tried to explain but I wasn't getting anywhere."

I don't know what to tell her. I can't give in and tell Rachel she can plan the wedding. It's out of my hands, and I wouldn't dare ask the members if she could have input. They've already made it clear that she is not to be involved, other than getting updates from the wedding planners.

"Did you ask your mother about the bridal shower?"

Rachel takes her legs off me and sits up. "Yes, but we haven't picked a date yet. A lot of my friends will be home for the holidays so that would be the best time to have it, but we'll be gone."

"We're coming back on the twenty-sixth. Why don't you fly out there and stay with your parents for a few days?"

"By myself?"

"Yes. Actually, it's good timing because I need to attend a client conference that week for Kensington Chemical."

"But your father fired you."

"That's not public knowledge. Our employees and clients haven't been told. They just think I'm taking time off." It's true, but I only found that out because I saw a memo about it when I went to pick up my things from my office. "I have close relationships with some of our clients so they expect me to be at the conference. I also have to go to dinner with them at night, so I won't be around much. It would be the perfect time for you to go visit your parents and have the bridal shower."

She considers it. "I guess it would be a good time to go back there. Once I get a job I won't be able to get home as much."

"Then it's settled. I'll get you a ticket."

The phone rings and Rachel reaches over to get it. "Hello." She listens. "Yes, this is Rachel." She smiles and nods. "No, we're not doing anything…okay, see you then." She hangs up.

"Who was that?" I ask.

"Victoria Lissfeld. She said she's Royce's fiancé. I thought they were just dating, not engaged."

"They're engaged now. So what did she want?"

"She invited us to have dinner with them tomorrow night."

"And you agreed?"

"Yes. We're not busy, and I thought it would be nice to have dinner with them. You're friends with Royce. I thought you'd want to go."

"No." I stand up, my anger rising. "I have no interest in having dinner with them, which is why you should've asked me before agreeing to it."

This is all Victoria's idea. I know it is. It's a ploy to get information from Rachel, which Victoria will twist into her own version of the truth that she will then gossip about to all her society friends. She'll turn them against Rachel before Rachel even has a chance to meet them. It'll be hard enough for Rachel to be accepted into that group of women, given that she's not one of us, but Victoria is trying to make sure Rachel is never allowed in.

"Pearce, I feel like you're trying to hide me from your friends again."

I sit back down beside her. "That's not it. I just don't care for Victoria. I've known her for years and she is not a nice woman."

"Why don't you let me decide that for myself? It's just one dinner. We're meeting them at the restaurant."

"Fine, but watch what you say around her. Don't tell her too much. She gossips constantly and I don't want her talking about us."

"If she's so horrible, then why is Royce marrying her?" She pauses, looking like she just figured out the answer to her own question. "It's an arranged marriage."

"Yes. But they're both okay with it."

"I still find that strange." She shakes away the thought and says to me, "So where were you this morning?"

"I was at the gym," I blurt out, unable to find a better lie.

"You always meet with your trainer at noon."

"He had a conflict today so he asked me to come in early. By the way, I got you a membership for the gym down the street. You should go check out the pool."

Her eyes light up. "You got me a membership? When did you get it?"

"Yesterday. I forgot to tell you."

She smiles. "Do you mind if I go right now? A swim would feel really good right now."

I kiss her. "Go ahead."

She goes to the bedroom to change. I recline back on the couch, relieved that she believed my story about the conference and that she went along with my idea for her to go home that week.

I don't know how I'll be able to keep doing this. When I have to go to a meeting for the organization or leave to complete an assignment, what am I going to tell her? Before, I could blame work, and I was able to do so just now. But I no longer have a job, so what will I do in the future? What excuse will I give her?

I feel like I'm running out of lies she'll believe. And we've only been married a few weeks. How will I be able to do this for the rest of our lives?

CHAPTER TWELVE

RACHEL

We just arrived at the restaurant where we're meeting Royce and Victoria. It's a seafood restaurant along the shoreline. Pearce has been here before and told me it's a very upscale restaurant, so I'm wearing a dress and Pearce is wearing a suit. I had to go out and buy the dress just for tonight. I didn't have one that was nice enough to wear to an expensive restaurant.

I really need some new clothes. Everything I own is casual, and Pearce said I'll need elegant dresses for the high-end events he goes to. On Friday I'm going shopping with that woman who picked out the clothes I wore in Las Vegas. Pearce told me to buy whatever I want and not look at the price tags, which will feel very strange given that I usually shop the clearance racks.

"Hello, Pearce." Royce stands up from the table. Pearce and I say hello and shake hands with him.

"And I'm Victoria," the woman next to him says. I've never met her so I didn't know what she looked like before now. She's a couple inches shorter than me, and thin, with dark brown hair that's pulled up behind her head. She's wearing a cream-colored fitted dress with a scarf draped over the shoulder and somehow tied at her waist. It seems very high fashion.

"It's nice to meet you," I say, shaking her hand.

Her eyes move over me, starting at my face and slowly moving down to my dress. I feel like I'm being inspected and judged, similar to how I felt when I met Pearce's parents. It's not a good feeling.

We all sit down, with Victoria across from me. She smiles at me, but it's a tight, strained smile. "So tell me how you met Pearce."

"They met at Yale," Royce answers, putting his arm up behind her chair.

"You went to Yale?" Victoria asks in a surprised tone, as if she couldn't imagine me going there.

"No. I went to Hirshfield. I was at Yale listening to Pearce give a speech on business ethics."

Royce laughs so hard he almost chokes on the water he was drinking.

"Pardon me," he says, blotting his napkin over his mouth. "Business ethics?" he says to Pearce. "They do know your family owns Kensington Chemical, correct?"

He laughs again, but I don't know why that's funny. Is he saying the company isn't ethical?

"Royce," Pearce says in a warning tone, which only makes me think Royce wasn't kidding.

Victoria ignores him and says to me, "I hear you're from somewhere in the middle."

I can't stand it when people call it that. It's the Midwest, not the middle.

"Yes, I'm from Indiana."

"And you're from a farm?" She almost laughs when she says it.

"Yes, I grew up on a farm." I probably said it a little too harshly but I hope she picked up on my tone. She's being rude and I don't want this to continue all night.

"Isn't that sweet, Royce?" She tilts her head. "Pearce found himself a sweet little farm girl."

"Victoria," Pearce says in a much harsher tone than mine. "Rachel and I will leave if you continue to act this way."

"What way?" she asks, batting her fake eyelashes at him. "I'm simply trying to get to know the girl."

Royce leans over to her and smiles. "Victoria, sweetheart, be nice." He says it like he's talking to a little girl.

Although I'm grateful to Royce for helping Pearce and me elope, I can't say that I like him. The first day we were in Las Vegas, Royce slept with multiple women, despite being engaged to Victoria. He doesn't respect women at all. He talks down to them, using a condescending tone like he did just now.

"I need to use the restroom," I say, already needing a break from this. I get up just as the waiter appears. "Pearce, could you please order me the salmon?"

"Rachel," I hear him say as I head to the restroom. I go in there and stare at the mirror as I take some deep breaths. I need to be tougher. I can't let these people walk all over me. If I do, I'll live up to their stereotype of the sweet, naive farm girl.

Victoria walks into the bathroom. "Is everything okay in here?"

Her face displays a smug grin, like she's pleased with herself for getting a reaction out of me. But I'm not letting her affect me again.

I smile. "I'm fine. Just freshening up."

I take my lipstick from my purse and reapply it, even though I don't need to. I don't even like lipstick, but I felt like I should wear it. At least it's a soft pink shade. Victoria's is bright red, which looks harsh against her pale skin.

"So are you happy with Pearce?" she asks, smoothing her hair as she looks in the mirror.

"Yes. Very happy." I put my lipstick back in my purse.

"He's such a naughty boy." She takes out her compact and blots her face with some powder. "But his looks make up for his bad behavior."

I don't respond, not wanting this conversation to continue.

"Royce is certainly no angel, but Pearce has been with far more women than Royce." She snaps her compact closed and drops it in her purse.

"I'm going back to the table," I tell her.

"Wait." She holds my arm. "You do know the men aren't faithful, don't you?"

"I need to go."

She won't let go of my arm. "It's in their nature. They're boys. They can't help themselves. And given their extreme wealth, they can have any woman they want, so why would they settle for just one?"

"Maybe because they're in love," I say, glaring at her.

She laughs. "They love their jobs and their money. Not their wives. We're just something to come home to. Someone to have their children."

"That's not how Pearce feels. Now would you let me go?"

"I'm just trying to be honest with you. This is your life now, Rachel. You'll be expected to stay at home with the children and do charity work, while Pearce spends his time at work and with other women."

"You don't know what you're talking about."

She smiles. "Do you ever wonder where he goes?"

"What do you mean?"

"Do you ever find that sometimes Pearce will be gone for hours and you're not sure where he went? Or he tells you where he went, but it seems like a lie?"

I DO feel that way, but I'm not going to admit it to Victoria. And even if Pearce doesn't always tell me where he goes, I know he's not off having an affair with another woman. He wouldn't do that to me.

She finally lets go of my arm. "It's just something to think about." She checks her hair in the mirror. "I enjoyed our girl talk. We should do it again."

I storm out of the bathroom and back to the table, stopping when I see a tall, gorgeous blond woman talking to Pearce. She's leaning down so that her cleavage is at his eye level.

I go and stand behind him. "Pearce, I'm not feeling well. Would you mind if we left?"

He quickly stands up and turns to me. "Are you okay?"

"I'm not sure. I feel kind of sick to my stomach."

He steps away from the table and puts his arm around me. "Let's go."

I notice the blond woman staring at me. She smiles. "Hi. I'm Rielle."

Rielle. Where have I heard that name? I know I've heard it before. From Pearce's father. That's where I heard it. Holton said Pearce had been with Rielle, and hinted that they were still together when Pearce and I were dating. But I'm sure Holton was lying. He had to be lying.

"Royce, we'll see you later," Pearce says.

We walk to the front of the restaurant, passing Victoria on the way out.

"Leaving so soon?" she asks.

We ignore her and keep walking. We get our coats from the coat check, then go outside.

Pearce stops just beyond the door, his hands on my shoulders, his eyes full of concern. "Are you really sick, or just upset?"

"A little of both."

He brings me into his arms. "I'm sorry, sweetheart. I told you Victoria was an awful woman. And Royce is just as bad. Those two are made for each other."

The way Pearce holds me, stroking my hair, kissing my head, I know that he loves me and I know he wouldn't cheat. So why did I even let my mind go there?

"Let's go home," he says, taking my hand.

When we're in the car, driving away, I say, "I'm sorry for making us leave. I should've stood up to her more."

He reaches across the seat for my hand. "There's nothing to be sorry for. You just saved us from a night of pure hell. Although that restaurant does have excellent lobster."

I laugh. "Then we'll have to go back sometime. Just the two of us."

"Since we didn't have dinner, would you like to stop and get something?"

"Could we maybe go to a pizza place?"

Now *he's* the one laughing. "In a suit and a dress?"

"Sure, why not?"

He lifts my hand up and kisses it. "Or we could get a pizza to go, eat at home in front of the fire, and see what happens after that."

"I like that idea even better."

So that's what we do. And it turns out to be a great night. I never asked Pearce about Rielle. I don't need to know why she was talking to him. I'm not letting Victoria plant seeds of doubt in my mind about Pearce. He's not like Royce. He's a good husband. And although it's true he could have any woman he wants, he chose me, and only me.

The next day I go to the gym and swim laps. It's a very nice facility. The pool is kept at a perfect temperature and the locker rooms are immaculate.

Pearce is at home, but later this morning he's taking his car in for maintenance. Speaking of cars, I'm now driving a brand new BMW. Pearce bought it for me soon after we got back from Vegas. He insisted I get a luxury vehicle, but I didn't want a Mercedes like his, so we bought the BMW. I've never had a new car, so anything new would've felt like a luxury to me, but the BMW *really* feels like luxury.

When I get back from swimming, I shower and dress and wait for Pearce to get home. We're having lunch together when he gets back. It's weird that we're both home all day. My job at the museum ended last week. Months ago, I told my boss when my last day would be, assuming I'd be moving away for a job in New York or somewhere else, so they had another grad student already lined up to take my place.

"Pearce, I'm in here," I say as I hear the elevator door open. "I'm in the bedroom, putting my earrings on."

He doesn't answer. That's odd.

"Pearce?" I leave the bedroom and see Holton standing in the living room.

"Hello," he says. As usual, he doesn't say my name. I don't think I've ever heard him say my name. Then again, I've only met him one time.

"Hello, Mr. Kensington." I walk over to him. "Pearce isn't home. He's getting his car fixed, but he should be home shortly."

"I'm not here to speak with my son. I'm here to speak with you."

A shiver runs through me. I don't know why, but Holton scares me. He shouldn't scare me. He's Pearce's father. But for some reason he makes me very comfortable.

I motion to the couch. "Would you like to sit down?"

He takes off his coat and holds it out in front of him. Then he sighs and lays it over the back of the couch. I guess I was supposed to take his coat, but right now I'm too nervous to follow all the proper etiquette rules. Why does he make me so nervous?

He sits in the chair next to the couch. He has on a black suit with a white shirt and a dark gray tie.

"Would you like something to drink?" I ask, trying to make up for the coat mishap.

"No. I won't be staying long."

I sit down on the couch. "What would you like to talk about?"

His eyes narrow. "How long do you plan to be married to my son?"

I can't believe he just asked me that. What kind of question is that?

"Well, hopefully forever," I say, trying to keep my voice even. "I don't know why you would ask such a question."

"A woman like you has a motive. Money. Fame. You're hoping to get something out of this. So name your price so we can end this."

Hurt and anger hit me all at once. Is that really what he thinks of me? That I married Pearce for something other than love?

"I don't think you understand," I say. "I married your son because I love him. I don't want his money and I definitely don't want to be famous."

"And yet you alerted the press about your engagement and are doing interviews for the papers."

"Yes, but only because Pearce said we should. I didn't—"

"By the way, does it bother you that you're not involved in planning your own wedding?"

"Yes, it does," I say honestly. "Maybe you could talk to your wife about that."

He lifts his chin slightly. "My wife? What does Eleanor have to do with the wedding?"

Holton doesn't know Eleanor is planning the wedding? How could he not know this? Or is she not really planning it? Did Pearce just say that so I wouldn't get involved? Why would he do that? Does he not trust me to plan it?

"That ring." Holton points to my engagement ring. "A woman who doesn't care about money wouldn't ask for a ring that size. I'm sure that will be the first thing you sell after the divorce."

I cover my ring with my hand. "There's not going to be a divorce."

He sits there, silently watching me, then says, "Pearce will not be faithful to you. No man with our kind of wealth is faithful to only one woman. I have never been faithful to his mother and Pearce will not be faithful to you. Women who are married to rich, powerful men understand this. But given your background, I feel the need to tell you."

I glance away from his penetrating gaze. "Was that all you needed to tell me?"

I really don't like this man and I just want him to leave.

"He lies to you." Holton's lips turn up just slightly as he crosses his legs. "He knows you're trusting and will believe anything he says."

"I think we should end this conversation." I get up and walk over to the window, wishing Pearce's car would appear at the gate so he could get up here and deal with his father.

"He tells you what you want to hear. It's what he's been taught. And it's how he gets what he wants."

I feel like I'm talking to Victoria again. Being told that Pearce is not the man I think he is. But that's not true. I know it's not. I may have only met him a few months ago and may not know

138

everything about him, but I know he's a good man. And I know that he loves me.

"Where does Pearce go when he's not with you?" Holton asks.

I turn back to him. "Pearce is a grown man. I don't keep tabs on him. And he doesn't keep tabs on me."

"Is that so? He has a man watching you every Saturday when you work at the homeless shelter in New Haven. Is that considered keeping tabs on you?"

A heavy, sick feeling gnaws at my stomach. "That's not true."

"Is he really getting his car fixed right now?" Holton smirks. "Or is he somewhere else?"

I can't take another minute of this. Holton is lying and I'm done listening to it.

"Mr. Kensington, if you're trying to make a point here, then do it. Otherwise, I'm going to go finish getting ready. Pearce will be home any minute now and then we're going to lunch."

"Do you know where Pearce was yesterday morning?"

I take a breath and close my eyes, then open them again. "He was at the gym."

Holton chuckles. "Is that what he told you?"

I don't answer, so he continues.

"Yesterday morning, my son was meeting with a friend of his. A friend of the family, actually. A man by the name of Jack Ellit."

I freeze, remembering the name. Jack Ellit was the man who came to my apartment. I was suspicious of him, so Pearce said he'd have his security guys find out who this man was. Pearce acted like Jack was a stranger, not a friend.

"Have you ever met Jack?" Holton asks, in a tone that implies he already knows the answer. I don't respond, so he says, "I've known him for years. He owns a communications company, but also dabbles in security and surveillance equipment. Jack and my son have developed a friendship the past year, and a few months ago, Pearce asked Jack to run background checks on you to see if you were just some con artist trying to steal his money. I'm surprised Jack didn't stop by your apartment to meet you in person. He usually does that, in addition to the background check."

That sick feeling intensifies. *It's not true*, I tell myself. *Don't listen to him.* But how does he know about Jack? Is Jack really a friend of the family? Why wouldn't Pearce tell me that? Is it because he sent Jack to spy on me?

"I'm sorry, I need to go," I say, racing off to the bedroom. I go in the bathroom and splash cold water on my face to alleviate the nauseous feeling in my stomach. Pearce wouldn't lie like that, would he? But he lied about Shelby. For months, he lied about knowing her. Oh, God, what if it's true? What if everything Holton said is true?

"Rachel, I'm home."

I hear Pearce's voice and quickly dry my face and hurry back to the living room. Holton is nowhere to be found.

"Where is he?" I ask, noticing his coat is gone.

"Where's who?" Pearce asks.

"Your father. He was just here a minute ago."

"My *father*?" Pearce takes his coat off. "My father was here?"

"Yes, but he must've left. You didn't see him leaving?"

"No." Pearce comes over and holds my arms a little too tightly. "Rachel, why was my father here? What did he want?"

My eyes drift to the floor. "He came here to talk to me. To tell me things."

"What things?"

"He said you..." I pause for a moment, trying to sort out everything Holton said.

"Rachel, tell me."

I feel Pearce's eyes on me, but I won't look at him.

"Do you have someone watching me when I go to the shelter?" I ask quietly.

He loosens his hold on my arms, but doesn't answer.

"Pearce. Do you?"

"Yes," he says in a quiet tone. "But only because I worry about your safety. He's not spying on you. He's just making sure you're safe."

I feel tears building and a lump forming in my throat. "Your mother isn't planning the wedding, is she? You just said that to keep my mom and me out of it."

"Why would you say that? Who—"

"Are you denying it?"

He hesitates, then says, "No."

More lies. How many are there?

My shoulders slump and I squeeze my eyes shut and say, "Jack Ellit."

"What about him?"

I keep my eyes shut. "You know him. You're friends with him."

I hear nothing but silence, so I open my eyes. And when I do, I see Pearce looking at me, his eyes desperate. But I don't know what they're desperate for. My forgiveness? My trust? Or are they just desperate for me to believe his lies?

"You sent Jack to my apartment to make sure I wasn't some con artist."

"What?" His brows furrow. "No. Jack went there on his own. I wasn't aware that he'd done that until after you'd told me."

Tears pour down my cheeks as it hits me that I really don't know Pearce. He's my husband, but I don't even know him.

"Rachel." He reaches for me as I back away from him. "Rachel, just listen to me. I've known Jack for years, but I promise you, I never sent him to your apartment. When I found out he did that, I was furious."

"Why did he do it?" I ask, wiping my tears.

"Because he doesn't trust people. Jack treats me like a son, and when he found out we were dating, he took it upon himself to make sure I wasn't getting involved with someone I shouldn't be. It was wrong of him and he never should've done it and I told him that."

"Why didn't you tell me you knew him?"

He sighs. "Because I was afraid of how you'd react. I had just met you and I knew we had something special between us and I didn't want anything ruining it. I assumed if you found out I knew

141

Jack, you'd assume I sent him over there and then you'd think I didn't trust you."

"You keep lying to me, Pearce. How do I know if anything you say is true?"

He's quiet. So what does that mean? That there are more lies? More he hasn't told me?

I look him in the eye. "Pearce. I want to trust you, but right now, I don't. I think we need some time apart." I turn and walk back to the bedroom, fighting back tears.

"Rachel, no!" He finds me in the closet, tossing clothes in my suitcase. "Rachel, you're not leaving."

"I need time to think." I drag the suitcase into the bedroom and zip it up. "I'll be at my apartment."

"We're married. You can't just walk out like this."

"I can't talk to you right now. I need time to think and figure things out. And figure out what I'm going to do."

He grabs the suitcase and sets it behind him, then pulls me against his body. "Don't say that. You're not doing anything. There's nothing to figure out." He holds me tighter and says in a hoarse whisper, "I love you, Rachel. Please stay."

"I'm sorry, but I can't." Tears are pouring down my face, soaking into his shirt. I place my hands on his chest and push away from him and look into his eyes. "You lied to me about Shelby. And I forgave you."

"Rachel." He tries to pull me into his arms again, but I press back, keeping us apart.

"I forgave you, Pearce, even though I didn't want to. You had sex with one of my closest friends and then acted like you didn't know her. You lied to my face and you did it for months. Most women would never forgive you for that...but I did. I just don't know if I can keep forgiving you."

I go behind him and take the suitcase and wheel it to the elevator. He silently follows me.

When the elevator door opens, I get on and see him standing there in the loft, his eyes filled with so much sadness it nearly breaks my heart.

142

"Please, don't," he says.
The elevator doors close and that's the end of our fight.
I just hope it's not also the end of us.

CHAPTER THIRTEEN

PEARCE

I watch the elevator doors close. Rachel is gone.

She knows I lied to her. Again. But this time she may not forgive me. This time could be the end.

This is all my father's doing. He came here and exposed all my lies to Rachel, hoping it would make her divorce me. And maybe it will.

"Fuck!" I yell as I slam my palm against the elevator door.

I hate him. I hate my father. I hate him so damn much.

I storm through the loft, down the hall to the room I use as an office. I open the bottom drawer of my desk and take out my gun. I load it and grab more bullets and storm back out of the room. I put my coat on, shoving the gun and bullets in my pocket and go down to my car.

I drive to my parents' mansion, speeding the entire way. When I get there, I sit at the gate, my heart hammering in my chest.

I squeeze my eyes shut and rub my forehead. What the hell am I doing here?

"Mr. Kensington?" The voice is coming from the speaker attached to the gate. It's one of the security guards. He can see my car on the cameras.

I roll my window down. "Yes, it's Pearce."

"I'm sorry, sir, but you're not allowed on the premises. Mr. Kensington has asked that—"

"Yes, I know. I was just turning around." I quickly back up, then accelerate down the street and turn onto the main road that goes into town.

What the fuck was I thinking? I can't kill my own father. It's wrong. I know it's wrong and yet I almost did it. It was pure instinct. I was driven by rage. I wasn't even thinking. What does that say about me? That I'm turning into him? I kill without even thinking?

I have to stop this. I am not my father and I will not become him. I will not let his actions dictate mine. He knew what he was doing by telling Rachel those things. He knew it would provoke me and maybe he thought I'd come after him. Maybe he wanted me to. Maybe he wanted to see how far he could push me before I'd go over the edge and do something drastic.

I'm not taking the bait. I am beyond enraged over what he did, but I will deal with it another way. And I will find a way to undo the damage he has done.

I drive until I arrive at the indoor shooting range. I always come here to practice, but I haven't had time the past few weeks. Now is the perfect time. I feel the need to shoot something.

I spend an hour there, shooting repeatedly at the target, imagining it's my father. My aim is perfect. I've never shot better in my life.

When I leave, I feel more at ease, but I still don't know what to do about Rachel. I can't show up at her place until I have a plan. I have to figure out what to say to her.

I drive to Jack's office, but when I get there, his secretary says he's at home. I head over there, and as I drive up to his house, I realize I forget to call and tell him I was coming over.

"You can't keep dropping in like this," he says as he opens the door. "I have a life, you know."

It's one o'clock and he's in a bathrobe.

I go inside. "Yes, I apologize. I wouldn't do this if it weren't an emergency."

"Someone better be dying because I was in the middle of—"

"Jack, get your ass up here and untie me," I hear Martha yell from upstairs.

He sighs. "You have horrible timing, Pearce."

"I'm sorry. I didn't realize you and Martha were—"

"Wait here." He goes up the stairs.

"Jack, are you coming?" Martha yells.

"Yes, but that idiot, Pearce, is here," he yells back.

This is embarrassing. For me, not for Jack. Nothing embarrasses him. It's the middle of a work day. Doesn't he need to be at the office?

Five minutes later he appears in his suit and tie and walks right past me. I just follow him like I always do, and we go to his hidden room.

"For future reference, I regularly schedule a little afternoon delight," he says, pouring himself a drink. "It's best not to stop by at this hour of the day." He takes a seat across from me. "So what the hell is the big emergency? Did you get a new assignment?"

"No. My father went to visit Rachel and told her I'd been lying to her."

Jack leans forward, almost spilling the drink in his hand. "He told her about Dunamis?"

"No. He told her some other things, one of which was that you and I are friends."

"Who did she think I was?"

"After you stopped by her apartment that night, I told her I had you investigated and found that you were just a wealthy old man who wasn't all there, mentally."

"All true." He swigs his drink.

"Perhaps, but it's not the whole truth. I acted like I didn't know you. It doesn't matter. The point is that she knows I lied to her on multiple occasions. She stormed out of the loft, saying she needs to think about what she's going to do."

"You think she'll divorce you?"

"I don't know, but I can't let that happen. I love her, Jack, and I can't live without her."

"What about Rachel?" He leans back, putting his feet up on the chair next to him. "Does she love you enough to forgive you?"

"Yes. At least I think she does. She has a big heart. She's very forgiving, maybe too much so."

"Meaning she shouldn't forgive your lying ass?"

"Yes." I pause, not wanting to admit this out loud.

"What is it, Pearce?"

"Maybe it's best if she didn't forgive me. Maybe if she didn't...she'd be safe. I worry about her, Jack. I worry what they might do." I burst up from the chair. "Fuck! What the fuck have I done? Why did I get her involved in this?"

"Because you were thinking with your heart instead of your head." He takes a drink. "Sit down."

I drop back in the chair, holding my face in my hands. "I don't know what to do. I don't want to lose her, but I also don't want to put her in danger. I thought I could protect her, but what if I can't?"

"It's a shitty world out there, Pearce. A pretty young woman like her? She'd be in danger whether she was with you or not."

"This is different. They could be planning something and I don't even know it."

"If you divorce her, they still might come after her."

"Why?" I look at him. "Why would they do that?"

He shrugs. "If they think you confided in her about Dunamis, or anything related to it, they'll kill her. And that'll be much easier to do if she's not married to you. If she's not your wife, she's a nobody. It's easy to get rid of a nobody. So as fucked up as it sounds, she might be safer *with* you than *without* you."

I hadn't thought about that, but it might be true.

"What do you want to do, Pearce?"

"I want to tell her the truth. I'm sick of lying to her. I want her to know the truth."

"Well, that's not an option, so what other ideas do you have?"

"I need to tell her *something*. I can't keep coming up with excuses every time I have to do something for Dunamis. We're

147

only a few months into our relationship and I'm already running out of lies."

Jack gets up and goes back to the bar to refill his drink.

"Jack, why were you willing to help me be with Rachel? You knew it wasn't allowed and yet you still agreed to help me."

"Because I'm tired of them fucking with people's lives. As I've told you before, they own us. We have no freedom. We have all this goddamn money, but for what? To give up our lives? Our freedom? To some power-hungry pricks who think they should rule the world?"

"What does that have to do with Rachel?"

He sits down again, looking at me from across the table. "You've had a shitty life, Pearce. The other members may complain about their childhoods, saying they weren't allowed to do this or that, but their problems are nothing compared to what you've had to put up with. Your father is a monster. I've watched how he's treated you over the years. Even when you were just a young boy, your father made your life hell. He punished you for just being a child. I remember being at your house when you were maybe four or five and you forgot to take your shoes off after coming in from outside. You got dirt on the tile and he screamed at you as if you'd just burnt the house down. He called you stupid and worthless and he almost..." He clears his throat. "Let's just say that I was never invited back to the house after that."

"Because you said something to him?"

He chuckles. "I did more than that. I punched him. He was so shocked he didn't even punch me back. He just kicked me out of his house and didn't allow me back until he was forced to years later for a Dunamis party he was hosting. I'm sure some people would say that I shouldn't have interfered like that, but I had to. I've done plenty of bad shit in my life, but I would never hurt a child or talk that way to a child, and I couldn't just stand there and let him treat you that way."

"I don't remember that incident." I take a poker chip from the table, holding it between my finger and thumb and tapping it on the table. I'm not comfortable talking about my childhood, and I didn't know Jack knew about it. His fight with my father explains why I didn't see Jack much when I was growing up. My parents had other members over for dinner, but not Jack. I'd only see him at parties or other social gatherings.

"You were probably too young to remember," he says. "Holton almost hit you that day, and he would have if I hadn't stopped him. Later, I met with your mother and told her what happened. She said he hadn't hit you before, at least not that she was aware of, and she told me she would never allow it to happen. And as far as I know, it didn't. Or did it?"

I keep my eyes on the poker chip. "Once. When I was older. But afterward, my mother wouldn't speak to him so he never did it again."

"He still treated you like shit. I bet that man's never said one nice thing to you, has he?"

I slam the poker chip down. "Are you making a point here, or do you just feel the need to remind me how much my father hates me?"

He takes a deep breath. "My point is that you deserve a better life, Pearce."

"Yes, well, don't we all?"

"True, but some of us have it better than others. I'm chained to Dunamis, but I still have Martha and the girls. And look at Arlin Sinclair. His wife, Grace, is the love of his life. Royce is a fuck-up, but their other son, William, is a good kid. What I'm saying is that the only happiness in our lives comes from our families, and I wanted you to have that type of happiness. I could see how happy you were with Rachel, but I realize now that I should've worked harder to keep you away from her."

"You just told me you wanted me to be with her."

"No. I told you I wanted you to have some happiness in your life, which you would've had if I'd been able to find you the right wife. One who was approved, but who you might actually grow to love. But then you went and married Rachel. I knew about that, by the way. I tracked you all the way to Vegas. Knew you

149

were getting married. What chapel you went to. The hotel you stayed at. All of it."

"You were spying on me? Then why didn't you stop me?"

"First of all, I make surveillance equipment. Of course I spy on you. I spy on everyone. And as for Vegas, I was torn. I wanted to stop you, and I almost did, but then I couldn't do it. At the time, your father was actively looking to set you up with a woman you would hate. He knew there were better options, but he wanted to find the woman who would make you the most miserable. If you hadn't married Rachel, you would've ended up with whoever he picked."

"And now you're telling me to stay with Rachel."

"That's up to you. We don't know if she'll even take you back. But if she does, then maybe we can find a way out of this."

"Out of what?"

"Your obligation to be part of the organization."

"What are you talking about it? I can't get out of it."

He takes a drink. "I hate the word 'can't.' It's so limiting. A dead end. It means you're giving up. I don't even let my employees say it." He swishes his whiskey around in his glass. "I'm making you my project, Pearce. I want to try to get you out of this. I don't know how, but I'm going to try."

"Doing so could get you killed."

"A lot of things could get me killed. And don't get too excited about this. It may take ten years, or twenty, or hell, I could die before it happens. But I'm still going to try."

"When did you decide to do this?"

"When you showed up at my door just now. You looked like hell. You still do. You look even worse now than before you met Rachel. Back then you were walking through life in a coma, but at least you had a flicker of light in your eyes. Now there's nothing there. Like you've given up all hope."

"Because I honestly don't know what to do. Not just about this fight Rachel and I are having, but about our relationship in general. She doesn't know me, Jack. Not all of me. She's married to someone she doesn't really know. She says she loves me, but the truth is she only loves part of me."

"Bullshit. The part she doesn't know isn't you. It's them. It's the organization and what they make you do. It's your father and the ideas he's put in your head. Rachel knows the real you. She knows you, the person. Not what you've done. She doesn't need to know what you've done because it's not you. If you were free from Dunamis, would you be going around killing people?"

"No. Of course not."

"I wouldn't either. Most of us wouldn't. But too many of us get caught up in thinking that we are what we do, even if we're forced to do those things."

"I can't keep lying to her, Jack. You told me I wouldn't be able to keep this a secret and you were right. It's impossible."

"It's not impossible. We have several members who have never told their wives. Jacobson's wife doesn't know. Her family isn't part of Dunamis. She was only approved to be his wife because we didn't have anyone else to set him up with. But we picked her because she fits in our world. She's extremely wealthy and is one of those wives who pays no attention to what her husband is doing."

"Rachel will notice. I can't hide this from her."

"I feel like we're talking in circles here. Just make a damn decision. What are you going to do?"

"I'm telling her the truth. Not the real truth, but a version of the truth. I'm going to admit that sometimes I can't be honest with her. I'll tell her I'm involved with something dangerous and I need to keep her out of it."

"If you tell her that, she'll be calling a divorce attorney."

"Maybe if I say it right she'll understand."

"Get your fucking head on straight, Pearce. The woman's not going to take you back if you tell her you're going to continue lying to her AND that you're involved in dangerous activities."

I sigh. "Then I either have to let her go or keep lying to her."

"So what's it going to be?"

I shake my head. "I can't let her go. I'll have to find a way to make this work. I'll just have to live a double life. Completely separate the Dunamis side of my life with the life I have with Rachel."

"You're finally thinking right. That's exactly what you need to do. It's just like I tell you to do with assignments. You need to separate yourself from your actions. It's not you. It's someone else. When you lie to her, it's that other side of you doing it. It's not you. If you weren't a member, you wouldn't lie to her, would you? I mean, besides the normal husband lies, like hiding the fact that you ate a pound of bacon for breakfast instead of whatever health food shit she tries to get you to eat."

I smile. "No. I wouldn't lie to her. Not even about the bacon."

"Then stop beating yourself up over this. You didn't ask to be part of the organization, but since you're forced to be, you have no choice but to lie. Accept that and move on. Live your life, but keep that part of your life separate. When you go home at night, don't think about it. I know that's not easy to do, but you have to in order to keep Rachel from suspecting anything. When you go home, you're her husband. A regular husband with a regular life. That's it. And when you have to lie to her about the other side of your life, you will believe the lie. Don't even let your mind think otherwise. If you do, she'll see right through you. And if you believe the lies yourself, it'll be easier to separate that side of your life from the other side." He stands up. "You think you can do that?"

"Yes. It won't be easy but it's my only option." I stand up and he walks me to the door. "Thank you for meeting with me on such short notice. I'm sorry to interrupt your day."

"No problem. But next time," he winks, "don't stop by in the afternoon."

"Agreed." I smile. "I'll see myself out. Goodbye, Jack."

I leave his house and get back in my car, not sure where I'm going. I keep thinking about what he said about getting me out of the organization. Is it really possible? Or did he just say that to make me feel better?

I like Jack. I really do. But as much as I like him, I know I can't trust him. I want to, but I can't. He has no reason to help me. I'm not his son. Of course, given that Jack's had sex with my mother, it could've been a possibility, but I know I'm not his son because I look just like my father.

Jack hates my father, so is that why he wants to help me? To anger my father? Or does he really feel sorry for me? I don't want Jack feeling sorry for me. I don't need his pity and I don't need him telling me about my childhood. I survived those years and I am stronger because of it.

I stop at a traffic light and realize I'm just down the street from Rachel's apartment. I don't even remember driving here, but I ended up here so obviously it's where I want to be. I have to see her. I need to tell her as much as I can, then hope she'll still want to be with me.

I park on the street and go in her building and up the stairs. I can hear her TV on.

"Rachel." I knock on the door. "Rachel, it's Pearce." I knock again, but there's no answer. I know she's in there. I can hear her walking around. "Rachel, I need to talk to you." I wait, but she still doesn't answer. "Rachel, please."

The volume on the TV goes up. So she won't talk to me. She doesn't even want to see me.

I sigh and drop my head, staring at the ratty green carpet that lines the hallway. I can't stand the thought of her staying here tonight, but if she's not even talking to me, then she definitely won't be coming back to the loft.

Shelby's door swings open and she comes out of her apartment wearing pink sweatpants and a black leather jacket, her blond hair in a ponytail.

"Hey." She locks her door. "She doesn't want to talk to you."

"Have you spoken with her?"

"Yeah." Shelby takes off down the stairs.

"Wait." I follow her, but she doesn't stop until she reaches the landing. "What did she say?"

Shelby goes out the door.

I follow her. "Are you not talking to me either?"

She turns to me. "I shouldn't be. But I will because you're helping my dad." She stares at my face. "You look like shit. It hasn't even been a day and you already look this bad? Damn, you really love her."

"She's my wife. Of course I love her. Now would you tell me what she said?"

"She didn't say much. She mostly cried." Shelby rolls her eyes. "I knew this would happen. I knew you'd hurt her."

"I didn't intend to, but you know I have secrets to keep."

"Which is why this will never work. You can't lie to her for the rest of your life."

She starts to walk off but I hold her arm. "Did she say she's leaving me? Just tell me."

"She said she needs time to think. But she's really upset, Pearce, even more than when she found my earring. And don't bother calling her. She said she won't answer your calls."

"Can you talk to her for me? Please, Shelby. Tell her I'm sorry and that I'll explain everything if she'll just let me."

"Why would I tell her that? It's just another lie. You can't explain *anything* to her. You'll just be telling her more lies."

I let go of her arm and stand back. "Like you're lying to Logan?"

She chews on her lip. "Yeah. Fine. But I didn't marry him, now did I?"

"You're still dating him, knowing he wants to get serious."

"We're not talking about me. We're talking about you. How are you going to fix this?"

"By talking to her, but she won't—"

"You really think you can keep this going? Lie for your entire marriage?"

"I will handle it. And how I do so is none of your business. This is between Rachel and me."

"She may not take you back." Shelby zips her coat up as the wind blows around us.

"Just please talk to her for me. Convince her to come back to the loft. I don't want her staying here. Tell her if she comes home, I won't bother her. I'll stay in the guest room."

"She won't do it. She doesn't want to be anywhere near you right now. I have to go." Shelby runs off to her car.

I want to go upstairs and knock on Rachel's door again, but I know she won't answer. She needs more time. I'll come back tomorrow. And the day after that. I'll keep coming back until she answers. I'm not giving up on her. Or our marriage.

She came into my life for a reason. We met because we were supposed to. And we didn't make it this far for it to just end.

CHAPTER FOURTEEN

RACHEL

I haven't seen Pearce in almost a week. I haven't talked to him either. The first few days after our fight he called me a million times, but I wouldn't answer. And he came to my door, but I wouldn't open it.

Then he gave up trying to contact me and now I haven't heard from him in days. It's Wednesday and my parents are coming here Friday for my graduation, which is Saturday. They fly home on Sunday and then on Monday, Pearce and I are supposed to leave for Italy for our honeymoon.

Now I don't know if that will happen. I don't know if Pearce is even coming to my graduation. I know I should talk to him, but I don't know what to say. I can't be married to someone who constantly lies to me. I can't be with someone I can't trust.

I talked to Shelby after I left the loft that day. She heard me next door and came over to say hi. She saw what a mess I was, so she stayed and we talked for hours. I told her how Pearce had been lying to me and how I felt like I couldn't trust him.

Part of what she said stuck with me and I keep thinking about it. She said that Pearce wouldn't hide stuff from me unless he had to, and that he'd never do it to hurt me. I know she's right. He would never purposely try to hurt me. He loves me. So then why would he hide things from me?

After we talked, Shelby tried to convince me to talk to him, but I couldn't. I wasn't ready to. I'm still not.

But I miss him so much. Being without him, I feel this overwhelming loss, like part of my heart is missing, and it only gets worse the more time goes by. I want to run back to him and be with him, but then what? Would he just keep lying to me?

I've been trying to keep busy the past few days to keep my mind off Pearce. I've spent most of my time applying for jobs, mostly around here, but I also applied for one in New York. But then I couldn't send the application. Sending it felt like I'd given up hope on my marriage, so I couldn't do it. The envelope is addressed and stamped but remains on my kitchen counter.

I've also spent time over at Shelby's house, sitting with her father and talking to him. He looks worse now than he did just a week ago, but I try to keep his spirits up by telling him funny stories or some of the corny jokes I used to tell on my tours. He always smiles when he sees me and thanks me for coming over, but his voice is so weak it's hard to hear him.

There's a knock on the door and it startles me.

"Rachel." It's a man's voice but it's not Pearce. "Rachel, it's Logan."

Logan? What's he doing here on a Wednesday night? He's usually in town on Tuesdays and Fridays. And why isn't he with Shelby?

I open the door. Logan has on jeans and a brown leather jacket. He looks really tired, his eyes heavy.

"Logan, where's Shelby?"

"At her mom's house. Can I come in?"

"Yes, of course."

He steps inside and I close the door. "Shelby wanted me to tell you in person."

"He died." I bring my hands to my mouth as tears fill my eyes.

Logan nods. "Yes."

I hug him, even though I don't know him that well. But I'm a hugger and I can't help myself. And I'm sure Logan could use a hug. I know he wishes he could've saved her father and feels bad that he couldn't.

"Is Shelby okay?" I ask, letting him go. "I mean, obviously she's devastated but…"

"She's having a rough time. She knew this was coming but she wasn't ready for it."

"Do you have to go back to Boston tonight?"

"No, I'm staying here. I need to be here for Shelby." He looks down at the floor, scrubbing his hand over his jaw.

"Logan, can I ask you something?"

He looks up. "Of course. Go ahead."

"Are you serious about Shelby? Or is this something…casual?" I didn't know how to say it. I probably shouldn't even be asking.

"I would like it to be serious, but Shelby isn't ready for that." He pauses. "Or maybe she doesn't want that. It's hard to tell with her."

"But I thought—never mind." I thought Shelby wanted something more serious, but I guess not. I wonder why.

"The funeral will be on Monday if you'd like to attend," Logan says.

"I'd like to, but I won't be here Monday." As soon as I say it, I remember that Pearce and I probably aren't going on our trip. I'm sure he canceled it.

"Shelby's mother is going to the funeral home tomorrow to work on the arrangements. Shelby didn't want to go so I'll be home with her. We'll be at the house. If you and Pearce would like to stop by, I'm sure she'd appreciate it. Maybe in the morning, around ten or eleven?"

"Yes. Of course. Tell her I'll be over."

He does a quick scan of my apartment. "Is Pearce here?"

"Um, no." I guess Shelby didn't tell him what was going on.

"Well, you can tell him the news. I should get going." He turns to leave.

"Wait. Logan?"

"Yes?" He turns back around.

"Would you mind calling Pearce?" I quickly shake my head. "No, forget it. I shouldn't be asking you to do that. I'll call him."

"Are you and Pearce not speaking?" He puts his hand up. "Sorry, it's none of my business."

"It's okay. And no, we haven't spoken for a few days."

"I'm sorry to hear that. I hope you two can work things out. Pearce has changed completely since I knew him back at Harvard and I'm sure that's because of you. So I hope it works out."

"What was he like when you knew him before?"

"Well, as you know he was married at the time but it wasn't a good marriage. He wasn't happy with her, or with himself. As a physician, I would've diagnosed him as being clinically depressed. He had all the signs. He was very withdrawn. Didn't sleep much. Didn't look forward to things. Drank too much. But given his life, that's understandable."

"What do you mean?"

"Pearce was under intense pressure from his parents, especially his father. Holton set such high expectations for Pearce, expecting him to always do everything perfectly. Has that changed at all?"

"No. His father is still that way."

"That's too bad. But at least he has you. You've obviously had a very positive effect on him. He seems like a different man. I can't believe how much he's changed. Anyway, I should get back to Shelby."

"Yes, go ahead. Tell her I'm thinking of her and that I'll be there tomorrow."

"I will. Goodbye, Rachel."

I need to call Pearce and tell him what happened. But once I hear his voice, I'll want to go see him and hug him and tell him how much I love him. Because I still do, even after he lied to me. And I want to forgive him, but not if he's going to keep lying to me.

I don't know how to fix this. I don't want to leave him. I don't want a divorce. I love Pearce and I want a life with him. So what are we doing? Why are we apart? How is this helping us?

I pick up the phone and call him. I need to talk to him. This fight needs to end. We need to work this out.

The phone rings and rings but he doesn't pick up. I lean against the kitchen counter, my eyes tearing up. I just want this to be over. I want us to be together again. It's the holiday season, my favorite time of the year, and I should be spending it with Pearce. Right now, we should snuggling by the fire with the Christmas lights all around us. I smile as I think of Pearce's face when he first saw all those lights I put around his loft. He had this huge grin on his face, like a little kid. He was so happy.

Logan's right. Pearce was someone else before I met him. He's changed so much the past few months. He used to be so sad and serious and stressed. I don't want him to go back to being that way again. I want him to be happy. I want to be happy too, and right now I'm not, because we're not together. God, I miss him so much.

There's a knock on the door. "Rachel. It's me."

The voice is deep and low and just the one I wanted to hear. My heart jumps to life at the sound of it.

"Rachel, if you're there, please open the door."

I race over and open it. Pearce is standing there, with no coat, even though it's freezing out. He's wearing jeans and the black polo shirt he bought the first time I made him go shopping. It looks good on him the way it stretches over his broad shoulders and muscular chest. I feel a tingling heat stirring inside me. I've missed him that way too.

He's looking at me with sad, regretful eyes. Without saying a word, he takes a step forward and brings me into his arms.

"Pearce," I say quietly.

"Please, don't," he says quietly back, his arms tightening a little. "Don't pull away. I need this. I just need to hold you. I need to feel you next to me."

When I first met him, he was so uncomfortable being close like this. He used to hesitate before holding my hand. He told me he'd never even had a hug, at least not a real one. And now he's hugging me, holding me, craving the closeness.

He rests his head on mine. "This can't go on. We have to talk about this."

"I know."

We slowly break apart, then go inside the apartment. He sighs and shakes his head as he looks around the room. It does look pretty bad compared to Pearce's loft. The walls are cracked. The paint's peeling. I never noticed how run-down this place was until I came back here.

"You shouldn't be staying here," he says. "This isn't your home anymore. The loft is ours, not mine, and you need to be there. You need to be home."

I want to agree with him because I feel the same way, but I want to hear what he has to say first. I go and sit on the couch, but he sits on the chair that's next to it.

"I don't know where to start," he says, his gaze on the floor. "I feel like nothing I say will make this better or change anything."

That's not what I wanted to hear. I want him to tell me why he lied and that he won't do it again.

"Pearce, why did you come over here?"

He looks at me. "Because you're my wife and I love you. And because I can't take another second of being apart from you. This separation, or whatever this is we're doing here, it needs to end. This past week has been one of the worst weeks of my life. You wouldn't talk to me. You wouldn't see me. I know you said you needed time alone, but this has gone on long enough and I'm not letting it continue." He pauses. "We're married, which means that even if we're arguing, we should be together, under the same roof. You can't run off like this. If you do, it just tells me you don't want this." He swallows. "Us."

I didn't think he'd say that. It's almost like he's already considered that might be an option.

"Is that what you want?" he asks quietly. "Are you telling me this is over?"

"I need you to explain yourself. I need to know why you can't tell me the truth."

He closes his eyes and squeezes the bridge of his nose. Then his eyes open again as he takes a deep breath. "You were right. I should have told you about Jack. But even looking back, I don't think I would've told you right away. I don't think you would've kept seeing me if you knew I had people in my life who would spy on you like that."

"Pearce, you can't assume how I'm going to react to things. That can't be an excuse for you to lie."

"Well, we can't go back in time and find that out, so let me just say that I'm sorry I didn't tell you that I knew Jack."

"What about the wedding? Why don't you want me involved in it?"

"The wedding is not for us. It's for everyone else. And I don't want you wasting time planning something that is just for show. It's a media event. It's something I'm expected to do because of my name. I have to have this big, elaborate wedding and invite hundreds of people, most of whom I either don't like or don't know. And if everything's not perfect on that day, people will talk. I'm not saying you couldn't plan a beautiful wedding. I know you could. But this is more than a wedding, and it will take a staff of people working around the clock from now until March to get it ready." He reaches over and takes my hand. "Rachel, I would love to give you a wedding. One that's for us and the people we actually care about. The Vegas wedding was an embarrassment and I feel terrible that that's all I was able to give you. So we'll do it again, and you and your mother can plan the whole thing. We could even have it in Indiana. You could invite all your friends. Invite the whole town if you want. Or we could go to an island and get married on a beach. Whatever you want, I'll do it."

"I don't want another wedding. And I understand what you're saying. I just wish you would've explained it to me instead of making up a lie." I pull my hand back from his. "I also wish you'd told me about having that man watching over me when I'm at the shelter."

He nods.

"Are you going to keep doing this, Pearce? Are you going to keep lying to me?"

"I can't promise you that I will never tell another lie. Married couples don't always tell each other everything. Ask your parents. I'm sure they have secrets they haven't shared with each other."

"I don't care what they do. We're talking about us, not them."

"You'll never keep something from me? You'll always tell me everything?"

"Yes. Of course I will."

"When I walked in here just now, I noticed something on your counter. It looked like an application for a job in New York. Were you going to tell me about that?"

I glance back at it. "No, I wasn't going to tell you, but I never sent it, so it doesn't matter."

"It matters because it means something. It means you thought of leaving me."

"I was just angry. That's why I did it. And part of me wanted to know if they would even call me back. If they thought I was good enough."

He leans forward and puts his hand on my arm. "Of course you're good enough. You're better than good. Those New York museums would be lucky to have you."

"Pearce, I need to be able to trust you, and I don't feel like I can when you keep lying to me." He doesn't say anything, so I continue. "I'm not going to put up with it. You are not going to lie to me and you are not going to cheat on me."

He shoots up from his chair. "What the hell are you talking about? I have never cheated on you!"

"Not now, but how do I know you won't in the future? Everyone keeps telling me that rich men like you always cheat. Like it's just a given and that I have to accept it."

"Who said that?"

"Victoria. And your father."

"And you're choosing to listen to them? The two most deceitful people on the planet?" He walks around to the back of the couch. "Men cheat. So do women. It's a fact, and it's true for many of the men I know, including Royce and my father. But I am NOT them! I wouldn't even THINK about being with another woman. Ever! And I'm disappointed that you would believe otherwise."

"I didn't say you would cheat. I know you wouldn't. I just..." I sigh. "Can we go back to what we were talking about before? I need to know you're done lying to me. So are you?"

"Yes." He looks at the floor as he says it. His head is down, like he's embarrassed and ashamed. It reminds me of how he looked when his dad was putting him down at the restaurant that night. But it's not the same. I'm not the bad guy here. Pearce did this to me. He lied. I didn't. So I'm not going to feel bad about this.

"Pearce, say something."

"I shouldn't have done it. And I'm sorry." He lifts his head and looks at me. "I don't like lying to you, Rachel. And when I did, I felt sick inside."

"Then why did you do it?"

"Because it's what I've been taught to do." He sighs and drops his head again. "It's all I know. My whole life is a lie." He takes a breath. "Just one big fucking lie."

I don't understand what he's saying, but I can tell he's not lying right now. I can feel the emotion in his words and the heaviness in his tone. He sounds angry and frustrated. Angry with himself for being this way and frustrated that he can't seem to change. And he sounds tired. Tired of living this way.

"What about your life is a lie?" I ask.

"Everything. The things I do. The things I say. How I act. Who I claim to be friends with. It's all a lie. And it's all I know. I've lied for so long that sometimes I don't even know the truth from a lie. It all blurs together."

I remain quiet because I want him to keep opening up to me. I need to know what got him to this point, why he felt he had to lie.

"I think you already know this but I'm going to say it again because I need you to know how much you mean to me, and how much of an influence you've had on me." He pauses. "I hated my life before you came along. I was a hollow shell of a man. I had

164

work and nothing else. I came home to an empty loft. I had no one in my life who even cared I existed. I, myself, didn't care if I was dead or alive. I felt dead inside, so I might as well have been dead."

I rub his hand. "Pearce, don't say that."

"It's true. I had nothing. I didn't even know who the real Pearce Kensington was. Growing up, I had to be the person my father expected me to be. I tried to overcome that and express myself, be my own person, but he wouldn't allow it. He beat me down to the point that I gave up trying to figure out who I was and just did what he told me to do. I was living a lie. Being someone else, just so my father would leave me alone." He looks at me. "I still do that, Rachel. I pretend to be someone else. Not just because of my father, but because of the world that I'm part of. The part that I tried to keep you out of when we were dating. Everyone in that world lies. Just think about the people you've met so far. Royce. Victoria. My parents. They don't seem genuine, do they?"

I shake my head. "No."

"That's because they're putting on an act. Royce and Victoria pretend they're in love when in reality they don't even like each other. Or consider my parents. My father hates pretty much everyone, but he still goes to parties and acts like those people are his best friends. It's the same way for everyone I know. They all live a lie. And I do the same."

"No, you don't."

"I do. When I'm around those people, living that side of my life, it's all a lie." He takes my hand. "I'm only myself when I'm with you."

"You can be yourself with other people besides me."

"It doesn't work that way." He glances down at our joined hands. "Since meeting you, I feel like I've been living a double life. One is good and the other is bad. And I will always have to live this way." He looks up again, his eyes on mine. "But it's better than what I had before. At least now, because of you, I can spend most of my life on this side. The good side."

After being exposed to his friends and his family, I understand what he means when he said he feels like he's living a double life. His life with me is so different than the side of his life that includes people like Royce and Victoria. And he does seem to become someone else when he's around those people.

"Rachel." Pearce squeezes my hand to get my attention. "I would never intentionally try to hurt you. I told you those things because I thought I was protecting you. And because…I was so afraid of losing you. That's what I fear more than anything." His hand lifts to my face and he cups my cheek. "Please say we can work this out. I love you, Rachel. And I need you in my life. We need each other. So please don't end this."

I need to think about all that he told me tonight. But would thinking about it change how I feel about him? Would I love him any less?

That's something I don't need to think about. I already know the answer.

CHAPTER FIFTEEN

PEARCE

"Rachel?" My heart pounds as I wait for her to respond.

"I'm not ending this, Pearce. I love you, and I want to be married to you."

I exhale and my shoulders relax. "Good. Because I wasn't going to accept any other answer."

She smiles. "Then why did you ask?"

"Because I needed to know how you felt about us. But if you'd answered differently, I wasn't going to let you go. I wasn't going to give up on us, Rachel. I'll always fight for us. And I'm never letting us be separated for this long again. If we're arguing and you need a break from me, I'll stay in the guest room. But we're going to remain under the same roof. You're my wife and I love you and we need to be together, even if you're angry at me."

"I don't like being angry at you. Or being apart from you. But in order for this to work, I have to be able to trust you. Which means you need to stop lying to me. You don't need to protect me from the truth. Even if I don't like it, I'd much rather have the truth than a lie."

I nod, but don't say anything. She wants me to tell her I'll never lie to her again, but saying that would just be another lie. There are so many things I can't tell her. And even if I could, would I really want her to know?

"When I found out you lied to me," she says, "it hurt me. It hurt me a lot, and I don't want to feel that way again."

It nearly kills me to know how much I hurt her. I never wanted that to happen, and yet deep-down, I knew it would. I knew someday, she'd eventually catch me in my lies and this would all come crashing down. I wanted to avoid that, or at least put it off as long as possible, but that didn't happen and now here we are.

This past week has been pure hell. I kept calling her and coming over here, begging her to talk to me, but she wouldn't. After a few days, when she refused to have any kind of contact with me, I thought it was the end. I thought she was telling me that she was done. That our marriage was over.

But I couldn't accept that. I wasn't giving up. I wasn't letting my father win. So I spent all of last week trying to figure out what to do. How to get her back. Flowers wouldn't do it this time. An apology wasn't enough either. The only way to get her back was to be as honest as I could. I know I lied to her tonight, but a lot of what I said was true. I *am* living a double life and I *was* taught to lie. Lying comes more naturally to me than telling the truth. When you can't trust people, you can't be honest with them so you become a good liar, and over the years, I've perfected it. And I will use those skills to hide the Dunamis part of my life from Rachel. But those are the only lies I will tell her.

I hold her face in my hands and look her in the eye. "I am so sorry I hurt you." I hold her gaze, letting her see my eyes, because my eyes always tell the truth. They tell how I'm feeling, and she knows that. So when she looks at them, I hope she can see how very sorry I am and how I would do anything to take away the pain I have caused her this past week.

"Just don't do it again." Her lips turn up just slightly. It means she's forgiven me, or at least is starting to.

"I love you." I kiss her forehead. "And I promise you, I will get better at this."

She smiles. "Better at what?"

"Being in a relationship. Knowing what to do. This is the first real relationship I've ever had, and obviously I have a lot to learn."

168

"I'm not very good at them either. I run at the first sign of trouble."

"No more running. This apartment is off limits." I glance at the peeling paint on the walls. "Actually, it should be condemned."

She laughs. "It's not that bad. But yes, I'm done running. I want to go home."

At least she's finally calling my loft 'home.' I know she feels like it's not really hers, but for now it's her home. Her home is with me.

"Pack your things and let's get out of here." I bring her face to mine and kiss her. "We have a lot of making up to do."

I start to back away, but she pulls me in for a hug. I hug her back, tightly, but not too tight, just like she taught me.

"I've missed this," she whispers.

I kiss her head. "You have no idea how much I've missed this."

We stay in the hug a few moments longer, then she goes to the bedroom to pack her bag. "Pearce?"

I go in the bedroom. "Yes?"

"Right before you got here, Logan came by and told me Shelby's dad died."

"Oh. I'm sorry to hear that. When is the funeral?"

"On Monday. Shelby will be at her mom's house tomorrow and he suggested we stop by and see her. I told him I would. Will you be coming too?"

"Of course I will." I walk over to the dresser where she's standing, and put my arms around her waist. "Rachel, this fight of ours is over. Don't act like we're not a couple."

"I didn't mean it that way. I just wasn't sure if you'd want to go."

"I'm going." I kiss her forehead.

She nods. "I feel so bad for Shelby. It's so hard to lose someone, and she was so close to her dad."

Rachel needs to end this friendship she has with Shelby. She can't be friends with an associate. If anyone from the organization saw the two of them together, it would not be good. I'd probably be punished for it. They would be angry and disgusted that Pearce Kensington's wife is friends with a whore. I shouldn't refer to Shelby that way, but in the eyes of the members, that's what she is, so she is not an appropriate friend for my wife.

"It's good she has Logan," Rachel says. "He's there now, and will probably stay there until after the funeral."

"Are the two of them becoming more serious?"

"I asked Logan that when he was here. Maybe I shouldn't have, but I did. He said that he wants to be more serious with her but that she doesn't want that. Shelby really likes him so I don't know why she doesn't want to get more involved with him."

I know why, but I can't tell Rachel. It's yet another secret I have to keep. Shelby needs to break up with Logan and not let this continue. He's already fallen hard for her and it's not fair for her to keep stringing him along, knowing she can't be with him.

Now I sound just like Shelby when she was telling me to stay away from Rachel. But Rachel and I were able to make it work. Shelby and Logan can't. Associates can't have serious relationships while they're actively working for us. There's no rule forbidding it, but it would never work. If an associate falls in love with a man, she won't want to have sex with other men. Even if she was willing to do so, the man she's with would end things once he found out. And my fellow members would make sure he found out. They need the associates to stay committed to the job. They know too much. They're in this for life. So Shelby needs to end her relationship with Logan. The two of them will never be able to be together.

Rachel and I go back to the loft and I finally feel like it's home again. When she wasn't here, it felt like just a big empty space. Rachel is what makes it a home, and I'm never letting her take off like that again. The next time we argue, we'll be doing it here. At home. Together.

"How's the water temperature?" I ask as I join her in the shower. I warmed it up for her before she got in.

"Perfect," she says, closing her eyes as the water cascades over her skin.

I take a moment to look at her. Her long, lean legs. Her hourglass curves. Her soft full breasts. Just the sight of her has me fully aroused.

Her eyes are still closed as I reach around her waist and draw her into me so that her body is pressed against mine.

Her lips curve into a smile. "I'm glad you suggested a shower. This feels really good."

"Turn around," I whisper in her ear. "And keep your eyes shut."

She does as I say, turning away from me as my arms remain around her waist, keeping her close. She leans her head back on my chest, and I watch as the water streams over her body. My hand is at her waist, and I slowly slide it up her ribcage to her breast, cupping it as my thumb skims over her nipple.

She lets out a breathy moan and pushes back into me, circling her hips, rubbing against the length of me.

It nearly sends me over the edge. It's been almost a week since I've been with her and I'm desperate to be inside her, but it's not time yet. I don't want to rush this. I want to look at her, feel her, kiss her, touch her. And then be inside her.

I reach up and get her shampoo and pour some in my hand, then turn her slightly so her head's not directly under the water as I gently massage the shampoo into her scalp.

She smiles, keeping her eyes shut. "That feels good."

After a few minutes, I lead her into the water again, being careful to keep the shampoo out of her eyes as it rinses away. I fill my hand with liquid soap, then tug her back against my chest and run my soapy hands along her slick skin, over her curves, between her legs. She moans again, her head collapsing to the side as I kiss her shoulder.

"I love you," I breathe into her ear.

She shivers from the warmth of my breath. "I love you too."

"I would do anything for you," I tell her, my voice soft.

She slowly nods. "I know you would."

171

I kiss her wet skin, just below her ear and whisper, "Please forgive me."

She turns to me. "I already have." Her eyes are open now and fixed on mine. She reaches up and puts her hand on my face. "I missed you. In so many ways."

I know what she means. I missed her so much, my body literally ached for her. I ached to hear her voice again. To feel her body against mine as I slept. To feel her presence in the loft, rather than the dark emptiness it is without her.

I take her hand and bring it to my lips, kissing her palm as I look at her. Then I release her hand and hold her face and kiss her. God, it feels good to kiss her. To feel her breath, her lips. It ignites the searing desire that has permeated the air around us since the moment she finally opened the door for me at her apartment. There's this heat, this attraction, this energy between us that was there from the first day we met. And when we're not together, it builds up, and now, it feels ready to explode.

Urgent kisses replace the soft gentle ones I gave her earlier and I lift her up and against the wall. I push inside her and we both breathe out at the feel of it. The relief of being together this way again. I'm convinced we were made for each other. Our bodies fit together perfectly. We both know it because we both feel it. Every single time we do this, we feel it.

"Pearce," she whispers, her arms around my neck, her hand gripping my hair as I move in and out. "Oh, God. Don't stop."

She's close. So close. I thrust into her until she gets her release. Mine hits me soon after. And then I set her down and kiss her, and our mouths remain joined for several minutes as the warm water runs over us.

"Let's go to bed," I say against her lips.

She nods, still kissing me, like she can't get enough.

I shut off the water. After we towel off, I take her to our bed and we lie there under the covers. I inhale a deep breath, filling my lungs with air, noticing the tightness is gone. Holding Rachel in my arms, I finally feel relaxed again. And at peace.

This past week, I realized even more how much I need her. Before she came into my life, I didn't know what I was missing. But then she showed me how much better my life could be, and now I can't go back to how it was before.

That's all because of her. She's the one who makes me feel this way and I can't fathom my life without her. It scares me that she has such an effect on me because it'll destroy me if she ever leaves. So I'll make sure that she never does. That she never wants to.

My father's plan didn't work. Telling Rachel those things was supposed to make her divorce me, but instead I feel like it made our relationship stronger. I told her things about myself that I've never told anyone else. Things I'm embarrassed and ashamed to admit. And she listened without judging me. Without telling me I was wrong or crazy for feeling that way. I felt like she understood me, which only brought us closer, not farther apart.

I haven't spoken to my father about what he did. All last week, I considered calling him or going to his office and having yet another fight. But then I decided against it. Doing so would give him what he wanted, which was to see me angry and panicked that I'd lost Rachel. I wouldn't give him the satisfaction of seeing me that way.

"Pearce?" Rachel's hand moves over my chest and I close my eyes and breathe, her touch soothing me.

"Yes, sweetheart."

"Are we still leaving for Italy on Monday?"

I open my eyes. "Of course we're leaving. Why wouldn't we?"

"I just thought with everything that went on that maybe you canceled the trip."

"The thought hadn't even crossed my mind." I lift her hand up and kiss it. "Even if you were still angry with me, I was still taking you to Italy. It's our honeymoon. We couldn't miss our honeymoon."

Her hand returns to my chest, making small circles over my skin. "If we were still fighting, it wouldn't be much of a honeymoon."

"Then I'd have to end the fight. Or at least distract you from it."

She smiles. "And how would you do that?"

I flip her over on her back and put my lips to hers. "Let me show you."

She laughs. "Again? Pearce, we just did it."

"And we will keep doing it until we've made up." I softly kiss her neck, working my way down to her chest.

"We haven't made up yet?" she asks, her hand moving over my back.

"I'm quite certain we'll have to do this several more times just to be sure."

So we do. And then we fall asleep. For the first time in a week, I'm finally able to sleep. Because Rachel is next to me. Where she should be.

The next morning we go to Shelby's house. Logan answers the door when we arrive.

"Come on in." He leads us to the living room. Shelby's on the couch, wrapped up in a blanket, her eyes red and puffy.

Rachel goes over and hugs her. "I'm sorry, Shelby."

"He's gone," she says, tears falling down her cheeks.

"I'm so sorry." Rachel keeps hold of her, rubbing her back.

Logan nudges me. "Let's give them some time."

We go out the sliding door to the back deck.

"She's not doing so well," I say to Logan.

"No. She's been crying all night. She knew this was coming, but it's still hard."

"How is her mother doing?"

"She's handling it better than Shelby, but I think that's only because she has to focus on getting the funeral planned and relatives called. Once all of that is over, I'm sure she'll be like Shelby is right now."

"It's good you're here for her."

He nods. "I'll be staying here through Monday, after the funeral, and maybe a few days after that if Shelby wants me to."

"So is this serious? You and Shelby?" I know Rachel already asked him this, but I want to see if his answer will be different when talking to me.

"She's told me she's not ready for a serious relationship, so I don't know what will happen. Honestly, I think she *does* want a more serious relationship, but for some reason she won't actually commit to that. Maybe she thinks she's too young."

"What do you mean by 'commit'? Are you thinking of proposing to her?"

He smiles. "No. I'm not quite ready for that. She hasn't even met my parents. But I have considered moving here to be closer to her. There's a job in Westport at a small private medical clinic. It's a good job and I know one of the doctors there."

"Do you prefer the private clinic setting over working at a hospital?"

"Yes, definitely. As I mentioned before, we're able to give better, more individualized care when we're not confined by the rules of insurance companies."

"And who are your patients? Mostly wealthy people?"

"Yes. They're the only ones who can afford it. At the clinic I work at in Boston, we see a lot of professional athletes, a few politicians, some businessmen. You should go to the one in Westport. You'll find it's much better than a traditional doctor's office."

"I never go to the doctor. I haven't been sick in years."

"Well, if Rachel ever needs to go, have her go to that clinic. They have some excellent OB-GYNs if you two are thinking of having children soon."

Children. It's something Rachel and I still need to discuss, but I'm trying to put it off as long as possible.

"Logan?" Rachel appears behind us. "Shelby asked for you."

He nods and goes inside. Rachel stays out on the deck with me.

"How's she doing?" I ask.

"Not well. Shelby and her father were really close. She wasn't ready for him to go. But she knows it's for the best. He was in bad shape and only getting worse." She glances inside. "We should probably leave. I think she wants to be with Logan right now."

"Let's go say goodbye." I open the door for her and we go inside. Shelby's still on the couch, tucked in Logan's arms.

Rachel goes over to her. "Are you sure you don't want us to stay?"

"Yeah, I'll be okay." She reaches up and hugs Rachel. "Thanks again for coming. I'll talk to you after your trip."

"I'll check in with you before we leave." Rachel looks at Logan. "Bye, Logan."

"Bye." He glances at Shelby in his arms, then looks at Rachel. "Don't worry. I'll take good care of her."

I go up to Shelby. "I'm very sorry for your loss. Please give your mother my condolences."

She nods, sniffling. "Thanks. I will."

"Next time I'm here, maybe we could have lunch," Logan says to me.

"Yes, we should do that. Give me a call and we'll set something up."

Rachel and I leave, but instead of going home, I drive to one of my favorite restaurants. I haven't taken Rachel there yet and I know she'll like it.

"Where are we going?" she asks when I drive past the exit that takes us back to the loft.

"I'm taking you out for lunch. You're graduating in two days and we haven't taken any time to celebrate. So we're starting now. It's a very nice restaurant. I think you'll enjoy it."

"I feel bad celebrating when Shelby is going through such a rough time."

"She'll be okay. She has Logan."

"Shelby told me he wants to move here, but she told him not to."

"Yes. He told me."

"I don't understand. I know Shelby really likes him, so I don't know why she's pushing him away."

"Maybe she's just not ready for a serious relationship. Logan is 28. He's ready to settle down."

"But I think she is too. I know she's only 22 but she's mature for her age. I could see her getting married in a year or two."

I pull into the restaurant. "Let's not worry about those two. We'll have lunch and then you can plan the rest of the afternoon."

We end up going to a movie. I've been to the movies several times since being with Rachel, and I've decided I don't like movies. It's not the movies themselves I don't like, but having to go to the theater to watch them. The sticky floors, the popcorn smell, the crowds of people. I'd much rather watch a movie at home. But Rachel loves going to the theater, so I go.

The next day, her parents arrive and we show them around Weston. Her mother brought up the wedding issue again, insisting Rachel be allowed to plan it. She seemed angry, but Rachel took her aside and talked to her about it. I don't know what she said, but her mother was in a better mood when they were done.

On Saturday we go to Rachel's graduation, then out for dinner. We drove down to Greenwich to a steakhouse that's considered the best in the state. I told Rachel we should drive into Manhattan to eat, but she thought it might be too much for her parents. She said her dad gets nervous in crowded, congested cities.

As we're finishing dessert, I hear Rachel say, "Mrs. Kensington."

I turn around and see my parents behind me. What the hell are they doing here? We're nowhere near when they live. But they do eat out on the weekends and I know they like this restaurant.

Rachel and her parents stand up, so I do as well.

"Mother. Father." I nod at them, but only my mother looks at me. My father is looking at Henry, assessing his suit. Henry's suit is a cheap, off-the-rack suit that doesn't fit him very well, but I'm sure it's all he has. He doesn't need an expensive suit working as a farmer.

"These are my parents," Rachel says. "Beth and Henry Evans."

I wish she would've just ignored my parents and let them continue out the door. I have no desire to speak to them. And I don't want them talking to Rachel's parents. I know this won't go well.

"Hello." My mother gives them her fake smile and shakes their hands. "Eleanor Kensington. And this is my husband, Holton."

He just stands there, silent, refusing to shake their hands.

"It's nice to meet you," Henry says. "We've enjoyed getting to know your son. He's a fine young man. And a fast learner. I taught him how to chop wood and he had it down within a couple tries."

My father glares at him, then says to my mother, "I'll be in the car."

He storms off. He's angry about what Henry said. Although my father hates me, he doesn't want anyone else stepping into his father role. He has to be in control of me, and he feels like he loses that control when someone else acts like a father to me. That's one reason why he hates Jack. And after Henry's comment, I'm sure he hates Henry as well.

Rachel's parents are quiet. They seem a little shocked that my father just left like that. My mother and I think nothing of it. That's typical behavior for him.

"I should go," my mother says. She gives us one last fake smile, then walks off.

The four of us sit back down at the table. Beth and Henry look very uncomfortable, like they're not sure what to say.

I feel the need to lighten the mood so I smile and say, "So those are my parents."

Rachel covers her mouth as she laughs. I laugh too. My parents are rude to the point that sometimes you just have to laugh and not take it too seriously.

"Did we do something wrong?" Beth asks in a concerned tone.

"No. It has nothing to do with you. That's just how they are. I apologize for their behavior."

"They can be a little difficult sometimes," Rachel says.

I chuckle. "Yes. Difficult. That's a nice word for it."

We return to the conversation we were having before my parents interrupted, and the evening is pleasant again.

I've decided I love Rachel's parents. I already thought that when I met them in Indiana, but the last couple days just confirmed it. They're good people and I'm always relaxed around them. My own parents make me nervous. They always have.

I feel blessed to be part of Rachel's family. I really lucked out. I married the woman of my dreams and received great in-laws as well.

CHAPTER SIXTEEN
Two Weeks Later

RACHEL

The past two weeks have been pure heaven. The best time I've had in my entire life. Like a dream. Or a fairytale.

Pearce and I have been all over Italy; staying at the best hotels, having fantastic meals, going to museums, churches, and other tourist sites. The weather has been chilly, but that's typical for December, and it's not nearly as cold as Connecticut. Pearce and I agreed that we need to come back here in the warmer months so we can do some of the outdoor activities we weren't able to do this time.

My favorite part of the trip has been spending time in the small villages. We spent our first week in the larger cities, going to all the tourist sites. Then this past week, Pearce took me to the smaller towns that he told me about when we first met. He's been here many times so knew where to go, but then a few days ago, we found a small village he hadn't been to before and we both fell in love with it. It's a cliffside town along the Mediterranean coastline and the views are magnificent. We were just going to come here for the day, but we loved it so much, we decided to stay, so we got a hotel and have now been here two days.

Today is Christmas and the entire town is covered in lights. It's so beautiful that Pearce and I have spent the past couple nights just strolling the streets, taking in the lights and the architecture and the people. The people here are very friendly. A lot of them don't speak English, but they try to communicate with us the best they can. We asked our hotel manager about restaurants, and although he knew some English, he still struggled to explain how to get to one of the restaurants he recommended. So he gave up trying to give us directions and just drove us to the restaurant, then came back later to pick us up. Pearce gave him a big tip for doing so, but the man wouldn't take it. He said he just wanted to make sure we had a nice evening. And we did. The restaurant was wonderful. We spent three hours there, drinking wine and enjoying a multi-course dinner.

It's our last night here and Pearce and I are spending it out on our private balcony. It's evening so the air is cool, but I'm wrapped up in the cashmere blanket Pearce bought me a few days ago when we were shopping in the open market. I'm usually not much of a shopper, but I couldn't resist shopping in these little Italian villages. I bought a couple scarves, a leather handbag, some leather boots, and some items for my mom. Pearce told me to buy whatever I'd like, saying it was my Christmas gift, but this whole trip is a Christmas gift. It's an experience I'll never forget.

"Merry Christmas," I say to Pearce.

"Merry Christmas to you as well." His arm is around me, my head resting on his shoulder, as we sit on the small bench that's on the balcony.

"I wish we didn't have to leave."

"So you enjoyed our honeymoon?" He leans down and kisses the top of my head.

"'Enjoyed' isn't a strong enough word. I don't even have words to describe it. It's better than I ever imagined it would be." I hug his chest as I reach up to kiss him. "And it's not just Italy. It's being here with you. I'll never forget this. Thank you for taking me here."

"You're very welcome. And since you enjoyed it so much, we'll be coming back here. Anytime you want to go, we'll make a trip."

"Could we come back to this village? I'd like to spend a whole week here. In fact, I could live here." I laugh. "Would you consider moving here?"

He isn't laughing. "Maybe we should retire here."

I sit up. "Are you joking?"

"Not at all."

"You would seriously consider retiring here?"

"We wouldn't have to live here year-round. We could buy a house and stay here for a few months out of the year."

"Oh, Pearce, I would love that! I think we should put it in our plan."

He smiles at me. "We have a plan?"

I smile back. "Yes. Our life plan."

He turns a little to face me. "And what else is in this plan?"

"Well, we should probably move out of the loft and get a house."

"I agree. I think we should start looking when we get back. We don't have to buy anything right away, but we should see what's out there." He holds my hand. "Anything else? So far, we've decided to buy two houses in different locations. That's not much of a plan."

The only other thing on my plan is to have a baby, but I don't know if I should bring that topic up now, or wait until later.

"What is it, Rachel?"

I should just tell him. We can't avoid this topic forever.

"I want us to have a baby." As I say it, his expression turns serious and a little concerned.

"You said you couldn't have children."

I take my hand back from his and wrap the blanket tighter around me. "That was just one doctor's opinion. I need to see someone else. A specialist. Someone who can run more tests and give me a second opinion. I just haven't done that because I'm afraid of what I'm going to find out."

"I didn't realize there was still a possibility..." His voice trails off.

"Maybe there isn't. But if there is...I want to try." I pause. "Even if we're only able to have one, that's okay. I'll take whatever God will give us." I squeeze my eyes shut, not wanting to cry. Crying implies I've given up. That I'm losing hope. And I refuse to do that. I still want to believe it's possible for me to have a child. I open my eyes and see Pearce watching me. "Pearce, you're not saying anything. You do want children, don't you?"

He's quiet, and a heaviness fills my chest. He doesn't want children. How could I not know this? How could we get married without talking about this? Truthfully, I think part of me knew he didn't want them. When I told him I couldn't have children, he didn't seem that upset. I should've known that was a sign he didn't want them.

"You don't want children," I say quietly, glancing down at the blanket.

Silence again. His silence is his answer.

Tears fill my eyes. I can't stop them. I feel like I did when my doctor told me I couldn't have children, except this time, my husband is telling me that.

"Rachel." He pauses. "It's not that I don't want them. I just..."

I look up at him. "You just what?"

"I just don't think I could do it. I can't be a father."

"Why not?"

He shakes his head. "I don't know the first thing about children. I get nervous around them. And they don't like me."

That's why he doesn't want kids? Because he's afraid of being a father? Relief washes over me because this is something he can overcome. A lot of men are afraid of being a father. I thought he was going to say he just flat-out didn't want them, and if so, I wouldn't be able to change his mind. But this is something he can work on. It's something we can work on together.

I smile. "Pearce, that's not true. Children like most anyone. And our child would *love* you. You would make a wonderful father."

He gazes out at the darkness. "No. I wouldn't. The only example I had was how NOT to be a father."

"Then you'll use that to know what *not* to do." I bring my hand out from under the blanket and place it on his face, turning him toward me. "Pearce, I want to have a child with you. I want us to at least try."

"I know you do." He kisses my forehead. "But we don't need to decide anything right now. Let's get home and have you see a specialist and find out what our options are. Then we'll talk about this again."

I nod, and lay my head back on his shoulder. We sit there quietly for a moment, listening to the soft breeze that's circling around us.

"Are you excited about going back to Indiana next week?" he asks.

"Yes. Although I'll be tired when I get there after all the travel. I might have to spend Monday catching up on sleep. But I'm excited to see my friends and spend time with my parents."

"I may not be able to call you much next week. These meetings tend to drag on and it's hard to get away."

"Meetings? I thought you said it was a conference."

He clears his throat. "It is, but in addition to speakers, we also have meetings with our clients."

"Do you think your father will talk to you when you're there?"

"Only if he has to, for business purposes. Otherwise, no, he won't talk to me."

I can't believe Holton is acting this way. There's something wrong with that man. Something seriously wrong. I've never met anyone who is that hostile and angry all the time. He's so unhappy, and he wants to make sure everyone else is as well, especially his son. He seems determined to break up Pearce and me, but it's not going to happen. In fact, part of the reason I was so forgiving of Pearce lying to me is because I knew his father intentionally told me those things so that I'd divorce Pearce. But instead, his father's actions caused Pearce to open up to me and tell me things that helped me understand him better. So if anything, his father just made my relationship with his son even stronger.

"Are you falling asleep?" Pearce asks.

184

I'm now nestled against him, my eyes closed. "No. I was just savoring our last few moments here."

"Let's savor them inside," he says, lifting my face up to his for a kiss.

I smile. "In bed?"

"It *is* our honeymoon. And after tomorrow, I won't see you for an entire week." He slides his hand under my legs and lifts me up, carrying me back inside the room.

"I don't want to leave tomorrow," I tell him as he sets me down.

"We'll come back here," he says, his lips over mine. He peels my robe back, gazing at my naked body, his eyes filled with desire.

His robe drops to the floor and my own desire erupts, firing up my core as I see him there, already aroused and ready for me. He holds my face and his lips move gently over mine, our bodies still not touching. He's too far away. I need to feel him. I step closer, placing my hands on his chest, then lowering them to feel the hard ridges of muscle that outline his abs.

My hand continues downward, stroking him. I hear him groan. I feel the rumble of it in my chest as his tongue sweeps over mine. His hand goes behind my head, tilting it up slightly as his kiss goes deeper, his other hand traveling down my body, teasing my breast. I moan and my head falls back into his hand. He holds it there, as his deep, slow, sensual kisses continue. I'm burning up. Wanting him. Needing him.

His hand slides down my stomach, and when he reaches the spot that so desperately needs his touch, he skims past it. I feel him smile a little as he kisses me. He knows what he did. He felt me tense up when he hit the spot, then relax in disappointment when he went past it. But it only made me more turned on. The waiting. The anticipation. He knows what it does to me and that's why he does it. He wants to please me. And he does. Every single time. Sometimes multiple times.

I gasp as his hand finally goes where I want it. I'm still stroking him, feeling him hard and thick in my hand. He steps forward, forcing me back against the bed. We lie down and I push on his shoulder until he's lying on his back, then straddle him, guiding him inside me.

He reaches behind my head and brings my mouth to his as my hips move over him.

"God, I love you," he says between kisses.

"I love you too."

He grabs hold of my hips, pulling me into him as he groans, low and sexy. He guides me with his strong, forceful hands, then lets me take control. I move my hips faster. I can feel it building. I'm so close, and I know he is too.

Pearce lifts up and flips me on my back and thrusts into me, hard and fast. And then it comes. Deep and intense. Hitting every part of me. Pearce is right there with me. I feel him tense up, then release, his body shuddering over mine.

We lie there a moment, breathing hard.

"That was amazing," I say.

"I agree." He rolls off me. "We should do it again in an hour."

I laugh. "Maybe we should wait until morning. I'm really sleepy." I yawn and snuggle up to him, my head on his shoulder, my arm over his chest.

"Then let's get some sleep." He reaches down and pulls the covers over us. His arm wraps around me, securing me in place as he kisses my forehead. "Goodnight, sweetheart. I love you."

"I love you too."

And that's how our honeymoon ends. A fairytale honeymoon that I will never forget.

CHAPTER SEVENTEEN

PEARCE

Today is only the first day of Dunamis meetings and I'm already finding it hard to stay awake. Even if I wasn't tired from the trip, I'd still find it hard to stay awake. The other members keep talking in circles about what to do with a man we put in the Senate a few years ago who isn't cooperating the way he should.

The politicians we place in office are supposed to do as we ask. That's their payment for us getting them elected. But this particular man has ignored our demands and is doing things his own way instead. If the man continues to not follow orders, he'll have to be terminated. But terminating a senator isn't easy. Senators are important people, so reporters will look into his death. If he has a heart attack, reporters will demand to know his medical history. If he's killed in a car crash, reporters might suspect someone tampered with his car. So if it comes down to having to terminate him, we'll have to have a well thought out plan.

The members have been discussing this for four hours now. They discuss it casually, as though killing someone is just a normal activity. There's no emotion involved. The senator is a problem, not a person. That's how our members have to see people in order to complete our kill assignments.

People are classified as either problems or obstacles. We even call them that instead of using their names. It keeps it from being personal. The senator is Problem 248. Each problem is assigned a number. Obstacles are assigned numbers as well.

"Problems" are defined as individuals who don't follow orders. They were given a task but didn't complete it. A freelancer could be classified as a problem, as could one of my fellow members. In fact, I have been labeled a problem because I didn't follow orders when I married Rachel. My problem number is my member number. When my punishment for marrying Rachel is complete, the problem label will be removed from my file.

An "obstacle" is someone who gets in the way of the organization's plans or puts us at risk of being found out. People who are obstacles usually have no idea they're being targeted for termination. The secretary I was assigned to kill was Obstacle 742. As with other obstacles, she saw something she shouldn't have, and therefore she was seen as a threat. Someone who might tell our secrets. Technically, Rachel could be considered an obstacle because she took the place of the woman I was supposed to marry, thus interfering with the organization's plans. But Rachel wasn't aware of their plans and didn't intentionally try to disrupt them, therefore, she can't really be considered an obstacle. But she could be if she knew about us and what we do, which is why I must be extremely cautious in what I say around her. She can never find out about us.

Today's meeting is being held in an underground facility that was built many years ago by our founders. To get to the meeting, you drive into what looks like a warehouse, park your car, then take an elevator deep underground, where the meeting rooms are located.

Jack installed top-of-the-line security to the underground area as well as the warehouse entrance and elevator. He installed the equipment himself because we couldn't risk having an outsider do it. It's another reason the members have to keep Jack around. They may dislike him, but he's extremely valuable to the organization.

When I arrived here this morning, nobody spoke to me except Arlin and Royce, who both said a quick hello. Everyone else avoided me, afraid to speak to me for fear of showing support to a "problem." I don't care. I'm glad to keep to myself. I'd rather

188

not talk to anyone. I'll be forced to when we're in a social setting later tonight, but for now, I'm sitting in the back of the room, trying not to be noticed.

While my fellow members have been discussing what to do about the senator, I've been letting my mind wander to Rachel and our honeymoon. I've always loved Italy, but going there with Rachel was like seeing it again for the first time. She was in awe of everything there. The food. The sites. The scenery. I've never seen someone truly enjoy something to that level. When you're used to having money, like I am, you lose some of the joy in life. You don't appreciate things as much. I've traveled all over the world and have always been able to afford whatever I wanted, so I don't have the same reaction to things as Rachel does. But seeing Italy through her eyes, I came to appreciate it more.

The last few nights we were there, we stayed in this tiny village. I can't say exactly what it was, but there was something special about it. Perhaps it was the friendly people or the fact that is was tucked away in a remote location, away from big cities and tourist spots. Whatever it was, we felt a connection to that place and we both want to go back. I told Rachel we should retire there, and I wasn't kidding. It's such a beautiful area and so relaxing.

On our last night there, she brought up the topic of children. It took me by surprise because it seemed like an odd time to talk about it. When she asked if I wanted a child, I didn't know how to answer. I don't like saying no to her, especially to something she desperately wants. But I feel guilty just thinking about bringing a child into this world, knowing what lies ahead for his or her future.

But perhaps the rules will change. I've heard rumblings from some of our younger members that it would be better to recruit people to be members rather than force our sons to join. Unfortunately, the older members would never go for that. They're determined to keep membership limited to the descendants of our original founding members. But if Rachel and I had a child, that child wouldn't know about the organization for twenty years, and by then, most of the older members would be dead, giving us younger members a chance to change the rules of membership, or at least bring it up for a vote.

Even if Dunamis weren't an issue, I still have fears about having a child. I've been trying to imagine myself as a father and I just can't see it. My parents didn't spend time with me growing up so I have no examples of what parents are supposed to do or how they're supposed to act. And children make me very uncomfortable. I don't know what to do with them. They're always running around, making noise.

I know Rachel would be an excellent mother, but I also know she would expect me to be a good father. And what if I couldn't do it? What if I acted just like my own father? What if the child hated me like I hate my father?

Despite my many reservations, there's a part of me that wants to have a child with Rachel. I find it shocking that I would even think that, given that I was completely against the idea just a few months ago. But I love Rachel so deeply that the idea of having a child with her is now appealing. I know it would make her happier than anything else in the world. And I think it would make me happy too. Maybe with Rachel's help, I could learn to be a good father.

"And that concludes today's session," I hear a man up front say.

Day one is over. Just four more days to go. After that, Rachel will be back and we'll celebrate New Year's together. I already miss her terribly and it's only been a day.

I feel someone nudge my shoulder. "Are you heading over there?"

I look back and see Royce behind me. "Yes."

Royce motions to the exit where people are filing out. "Hurry up. You need to get your reservation card before all the good ones are gone."

"Reservation card?" We walk to the elevator. "I don't know what you're talking about."

He smiles. "You'll see when we get there."

There's a line of men waiting for the elevator. The doors open and we all file on. As we ride up to the garage level, I glance around at my fellow members. We're all in the same black suit, same white shirt, similar ties. We look identical. Jack was right when he said we're like soldiers. We're told what to wear, what to do, how to act. We think we have power, but if you really stop to think about it, we're powerless. We act based on fear, not by our own decisions. It's this fear that keeps us in line. Fear of what they'll do to us or our families if we don't follow orders.

We get in our cars and stream out of the warehouse, one by one. We all drive black cars, mostly black Mercedes. The cars are provided to us and are equipped with bulletproof glass in case one of our enemies comes after us.

I head to the hotel where we've having the banquet and cocktail hour. The hotel is owned by one of our members. His great-grandfather built it and it's remained in the family ever since. It's a gilded age mansion that is extremely ornate.

As I walk into the lobby, I immediately think of Rachel. She would love this place. There's so much history here, in the architecture and furnishings and artwork. She could probably give a tour of it without even having to do much research. She always amazes me with her extensive knowledge of all aspects of American history.

I follow the other men to the back of the hotel where the ballroom is located. The hotel is reserved all week for our group. Since many people are from out of town, they'll be staying here overnight. And some, such as Royce, will stay so they can get drunk and not have to worry about driving home.

I enter the ballroom and head straight to the bar. I dread these social events. They're almost worse than the meetings. I have no interest in talking to any of these people. I don't trust any of them so just being around them makes me tense. But I'm getting better at hiding it. I've had months of training with the body language coach that Jack set me up with, and I'm now much better at hiding my emotions. I was already somewhat good at it because I was raised in a house in which showing emotion was not allowed, but I need to work on not reacting when something unexpected happens. For example, when my father disowned me and fired me, I'm sure he could see the shock on my face and hear it in my voice. It's those reactions I need to get control over, because if I don't, they'll be used against me.

I order a scotch and water and drink it while still standing at the bar. Then I ask for another, and drink it down as well, feeling it warm and relax my body. I order a bourbon, and after the bartender hands it to me, I turn and face the room, deciding who to talk to. I go over and stand next to a group of eight men who are deep in conversation. Maybe they won't notice me and I can just blend in and not talk.

"Pearce." I look to my right and see Leland Seymour standing two men down from me. I didn't notice him when I walked up to the group. I can't stand Leland.

He grins. "Katherine was asking about you at dinner the other night."

The other men laugh. Everyone knows about Katherine's teenage crush on me.

"You should encourage your daughter to find a young man her own age," I say, then take a drink of my bourbon.

"I've tried," Leland says, "but she says she prefers mature men."

"Perhaps Pearce could take her to prom," Canton Stillwell says, chuckling. Canton is the man who owns the hotel.

"Or perhaps you should tell her I'm married," I say, "and end this ridiculous crush once and for all."

The men stop laughing. They look at each other, almost like they're hiding something from me.

My eyes move over all eight of them. "Gentlemen, is there something you'd like to tell me?"

"No. Nothing at all." Leland gives me an overly wide smile that's extremely fake.

These men could use some body language classes. They're giving themselves away. They're definitely hiding something.

"Speaking of your wife," Leland says. "I can't wait to meet her. I've heard so much about her. The little farm girl from Iowa. Or was it Idaho? Ohio?" He laughs. "It doesn't matter. It's somewhere in the middle."

I fight any kind of reaction. I'm not letting Leland get under my skin.

"Anyway," he says, "we're all looking forward to meeting her at the party."

"What party?" I ask.

"The one Audrey and I are hosting at the new house."

"I wasn't aware of the party, but Rachel and I will not be able to attend."

"You don't have a choice in the matter. It's mandatory. Weren't you listening during today's meeting?"

"I must've been in the restroom when they mentioned it."

"You'll be getting an invitation shortly. Be sure to mark it on your calendar. As I said, it's mandatory. You wouldn't want to miss it and face additional punishment." He smirks.

The other men just stand there, watching me, waiting for a reaction.

"If you gentlemen will excuse me, I need to refill my drink." I still have some bourbon in my glass but I needed to get away from them. In my hurried escape to the bar, I bump someone's shoulder and hear him curse.

"Pardon me," I say, continuing on.

"Pearce!"

Shit. It's my father. I've managed to avoid him all day.

I turn back. "Yes, Father."

"Apologize for your behavior! Obviously being in the company of those cretin in-laws of yours has affected you to the point that you no longer have manners."

I clench my jaw. "I said 'pardon me.' Perhaps you didn't hear me."

"That is not an appropriate apology. You made me spill my drink, you imbecile." He swipes his hand over his lapel.

"I'm sorry, Father. I will make sure to keep a safe distance from you for the remainder of the week so as not to disturb you again."

He steps up to me, glancing left and right, then back at me. He lowers his voice. "The story I told them is that I encouraged you to find work elsewhere in order to diversify your skills and knowledge."

"What story? What are you talking about?"

"The story about why you left the company," he says, even quieter.

"I didn't leave the company. You fired me."

"Quiet!" he says, through gritted teeth. "You are not to tell anyone that. I could be punished. You're supposed to work for the company. But I convinced the members that your brief departure would look good to outsiders. You'll be seen as hard-working, wanting to make it on your own rather than being handed a job."

"And they were okay with that?"

"Yes. They thought it was brilliant. Then, later, you'll return to Kensington Chemical with a commitment to make it an even greater success."

"I thought you didn't want me there."

He checks that no one's around us. "I don't have a choice. If I could choose anyone else as a son, I would. You're a complete embarrassment to this family and I have never been more ashamed of you. But there are rules and traditions that must be followed, and so you will do as planned, and take over the company someday."

"If I'm as worthless as you think I am, then have someone else take over the company. I have no interest in taking it over."

"You will run the company and you will be happy to do so."

I keep my voice down. "What if I told the other members the truth? That you fired me?"

He narrows his eyes at me. "Don't even think of challenging me, Pearce. Your fate is in my hands."

He's right, and I hate that he's right. I hate that he's been given influence over my punishment for marrying Rachel. He holds all the cards and I can't do anything about it.

"You will work for Leland during your departure from Kensington Chemical," he says. "I've already spoken to Leland and he has agreed to let you work in the finance department at MDX Aerodynamics."

"I'm not working for Leland."

"What did I just say about challenging me?"

"I can't work for Leland. I already accepted a job."

He straightens up. "What job are you referring to?"

"Jack offered me a job at his company."

My father's face becomes red, his lips purse, and his brows furrow. "You will NOT work for that man! Not now! Not ever! You know how much I despise him."

"I do," I say calmly. "But despite your personal feelings toward him, he's an excellent teacher and I know I could learn a great deal under his guidance."

My father is already furious, but for some reason, I felt the need to add flame to the fire and I knew that comment would. It's bad enough Jack is my mentor for Dunamis, but having him teach me about business as well? That's my father's worst nightmare.

"It will never happen," he says. "I'll speak to him myself right now and let him know that you will not be working there."

"I don't think that's a good idea." My father waits for me to tell him why, but instead I take a drink. I want him to stand there, wondering and waiting.

"Are you going to explain yourself, Pearce?" he finally asks.

"I wasn't aware that people weren't supposed to know about you firing me, so I mentioned it to Jack. If you don't allow me to work for him, there's a chance he might let it slip that you fired me simply because you were angry, without considering the impact it might have on the organization."

"Fuck," he mutters under his breath as he searches the room for Jack. His eyes dart back to mine. "Who else did you tell?"

"Royce Sinclair."

He huffs. "I'm not worried about him. He lies so much that nobody would ever believe him."

"I need to speak to some of the other members. Tell Mother I said hello."

I walk off to the side of the room, then stop to finish my drink. I scan the area around me for a place to set my glass.

"I'll take it." A tall blond woman walks up to me, holding a tray. She's dressed in a very short black skirt and a white blouse that can barely contain her breasts. She looks familiar. I glance down at her long legs, down to her very high heels. I notice a fake diamond bracelet on her ankle, and that's when I remember her. I rarely looked at their faces. I always focused on their bodies, and I remember seeing that bracelet before.

She's an associate. I've slept with her. Many times.

She leans over and whispers in my ear. "Do you want my card?"

"What card?"

"My reservation card."

"And what am I reserving?"

"Me." She says it in my ear, then backs away. "It's something new they're trying. They want to make things more organized. You reserve a girl now, then meet up with her after dinner. That way, there's no fighting over a certain girl. You get whoever's card you reserved." She smiles. "Come on, Pearce. We always had fun together. And you're running out of options. The cards are going fast."

"I'm married. I won't be taking a card this evening."

She laughs. "Almost every guy in here is married."

"Well, regardless, I will not be taking a card."

She shrugs. "Whatever." She walks off toward another man who's looking for a place to put his empty glass. I'm sure he'll accept her offer.

I glance around, wondering who else I could talk to in order to pass the time until dinner starts. As my eyes wander the crowd, I see Shelby. Shit. I totally forgot about her being here. I'm so

196

used to seeing her as Rachel's friend and not an associate that I didn't even think about her being here.

I make my way over to her. She's taking empty glasses from a group of men. They're talking and not paying attention to her.

I walk up to her. "I need to talk to you."

She seems surprised seeing me here. I guess she, too, forgot about this secret we share. I think we both try to pretend this part of our lives doesn't exist.

I move off to the side and wait for her to come over. When she does, I say, "Give me your card."

"What?" She looks at me with disgust. "You're already cheating on her? And you're choosing *me*?"

I sigh. "No. I'm not interested in that." I lower my voice. "I need your card so you don't end up with someone else. After dinner, we'll go to one of the rooms, then wait for an hour and leave."

She nods, looking nervous as she takes the card from her pocket. "What if someone sees us?"

"They all cheat. They won't think anything of it."

"That's not what I mean. What if someone tells Rachel?"

"That can't happen. Nobody is allowed to talk about this." I step closer to her and lower my voice to just above a whisper. "I'm only doing this to help you. Now do you want my help or not?"

"Yes," she says quietly.

I step back. "As for your friendship with Rachel, it needs to end. If anyone saw the two of you together—"

"No. I can't lose her. She's one of my only friends."

"You know they won't allow it. My wife cannot be friends with someone like you."

She drops her head in shame.

"Shelby, I'm very sorry. I didn't mean to say it that way."

"No, it's true. I just don't want to stop being friends with her."

"I know you don't, but you need to end the friendship. You also need to stop seeing Logan."

She frowns. "I know. But I don't want to let him go." She looks up at me. "I love him."

I check around me, making sure nobody's listening. "You love Logan?"

"Yes. And he loves me. He told me the other night. He's moving here in a month. Well, to Westport. He took a job there."

"It'll never work. You know that."

"It's not against the rules."

"It doesn't matter. Once he finds out about you, your relationship will end, and the longer you keep this going, the harder it'll be when it's over." I see William Sinclair coming toward me. "I have to go," I say to Shelby. "I'll see you after dinner."

She walks off and I turn to William. "William, good to see you again."

We talk for the rest of the cocktail hour, then everyone goes in another room for dinner. Afterward, I sneak out and meet Shelby in the hall.

"Nobody's watching," I say to her. "They're all still in the dining room and too drunk to notice I left. Just go. You'll be fine."

She points to her outfit. "I need to change clothes. Can you let me into one of the rooms?"

"Of course." I take her bag that contains her clothes and we go down to my room. We were all given a hotel room to use for when we were ready to be alone with our chosen associate. I open the door and step inside, setting the bag down. "Goodnight, Shelby."

"Goodnight."

I exit the room and go out to my car. I'm sure I'm the first one to leave, but I want to go home. It may be an empty home without Rachel there, but it's better than being here. And as soon as I'm home, I can call her. Because I need to. I need to hear her voice.

After a day immersed in the darkness that is Dunamis, I need some light. And that light is Rachel.

CHAPTER EIGHTEEN
One Week Later

RACHEL

It was great being in Indiana last week, seeing my friends and family, but I couldn't wait to get back home to Pearce. While I was away, I realized that even though I've lived in Connecticut for a year and a half, I never considered it home until I married Pearce. But now that we're starting our life together here, it truly feels like home.

Last weekend, Pearce and I celebrated New Year's. We could've gone to one of the numerous parties Pearce was invited to, but instead we went out for a nice dinner, then rang in the New Year at home. After a week apart, we wanted to be alone together. I'd really missed him. I wasn't able to talk to him much last week because he was at that conference.

I didn't ask Pearce much about the conference because I could tell he didn't want to talk about it. He seemed really stressed when I got home on Saturday so I'm wondering what happened. I'm guessing he had a fight with his father, and if so, I need to wait for him to tell me about it. Or maybe he just wants to forget it. I know this is hard on him, having his father reject him this way. But I keep thinking it's for the best. Maybe the two of them need some time apart. Maybe it will help his father realize what a huge mistake he made by cutting Pearce out of his life. And if not, then his father should just stay away. If Holton can't see what an amazing person his son is, then I don't want him anywhere near Pearce.

Now that I'm back in Connecticut and done with school, I'm eager and ready to find a job. I heard back from two of the museums I applied at. They're both within an hour's drive from here, which is a long commute but manageable. My options are limited so I can't be picky. I'll take what I can get. My first interview is tomorrow and the second one is Thursday.

Pearce has a new job. He'll be starting it later this week. He's working for his friend, Jack Ellit. Pearce told me about the job last weekend and he seems really excited about it. I met Jack when he came to my apartment a few months ago. He didn't tell me he knew Pearce and he lied about donating money to the shelter, so I wasn't thrilled that Pearce was going to work for this man. Pearce assures me Jack is a good guy, but I'm still leery of him, so we're having dinner with Jack and his wife tonight so I can get to know him better.

We're heading over there now. Jack picked the restaurant. It's a nice place, so I'm wearing a new red dress and Pearce is wearing a suit.

"Before we get there, I should warn you about Jack," Pearce says.

"*Now* you tell me this? Right before I meet him?" I shake my head, smiling. "So what do I need to know about him?"

"He's a little unconventional. And he doesn't have the best manners. He curses a lot. Talks with his mouth full. Doesn't filter what he says."

I laugh. "That's it? You had me all worried it was going to be another Royce and Victoria dinner."

"No. Not at all. Royce is disgusted by Jack. All the members—" He stops suddenly, then says, "Jack is not popular among the high-society crowd."

"What were you saying before? The members of what?"

He hesitates. "The country club. Jack belongs to a very exclusive country club and the members frown upon his behavior."

"Then I'm surprised they gave him membership."

"He's very wealthy and very successful, so he fit the criteria." Pearce parks the car and we go inside.

The restaurant is dimly lit and I have to hold onto Pearce until my eyes adjust. The hostess leads us to the table where Jack and his wife are sitting. They both stand up.

Jack smiles as he shakes my hand. "We meet again. Sorry for that little show I put on at your apartment." He pats Pearce's back. "I was just looking out for this guy. But he made sure to yell at me when he found out what I did." He laughs.

At least Jack isn't pretending it didn't happen. I'm glad he came out and addressed it. It helps relieve some of the tension I was feeling upon seeing him again.

"You'll have to excuse my husband," his wife says. "He acts first, thinks later." She smiles. "I'm Martha."

I smile back. "It's very nice to meet you."

We sit down and Jack says to me, "How do you like your steak?"

I'm confused. I haven't even opened my menu. "Oh, um, I don't know if I'm ordering a steak."

"I don't care what you order. I'm asking how you like your steak."

Pearce leans over to me. "He asks everyone this question. Just go with it."

"Okay, well, I like it medium rare," I say.

He smiles at Pearce. "You picked a good one."

"What does that mean?" I whisper to Pearce.

Jack answers. "It means you know how to eat a steak. I was hoping you weren't one of those well-done people. I hate those people. Ruining a good steak by cooking it to death."

Martha rolls her eyes, pointing at Jack. "He eats meat practically raw. Most restaurants won't even serve it that way."

"Fucking food safety shit," he says. "If I want to risk getting tapeworms, or whatever the hell they think I'm going to get, it's none of their damn business."

I smile, remembering Pearce's warnings about Jack. He is definitely different than what I expected.

"Jack," Pearce says. "There are ladies present. Perhaps you could tone down the language tonight."

"I'm not the one you have to worry about. Get a few drinks in Martha and she'll be swearing like a sailor."

She just shakes her head.

I'm trying not to laugh. These two are quite the pair. We've only been here a few minutes and they're already way more entertaining than Royce and Victoria.

Jack is holding a glass of some kind of dark liquor. He takes a swig of it and some of it splashes on his shirt.

"Goddammit," he mumbles, dabbing his shirt with his white cloth napkin. His wife doesn't even react. He must do this all the time.

My eyes keep going to his tie. It's bright yellow so it really stands out against his navy pin-striped suit. His wife is wearing a yellow dress that's almost as bright as Jack's tie. The dress is a little too tight on her, the fabric clinging to her body and creating wrinkles around her chest. She's rather overweight so maybe the dress used to fit but now it doesn't.

After we order, Martha asks me about Indiana. Unlike Victoria, Martha actually seems interested in what I'm saying. And she doesn't make any rude comments like Victoria did.

Our meals arrive and as we're eating, Martha says to me, "You should come over to the house sometime. I'm usually around in the mornings. Stop by next week and we'll have coffee."

"Just don't let her make it," Jack says, gnawing on his pork chop. He wouldn't order the steak after the waiter said the cook refused to serve it still bloody inside. "Martha makes terrible coffee. Worst you ever had."

"It's true," she says. "But I'll have the housekeeper make it. Or we could skip the coffee and have a gin and tonic."

I'm not sure if she's kidding, so I smile and say, "In the morning?"

She shrugs. "It's the only way I can put up with Jack. Always have to have a few drinks in me."

"Ain't that the truth." He laughs and leans over to kiss her cheek. "But you still love me, woman."

"Unfortunately." She kisses him back.

Jack turns to Pearce. "So are you ready for tomorrow?"

"I thought you said Thursday."

"What the hell day is it?"

"Today is Monday."

"Is it really?" He stops to think. "Doesn't matter. I want you there tomorrow."

"What time?"

"Ten. Is that too early?"

Pearce chuckles. "That's practically the afternoon to me. Are you sure you don't me there earlier?"

"What the hell for?"

"To get started. I'm sure you have things for me to work on."

"You can work on them after ten. Before that, you should be asleep. Or making love to your beautiful wife."

I feel myself blushing. I can't believe he said that. But like Pearce said, Jack doesn't filter his words.

"All right then," Pearce says. "Ten it is."

We finish our meals, then have dessert and coffee. Pearce and I tell them about our trip to Italy and then Martha tells us about some of the trips she and Jack have taken.

By the end of the evening, I've decided I really like Jack and Martha. Even though they're much older than Pearce and me, I'd like to have dinner with them again. And I told Martha I'd come over for coffee. But just coffee. Not gin and tonics.

When we get home I turn on the TV and see a photo of Pearce and me from the photo shoot.

"Pearce! We're on TV!"

He comes over as I turn up the volume. It's a celebrity news show and the woman at the desk says, "It's almost like a fairytale. A regular, small-town girl falls in love with a billionaire. And not just any billionaire. Pearce Kensington, one of the world's most eligible bachelors."

"Not anymore," the man next to her says. "He's now off the market. And engaged to a very beautiful woman."

"Yes, she's simply stunning," the woman says. "They're such a gorgeous couple." She turns to face the camera. "The wedding is set for mid-March and will include six hundred guests. We'll be following the wedding preparations up until the actual day. Be sure to tune in to see the flowers, the dress, plans for the reception, and more."

They move on to another story and I turn the volume down.

"They're doing stories on the wedding plans?" I ask Pearce.

"I told you this would get a lot of media coverage. This happened with my last wedding as well, but this one is getting even more publicity." He goes over to our stack of mail and pulls out a magazine and holds it up. "This just came today. I didn't have a chance to show you before we left."

"We're on the cover?" I take the magazine from him. "This is crazy." I flip through to the story and see a two-page article about us, along with more photos. Most of the article is the interview we did, but there's also a sidebar with information about me; my hometown, my age, where I went to college, my swimming awards. "Where did they get all this information?"

"It's all public records," Pearce says.

I set the magazine down. "I don't like having all my personal information out there like this."

"Unfortunately, you'll have to get used it. This is how it is, being a Kensington."

He keeps saying that, but I'd never even heard of Pearce or his family until I met him. I never saw anything about his previous wedding on TV or in magazines, but I don't really pay attention to that type of stuff.

I've been starting to get updates about the wedding. Even though I'm not directly involved in the plans, the wedding coordinators send me packets in the mail. So far I've seen sketches of what the ballroom for the reception will look like, a list of the flowers, the menu, pictures of the cake, and photos of bridesmaid dresses. Just yesterday, they sent me photos of the wedding dresses they picked out. In a few weeks, I have to go try them on.

I love everything I've seen so far. It's like the wedding coordinators did research on me and picked out exactly what I would like. They're doing an amazing job. Much better than I would do. This wedding is going to be gorgeous.

The next day I go to my first job interview. It's at a medium-sized museum and includes a mix of job duties, including planning museum events. I've never done that before but I'm sure I could figure it out.

"Have a seat," the man interviewing me says. He's an older gentleman with white hair, wearing dress pants and a tweed sport coat.

I sit across from him and wait as he looks over my resume. I hope this isn't the first time he's reading it.

"Rachel Evans." He glances up and to the side. "That name sounds familiar."

I had to use my maiden name since nobody knows I'm already married.

"I'm very impressed with your collection," I say. "I've been here many times and—"

"Were you recently on TV?" he asks.

"No, I don't think so," I say, not wanting to start a discussion about my wedding during a job interview. And how would this man possibly know about that? He doesn't seem like someone who follows celebrity news.

He leans forward and waves his finger at me. "Yes. I saw your picture on TV. It was just last night. My granddaughter was over for dinner and she made us watch some show about celebrities. That's where I saw you. I remember now. You're engaged to Pearce Kensington."

I nod. "Yes. So anyway, I'd love to learn more about the position. Could you tell me about it?"

He stands up. "I'm sorry, Miss Evans, but we have many other candidates."

I stand up as well. "I'm sorry, but what does that mean?"

"It's a tough job market right now. This position needs to go to someone who actually needs a job. I can't offer it to someone who's marrying a billionaire. Just think of all the negative press we would get."

"But I'm a very hard worker. And you don't have to pay me much. I could—"

"Miss Evans." He walks around his desk to the door, holding it open for me. "I don't want to take up any more of your time. I'm sorry, but I can't hire you. If you'd like me to put you in contact with our volunteer services, I'd be happy to do so."

"Thank you, but I'm hoping to find a full-time job." I shake his hand. "It was nice meeting you."

I hurry out of there before I scream at the guy. He didn't even give me a chance to go over my experience or explain the ideas I had if I were to be hired. I spent hours preparing for this interview, only to be kicked out of his office in less than five minutes.

At dinner, Pearce asks me how the interview went and I just say it went fine. I don't want to talk about it. That man was really old and grew up in an era when women didn't work if they didn't have to, so maybe that's why he reacted that way.

"So how's your new job?" I ask Pearce.

"Good. But I feel like I didn't get much done." He smiles. "Jack sent me home at five. I felt as though I had just got there and yet he was telling me my day was over."

"What did you do while you were there?"

"Met with the product team. We went over their budget and timeline for the new product launch. Then I met with the marketing team and we talked through their initial strategy for introducing the product to the client."

"Sounds like you did a lot."

"I mostly just listened. I didn't do a lot of hands-on work. That will come later."

"I know it's only the first day, but do you think you'll like working there?"

"Definitely. It's interesting. Challenging. And I actually look forward to going back there."

I reach over and kiss him. "I'm really happy for you. It sounds like a great job."

He continues to tell me about it, and it really does sound great. I just wish I could find a job as well. But after today's incident, I'm starting to get worried.

On Thursday, I go to my second interview. The job is only part-time but it might become full-time in a few months.

"Would you like some coffee or water?" the man interviewing me asks as we take a seat in his office. His name is Curt.

"No, thank you."

He coughs. "I really need some water. I'll be right back." Curt gets up and opens the door. "Sandra, would you mind grabbing me some water?"

She agrees, and he comes back to his desk. Curt is around 30, with dark hair and black-rimmed glasses. He's wearing casual pants and a plaid button-up shirt. He looks like a teacher I had in junior high.

"So tell me about your background," he says, picking his pen up to take notes.

"Well, I've always been interested in history, particularly—"

"Hold on." He waves at someone to come in the room. It's the woman who was sitting at the desk out front. She hands him a bottle of water.

"Oh my God!" she says, startling me. "Rachel!"

She's staring at me, so I say, "I'm sorry, do I know you?"

"No. But I know you." She smiles and comes around to shake my hand. "You're the lucky woman who snagged Pearce Kensington. I have the magazine with you two on the cover."

"You're dating Pearce Kensington?" Curt asks.

"They're engaged!" Sandra answers before I can. "They're getting married in March."

"Sandra, could you give us a moment?" Curt says.

"Oh, yes, certainly. Sorry, I didn't mean to interrupt." She takes off, closing the door behind her.

Curt clears his throat and looks very uncomfortable. I'm getting a bad feeling about what he's about to say.

"Rachel, I'm sure you're very qualified for the job, but given the fact that you're, um..."

"Going to be the wife of Pearce Kensington," I say, finishing his thought.

"Yes. That, um, changes things." He points to a stack of resumes on this desk. "I have a lot of applicants and I need to give this job to someone who needs it. I'm sorry, but I can't consider you, knowing your situation."

I nod, eyeing the resumes. There must be at least thirty of them in that stack. Thirty people want this job. Most of them are probably living paycheck to paycheck, like I was doing before I met Pearce. Would I be mad if a job I really wanted and needed went to the wife of a billionaire instead of me? The answer is yes. I would.

Dammit. My Hirshfield advisor was right. I can't get a job, at least not a paying one. Even if I'm the most qualified person I won't be given the job, because I don't need one. I'm a billionaire. I don't need the money. If I want to work, I have to work for free. I have to volunteer. That's my only option.

I stand up. "Thank you for your time."

He walks me to the door and I leave, feeling completely deflated.

When Pearce gets home, I tell him about both of my interviews.

"I'll never have a job, Pearce."

We're sitting together on the couch. I'm leaning back on his chest and his arms are around me.

"You've only been on two interviews. You need to go on some more. Didn't you say you had one next week?"

"Yes, but the same thing is going to happen. Nobody wants to hire Pearce Kensington's wife. Or fiancé."

He doesn't argue the fact. He knows it's true.

"I feel stupid for even going on those interviews. They're right. There are so many people out there who need the money more than I do. It would be wrong of me to take a job. But I don't understand why it's different for you. Is it just because you're a man? You get to work and I have to stay home?"

"Rachel, I only have this job because I know Jack. If I went out and tried to get a job anywhere else, I'd have the same issues you're having. People would tell me I don't need the money or that I should go work for my father. That's why wealthy people who want to work end up working in the family business. It's the only place they can get hired."

"So now what do I do?"

"I think you should go on a few more interviews. You never know what will happen until you go."

"Yes, but like I said, I don't want to take a job from someone who needs it. Maybe I should try volunteering."

"At a museum?"

"Yes. And maybe I should get involved in some organizations."

He kisses my head and pulls me closer. "Whatever you want to do. I'll support you any way I can. I just want you to be happy."

I tilt my head back to kiss him. "I know you do. I love you."

"I love you too."

The following Monday, I go to another interview and see two women in their thirties waiting to be interviewed. The job barely pays anything and yet they still applied. They really need this job. I don't. I tell the person at the front desk that I've changed my mind and then I leave, deciding that my job search is over.

My career ended before it even started.

CHAPTER NINETEEN

PEARCE

I've been working for Jack for a week now and it's going better than expected. Truthfully, I wasn't sure what to expect. I know Jack is successful, but given his odd personality I wasn't sure what type of boss he would be. It turns out, he's an excellent boss. Rather than hovering over his employees and telling them what to do every second of the day, Jack trusts them to do their job and do it well. And if they don't do it well, they get called into the corporate dining room for a steak lunch, after which they have to give a presentation to Jack regarding why their job performance isn't up to par and and what they can do to correct it.

It's an unusual approach, but it seems to work. The employees I've talked with said the steak lunch seems like less of a disciplinary session and more like a coaching session. And having to give the presentation forces them to find a way to fix whatever problem led them to the steak lunch meeting. They also like that Jack tells it like it is. He's not afraid to tell someone what they need to work on, but he does so in a way that's supportive, rather than yelling at them, like my father would.

Since working here I've spent most of my time in meetings, but instead of just sitting there, as I did at Kensington Chemical, I'm actually allowed to participate in the meetings. I'm able to have an actual discussion and leave the meeting feeling like I accomplished something.

My work day is so short that I feel like I'm hardly ever at the office. But I like this schedule. It gives me more time with Rachel, who is feeling depressed right now. She's given up looking for a job and now she's searching for volunteer opportunities. I think if she found the right organization, she'd like volunteering, but right now, she's not thrilled about it. She really wanted to work at a regular job.

Last night she brought up the baby topic again, saying she's ready to see a doctor to find out if she might be able to have a child. I worry that the results she gets back will just depress her even more, but she really wants to do this so I told her about the clinic Logan suggested. This morning she called to get an appointment but the first one they had available is a month away.

I was relieved. I'm not ready to get the results. If they confirm she can't have children, she'll be devastated. But if they find that she can, we'll end up having children, and that scares me. I went to bed last night thinking about this and had a dream in which I had a son. It turned into a nightmare because Dunamis took him. They took him as a baby and wouldn't give him back. That would never happen because initiation doesn't occur until age 20. But still, just the image of them taking my son nearly stopped my heart. I woke up in a panic, breathless and sweating.

"What are you still doing here?" Jack asks as he walks into my office. He plops down on the small couch that's off to the side.

"It's only five. The day just ended."

"It's ten after five. You should be heading home to that beautiful wife of yours. I wish I had a woman like that to go home to."

"Jack, don't put down your wife. You're lucky the woman puts up with you."

"I'm not saying anything against my wife. I'm saying I'm jealous of you, you lucky bastard. I see why you risked it all to be with her. How's she doing, by the way?"

"She's upset that she isn't able to find a job."

"A job? Why the hell would she want a job? Having to put up with shit. Dealing with idiots all day. Wasting your life at an office. If I could retire tomorrow, I would."

"She's always been a hard worker, and now that she can't find a job, I think she's feeling lost."

"So have a kid. That'll cheer her up. She seems like someone who likes kids."

"Actually, I wanted to ask you about that."

"About whether you should have a kid? You should probably be asking your wife about that." He slips his shoes off. "My feet are killing me. These damn shoes. The sales guy said they'd stretch out, but I've been wearing them for three days now and they feel even tighter."

"Jack, I don't think I can have children."

He rubs his feet. "Wear looser underwear and stay out of hot tubs. Those two things will work wonders for your sperm count."

"No. That's not what I'm referring to. I'm saying I don't want my children to be part of what you and I are part of. If that's their future, then I don't want to have children."

He sighs as he gets up and closes the door. "None of us want that, Pearce. But if that's your reason for not having children, then you're just letting them take away even more from you. If you want children, you should have them. There's no way I would've let those assholes deny me the experience of being a father. I love my girls. They're the light of my life."

"But you knew your daughters would be forced to marry members. Didn't that bother you?"

"I didn't worry about it. Not all the members are bad. Look at you and me. We're good husbands. Well, you more than me, but still. Both my girls ended up with decent men. Maybe not the most handsome, but my girls aren't exactly beauty queens."

"I wouldn't want my daughter being forced to marry someone."

"My daughters weren't forced. There was a selection process, and Martha and I were allowed to have input. Then the girls dated several of the men before deciding."

"Yes, but in the future, the organization could change the rules and take away any choices."

"If anything, the rules will become less strict as time goes on. Once some of those old bastards die off, things will start to change. You were at the meeting. You heard the younger members. They all want change, but the older members won't allow it."

"If I had a son, I wouldn't want him to be a member."

"Well, that's a problem. They might loosen the rules for daughters but I doubt that the rules regarding sons will ever change. They're determined to keep membership limited to the families who are already members."

"Then I can't have children." I sigh and shake my head. "Rachel will never accept that. If she's able to have them, she will."

"She can't have children?"

"We don't know yet. She's going to have some tests run to find out."

"Pearce, if you can have a child, you should. You don't want to miss out on being a father. Having children brings light to your life, and you need that. I did too. I don't know if I would've survived all these years if it weren't for my girls."

"I can't bring children into this world knowing what their future will be."

"You can't predict the future, Pearce. Things may change in twenty years. And if you really want that change, then go create it yourself. Start talking with the younger members. See if they, too, have concerns about their sons. Find the ones that do, and start a discussion with them. Come up with a plan to try to get them out of this."

"You think that would be possible?"

"Anything's possible. I've done the impossible before, and so can you."

"I don't know, Jack. I think it's better if I just didn't have children."

"But the woman you love wants them. So how will you tell her no?"

"I can't." I shake my head. "I can't tell her that."

"Would you want children if you didn't have to worry about the organization?"

I nod. "Yes. Although I have concerns I won't be a good father."

He chuckles. "All us men have those concerns. But you'll get over it." He gets up and stands in front of my desk. "Now get out of here. Get your ass home and practice making some babies."

He picks his shoes off the floor and walks out of my office.

I leave thinking maybe he's right. Maybe the rules will change when the older members die off, and maybe younger members like myself can be the catalyst for those changes. It's not likely, but it's possible. It gives me hope.

When I get home, I find Rachel at the kitchen table with a pad of paper, writing something down.

"What are you up to?" I come up behind her chair and rub her shoulders.

"I'm making a list of organizations where I could volunteer. I already contacted the museums in the area. I was hoping they'd let me give tours, but the only volunteer work they have available is putting together mailers for potential donors and I don't want to do that." She sets her pen down. "Sorry I don't have dinner ready. I didn't realize what time it was."

"Don't worry about dinner." I pull her up from her chair and kiss her. "Rachel."

"Yes?" She looks sad. It's a look I rarely see on her and I don't like it. I want her to be happy and now she's not.

"Rachel, I love you, and I'm sorry you're feeling this way. I wish I could do something to make you feel better."

"I just need time to reevaluate what I'm going to do. For so long, I had this image in my head of what I'd be doing after graduation, and now that it's changed, I need to let that go and make a new plan." She softly smiles. "It'll all work out. I know it will. I always believe that things happen for a reason. So maybe I wasn't meant to work at a museum. Maybe I was meant to do something else." She kisses me. "I didn't plan on marrying Pearce Kensington, but look how that turned out."

I smile. "How did it turn out?"

"Better than I could've ever imagined. I ended up with a hot, sexy, charming husband who I love more and more each day."

Even when she's feeling down, Rachel finds something to be positive about. She's always hopeful. Always looking for the silver lining. I need to be more like her. I need to believe that things will work out. Because sometimes they do. We're proof of that. I never thought I'd be able to be with her, and yet here we are, together and married.

I hold her face in my hands, tilting it back slightly to kiss her. My lips move over hers and I hear her softly moan. I keep kissing her until she stops briefly to say, "Don't you want dinner?"

"Not now. I'm busy." I undo the top button on her shirt and keep going.

"Busy doing what?" She loosens my tie.

"Practicing," I say, my lips returning to hers.

She pulls back, looking confused. "What?"

I don't explain. I just continue to kiss her as I walk her to the bedroom. And then I do as my boss suggested, and I make love to my beautiful wife, practicing making that baby we might have someday.

I still have my doubts, but that part of me that wants to have a child keeps shoving those doubts aside.

On Saturday, I wake Rachel up at seven, which is earlier than we normally wake up on the weekend.

"What time is it?" she asks, rubbing her eyes.

I kiss her. "Time to find a house."

"A house?" She yawns. "What are you talking about?"

"Come on. Get up." I pull the covers back. "I'm taking you to breakfast and then we're meeting with the real estate agent."

"We're looking for houses? Today?"

"Yes. We didn't have any plans for today and Jack bans me from the office on the weekends, so I thought we should go out and look at some houses."

"Okay, but why so early?"

"There's a lot to look at. And I asked the agent to take us to some different towns. I didn't want to limit our search to just around here. So hurry up. Get in the shower."

She steps out of bed and slips off her silky nightgown, tossing it aside. "Are you showering with me?"

My eyes drink her in. Her curves. Her skin. God, she turns me on. "I'd be happy to shower with you, but that will slow us down."

"Then forget it," she says, walking toward the bathroom, completely naked.

"Hey!" I come up behind her and scoop her up in my arms. "I'm not in *that* big of a hurry."

We shower and dress, then go to breakfast and meet up with Elana, the real estate agent, in her office. She gets a map out and points to the areas she'll be taking us to and tells us a little about each one.

"Are you hoping to move in right after the wedding?" she asks Rachel.

Rachel looks at me to answer.

"It's up to you," I tell her. I want Rachel to make the decision. I want her making all the decisions about the house. What style it is. The layout. How it's decorated. The only decision I'll weigh in on is the location, but I'm flexible on that. I want Rachel to have the house of her dreams.

She looks back at Elana. "I guess right after the wedding would be good, but it could be later too. April or May would also be fine."

"I'm sure we could get you in any of these houses whenever you'd like. There's no need to wait." Elana smiles at me. She knows how it works. She only deals with wealthy clients. She knows we have the money to make things happen. If Rachel wants the house in March, we'll convince the sellers to be out of there in March.

We get in Elana's car and she takes us to the first property. It's a ten-bedroom house set back in the woods, surrounded by a large iron gate. The property also includes a guest house, an outdoor pool, and a tennis court.

"It's very large," Rachel says as we walk inside the house. The ceiling in the foyer extends to the second floor and off to the right is a large winding staircase.

"Would you like to go upstairs first?" Elana asks Rachel.

She bites her lip as she glances around the downstairs. She seems nervous. Why would she be nervous?

"Could I talk to Pearce for a minute?"

"Certainly," Elana says. "I'll go wait in the kitchen. It's just down the hall to the left. Meet me in there when you're done."

Once she's gone I turn to Rachel. "Is something wrong?"

"Are they all like this?" she whispers.

"Sweetheart, you don't have to whisper. She can't hear us. Now what were you asking?"

"Are all the houses she picked like this? Are they all mansions?"

"This isn't a mansion. It's just a large house. My parents' house is a mansion." As I say it, I realize Rachel's never even been there. She's my wife and yet she's never been to the house I grew up in. I'm sure if I brought her there, my parents wouldn't even let her inside. They're still not speaking to me.

"It's a mansion, Pearce. It's huge. It has ten bedrooms. What would we do with ten bedrooms?"

"So you don't like the house."

"No." She frowns. "I'm sorry."

I take her hand. "There's nothing to be sorry about. You don't have to like this one, or any of the ones we see today. We're just looking. We don't have to buy anything today."

"If they're all like this, I don't think I want to look at the others."

217

"They'll all look different. This one feels too ornate for us, with the crystal chandelier and the gold banister on the staircase. We'll just go to the next house."

"I wasn't referring to the way it's decorated, although yes, it's too ornate. But what I meant is that it's just too big. I feel like I'm in a hotel."

"How big of a house would you like?"

"I don't know. Maybe four bedrooms? And I'd like it to be in a neighborhood, not hidden away behind a gate. I want to have neighbors. I don't want to be all by ourselves with nobody else around."

I guess we should've discussed this before I talked to the real estate agent. I just assumed Rachel wanted a large house like this. And I didn't even think about living in a neighborhood. I've never lived in a neighborhood. Having neighbors? That would be a huge change for me. But if that's what she wants, I'm willing to try it.

"I'll go talk to Elana," I say.

"Pearce, maybe we should look at a few more houses before you tell her. I feel bad that she did all that work, finding places for us to look at."

"There aren't many properties in this price range. She didn't have to work that hard." I kiss Rachel. "Don't worry about her. This is her job. Wait here and I'll go explain what we decided. Or do you want to go tell her?"

"You go ahead."

I walk down the hallway to the kitchen. "Elana," I say getting her attention. She was gazing out the window. "There's been a change of plans. Rachel would like to look at some smaller houses."

"Smaller than this?" She seems surprised. "This is the smallest house I'd planned to show you today."

"Yes, I assumed that was the case. And I know you generally only show higher-end listings, so if we need to find someone else, I understand."

"No. Of course not. I have access to other listings. What type of house is she looking for?"

"She'd like to see something in a neighborhood. Something with maybe four or five bedrooms. Could you show us anything today? Or do we need to reschedule?"

"Hmm." She taps her fingers on the kitchen island as she thinks. "I might have something she'd be interested in."

We go back out to her car and she drives east, through some small towns a little inland from the coast. About twenty minutes later, we arrive at a town square with stores all around it.

"So this is the town," she says. "There's a small grocery store, a drugstore, some shops. There's not a lot here, but you're close to some bigger towns."

Rachel smiles as she sees it. "I love it. It feels just like Indiana."

"Would you like to get out and walk around?" Elana asks Rachel.

"No, that's okay. Let's go see the house."

We drive along a winding road with woods on both sides and eventually turn onto a small street lined with houses.

"It's a very family-friendly neighborhood," Elana says, as we pass two young girls playing in one of the yards. "Your neighbors here would be mostly doctors and lawyers or people in business."

She parks in front of a brick colonial-style house with black shutters. There's a large tree out front that's bare now because it's winter. It must be an older neighborhood because all the houses have full-grown trees in the yards. But the houses don't look old or dated. They're all traditional styles that hold up over time. I like that they're spaced far apart. I didn't want our house to be only a few feet from our neighbor's house.

We follow Elana up the long sidewalk to the front door. Elana opens it for us and Rachel and I go inside and stand in the foyer.

I look over at Rachel. She's smiling and her entire face is lit up. I've seen that look. She had that look when we got married.

I think we just found our house.

CHAPTER TWENTY

RACHEL

This is it. This is the house. I could feel it the moment we walked in. I haven't even seen all of it yet, but something just feels right about it. I love the little town it's in and I love the street it's on. And I love the outside. There's a big tree out front that would offer some shade in the summer, and along the sides are some azalea bushes that will flower in the spring, framing the house in beautiful pink blooms.

"Come look around," Elana says, leading us into the house. "To the right is the dining room and to the left is the formal living room. There's also a family room off the kitchen at the back of the house."

"Could we go upstairs first?" I ask, pointing to the staircase.

"Of course. Go ahead."

I walk up there, with Pearce and Elana following behind.

"There are four bedrooms total." Elana motions me to follow her and we go in a large room with a king size bed. This is the master. It doesn't have a walk-in closet but you could always build one. The master bath has been updated with a new walk-in shower, new sinks, and new counters."

I go in the bathroom. It's very spacious, and it does look brand new, with granite counters, a large soaking tub, and a tile shower with multiple shower heads, similar to the one at our loft.

Next, she takes us down the hall and shows us the other three bedrooms. One has a crib in it and the another one has a tiny bed and lots of stuffed animals. The last bedroom looks like a guest room with a dresser and a queen bed.

It's a basic layout upstairs but it's just what I wanted. We go back downstairs to the living room.

"The floors are cherry wood," Elana says. "I think it adds a rich warm feel to the house."

I've always loved cherry wood floors. My parents' house has oak floors but I prefer the cherry.

"The kitchen has also been recently renovated." Elana waves at me to follow her. "Do you like to cook?"

"Yes, I love to cook."

"Then you'll love this kitchen. Granite countertops. All new appliances. Two ovens. And one is a convection oven."

She continues to talk, but I lose track of what she's saying. I'm too busy taking it all in. There's a huge kitchen island with stools along one side and the other side is a work area with a built-in sink. It's the perfect place for rolling out dough or preparing cookies. I turn around and along the back wall there are tons of cabinets to store things.

"Rachel, open the drapes," Pearce says. I look back and see him smiling at me.

I'm standing over the sink, and above it is a window covered in a short cotton drape. I move the drape aside and see a big back yard with an in-ground pool. "It has a pool!"

Pearce comes up behind me, his arms going around my waist. "And it's heated, so you could get more use out of it during the year."

I flip around to face him. "This house is so great."

He just smiles, then leans down and gives me a kiss.

"Would you like to see the office?" Elana asks.

We go down a short hall to a room that has a desk and built-in bookshelves just behind it. It's a big room. All of the rooms in this house are much larger than I thought they'd be.

"This would be a great home office," Pearce says.

He likes the office, but I can't tell if he likes the house. It's not as modern looking as his loft and it's not a mansion like he grew up in.

We return to the kitchen and continue on to the family room. I like how it's open to the kitchen. I could be making dinner while Pearce is reading a book or watching TV and it wouldn't feel like we're in separate rooms. There's a fireplace in the family room and the back wall has several windows, letting a lot of light in.

When we're done with the tour, Elana says to me, "Is this more like what you were looking for? Because I have several other houses this size that I could show you, although the neighborhoods aren't as nice as this one."

"Could we have a minute?" Pearce asks.

"Absolutely. Feel free to look around again if you'd like. I need to run out to the car to get something."

When she's gone, I smile at Pearce.

He knows what it means. "You want this house, don't you?"

"I love this house. I love the layout, and the kitchen is incredible! And the yard. Did you see the yard? It's huge. And the pool. Did you know it had a pool?"

He nods, smiling. "Yes, but I wanted it to be a surprise."

"I love the pool. I love everything about this house. And I love this street and the little town square. It all just feels right."

"Then let's buy it."

"Pearce, this isn't just my decision. I want you to be happy with it too. I know this isn't what you wanted, so we should keep looking. We don't have to decide today."

"Rachel." He holds my shoulders and looks me in the eye. "Do you really love this house?"

"Yes. It's perfect."

"Then there's no need to keep looking. If you love it, then we're buying it."

"But *you* don't love it."

"I don't care what type of house we have. You'll make any place we live feel like home. As long you're there, nothing else

222

matters to me. And I want you to be happy. So would you be happy living here?"

"Yes. Absolutely. And if we have a baby, this would be the perfect place to raise a child. It's a safe area and there are other families around and I like the small-town feel. It reminds me of where I grew up."

"Any questions?" Elana is back.

"Yes," Pearce says, putting his arm around me. "How soon could we move in?"

An hour later we're back at Elana's office filling out the paperwork to buy our first house. I thought it'd take months to find a house, but instead it only took one day. It's like when I met Pearce. I didn't need months or years to get to know him. I knew right away that I liked him. There was something about us that just felt right. Like we belonged together. Sometimes you just know. And today, I knew that was our house.

Elana talked to the sellers and they said they'd be out of the house at the end of January. Pearce and I decided we wouldn't move in until after the wedding. Even though we're already living together, moving into a house is different, and for appearance's sake, it would look better if we waited until after our fake wedding.

The timing will work out well. I'll have plenty of time to get the house ready before we move in. I think I want to paint some of the walls. Pearce told me to buy all new furniture, saying he'll just sell the loft furnished. But I want to keep some of his things, like maybe his leather couch and his living room tables. They're only a year old and they'll look good in the new house. Plus, those things will always remind me of the loft and when we were dating, so I don't want to give them up.

"We need to celebrate," I say to Pearce as we're driving away from the real estate office.

"We can't tonight. We have that party to go to. And we're going to be late if we don't hurry. With traffic it'll take us over an hour to get there."

"I forgot about that. We'll have to celebrate tomorrow."

The party we're going to is in Scarsdale, New York, one of the wealthiest towns in the country. It's hosted by the Seymour family. I've never met them, but Pearce said his family has known them for years so he's expected to be there.

I'm nervous about going. A lot of high-society people will be there. People like Victoria, who will spend the evening tossing insults at me. I'm sure Holton and Eleanor will also be there.

We arrive at the party at eight. The house is hidden behind a gate, and it's an even bigger mansion than the one we looked at today. But it looks similar inside, with shiny white marble floors and a large crystal chandelier in the foyer. It's not my style. It feels cold. I prefer a warmer look.

A maid comes up to us and takes our coats. She says nothing. She just takes them and disappears. Pearce wore a black suit and I'm wearing one of the new dresses the shopper picked out for me. It's a cream-colored long sleeve dress with a thin black belt and black trim along the neckline.

A woman with bright blond hair, wearing an elegant black crepe dress comes up to Pearce.

"Welcome to our new home," she says, smiling at him. She's probably in her mid-forties. I think she's had plastic surgery. The skin on her face looks like it's been pulled tightly back. So tight that it doesn't look right. She has her hair up in a twisted bun that's neatly tucked behind her head. Sparkling diamond earrings shine from her ears and match her diamond necklace and bracelet.

"Hello, Audrey," Pearce says. He puts his arm around me. "This is Rachel Evans, my fiancé."

I have to keep reminding myself to pretend we're not married. I keep wanting to call Pearce my husband.

"Rachel, this is Audrey Seymour," Pearce says.

"It's nice to meet you," I say, shaking her hand. Her hands are cold and bony. She's very thin. Too thin. I can see the outline of her collarbone through her dress. "You have a beautiful home," I tell her. Even if it's not my style, it's still a very nice house.

"Thank you." She smiles weakly, then looks back at Pearce. "Your parents arrived a few minutes ago. I believe they're back by the bar."

"Pearce." A man walks up behind Audrey. He's about her age with dark hair that's streaked with gray. He's wearing a black suit and his skin is very tan for this time of year.

"Leland," Pearce says, shaking his hand. "This is my fiancé, Rachel."

"I've heard a lot about you," he says as he shakes my hand.

Why would this man have heard about me? Pearce said he never talks to these people.

Leland and Audrey are both looking me over, assessing my dress and my shoes, just like Victoria did. What is *with* these people? If they're going to assess my clothes like this, they could at least be more discreet about it. Or maybe they do it on purpose to make me uncomfortable.

"I'm glad you could make it," Leland says. "Enjoy your evening."

They walk away and Pearce places his hand on my lower back and leads me farther into the house. There are a lot of people here. Some old, some young. All of them are very well-dressed and the women are covered in diamond jewelry, like it's a contest to see who has the most.

Everyone's watching Pearce and me as we walk by. Some are whispering to each other.

"Pearce," I say quietly to him. "Everyone's staring at us."

He leans down to whisper in my ear. "They're staring because you're beautiful. They've never seen such a beautiful woman."

"I don't think that's the reason," I whisper back.

"Just ignore them." He leads me to the bar. "Let's get a drink. What would you like?"

"A glass of white wine. Any kind."

Pearce goes up to the bartender. "A glass of Chardonnay and a bourbon, neat." He waits for our drinks, then hands me mine.

"Shall we go see if we can find Jack?" Pearce has that formal tone he used when we were first dating. And he said 'shall' which

225

he hardly ever says anymore, at least not around me. But as he's told me before, he changes when he's around these people.

We sneak through the crowded area near the bar. We go around a corner to another room and there are Pearce's parents, right in front of us.

Pearce stops, holding me at his side. "Mother," he says to her, ignoring Holton. "How have you been?"

"Fine. And you?" She smiles a little.

"Excellent. I'm sure Father informed you that I have a new job."

Holton clears his throat, then says to Eleanor. "I see the Prescotts just arrived. We need to go speak to them."

He tries to leave, but she holds him back. "We'll speak to them in a moment. Right now, we are speaking to our son."

She uses a harsh tone. Interesting. Maybe Eleanor doesn't want to be fighting with Pearce. Maybe she's only doing it because Holton is making her. She shouldn't listen to him. If she wants to talk to her son, she should do so, and end this ridiculous silent treatment that's been going on for way too long.

Eleanor doesn't look happy to see me. That slight smile that appeared when she saw Pearce has now turned to a frown as she looks at me. She hasn't even said hello to me, so I say it to her.

"Hello, Eleanor."

She ignores my greeting and eyes my dress. "I see you hired a stylist."

I look down at my dress. "Yes. She took me shopping a few weeks ago."

"She shouldn't make you shop with her. It's her job to find you the right items and have them delivered."

"I didn't mind shopping with her. It was kind of fun, actually."

That was the wrong thing to say. I know because Eleanor is giving me a look of disapproval, which I think means that I should not be doing things with people that I hire. Eleanor likes to place people in a hierarchy, with her at the top and her hired help at the bottom, and she only associates with the people who are at her level. I wonder what level I'm at.

She holds her gaze on me for a moment, then turns to Pearce. "What have you been up to besides work?"

Holton's standing there, mumbling something, his eyes on the other people in the room.

"Rachel and I bought a house."

Holton's eyes dart to Pearce. Narrowed eyes that match his very angry expression.

"Why the hell would you buy a house?" he asks.

"That's what you do when you get married," Pearce says calmly. "You buy a house."

"You're not married," he says, playing along with the fake story, although I know he wishes it were true.

"We won't be moving into the house until after the wedding."

"Which property is it?" Eleanor asks, as though there are only a few to choose from. And I'm sure that's true for the mansions Elana wanted to show us.

"It's a four-bedroom house in a neighborhood," Pearce says.

Holton laughs under his breath. "You're not serious."

"It's a brick colonial located in a small town, about a half hour east of your house."

Holton realizes that Pearce isn't kidding and I see his jaw clench. I think he'd blow up at Pearce if we weren't in a room full of people, but since we are, he lowers his voice and says, "Goddammit, Pearce. Haven't you done enough to destroy our family?"

"Father, I have not—"

"Pearce, you cannot live in a house like that," Eleanor says.

"And why is that, Mother?"

"You know why," she snaps, sounding almost as angry as her husband. "It doesn't look good. People will think we're struggling."

He sighs. "Nobody will think that, Mother. And Rachel and I looked at some larger houses but they just didn't suit us. We wanted something smaller."

"SHE wanted something smaller," Holton says, glaring at Pearce. "YOU didn't."

227

Pearce remains calm. "We *both* did. We have no need for a mansion. It's too much space."

"And how do you expect to host parties at a house that small?" Eleanor asks.

"I will not be hosting large parties like this one."

"As a Kensington, you are expected to," Eleanor says. "You know that, Pearce."

I can't believe how angry they're getting over this. It's none of their business what kind of house we live in. They're completely overreacting.

"Mother, perhaps we could talk about something else. Rachel is looking for volunteer opportunities. Why don't you tell her about some of the charity committees you serve on?"

She keeps her eyes on Pearce. "I am asking you to reconsider your purchase of this house. This is a decision that affects all of us and it's selfish of you to think otherwise."

"It's a very nice house," I say, because I think they forgot I was here. "And it's 4200 square feet, so it's not small."

Eleanor finally turns to me. "The house Pearce grew up in is 22,000 square feet. So in comparison, the house you purchased is small. Embarrassingly small. And the location is not appropriate either. Location is everything. Where Pearce lives reflects on my family. But you chose not to consider that."

"I didn't mean to cause problems," I say to Eleanor. "I just—"

"Then FIX the problem by calling your agent and telling her you will not be buying that house."

"Mother, we're not doing that," Pearce says. "We love the house and that is the house we will be living in."

"Your father is right," Eleanor says. "You're nothing but a selfish child." She turns and storms off, leaving Holton there.

"How dare you upset your mother like that," he says. "Stay away from us. We want nothing to do with you." He follows after his wife.

Once again, I'm shocked at how horribly they treat their son. I don't think I'll ever be used to it.

"I'm sorry, Pearce."

He drinks his bourbon. "It's fine. I knew they'd react that way."

"Then why did you tell them?"

"Because it's better than having them find out from someone else." He holds his glass up. "I need another one. Let's go back to the bar."

"You go ahead. I'll just wait here. It's too crowded by the bar."

He heads over there and I wait in the living room, which is full of people. None of them look happy to be here. Their smiles look forced and their laughter sounds fake. Why do these people spend time with people they don't even like? I guess it's just something rich people do. No wonder Pearce doesn't like this side of his life.

"Are you Rachel?"

I turn and notice a young girl standing next to me. She's very pretty. Long blond hair. Bright blue eyes. She's maybe 14 or 15 and very thin. She's wearing a black cocktail dress with thin straps at the top.

"Yes, I'm Rachel. And you are?"

"Katherine Seymour."

When she says it, I see the resemblance. She looks very similar to her mom.

"It's nice to meet you." I smile at her. "I met your parents earlier. Your family has a beautiful house."

She shrugs. "It's not that great."

Is she kidding? Most kids her age would love to grow up in a house like this.

"I'm guessing you're in high school?"

"When did you start dating Pearce?" She says it in an accusatory tone, almost like I'm dating her boyfriend.

"Last September. So what grade are you in?"

"You know you can't be with him."

I raise my brows. "Excuse me?"

"He has to be with a daughter of a member. Someone like me."

"You? You're a teenager."

She straightens up. "I'm 15, and I turn 16 in a few weeks."

"And Pearce is 25, almost 26."

"So? That's not that big of an age difference."

"It is when you're 15." This girl is getting on my nerves. I don't like her tone or the way she's looking me up and down, assessing me just like her parents did.

She sets her hands on her hips. "You can never be with him, so you might as well end this now."

"Pearce and I are engaged. We're very happy together. We're not breaking up."

"The wedding will never happen. They won't allow it."

"Who's 'they'? Who are you talking about?"

"The organization." She smirks. "He hasn't told you about it?"

"What's going on here?" Pearce asks, as he comes up behind me. "What do you need, Katherine?"

"I was just saying hello to Rachel." Katherine tilts her head and smiles at him. She's trying to play sweet and innocent, but I won't let her get away with it.

"Katherine was saying how we couldn't be together," I tell Pearce. "She said some organization won't allow us to get married."

Pearce starts coughing, almost like he's choking.

"Are you okay?" I ask.

He nods. "Yes."

I turn back to Katherine. "So, Katherine, what organization are you referring to?"

Before she can answer, Pearce says, "Katherine has a very active imagination. She always has, haven't you, Katherine?"

She smiles at him. A flirtatious smile. "You look good, Pearce. I like your suit."

"Katherine, why you don't run along and find someone your own age to talk to?"

"Call me sometime," she says, stepping closer to him and running her hand down his tie.

He backs away from her. "Katherine," he says in a warning tone.

She smiles and looks back at him as she walks away.

I move closer to Pearce. "Wow. She has quite a crush on you."

"She has for the past three years. I thought she'd grow out of it, but it seems to be getting worse."

"She kept telling me I couldn't be with you. Something about how you have to be with a member's daughter. Do you have any idea what she meant by that?"

"I told you, she has a very active imagination." He says it quickly, in an angry tone.

"Pearce, is something wrong?"

"No. Nothing." He nods toward the back of the room. "Jack and Martha are back there. Why don't you go talk to them? I need to find a restroom."

Pearce leaves and I make my way over to Martha. She smiles when she sees me.

"Rachel." She gives me a hug. "I'm so glad you came."

Finally. Someone who's happy to see me. If I could, I'd stay here the rest of the night. It's the only place I feel comfortable.

CHAPTER TWENTY-ONE

PEARCE

I've been searching for Katherine for nearly ten minutes, furious at her for saying those things to Rachel. How does Katherine even know about the organization?

I spot her going down a hallway on the far side of the house, away from where the guests are. I hurry over there before she disappears into one of the rooms.

"Katherine." I know she hears me and yet she keeps walking. "Katherine! I need to speak with you."

She looks back and smiles. "Come to my room."

"I'm not going in your room." I meet up with her in front of a door that I'm guessing leads to her bedroom.

"You tracked me down." She leans back against the door, sticking her chest out. "I knew you liked me." She grabs my tie, pulling it toward her and lifting her face up like she expects me to kiss her.

"Katherine." I take her hand and remove it from my tie. "For the last time, I am not interested in you. You're a child. I'm an adult. Go find someone your own age."

"I don't like boys my own age. They're disgusting and immature. I prefer men." She puts her hand on my chest, gazing up at me. "Men like you, Pearce."

"Stop it." I take a step back. "I've had enough of this ridiculous crush you have on me. It needs to end."

"If you were 35 and I was 25, it would be okay, so what's the difference? It's still ten years."

"I'm not discussing this. We have more important things to talk about." I check to make sure we're alone. "Who told you about the organization?"

"My father." She folds her arms over her chest, annoyed that I didn't give in to her advances.

"When did he tell you?"

She shrugs. "I don't know. Maybe a year ago? Why do you care?"

"You're not supposed to know about it until you're at least 20."

"My father says I'm mature for my age."

"Did he tell you never to tell anyone?"

"Yes. But I don't always listen to my father." She takes hold of my lapel and smiles up at me. "You don't have to be afraid to be with me. I'm not a virgin."

I move back and put my hands on her shoulders, holding her away from me. "Katherine, I need you to listen to me. And I need you to listen very closely. What your father told you is never to be told to anyone. Ever! Do you understand?"

"That girl needs to know she can't marry you. She needs to know the rules."

I'm surprised Leland didn't tell Katherine that Rachel and I are already married. Telling her might've stopped her obsession with me. But maybe Leland wanted it to continue. He seems to find it humorous.

"Rachel is my fiancé," I say. "And we ARE getting married. It's already been approved."

She pouts. "But that's not—"

"Listen to me! If you told Rachel about the organization and one of the members found out, your father would be punished."

"So? They'll give him less money. Big deal."

"No. The punishment could be far worse than that. Your father could be killed."

Her eyes drop to the floor. "Oh."

I don't think it's true, but I need Katherine to take this seriously. Honestly, I don't know what would happen if she told

Rachel about Dunamis. Her father would be punished for her actions, but I don't know what that punishment would be. The organization constantly reminds us that any member who tells an outsider about us will face severe punishment. I don't know if that punishment would be death, but I know for a fact that they would kill an outsider who finds out about us. And even though Rachel is my wife, they still consider her an outsider.

I hold Katherine's chin up, forcing her to look at me. "You must never EVER tell Rachel, or anyone else, that the organization exists. Do you understand me?"

She nods.

I let go of her. "Goodnight, Katherine."

I walk off, but hear her talking. "You still can't be with her."

I turn back and see Katherine watching me. Then she goes in her room and slams the door.

"Have you seen Katherine?" Leland asks as he walks toward me.

"Yes, she just went in her room."

He walks past me. "She needs to get back to the party."

"Leland."

He stops. "What is it, Pearce?"

I go up to him. "Why the hell did you tell Katherine about the organization?"

"So she wouldn't waste her time on boys she can't be with."

"That is NOT something you tell someone her age."

"Your father told you when you were 16."

"Yes, and he never should've done that. I was too young to be told something like that."

"Katherine is very mature for her age."

"She almost told Rachel about it!"

He pauses, and I see a hint of a smile. "That would've been a shame. Your bride terminated because of a simple misunderstanding?"

I get in his face. "What the fuck are you saying? You did this on purpose? Did you tell Katherine to tell Rachel?"

"Of course not." He backs away. "Katherine simply didn't know the rules."

"It's your job to tell her the rules."

"I'll be sure to have a talk with her." He turns toward her room, but then turns back. "I assume you heard the news."

"What news?"

"Your punishment has been decided." He smirks. "Well, it still has to be voted on by the higher level members, but I'm sure it will be approved."

"How do you know this?"

"Your father told me. It's too bad you two aren't speaking. Perhaps if you were, he'd keep you up to date on such matters."

"What is it? What's the punishment?"

"I'm not allowed to say. Now if you'll excuse me." He walks away.

"Leland, wait!"

He ignores me as he knocks on Katherine's door. "Katherine, open the door. Your mother is looking for you."

She opens the door and he goes inside.

I can tell when Leland's lying and he wasn't lying just now. He knows what my punishment is and he refuses to tell me. I wonder who else knows. Would Jack know?

I go back to the party. Rachel's probably wondering where I am. I've been gone for at least fifteen minutes. I see Jack by the bar, laughing too loud and getting dirty looks from people. He's clearly drunk.

"Jack." I hold his arm. "I need to talk to you. In private."

"Where's that bride of yours?" he asks, stumbling a little as I lead him to the study that's just off the living room. "She's a nice girl, that one. Martha already loves her like a daughter. She goes on and on about her."

I close the door to the study. "What's my punishment?"

Jack sits down in one of the leather chairs. "Punishment for what?"

"Marrying, Rachel! Dammit, Jack, how drunk *are* you?"

"Drunk enough to tell off your father." He chuckles.

"You were fighting with my father?"

"He's furious that you're working for me. I told him to get the fuck over it." Jack yanks off his shoe. "Damn shoes. They still haven't loosened up."

I take his shoe and toss it on the floor. "Jack, pay attention. Do you know what my punishment is or not?"

"How the hell would *I* know that? Only the people at the top know." He yanks his other shoe off. "I'm walking around in my socks the rest of the night. If they want to complain, they can throw my ass out of here."

"Leland said he knew."

"Knew what?" Jack's rubbing his foot.

I sigh. "What my punishment would be. Leland said my father told him. Why would my father tell Leland and no one else? Or do you think other people know?"

Jack sits back in the chair. "No. I think it's just Leland."

"Why Leland?"

"Because your punishment could affect the future of Kensington Chemical, which he has a vested interest in."

"Since when does Leland have a vested interest in the company? What are you not telling me, Jack?"

"Last year, Leland and your father were trying to work a deal between Kensington Chemical and MDX Aerodynamics."

"What kind of deal?"

"I don't know the details. I shouldn't even know about it. I only do because I overhead them talking about it after one of our meetings. But I don't think the deal ever went through. At the meeting in December I noticed the two of them arguing and your father looked even more angry than usual."

"You think Leland was the one who called off the deal?

He nods. "I'm assuming he refused to do business with your father after you married Rachel. Leland thinks she's trash. He even calls her that. Then again, most everyone here tonight thinks that way about people without money so it's not that surprising."

It's true, but it still fills me with rage to know that people think that way about Rachel.

"If there's no deal, then why would my father tell Leland my punishment? Leland wouldn't care."

"Why are you asking me this shit?" Jack raises his foot up and adjusts his sock. "I have no idea if any of this is true. It's just a theory."

I take a moment to think this through. What kind of deal would Leland have with my father? I know both of them want to get contracts with the military. So is that what the deal was? To somehow work together to get government contracts?

"I was supposed to go work for Leland," I say, thinking aloud.

"Work for Leland? Why would you work for that asshole?"

"My father set it up. But why would Leland want me working for him if he's so disgusted with me being with Rachel?"

"Huh." Jack glances to the side, rubbing his hand over his chin. "That doesn't make sense, now does it?"

"No. It doesn't. Do you have any idea why he might do that?"

"Maybe. But I don't care to share it."

"Jack. Tell me."

He looks back at me. "Again, it's just a theory, but if Leland wanted you working for him, maybe it's because he thinks the deal with Kensington Chemical will still happen. Which it will if Rachel is gone."

"You're saying that's my punishment? No. That doesn't make sense. Why would they go through with a big public wedding if they were just going to force me to get a divorce later?"

Jack's expression turns dark, his eyes fixed on me. "I'm not talking about a divorce."

My breath catches in my throat. "No. They wouldn't do that. My father wouldn't let them. He'd find a different way. He has no problem killing people he doesn't know, but he wouldn't harm my wife. And he wouldn't let them do it either."

"Maybe not. But Leland would. He'd do it himself. Especially if doing so would benefit his company."

"Jack, no. That's taking it too far. He wouldn't do that."

"You need to see people for who they are, Pearce. Leland has no connection to Rachel. He doesn't care about her."

237

"Shit." I clench my fists, prepared to walk out the door and go kill that asshole right now. "I won't let him near her."

"Pearce." Jack is in front of me now. "Don't act on this. It's just a theory. I could be completely off-base. But as I've told you many times, trust no one."

I stand there, trying to put this together. Seeing if it could be true.

"Do you really think that's my punishment?" I ask.

He shrugs. "Maybe your punishment has nothing to do with Rachel, which would explain why Leland might come after her. He has to take matters into his own hands."

"But doing so would get him in trouble with the organization. With all the wedding coverage in the media, Rachel is becoming well-known. If Leland did something to her, reporters would investigate, and that's the last thing the organization wants. Leland wouldn't put himself at risk like that, would he?"

"Goddammit, Pearce. I don't have all the answers." He sits down again and forces his shoes back on his feet. "I'm just making shit up here. And the fact that you believe me without question is concerning." He stands up, adjusting his feet in the shoes, then walks over to me. "You need to start thinking the way *they* do. The way all the members do. You have to constantly be on the lookout, questioning your fellow members' actions, listening closely to what they say, searching for ulterior motives. I know it's a shitty way to live, but it's what you have to do. It's every man for himself, and you're dealing with some ruthless bastards who will do most anything to get ahead. I've done my fair share of bad shit to get where I am and I don't regret it. If I hadn't done those things, those bastards would've walked all over me. They already don't respect me, so I sure as hell wasn't going to let them win. I've fought for everything I have, and now I own one of the most successful companies in the world. But it wouldn't have happened if I hadn't played dirty."

"So what do I do about Leland?"

"Just act normal. You don't know anything for sure, and you don't want Rachel suspecting something's wrong. When you see

Leland at the meetings, be overly friendly to him. It'll take him off guard. Say something about Rachel and see how he reacts. Watch his eyes. His mouth. Look for the slightest movements, because those are the most telling. If he reacts, then you'll know he's up to something."

"I might already have the answer," I say, remembering my earlier conversation with him. "When I talked to Leland just now, he said it would be a shame if something happened to Rachel. He was being sarcastic, which just proves he's planning something. Fuck!"

"No! That's not what it means. Dammit, Pearce! What did I just say? You need to think like them. They're cunning. Deceitful."

"What are you saying?"

"Leland was just playing you. Wanting you to think he'd come after Rachel. If that's really what he was planning, he wouldn't come out and admit to it. You should've told me this earlier. Now my whole theory is shit."

"You said it was shit anyway."

"Yes, but at least it was something." He sighs. "Maybe Leland's just planning a way to get you to divorce her. Or for her to divorce you." He nods. "Yes, that makes more sense. They know you won't leave her, but she might leave you, if she were presented with the right evidence."

"What evidence?"

"Evidence that you're cheating. Or doing something else she doesn't approve of."

"They'll never have evidence of that. And your theory still doesn't explain why Leland would offer me a job."

"Maybe he owed your father a favor. Holton *did* bail Leland out of that financial scandal a few years ago."

"I suppose it's possible. But I'm still worried that Leland might be up to something."

"Then keep a closer eye on Rachel. Or I'll do it. I'll install cameras on her car. See if anyone's following her."

"Can you do it soon?"

"Drive her car to the office on Monday and I'll do it then." Jack opens the door. "Come on. I'm sure our wives are wondering where the hell we are."

We meet up with them back in the living room.

Rachel's smiling and seems much happier than when we arrived, probably because she's talking to Martha, the only nice woman here. The rest of the women won't even speak to Rachel. Instead, they stand around gossiping about her.

"Where have you been?" Rachel asks. "I was starting to think you weren't coming back."

"Sorry. I got stuck talking to some people."

"It's fine. Martha's been keeping me company."

"Can we adopt her, Jack?" Martha says kiddingly. "I love this girl, and I always wanted another daughter."

"After all the headaches our girls gave you?" He shakes his head. "Two was plenty."

"You'll have to meet our daughters sometime," Martha says to Rachel.

"Yes, I'd love to. Do they have any children?"

"No," Jack answers. "And they better hurry the hell up. I want grandchildren before I'm dead. And the way I drink, I could go at any time."

Martha rolls her eyes.

"I think we'll head home," I say, securing my arm around Rachel's waist.

"Are you sure?" she asks. "We haven't been here that long."

"I know, but I have a headache and the noise in here is getting to me."

"Okay." She hugs Martha. "I hope to see you again soon."

"Yes. We'll have you over for dinner."

"Steaks." Jack points to Rachel. "Medium-rare."

She laughs. "Yes. Medium-rare."

"Goodnight, Martha," I say to her. "Jack, I'll see you Monday."

We make our way back to the front of the house. I flag down the maid and we wait for our coats. Then I tell the valet to get our car.

"Leaving so soon?" Leland comes up next to me.

I give him a big, friendly smile. "Yes, we need to head out. But perhaps we could meet for drinks next time you're in town."

"Yes, I'd like that. I'll give you a call."

He didn't react to my invitation or my over-the-top smile. No pause. No change in facial expression. Nothing.

"Rachel, it was good to finally meet you," he says, shaking her hand.

Again, nothing seems odd about their exchange. He's acting completely normal.

The maid brings our coats and we say goodbye to Leland and go out to the car, which is waiting for us out front.

I'm quiet on the drive home. I tell Rachel it's because of my headache, but it's really because I'm thinking. Trying to figure out what went on tonight. Am I just being paranoid? I didn't think so when I was at the party, but now I do. Leland wouldn't hurt Rachel. Because he knows if he did, I'd kill him, and I'd have no problem doing it.

So he must have said those things just to rile me up. He does that all the time. With everyone. I know that about him, so why did I let him get to me like that? Jack's right. I need to be more on guard around these people. I need to see through their conniving ways and be just as conniving back. I don't want to be that way, but if I'm not, I won't survive.

Almost two weeks have gone by and nothing has happened. By nothing, I mean nobody has been following Rachel. Jack installed those cameras on her car and I've been monitoring them, but haven't seen anything unusual.

I met Royce for lunch last week and told him about Leland. I don't know if I should've done that. I know I can't trust Royce, but I can't trust any of them and I needed information and Royce always seems to know things he shouldn't. He's able to get people to talk and spill secrets, so he can be quite useful sometimes.

Royce told me Leland's company was just awarded two government contracts but it hasn't been announced publicly yet.

So if that's true, then Leland doesn't need whatever help my father offered him. Which means he has no motive to go after Rachel.

When I told Royce my suspicions about Leland, he laughed and said Leland has better things to do than concern himself with my love life. It's true. And by the time our lunch was over, I'd convinced myself to stop obsessing over Leland.

Since then, I've felt somewhat relieved, but I'm still nervous about what my punishment will be. Leland said it's been decided but not approved. So when will it be approved? Why is it taking so long? I wish they'd just punish me and get it over with. I don't want this hanging over my head for the next six months or however long they might take to do this.

"I'm nervous," Rachel says, squeezing my hand.

"I know, sweetheart." I pick up her hand and kiss it.

We're sitting in the doctor's office. Rachel had her appointment the other day and now we're here for the results. She's been so anxious about this she's barely slept. I haven't either. I keep switching back and forth between wanting a child and not wanting one. There are pros and cons to both sides, but the cons usually win out because of the organization and what it could mean for my child's future.

"Good afternoon." The doctor walks in the room, closing the door behind her. She says hello to Rachel, then says to me, "I'm Dr. Perkins. I assume you're Rachel's fiancé?"

"Yes. Pearce Kensington."

I haven't met the doctor before. I offered to go with Rachel to her appointment the other day, but she wanted to go alone.

Dr. Perkins sits at her desk, setting a file down in front of her. "So, I have some good news and some not-so-good news."

"Start with the good," Rachel says.

Dr. Perkins smiles. "The good news is that getting pregnant shouldn't be a problem. Everything looks good in that regard."

"And the bad news?" Rachel asks as she squeezes my hand.

"I didn't say it was bad. It just isn't as good as I'd hoped it would be." She sets the folder aside and focuses on Rachel. "Your previous doctor was incorrect in saying you could never have children."

Rachel exhales a breath and loosens her grip on my hand.

"But it will be difficult to carry a baby to term. Not impossible. But difficult. Given your condition, your risk for miscarriage is much higher than for other women. In fact, it's possible that you'll have multiple miscarriages before you have a successful pregnancy. That can take a toll on both of you and can sometimes drive couples apart. So that's something to think about."

"Is there anything we could do to reduce the chance of a miscarriage?" Rachel lets go of my hand and I put my arm around her.

"Yes. We could try limiting your activity to as little as possible, especially in the early stages of your pregnancy."

"Do you mean bed rest?"

"Yes. Complete bed rest until you're at least sixteen weeks along, maybe longer. I can't say for sure until we're at that stage. We'd closely monitor you and make decisions as we go along. This won't be a typical pregnancy, but it's not something we haven't dealt with before."

"So other women like me have had success?"

"Yes. Many women just like you have given birth to healthy babies, but it sometimes takes several tries and you have to be willing to spend all those months in bed. I had one woman who spent nearly her entire pregnancy in bed."

Rachel nods. "I'm willing to do that. I'll do whatever it takes."

The doctor opens the folder and goes over Rachel's test results in more detail. I should be listening, but instead I'm trying to accept that this is really going to happen. We're going to try to have a baby. We have to. I can't tell Rachel no. She wants this way too much.

I'm still torn about what I want. Part of me was hoping the news would be bad so that having a child wouldn't even be an option. That's horrible of me to think that, knowing how devastated Rachel would've been. But if she knew the truth about

243

the organization and what it might mean for our child's future, would she still want a baby? She probably would. Her positive outlook would convince her we could get our child out of it. So that's what I need to do. I need to think that way. I need to hold out hope. Otherwise, I can't go through with this.

"It will be a high-risk pregnancy."

The words 'high-risk' catch my attention and I focus back on the doctor.

"What does that mean?" I ask her. "Rachel's health could be at risk?"

"Most likely the baby's health," she answers. "Although there could be complications for Rachel as well. Bed rest can be hard on the body and she could have a difficult delivery."

Rachel glances at me. "It's okay. I'm willing to take the risk."

I'm not. But I keep quiet as the doctor explains the other complications that could occur. By the time she's done, I'm not feeling good about this. My fears about the organization and about being a father have been replaced by my fears about what could happen to Rachel. The doctor assured us that the risk of serious complications is small, but that doesn't calm my fears.

"So what are the next steps?" Rachel asks.

"You and Pearce should take some time to discuss this. If you decide to move forward, we'll start you on prenatal vitamins and get you off the pill. But before we do that, I want you to eliminate the stress in your life. I know it's not possible to eliminate all of it, but you need to reduce it as much as you can. Doing so will increase the chances for pregnancy, and later, decrease the chance of a miscarriage."

"We're getting married in March and then moving into a house," I say. "I assume that's too much stress?"

"Yes," the doctor says to both of us. "A wedding and a move are both stressful, even though they're happy events. I would suggest maybe waiting until this summer, when you're settled in the house and things have calmed down. But that's up to you. I wouldn't wait *too* long because things will only become more difficult the older you get." She checks her folder again. "Rachel, you'll be turning 25 this summer?"

"Yes."

"That's a good age to start trying. I wouldn't want you to wait much longer than that."

She wraps up by giving us some information to take home and read over. Then we leave and go out to the car. I hold Rachel's door open for her, but instead of getting in, she hugs me and I hear her sniffling.

She's crying. I don't know what that means. Is she happy or sad?

CHAPTER TWENTY-TWO

RACHEL

I just got my test results and the results showed that I can have a baby. It's possible. It's really possible!

We just left the doctor's office and I'm a crying mess. Pearce probably thinks I'm crazy, but I couldn't help it. As soon as I walked out of the clinic, it hit me that I could be a mom, and my emotions just overwhelmed me.

"Rachel," Pearce says as he hugs me. "What's wrong?"

I pull back and smile at him. "Nothing's wrong." I wipe my eyes. "These are tears of joy. I was prepared for bad news, but instead I found out we can have a baby. Pearce, I'm so happy." I hug him again.

He's not saying anything. Is he not happy about this? What if he's not? What if he didn't want this?

I let go of him and look at his face. It's not showing any emotion. And he's still not saying anything.

He holds open my door and I get in the car and wait until he gets in on the other side.

"You aren't happy," I say quietly, my eyes on my lap.

"What?" The car is running and I don't think he heard me.

"You aren't happy about the news." I say it louder this time.

He puts his hand on my knee. "Of course I'm happy."

"No. You're not. I can tell."

"Can we talk about this at home?"

I nod, and focus out the side window as he pulls out of the parking lot. The silence makes the drive back to the loft go painfully slow. And as we drive, I get more and more angry. How could he not want this? I know he's afraid to be a father, but he needs to get over it. All men are scared of fatherhood. My mom said my dad was scared to death. He was even afraid to hold my sister and me because he was sure he'd drop us on our heads. But he got over his fears, and then he loved being a dad. I know Pearce would too.

When we're back at the loft, we both sit on the couch and I wait for Pearce to speak.

"I know how much you want a child," he says, "but I don't like what you'll have to go through in order to *have* that child."

"Pearce, I've already thought about this. I knew if this was possible that it wouldn't be easy, and I'm okay with that."

"Well, I'm not sure that I am."

"You're not the one going through it. I am. And I'm ready for whatever happens."

"We'll be going through this together, Rachel. It's not just you. And I don't want to watch the woman I love suffer for nine months."

"Bed rest is not suffering."

"The doctor mentioned numerous complications. Not just for the baby, but for you."

It's true, but I want a baby so much that I don't care about myself. I'll suffer through anything to have a child.

"And what about the risk for miscarriage?" Pearce asks. "Do you really think you can go through that again?"

"Yes," I say, but my voice lacks confidence. Because honestly, I fear that most of all. I was devastated after my last miscarriage and I don't want to go through that again. But I'm prepared to.

"It's different than when it happened before," I tell him. "This time I have you. Before, I had my parents, who were a huge help, but I needed Adam, and he left me. You won't do that. So it'll be different this time."

"It will still be a huge loss. It won't be any easier, even with me here to support you."

247

"You're right," I say, admitting it to both him and myself. "It won't be easy, and I don't want to go through that again. But I know I can do it. And I know that once I hold our baby in my arms that everything I had to go through to get to that point will be worth it." A tear slides down my cheek. "Please don't deny me this, Pearce. I love you, and I want us to have a baby. Whatever it takes to have one, I'll do it. And if it doesn't happen, we at least tried."

He doesn't say anything. He looks down at my hand and holds it, lightly rubbing it with his thumb.

He's quiet. Too quiet. Because he doesn't want to say what he's thinking. Another tear slips down my cheek. He doesn't want this. He doesn't want a baby. I finally found out I can have one, and now the man I love doesn't want one.

I shut my eyes, trying to hold back the tears. Pearce kept hinting that he may not want this so I shouldn't be surprised, but that doesn't make it hurt any less.

Why didn't he tell me this before? How could he make me go through all those tests, knowing he didn't want children? How could he do that to me? Was he hoping the tests would show I couldn't have a baby so that he wouldn't have to tell me no?

We should've talked about this before we got married, but now it's too late. And as much as I want a child, I'd never divorce Pearce because of this. I'm angry with him, and his decision hurts me, but I still love him. I'll always love him, and I have to accept his decision. We both have to want this. I would never trick him into it, or threaten to leave if he didn't agree to it. I want him to *want* a baby, not be forced into having one.

But he doesn't want one. *He doesn't want a child.* The words echo in my head and my throat burns as I try not to break down sobbing for the intense loss I'm feeling right now. Loss for what I could've had.

"I don't know how to change a diaper," he says, still gazing down at my hand.

"What?" I ask, not sure I heard him right.

His eyes return to mine. "I don't know how to change a diaper. I don't have the slightest idea how you even put one on."

More tears slide down my cheeks, but I'm smiling. "What are you saying, Pearce?"

"I'm saying that I'm going to need some instruction. I don't even know how to hold a baby. They're so small and their heads don't seem very stable."

I swallow and wipe my tears. "Are you saying we can try?"

"Yes. We can try."

I reach around him and tightly hug his chest, my tears soaking into his shirt. They're happy tears because I'm so relieved. So happy he wants this.

He kisses my head and I lift my face up to his. He looks serious again and I worry about what he's thinking.

I sit back. "Are you only doing this because you know how much I want a baby?"

"No. I want one too. But I still have concerns about what you'll have to go through. I'm willing to try this, but if it gets to the point that your health is suffering, either emotionally or physically, then we're not going to continue trying."

I nod. "Okay."

"And if you become pregnant and there are complications, with either the pregnancy or the delivery, that put your health at risk, then we are not doing this again. If that's the case, then we are only having one child."

"I would be happy with one." I smile. "Can we celebrate now?"

He smiles back. "Yes. I'm sorry I wasn't more enthusiastic earlier. I know how much this means to you and I should've reacted differently when we got the results. I was just feeling a little overwhelmed at the doctor's office. What would you like to do to celebrate?"

"Maybe go out to dinner?" I kiss him. "And then maybe do a little practicing?" I smile. "If we want to make a baby this summer, we really should start practicing."

He kisses me and leans me back on the couch. "We're going to practice right now."

"Let's do it later. I'm starving and I want to call my mom quick and tell her the news."

He sighs and sits back. "Go ahead."

I get up, but lean down to his ear and whisper, "I promise we'll do lots of practicing tonight. Lots."

He swats my butt. "Then hurry up so we can go to dinner and get home."

I call my mom and she's thrilled. She always told me to get a second opinion but I kept putting it off. I didn't tell her the risks because she'd worry too much. She's not as overprotective of me as she used to be, but when it comes to my health, she still worries.

The next day I meet Shelby for lunch to tell her my news. Since I invited her, I told her I'm paying. I picked a really nice restaurant. She's probably still eating mac and cheese every night so I wanted her to have a good meal at lunch.

Shelby is doing much better now. She's still sad about her dad, but she's working through her grief and slowly getting back to her old self. Logan's been helping her get through it. He lives here in Connecticut now so they see each other all the time.

"Is Pearce excited that he might be a dad someday?" she asks, as we're waiting for our order.

"Excited probably isn't the word." I laugh. "More like scared. Or nervous. He worries he won't be a good dad. He's never spent any time around babies or kids."

"I haven't either. I don't think I could take care of a kid."

"Really? I thought you wanted kids someday."

"No. I'm not the mom type. I'm not nurturing."

"Yes, you are. You'd be a great mom."

"Why?"

"You're fun. You have lots of energy. You don't overreact to stuff. Those are all good qualities for being a mom. And I bet your mom would love to have grandkids."

She rolls her eyes. "She tells me that all the time."

"How does Logan feel about kids?"

"He wants them. He says he wants two, but I think he'd take three or four if his wife would give him that many."

I smile at her. "So are you willing you to give him that many?"

She laughs. "Yeah, right. I just told you I'm not the mom type. So three or four kids? Not going to happen. Neither is one or two."

"Have you told Logan that?"

"Why would I? I'm not marrying him."

"Then why are you two still dating?"

"Because I like him. We have fun together and he treats me well."

"You can't date him forever. Eventually he'll want to get married."

"Then I guess that's when we'll break up."

"Shelby, why wouldn't you marry him? Are you afraid to get married? Or is he just not the one?"

"Why do you always ask such personal questions?" She sounds annoyed.

"Because I'm your friend. Friends always ask personal questions. If I didn't, we wouldn't be friends. We'd just be acquaintances." I take a sip of my iced tea. "So is he the one or not?"

She sighs dramatically. "Fine. He's the one. Are you happy now?"

I can't tell if she's being serious or joking with me.

"Aren't you going to say something?" she asks.

"Yes. I'm just surprised that you said that. I thought you'd say he's not the one. But if he is, then why wouldn't you marry him someday?"

"Because I don't want to get married. I'm not the marrying type. Just like I'm not the mom type. That lifestyle just doesn't fit me. I'm meant to be single."

"You only feel that way because you're 22. In a few years—"

"I'm 23, but that doesn't mean I want to get married."

"Did you just have a birthday?"

"It was in December. Right after the funeral. I didn't feel like celebrating."

"You should've told me you had a birthday. I would've got you a gift."

"You're buying me lunch. That's good enough."

"No, it's not. I'll get you something and give it to you later. So going back to Logan, maybe you should move in with him. Test out living together."

"He asked me to but..." She messes with the napkin in her lap. "It's not a good idea."

"Why? Because you'd have to move? It's just a half hour away. You could still go visit your mom. And I'm sure you could get a job there. Maybe one with full time hours."

Our food arrives and she changes the subject. She doesn't want to talk about Logan, but she won't tell me why. We've been friends for months and she still won't open up to me.

"Is everything ready for the wedding?" she asks.

"Yes. I had a final fitting for the dress last week. It's such a gorgeous dress."

"And you didn't even have to pay for it."

"I know. But the designer is getting a ton of press so he's coming out ahead. We're also getting the cake for free because the bakery wants the publicity."

"Isn't it weird how rich people always get free stuff? The people who can most afford it don't have to pay for it."

"I wish you were coming to the wedding."

"I can't cancel this trip. I've had it planned for months."

"I know, but I still wish you were coming."

Shelby is going to Florida the weekend of my wedding. She's staying with her cousin in Fort Lauderdale. She said she planned the trip months ago, yet she never even mentioned it until I told her the date of the wedding. And she didn't seem upset that she was missing it, which kind of hurt my feelings. But maybe she just doesn't like weddings.

"Rachel. We meet again."

I look up and see Leland Seymour standing next to me. I haven't decided what I think of this man. He tries to act nice, but I think it's a fake nice.

"Hello, Mr. Seymour."

"Please. Call me Leland." He smiles. "And who is your—" He stops when he sees Shelby. "Your friend." He says it slow and grins even wider.

Shelby's reaching under the table for her purse.

"Leland, this is Shelby."

"Shelby." He rubs his thumb and finger over his chin. "What an interesting name. You know, you look more like a Sophia."

She abruptly gets up, almost falling off her chair. "I have to use the ladies' room."

Leland watches her leave. "Are you and Shelby good friends?"

"Yes. I met her back in September. We lived in the same apartment building."

"Is she coming to the wedding?"

"No. She'll be out of town."

"What a shame. I'm sure you'd love to have her there." He gets that big grin on his face again. It's strange, and making me uncomfortable.

"So what are you doing in New Haven?" I ask. "That's a long drive from your new house."

"My daughter wanted to look at colleges."

"Katherine is here?"

"Yes, we're on the other side of the dining room." He points to their table and I see Katherine sitting there, applying her lipstick. "She just turned 16 and she wants to start looking at schools. Her sister, Caroline, will be starting Yale in the fall."

"Is that where Katherine wants to go?"

"Yes, but..." He lowers his voice. "She's not Yale material. We're looking at some other colleges in the area. Maybe Moorhurst. That's about a half hour from here."

"I've heard that's a very good school."

"It's not Yale, but it would be a better fit for Katherine. Well, I'll let you and your friend get back to lunch."

Shelby takes forever in the bathroom, and when she finally comes out, she stands by the table and takes her keys from her purse. "I'm not feeling well. I have to go. I'm really sorry I couldn't finish lunch."

I stand up. "That's okay. We'll just try again some other time. Do you need me to drive you home? You shouldn't drive if you're sick."

"I'll be fine."

I hug her. "I'll call you later to make sure you're okay."

She smiles. "See? That's why you should be a mom and I shouldn't. I'd never tell someone that."

"You need to call your doctor boyfriend and ask him to come stay with you. I bet he could make you feel better," I tease.

"You need to stop with the matchmaking."

"I'm not matchmaking. I don't need to. You two are already a match."

She rolls her eyes. "Bye, Rachel."

"Bye."

I've only eaten half of my lunch but I'm full so I ask the waiter for the check.

"It's on us," he says, smiling.

"Um, that's okay." I get out my wallet. "I'll just pay."

"Miss Evans, the manager would really like to pay for your meal. And if you enjoyed it, perhaps you could tell your friends."

So this is a business deal. A free meal in exchange for my help in getting more people to come to this restaurant. The manager knows who I am and he assumes I know other rich people. The kind of people he wants at his restaurant. I don't want to argue with the waiter, so I thank him, then get my coat and leave.

I've had a lot of these encounters recently. There's been a lot of press about the wedding so people are starting to recognize me. I'll go to a restaurant or just out for coffee and the manager offers to pay my bill. I even had this happen at the dry cleaners. They wouldn't let me pay. Pearce said I shouldn't even be going to the dry cleaners because it looks bad. I'm supposed to have the dry cleaning picked up and delivered. I wondered why they looked at me funny when I went there and told them my name.

I'm still not used to living this way. Not being able to do things for myself. Having people know who I am. And things will change even more once I'm officially Mrs. Kensington, which will happen in just a few short weeks.

CHAPTER TWENTY-THREE
The Wedding

PEARCE

It's the middle of March and today, Rachel and I are getting married. Again. This time in front of six hundred people. The guest list includes some of my fellow Dunamis members and their families, some friends of my parents, and a few celebrities tossed in to attract more media attention to the event. I don't know who else was invited. The organization sees this as a high-level networking event, so I know there are prominent businessmen and politicians here as well.

Rachel's parents are here, of course. They've been here all week. Jack gave me the week off so I could spend time with them, as well as take care of anything that needed to be done for the wedding. But everything was basically done. All I had to do was have a final tux fitting.

Rachel and her mom have spent the past week getting the new house ready. We've owned the house since early February, and Rachel has spent the past month painting the walls and putting up new window treatments. I told her we could hire people to do those things, but she wanted to do them herself.

We bought new furniture, which was delivered a few weeks ago, and Rachel has stocked the kitchen with mixers and blenders and other things we don't have and won't receive as wedding gifts. The people I know don't give toasters for wedding gifts. They give vacations or expensive paintings or rare antique items we'll have no use for.

I'm looking forward to moving into the house. I like my loft, but the house feels more like a home. It's warm and inviting and I can see Rachel's personality in how it's decorated. I like that. I'll feel like she's there even when she's not.

We kept my leather couch and chairs for the living room, then bought a navy fabric-covered couch for the family room, along with several tables, including ones for the dining room and kitchen. Rachel prefers wood furniture, like I do, so all the tables are wood.

I grew up in a house filled with glass tables, which I hated because if I touched them I would get yelled at for leaving fingerprints behind. Everything at that house was breakable or too valuable to be touched, so I had to be extremely cautious growing up. And my parents' furniture is either beige or white so I always had to be careful not to spill anything.

My parents would cringe if they saw my house. Actually, most everyone I know would, even people my own age. They prefer to live in a house like my parents have; one with glass tables and crystal chandeliers and beige furniture. If I'd been forced to marry someone else, I'd be living in that type of house.

"Your bride would like to see you." Henry walks into the groom's dressing room, where I'm ready and waiting in my tux. The ceremony starts in ten minutes.

Rachel and I are getting married in a large historic church. My first marriage also took place in a church, which is odd because my family is not religious. The only time we go to church is for weddings and funerals.

"Is she almost ready?" I ask.

"She's ready, but she's nervous having all those people out there. She said you're always able to calm her down."

"I'll go see her." I stand up, straightening my tux jacket.

"Pearce." Henry smiles. "I just wanted to say that I'm glad my daughter found you. You're a good man, and I've never seen Rachel this happy before."

"I promise to *keep* her happy. I love her very much."

"I know you do." He smiles even wider and pats me on the back. "Now go see your girl."

I spent most of last week with Henry while Rachel and her mother were out shopping for things for the house. Henry and I went to a few sports bars and watched basketball. We also played pool and he gave me some tips to improve my shots. Then after dinner every night, we'd play a few games of poker.

It's sad that I've never done those things with my own father. I've only known Henry a few months, but he feels more like a real father to me than my own. My father hasn't spoken to me since the party at the Seymour mansion. My mother hasn't either. I'll see them today and they'll smile for the crowd, but by tomorrow they'll go back to not speaking to me.

I walk down the narrow hallway to the bride's dressing room. Rachel and I already had our photos done so I've seen her in her dress, but when I knock on the door and she answers, I'm once again taken aback by how beautiful she looks.

Her dress is strapless and fitted on top, then goes out at the waist into a full skirt. It looks like something a princess would wear. It's a simple design but has intricate beading on the upper half.

It's not just the dress that makes her beautiful. It's her. She has such a glow about her today. She had it at our first wedding as well. But today it's back and even brighter than before, because now she's with her family and some of her friends. And in less than an hour, everyone will know her as Rachel Kensington. We'll no longer have to pretend. I think I'm glowing a little too because of that. I'm so proud to call her my wife, and soon I'll finally be able to do that.

"Pearce." She gives me a loose hug, not wanting to mess up her dress or her hair. Her hair is up and fitted with the veil.

"Your father said you wanted to see me."

"Yes." She steps aside, and when I go in the room I see all her bridesmaids there. They smile at me as they get up and leave. At least Rachel was allowed to pick her bridesmaids. I was allowed to pick my groomsmen, but I didn't really have anyone to pick. I'm not close friends with anyone and I haven't stayed in touch with my college friends. So Royce ended up as my best man and the remaining groomsmen are other men my age from the organization. I know all of them and went to high school with a couple of them but we aren't really friends.

"I'm nervous," Rachel says once the girls are gone. "Did you see how many people are out there?"

I hold her hands. "You'll do fine. You just have to repeat what the minister says, then say 'I do.' It's as simple as that. Just ignore all those people."

She smiles and squeezes my hand. "Soon I'll be your wife."

"You already are my wife."

"But now everyone will call me that. Maybe they'll accept me now."

"Rachel, don't worry about them. Those people aren't your friends and they never will be. You're far too good for them."

She gazes at me with those bright blue eyes. "I love you."

"I love you too." I lean down and softly kiss her. "Now are you ready to do this?"

"Maybe one more kiss for good luck?"

I kiss her again.

"Okay," she whispers over my lips. "Now I'm ready."

I go around her to the door, but stop when I see an envelope lying on the small table in front of the mirror where the girls were doing their makeup. The envelope is the size of a greeting card, but it hasn't been opened.

"Is this from your parents?" I ask.

She turns around. "No. They put their card with all the other ones. Where did you find that?"

"It was on this table, but it only has your name on it, not mine."

"Go ahead and open it. I need to put my shoes on." She sits down on one of the chairs and reaches for her shoes.

I open the envelope, but instead of a card being inside, there are three photos. The photos were taken the night of the banquet that was held after the Dunamis meeting in December. They show Shelby and me talking during the cocktail hour, then us walking down the hall, then going into the hotel room together. The photos are stamped on the back with the time and date of when they were taken.

My muscles tighten and I clench my hand into a fist as rage consumes me. Someone planted these photos here, hoping Rachel would see them and call off the wedding. It was obviously one of my fellow members, but which one? Who would do that? And how did they get access to this room?

"Pearce, I think I need my mom to help me with the shoes. I can't even find my feet with this dress on."

I shove the photos and the envelope in my pocket. "Yes, I'll go get her."

"Wait. Who was the card from?"

"It wasn't a card," I say, trying to sound calm, despite feeling like I want to go kill someone. "It was just a note from the church, telling you when services are, in case you want to attend sometime."

"Maybe we should."

I open the door and see both our mothers there.

"Rachel could use some help with her shoes," I say to Beth.

She walks in the room, but my mother stays at the door. "They need you to go line up."

My mother hasn't been in this room yet, so she couldn't have planted those photos. And I've had Jack keeping an eye on my father all day.

Who else could it be? I suppose anyone could've paid someone to drop off that envelope. I just don't know who did it, unless...

"Is Leland here?" I ask my mother.

"Of course he is. The whole Seymour family is here."

"Oh, Pearce," Rachel says. "I forgot to tell you that I saw Leland a couple weeks ago when I was out having lunch with Shelby."

I turn back to her. "Leland saw you and Shelby?"

"Yes. He came over and talked to us."

So he knows they're friends. Even more reason for him to share those photos. He knows it would be even worse if Rachel thought I was having an affair with her friend. And he's right. If Rachel saw those photos, I don't think she'd believe me when I told her there was nothing going on between Shelby and me. Not after the earring incident. Rachel knows I slept with Shelby and those photos would convince her that it's still going on.

"Was Leland with anyone else?" I ask her.

"He was with Katherine. They were looking at colleges."

"Pearce." My mother tugs on my arm. "You need to go."

"Yes. I'm going. Rachel, I'll see you out there."

I'm livid about those photos, but I have to shove my anger aside and focus on the ceremony. So for the next half hour, that's what I do. I focus on Rachel's beautiful face. Her radiant smile. Her voice as she says our vows.

The ceremony goes flawlessly. Neither one of us even stumbled on our vows. To the people watching, I'm sure it looked like the perfect wedding. I would've thought so too, if it weren't for those photos.

If Rachel had seen them, we wouldn't be standing here now, holding hands and facing our guests, as the minister says, "And now, for the very first time, I am pleased to introduce Pearce and Rachel Kensington. Pearce, you may kiss your bride."

I give her a kiss, then look in her eyes and whisper, "I love you."

"I love you too." Her whole face is beaming, even more so than before the wedding.

As I lead her down the aisle, Rachel is smiling the entire way. This may have been a fake wedding, but it's still a wedding and I can see how happy it's made her. Unlike our Vegas wedding, this one is in a beautiful setting and Rachel has her parents here.

When we get to the hotel ballroom where we're having the reception, Rachel stops for a moment, trying to take it all in. It really is incredible. It's a very large ballroom and there are flowers everywhere. We could smell them as soon as we walked in.

Rachel loves flowers, so this is perfect for her. There are flowers on the tables and in tall planters all around the room and along the perimeter of the dance floor. And tall green topiaries are scattered about, adorned with twinkling white lights.

"What do you think?" I ask her.

"It's absolutely beautiful. And the scent." She inhales it. "It smells just like a flower garden."

We're introduced again, then have our first dance to music played by a live orchestra. The reception continues with a cocktail hour, followed by dinner.

After dinner, I see Leland leaving the ballroom. I tell Rachel I need to use the restroom, then hurry to find him.

"Leland!" I say, stopping him.

He turns around. "Pearce." He shakes my hand. "Congratulations."

"Yes, unfortunately for you, your plan didn't work."

"What plan are you referring to?"

"Why did you do it?" I know why, but I want him to admit it.

"I have no idea what you're talking about. Have you been drinking?"

"The photos. The ones in her dressing room."

"What photos?"

"She said you saw her with Shelby."

He chuckles. "Yes, how ironic that your wife is close friends with one of our associates. Although I know her as Sophia. You've been with her, haven't you, Pearce?"

"So you admit it. You planted those photos, hoping it would end my relationship with Rachel."

His eyes narrow. "Your marriage will end on its own, without my help or anyone else's. You don't belong with her, Pearce. Everyone knows it. Even you. I don't know if this is some attempt to get back at your father, or what your motives are, but this marriage will never last. You're a blue blood. She's white trash. So if—"

"Get out!" I try to keep my voice down because people keep going past us on their way to the restroom. "Leave. Now."

"I will leave when the rest of my family is ready to go." He walks around me, then stops. "I didn't give her any photos, which means someone else is trying to end this." He smirks. "Enjoy your evening."

I return to the ballroom and see Rachel talking with one of her bridesmaids.

Henry comes up next to me and puts his hand around my shoulder. "Well, son, how's it feel to be married?"

He's already calling me 'son.' I don't mind it, but my father would be furious if he heard Henry call me that.

"It feels good," I tell him.

"You didn't seem nervous up there at the altar."

"No, not at all. I don't think Rachel was either."

He smiles. "I know you two will have many wonderful years together. I better get back to my *own* bride. I promised her a dance."

As he walks off, I look over to the side and see my father watching me. I notice his tense stance, his body straight and rigid. He must've seen me with Henry. Or maybe my father is angry because the wedding went on as planned. I'm sure he was hoping it wouldn't. It makes me wonder if he's the one who planted those photos.

I make my way over to him. He's standing a few feet from the bar, a drink in his hand.

"Father," I say, standing in front of him. This is the first time I've spoken to him all day. We passed each other several times, both at the church and here at the reception, but he wouldn't acknowledge me.

"What do you want?" he says.

"You can't even give me a simple congratulations?"

"Congratulations for what? Disgracing our family? Tarnishing our family name? Embarrassing your mother and me? Destroying your future? Yes, Pearce, congratulations on all those things. You did a fine job tearing apart this family and everything we've worked for over the course of several generations."

"I did no such thing. Marrying Rachel has not harmed you or Mother in any way. In fact, this wedding is bringing publicity to the Kensington name. *Good* publicity. I'm guessing it even brought in new business to Kensington Chemical. Am I correct?"

He takes a drink instead of answering, which means I was right.

I remember why I came over and say, "Did you give her those photos?"

"What photos?" His eyes are on someone behind me.

I look back and see one of the waitresses. A very pretty woman with large breasts and long blond hair. She's half my father's age.

I turn back to him. "Did you give those photos to Rachel or not? Answer me."

"I don't know what you're talking about," he says, his eyes still on the waitress. "Why the hell would I give her photos? Photos of what?"

So it wasn't my father. If he'd planted those photos, he would've given me a smug grin. He would've been proud of what he'd done and even bragged about it. So if it wasn't Leland and it wasn't my father, then who the hell left those photos?

CHAPTER TWENTY-FOUR

PEARCE

"You were seen going into a bar with her father last week," my father says.

"You were spying on me?"

"Cecil Roth saw you. He was on his way to a meeting, and when his driver stopped at a light, Cecil saw you going into a bar. He said it was one of those places with all the TVs."

"It was a sports bar, where people go to watch games, so yes, they have several TVs."

"This is what I'm talking about. You continue to embarrass our family without any concern for how your actions affect your mother and me. You know better than to be seen at a place like that. If you want to drink, you do so at the country club, or in one of the other private clubs we belong to. Or you go to a decent restaurant and sit at the bar and discuss business with a colleague or a client. You do not go to a low-class watering hole with some idiot farmer and watch men toss a ball around on a giant screen while eating God-knows-what and drinking beer." He huffs. "It's a disgrace. A complete and utter disgrace."

He takes another drink.

"There was nothing wrong with that bar. And there is nothing wrong with watching basketball. Just because you don't like it, doesn't mean it's bad."

"So is this the effect that man has had on you? Turning you into someone like him? A beer-drinking, backwoods hick?" He raised his voice and the bartender looks over at us. I catch him staring and he looks away.

"Henry is not a hick. He may not have money or a college degree, but he's a good man. He's honest and a hard worker and a good father."

My father narrows his eyes. "What are you saying, Pearce?"

"Nothing. It's just a general statement."

"That man is NOT your father and you are NEVER to call him that."

"He is my father-in-law and what I call him is none of your business."

He steps closer, his eyes fixed on mine. "You have ONE father and that is ME, and only me. You will not fraternize with that man. You will not allow him to teach you things. And you will most definitely not call him your father."

"You cannot dictate my relationship with him. Beth and Henry are my family now."

"They are NOT your family. You are a Kensington. Your mother and I are your family. No one else!"

"Well, given that you and Mother disowned me, that's no longer true, now is it?"

His face tightens, his anger escalating. "This conversation is over. Your mother and I have put in enough time here. We're leaving. And we do not want to hear from you or the girl ever again. As far as we're concerned, you no longer exist."

He turns and walks off toward his table. I follow him.

"What are you doing?" he asks.

"Saying goodbye to Mother."

He shakes his head and continues walking until he reaches the table. "Eleanor, we're leaving."

She was sipping her coffee but sets it down. "We're not leaving. I'm waiting for Cecil's wife to return from the powder room. We're discussing plans for the symphony fundraiser in May."

"You can discuss that with her later. Now get up. We're leaving."

266

"Holton. You have barely worked the room. Go talk to Cecil. He was looking for you earlier. He wanted to introduce you to someone who is interested in doing business with us."

My father storms off. He's only listening to her because she mentioned the company. She knows that's the only reason he'll stay here. There are a lot of important people in this room and my father should be talking to them rather than yelling at me.

"Mother, would you like to dance?" I told the wedding coordinators to skip the mother-son dance because I didn't think she'd do it, but it doesn't hurt to ask.

"Pearce, didn't you hear me? I'm waiting for Marienne to get back."

"I'm sure she won't mind if you dance with your son. It won't take long." I offer her my hand, but she doesn't take it. "Please, Mother. Just one dance."

She hesitates, but then scoots her chair back and takes my hand and we go over to the dance floor. The orchestra starts playing a waltz and I lead her around the floor alongside the guests, who all know the steps and move gracefully to the music. We've all been trained in ballroom dance, with instruction beginning at a young age.

"You look very nice tonight, Pearce."

"Thank you, Mother."

"The girl looks nice as well."

"I appreciate you saying that." I'd like my mother to use Rachel's name rather than always calling her 'the girl' but I don't want to push the issue. Not now. Not when my mother is actually being somewhat pleasant to me.

"So you're moving into the house soon?" she asks.

"Yes. Next week. I would love to have you come over sometime."

"You know that won't happen, Pearce."

"You don't have to bring Father. You can come over without him." I turn and step to the side as we approach the edge of the dance floor, leading her back to the center.

"How is your job going?" she asks. "Do you like working for Jack?"

"Yes. Very much so. Jack is an excellent boss."

"Good. I've always liked Jack."

She smiled when she said his name. Does she still have a crush on him? He certainly has one on her. He's told me that many times. I wonder if Martha knows. Jack and Martha aren't faithful to each other, so maybe Martha wouldn't care, although I find that hard to believe.

I spot my father out of the corner of my eye. He's talking to someone but he keeps glancing over here.

"I see him," my mother says, referring to my father.

"He'll be angry that we're dancing."

"I am quite aware of that, Pearce, but your father can go to hell."

I'm so surprised by her words that I stop for a beat, then continue with the dance.

"Are you fighting with Father?"

"You know we don't fight. We disagree."

It's true. They never raise their voices, as most people do during a fight. Instead, they give each other the silent treatment, or they make snide remarks, or they do something they know will irritate the other person but then deny they had any ill intentions. The passive-aggressive approach has always been a favorite of theirs.

"What happened?" I ask.

Her eyes go behind me to where he's standing. "Your father came home last night with lipstick on his collar. The associates know better than to leave evidence like that, so it had to have been his secretary. She started just last week. A tall blonde. Younger than you." She looks away from him. "It's completely inappropriate."

My mother knows he cheats. She acts like she accepts it, but it clearly upsets her. I don't think she loves my father, but she does have *some* feelings for him. If she didn't, this wouldn't bother her.

"You'd think he'd have enough decency to change his shirt before he came home."

She's never talked about this with me in the past and I don't know why she's doing it now. Is it because she's so angry that she can no longer hold it in? She can't tell her friends about it. They'd never talk about such things, even though they all have cheating husbands. I guess that's why she feels the need to tell her son.

"I've never denied him anything," she says. "I've never told him no. And yet he still goes outside the marriage."

I don't want to hear this. I don't even want to think about my parents having sex. In my mind, they did it once to have me and that was it.

"Mother, why don't we talk about—"

"I see Jack over there," she says, smiling. "Perhaps I'll see if he'd like to dance. Your father refused to dance with me but I know Jack would say yes."

"Mother, are you drunk?" I don't smell alcohol on her but she's acting out of character.

"Of course I'm not drunk." She abruptly stops dancing. "The song has ended. We should return to our seats."

We move off the dance floor. "Are you going to speak to me after today?"

"It's not likely," she says, smoothing her hair as we walk back to the table.

"Why? We just had an enjoyable dance."

"We danced because it's your wedding and we're expected to. But the fact remains that you married a woman no one approves of, thus disgracing the Kensington name."

"Now you sound like Father."

"Your father is correct in that regard. You never should have married that girl. You should've married Sydney St. James. She was a very suitable mate for you. You would've made a lovely couple."

"I married Rachel because I love her. She makes me happy. Don't you want me to be happy, Mother?"

We stop at her table and she sits down, not answering me.

"Mother, this silent treatment cannot continue. Maybe with Father, but not with you. We've always had a decent relationship and I don't want it to end. At least say that you'll talk to me if I call."

"I don't know, Pearce. We'll see."

One of her friends approaches the table. My mother ignores me and talks to the woman.

I turn and walk away. I need to get back to Rachel. But then Jack comes up to me, hanging his arm off my shoulder. "Pearce. Let me buy you a drink."

"The drinks are free, Jack."

He chuckles. "Yes. And I have taken advantage of that tonight." He drags me to the bar. "Scotch and water," he tells the bartender. He nudges me. "See that? I added water this time. You should be proud of me."

"I'm sure that's your tenth drink tonight and the other ones didn't have water."

He slaps me on the back. "You know me too well, Pearce." He takes his drink from the bar. "I danced with your wife earlier."

"Do you know where she is? I was looking for her."

"She's around here somewhere." He swigs his drink. "God, she's a beautiful woman. You're a lucky man. I bet you can't wait for the honeymoon. Did you tell her about it yet?"

"No. I'm keeping it a surprise."

"Well, enjoy it. Just relax and spend the week making love to that gorgeous woman." He finishes his drink. "Speaking of gorgeous women, did you see your mother tonight?" He smiles. "Damn, that woman gets me going. In all the right places, if you know what I mean."

"Jack, we've talked about this. Do not talk about my mother."

"Yeah, yeah." He waves his hand around. "I always forget how that bothers you."

I see Leland across the room. He's getting up to leave. My mind goes back to those photos.

"Jack, I need to ask you something." I move away from the bar. "Over here."

He comes over. "What is it?"

I lean down and lower my voice. "Someone left photos in Rachel's dressing room. They were in an envelope with her name on it."

"Photos of what?"

"Me, with one of the associates. They were taken the night of the banquet after our first day of meetings."

"You were with one of the associates?"

"No! She wanted to change clothes so I let her into the hotel room I was given, but someone took photos of us going into the room, making it look we were together. Luckily, I found the photos before Rachel did, but if she had, we wouldn't be here right now. She'd be filing divorce papers as we speak."

"So who did it?"

"I don't know. That's why I'm asking you. I thought it was Leland, or maybe my father, but I asked them and they both denied it."

"They were lying."

"No. They weren't. I could tell. Someone else did this, Jack, and I need to know who."

"Why? What difference does it make now? She never saw them and she never will."

"I'm sure this person has copies. They'll just send them to her again."

"I doubt that. The members don't want you involved in a messy divorce, especially after the success of this wedding. I've already heard from several members who have made business deals just within the past hour. If you got divorced right away, the wedding would look like a set-up. Just an event to get the right people in the room, which it was, but that's our little secret." He chuckles. "Howard!" Jack waves at a man as he passes us. "I have to talk to this guy," Jack says to me. "I'll see you later."

Jack could be right. The photos may be useless now. They were meant to stop the wedding but the plan didn't work. But I still want to know who took those photos and left them in Rachel's dressing room.

271

I make my way back through the ballroom and feel someone's arm wrap around mine. I look back and see Rachel.

"Excuse me, sir, but I'm looking for my very handsome husband. Have you seen him?"

I smile and pull her into me and give her a kiss. "I haven't seen him, but since he's not around, would you like to dance?"

"I would love to."

We dance, and keep dancing until her parents come over to say goodbye. They're flying home tomorrow. We're all staying overnight in this hotel, but they have an early flight so we won't see them in the morning.

After they leave, Royce stumbles over and says goodbye. He's been drunk for hours. He's also staying at the hotel and probably has a girl waiting in his room. Victoria was here earlier, but left hours ago. I'm sure she knows Royce will be spending the night with another woman. She knows he cheats and yet she looks the other way and pretends it isn't happening. I'm sure she'll do the same when she's his wife. Royce and Victoria are getting married in June and the wedding is going to be even larger and more extravagant than mine.

More people leave, and Rachel and I decide to go up to our suite on the top floor. It's the nicest room at the hotel.

"I guess this is our second honeymoon," Rachel says as I stand behind her and unzip her dress. "Or our third if you count Vegas."

"A night or two in a hotel room is not a honeymoon. Italy was the honeymoon." I kiss her neck as I slide the dress off her. "And I'm taking you back there next year."

She turns around and my eyes shift down to the lingerie she's wearing. A white lace bra and matching panties.

She smiles. "We're really going back there?"

"For our one year anniversary. Our *real* anniversary."

She steps out of the dress and puts her arms around my neck. "I can't wait to go back."

"I can't wait to get you out of this lingerie." I unhook her bra.

272

She laughs. "Pearce, you didn't even look at it. I bought it special for tonight."

"It's beautiful, but it's covering up areas of you that I would very much like to see." I kiss her. "And touch." I slip my hand under her white lace panties.

She closes her eyes and smiles. "I love you, Pearce."

"I love you too."

And then I show her how much. And I will show her several more times over the course of the night.

This has been a day of ups and downs, highs and lows, but it ended well.

Rachel is finally my wife. In the minds of the organization and the minds of the public. She's mine. And I am hers.

Forever.

CHAPTER TWENTY-FIVE

PEARCE

Rachel and I left for Grand Cayman the day after the wedding. She had no idea we were taking a trip. I wanted it to be a surprise. A second honeymoon. We'd talked about going somewhere, but then she decided she just wanted to stay home and spend time together in our new house. But we needed to do more than that. After such an extravagant wedding, we couldn't just go home. We still have the media watching us and they expected us to go on a honeymoon. So we went to Grand Cayman for a week.

We're back now, but I wish we'd stayed longer. We had our own private bungalow located right on the white sand beach with beautiful views all around us. It was very secluded. We spent all our time on the beach or in bed. Rachel had never been to the Caribbean. She loved it. The weather was perfect, the ocean water was clear and warm, and best of all, we didn't have anyone bothering us.

I liked being away. It was relaxing, and I needed to relax after the stress of finding those photos at the church. I still don't know who left those photos and I'm worried that whoever it was might do it again. I tried not to think about it when we were on vacation, but I couldn't stop my mind from going there. I considered every member, trying to figure out who did it, but it could've been anyone.

"Nice office." Royce walks into my office, glancing around at it. "Much better than the one your father gave you."

Royce and I are going to lunch. He invited me. He assumes we're friends. I'm not sure why. I never call him. He's always the one calling me and inviting me to do things with him. Even though we went to college together and he helped me elope, I don't consider Royce a friend. I'm always wary of him.

"Did you have a restaurant in mind for lunch?" I ask him as I stuff some paperwork into a folder.

"I was thinking we'd go to the gentlemen's club." He smiles. "An old married man like youself must be craving the sight of other women by now."

"I am not going to a strip club for lunch," I tell him. The club he's referring to is a private upscale club that I went to many times when I was single. The women there are all very beautiful, but I have no desire to look at them. I have my own beautiful woman at home and she's the only one I want to see.

He drops down into the chair across from me. "Come on, Pearce. You can't tell me you plan to be with just one woman for the rest of your life."

"That's exactly what I'm telling you." I write myself a note to call the head of marketing when I get back. He left me a message and I forgot to call him.

"You're too young to settle down. And you need other women in your life. Rachel can't meet all your needs. No woman can."

"She more than meets my needs." I get up and go around my desk and take my coat from the hook on the wall. "Are you ready?"

He stands up and walks over to me. "If she meets your needs, then what were you doing with Sophia?"

I shut my office door and lower my voice. "What are you talking about?"

He smiles. "Last December. After the first day of meetings, when we all went to the hotel for the banquet, you got together with Sophia."

"How do you know that?"

"One of the other associates told me. The blond chick that always wears that fake diamond ankle bracelet. I asked her if she'd seen you with anyone and she said you took Sophia's reservation card." He smiles. "So that's why you don't want me to be with her? Because you've claimed her as your own?"

I throw my coat on the chair. "I was NOT with Sophia that night."

His brows rise at my angry tone. "Relax, Pearce. I won't tell Rachel."

"I am telling you that nothing happened."

"Then why would you take her reservation card?"

"She was feeling ill and unable to perform her duties. I gave her my room so she could rest."

"Of course you did." He smiles and pats my shoulder. "Because we both know what a saint you are." He buttons his suit jacket and picks a piece of lint off it. "Isn't Sophia friends with Rachel?" He laughs a little. "That's rather dark and twisted of you, Pearce. Fucking the best friend? I'm sure Rachel wouldn't approve." He smirks.

The photos. Was Royce the one who took them? Did he put them in her dressing room?

I get in his face. "You fucking did it, didn't you?"

"What the hell?" He steps back, straightening his jacket. "What are you talking about?"

"The photos! You planted them in Rachel's dressing room at the church!"

"What photos?" Royce is a good liar, but right now I don't think he's lying. He looks confused, and not a fake confused, but like he really doesn't know what I'm referring to.

"Someone left photos in Rachel's dressing room before the wedding. They were photos of Sophia and me that night at the hotel. They showed us going into a room together."

"What did Rachel do when she saw the photos?"

"She didn't see them. I found them before she did."

"So someone was hoping she'd see them and call off the wedding," he confirms.

"Yes. But who would do that?"

"Your father," he says casually, sitting back down in the chair.

I remain standing. "No. It wasn't him. It was someone else. Who else would do it? Who was taking photos that night?"

"No one. They're not allowed to. There's no photography allowed at those events. They reminded everyone of that at the meeting."

"I don't remember hearing that. Regardless, someone broke the rules because photos were taken that night, at least of me. Who would do that?"

"Someone who doesn't care about breaking the rules." He sees my accusatory expression and says, "Pearce, I swear to you, it wasn't me. Yes, I break the rules but I didn't do it." He leans back in his chair, pausing to think. "The camera would've had to have been extremely small in order for this person to hide it. And he'd have to mount it on the wall or the ceiling so no one would see it." He slowly smiles. "I know who it was."

"Who?"

"Your boss. Maker of the world's best surveillance equipment."

"No," I say, quickly dismissing the idea. "Jack wouldn't do that. He'd never do that."

"He's the only one who has the equipment. It makes sense. He's your mentor. He's supposed to keep you in line. Make you follow the rules. And marrying Rachel was definitely against the rules." Royce shrugs. "Jack's just looking out for himself. You screwed up and made him look bad. With those photos, he was trying to get Rachel out of your life so he could earn back some respect from the other members."

It seems plausible, but it's not true. Jack wouldn't do that. He likes Rachel. He wants me to be with her. He wants me to be happy. He's told me that several times. He wouldn't betray me like this. I know he wouldn't.

Royce yawns. "Are we going to lunch or not?"

"No." I hold open my office door, suddenly feeling very agitated and anxious. "You need to leave. I have things to do."

He gets up from his chair. "Then I'm going to the strip club."

"Fine. Then go." I wait for him to leave.

"What are you going to do?" He laughs. "Kill Jack?"

"I don't know. But don't tell anyone about this."

He walks out of my office.

"Royce," I say, stopping him. "Do not tell anyone."

He smiles. "Your secret's safe with me."

I know that's a lie, but he has no reason to tell anyone. He only spills secrets when it benefits him and he has no use for this information. But he'll still use it against me. Royce loves keeping score, and if he does you a favor, you owe him. Helping me marry Rachel was a huge favor, and keeping quiet about these photos is another, so someday in the future I'll have to pay him back.

I hurry down to Jack's office, trying to remain calm. Royce's theory could be completely off-base and I don't want to blow up at Jack for something he may not have done. When I reach his office, he's standing at the door with two of his salesmen.

"Pearce, you're back," Jack says when he sees me. "That's it for today," he says to the two men. They walk off and Jack says, "How was the honeymoon?"

"Good. Very good." I go into his office. "Can I speak with you?"

He joins me in his office, eyeing me suspiciously. "What's wrong with you? You're acting strange. Did something happen?"

"The photos," I say quietly because the door is open. "Did you take those photos?"

"Pearce, why would you—"

"You're the only person who would have cameras small enough to hide. Did you do it, Jack? Tell me!"

He doesn't answer but I see his mind working, like he's trying to come up with an excuse. A reason why he did it. A lie.

Royce was right. It was Jack.

"How could you do that?" I yell it.

He closes his office door. "This is a place of business. Keep your goddamn voice down."

"Tell me why you did it," I say, my body burning up with a rage so intense I feel like I'm about to explode. "I trusted you,

Jack. And you went behind my back and betrayed me. I asked you about those photos and you lied to me!"

He stands right in front of me, his eyes on mine. "I TOLD you to keep your voice down. I will explain everything, but you need to shut the fuck up. I mean it." He's breathing hard and his eyes are dark. He holds out his hand. "Cell phone."

"What?"

"Give me your cell phone."

"I can't. We have to—"

"Give me your goddamn cell phone!"

I reach in my pocket and give it to him. He takes it, and his own phone, over to the safe in the wall. He punches the code in, opens the safe, and sets the phones inside.

Then he comes back and grabs my arm and shoves me toward the door. "Elevator! Now!"

I open the door and he goes past me and down the hall. He's walking fast and I hurry to catch up. When we reach the elevator, he waves his badge over the panel on the wall and the elevator opens. We get on, and as the doors close he waves his badge over another panel and we start descending. He didn't push any of the buttons for the lower level floors so I don't know where we're going, but the elevator continues its descent, down and down like it's never going to stop. Finally it does and the doors open to a long hallway made of concrete. He says nothing as I follow him down the hall, ending at a room. It's small and also made of concrete. Concrete walls. Concrete floors. And in the center is a table and four chairs.

"Sit down," he orders.

We both take a seat and I look around the empty room.

"Jack, where the hell are we?"

"Deep underground where no one can hear us. Tracking devices? Listening devices? None of them work down here."

"Why are we—"

"Just shut up and listen." He looks at me across the table. "I took the photos. And I hired a freelancer to plant them at the church."

I bolt up to standing. "Jack, why the—"

"I said SIT down!"

I want to kill him but I also want to hear his explanation, so I lower myself back down on the chair.

"I heard a rumor," he says. "There was a rumor that she was going to be killed."

I freeze, my body going rigid as every muscle tightens. Blood pumps hard in my chest, adrenaline flooding my system as I hear his words repeat in my head. *She was going to be killed.*

"No one actually told me," Jack says. "I saw a piece of paper. An order from the ruling council saying Rachel would be killed in May."

I take a deep breath. "Where did you see this piece of paper?"

"It was in a room. I was attending a sentencing, and during a break, I was walking down the hall and noticed a door was slightly open. There was a bar in the back of the room and I was dying for a drink, so I snuck in there to get one and saw a piece of paper on the floor, like someone dropped it. And that's when I saw the order."

"When did this happen?"

"Right before your wedding."

I slam my fist on the table. "Why the fuck didn't you tell me?"

"Because you can't control your damn temper. When you're angry, you make rash decisions that end up making things worse. If I'd told you, you would've gone on a rampage, getting yourself killed, and her as well. The order turned out to be a fake, but if it had been real, my plan would've saved you both."

"What plan? The photos?"

"Yes. Planting those photos would've saved Rachel. She wouldn't have gone through with the wedding. As for your real marriage, she would've ended it. And if she divorced you, she would've been safe."

"No." I shake my head. "You wouldn't do this, Jack. You wouldn't betray me like this."

"Betray you?" He slams his hand down in front of me. "Did you not fucking hear what I just said? If this had been true, I would've saved your ungrateful ass! I would've saved Rachel! And risked my own ass in the process."

"What do you mean if it had been true? How do you know it's not?"

"It was a test. The higher level members set me up. Given that I'm your mentor, they wanted to test whether I would betray the organization in order to save you from the heartache you would suffer if they killed Rachel. They made that fake order and planted it in that room right by the bar, knowing I would go in there to get a drink. They knew I would read it, then waited to see if I would try to save her, thus betraying the organization. And I took the bait. I tried to save her, not knowing what was really going on. Luckily, nobody found out what I'd done. Rachel never found those photos so the wedding went on as planned. Your wedding was my test. That was my chance to get Rachel to call it off, and to divorce you, thus saving her. But as far as Dunamis knows, I didn't interfere. I let you two get married, knowing what would happen in May and knowing it would destroy you."

"They were testing your loyalty. Making sure you were loyal to them and not me."

"Yes. But I didn't know that until after the wedding. As I was standing outside the church, watching you two get in the limo to go to the reception, I got a phone call. It was on my Dunamis phone. The man on the other end of the phone told me the truth. That there were no plans to harm her and that it was simply a test, and that I'd passed it. Then he gave me a warning."

"Which was what?"

"The same warning they give all of us. That we are never to interfere with their plans. Because if you do, you'll be punished and possibly killed. Thank God they didn't find out about those photos."

"I told my father about them," I say.

Jack bursts up from chair. "You what?"

"I didn't explain anything. I just made a comment about the photos to see how he'd react. He didn't know what I was talking about, so I didn't go into details."

"Did you tell anyone else?"

"Yes. Leland and Royce."

"Fuck!"

"They don't know it was you who took the photos. Well, Royce does, but he can't prove it and he has no reason to tell anyone."

"He doesn't need a reason. Royce does shit just to cause trouble. The kid's fucked in the head." He shakes his head. "Doesn't matter. I have plenty of things to blackmail him with. If he wants to be president someday, he'll keep his mouth shut about this. I'll have a talk with him later. And Leland's too stupid to figure out it was me."

"Why did you take those photos of me with Shelby?"

"I took photos of everyone that night, in case I need them someday. It's blackmail. Sometimes you need to save yourself or make someone be quiet, and the only way to do that is with blackmail."

"So you planned to blackmail me?"

He shrugs. "Maybe. If I needed to. I think you're a decent guy, Pearce, but when backed into a corner, you'd do anything. All of us would. It's how we're trained. Nobody's loyal. Nobody's your friend. Trust no one."

"How do you know Rachel won't be harmed? You can't trust what they say."

"No, but I have inside information that—" He narrows his eyes at me. "Don't you dare tell anyone this."

"I won't. Just continue."

"I recently discovered the identify of one of the men on the ruling council. He heard that your punishment has not yet been decided, but that it will not involve her."

"Leland said it *had* been decided. He told me that months ago."

"He said it had been *decided,* but not approved. And if it's not approved, then they could change their minds."

"They could still come after her."

"Yes, but I don't think they will." He pauses. "I've been feeding them information."

"So now you're spying on me? For THEM?"

"It's called being a double agent, and once again, I'm risking my ass for you so maybe you could show me some goddamn appreciation."

"I would if I trusted you, but you've made it clear that I shouldn't. So what did you tell them?"

"That having Rachel in your life has made you more focused and more committed to your assignments."

"That doesn't make sense."

"It makes perfect sense. Your constant fear that they might harm her is a way for them to keep you in line. Before Rachel came along, they had no way to incentivize you. If you refused an assignment, they couldn't threaten to hurt someone you loved because you loved no one. They couldn't threaten to kill you, because sadly, before meeting Rachel, I think you might've found death a welcome relief. So their threats would've meant nothing."

"That's great, Jack. Now they'll make me do even more horrific things, threatening to kill Rachel if I don't."

"No. The assignments are randomly assigned. When your number comes up, you get whatever assignment is next in line to be done."

"So going back to what you did. You're saying you tried to end my marriage to save Rachel."

"And you. But I had to focus my efforts on Rachel, because if I'd told you what was going on, you would've gone after them and you'd both be dead right now."

"Are you positive they aren't coming after her?"

"You can't be sure of anything when it comes to them. They do what they want. You know that."

I don't know if I should believe Jack's story, but that's an elaborate story to just make up. And faking a document? Testing someone's loyalty? It's exactly the type of the thing the organization would do.

"Even though they said Rachel is safe, I still feel like she's not," I tell Jack. "And I don't know how to protect her."

"Start with the basics. Get an alarm system. Put cameras around the house. Give her an alarm to keep on her keychain. You both need to get cell phones so she can always reach you. Tell her these things are necessary because of your money. People with money get robbed and attacked. That's a fact, so if you tell her that, she won't question it."

"That doesn't seem like enough. What else can I do?"

"Have a child with her."

"Why? What would that do?"

"It makes her more enmeshed with us. If she has your child, they're more likely to accept her. They wouldn't harm the mother of your child."

"That's not a reason to have a child."

"It's not the only reason but it's something to consider."

"You wanted her to divorce me just a week ago and now you want me to have a child with her?"

"I'm trying to save her, Pearce. I'm trying to save both of you. And sometimes you have to take drastic measures to do so. I didn't want to take her from you, but having her divorce you is better than having her dead, isn't it?"

"Yes. Of course it is."

"Now that we know that document wasn't real, you need to go on as if this never happened. Live your life with her. Have a child together."

I don't respond.

"Pearce." He pauses until I look at him. "I know you want children. At least one. Stop telling yourself you don't."

"I already told Rachel we would try. I just...I can't stop worrying about the child's future."

"Fuck the organization. You are NOT letting them deny you this. You already defeated them once by marrying Rachel, and you can do it again. You can get your child out of this. You have at least twenty years to figure out how."

"Even if I could, I still fear having a child. What if I become HIM? What if I have a child and become my father?"

He sits back. "You are not him. And don't ever assume that you will be."

I nod, but the worry is still there. I would hate myself if I treated my child the way I was treated. But what if I couldn't stop myself?

Jack motions to the door. "We need to get out of here. Our damn phones might ring and God forbid if we're not there to answer them." He rolls his eyes as he stands up.

I stop him before he reaches the door. "Jack, if you come across information like this again, I want to be told."

"You can't handle that kind of information." He continues to the door.

"Jack." I stand in front of him. "I'm not sure I believe what you told me just now."

"I don't expect you to," he says casually. "You should always question what people tell you. Always wonder if someone is telling the truth."

"But the order was fake, correct? You wouldn't lie about that, would you?"

"Of course not. I like Rachel. I don't want to see any harm come to her. You know how much I hate it when they hurt an innocent. Now let's get out of here."

We go upstairs and return to work. As I sit at my desk, I keep thinking about that test. Why would they test Jack? Do they think he's getting too close to me? Treating me more like a son than a mentor? It's true that he treats me that way, but nobody knows that except me. And my father. My father hates that Jack and I have this kind of relationship. So did my father suggest the test? But it came from the higher level members and my father is a regular member, like me, so he's not allowed to talk to them.

There was a reason for that test. They don't trust Jack. Or maybe it's me who shouldn't trust him. What if the order was real? Or what if that story Jack told me was just something he made up to explain why he left those photos for Rachel?

I really can't trust anyone but myself. I can't believe what anyone says. But I do believe that if they really wanted to harm Rachel, they would've done it by now. Why would they wait? There's no reason to.

That doesn't mean I won't take precautions when it comes to her safety. I pick up the phone and call a security company and tell them to install alarms and cameras at the house. Then I call Rachel and tell her it's being done, explaining that criminals often target people with money. As Jack predicted, she doesn't question it, and even seems relieved to have the extra security.

As for the other security measure he suggested? A child? I still have concerns about it, but I've given it a lot of thought and I know it's something I want. It might not happen, but I want to at least try.

Sometimes none of this seems real. Living in a normal house in a normal neighborhood. Being married to Rachel. Planning to have a child. For years I imagined a life like this but never thought I would have it. And now that I do, I will fight like hell to keep it.

CHAPTER TWENTY-SIX
The Following November

RACHEL

I don't know how the past year went by so quickly, but it did, and now Pearce and I have already celebrated our one year wedding anniversary. It's hard to believe that a year ago I was still in grad school and now I'm married and living in my first house.

I love this house. I loved it when I first saw it, but I love it even more now that Pearce and I are living here. And I love the neighborhood. Our neighbors are all very friendly. In the house next to ours is a family with two kids. We don't see them much because the kids are in so many activities that the family is rarely home.

Our neighbor on the other side is a retired school teacher. She's 78 and a widow. I stop by her house every day just to say hi and check on her. She always tells me how handsome Pearce is and then winks. She's funny, and a very sweet lady.

As for our house, the inside didn't need any work but the outside needed some sprucing up. Last spring, I trimmed all the bushes and planted flowers. I went a little overboard on the flowers, but once I started I couldn't stop. I put flowers around the front of the house, along the sidewalk that leads to the street, and in pots on the back patio. Then I had flower boxes installed on the windows and filled those with even more flowers. Pearce kept asking me if I was ever going to stop or if I had plans to tear up the whole yard and replace it with flowers. He was just kidding. He told me to plant as many as I'd like.

Last summer, Pearce and I spent most of our time in the back yard, swimming in the pool or just lounging on the patio. I bought Pearce a hammock and on the weekends I'd find him out napping on it in the afternoons.

Pearce doesn't go into the office on weekends anymore, like he did when we were dating. Since working for Jack, Pearce only works weekdays, and his schedule is a normal nine to five, sometimes ten to five. It's made such a huge difference in how he feels. Pearce used to be so tense all the time, but now he's relaxed, he sleeps through the night, and his mind isn't constantly thinking about work. And when he *is* at work, he likes being there. He's allowed to have input on things and make decisions, which he wasn't able to do when he was working for his controlling father.

As for his father, he's still not speaking to us. Neither is Eleanor. I feel bad for Pearce, but then I consider how they treated him and think maybe it's better if they don't talk. We see his parents when we go to parties or other events, but they don't acknowledge us. They'll walk right past us and not even say hello.

We got that reaction from a lot of people in the months that followed our wedding. We'd go to parties and people would ignore us, or at least me. But it's been getting better. The other women are finally talking to me. I wouldn't say they're friendly, but they're not ignoring me anymore. I think the reason for that is because I'm becoming more involved with various charitable organizations. I volunteer on several committees, and some of these women are on the same committees as me, so they have to be somewhat friendly in order for us to work together.

A lot of my volunteer work is with the Leukemia and Lymphoma Society. I work with the local chapter and I've helped plan several events. Being part of this group, I've met a lot of people who lost someone to leukemia and it's helped me get through some of my own unresolved grief over losing my sister.

Between the house and my volunteer work I've kept busy the past few months, but not too busy. I'm doing what the doctor said and keeping my stress level low. I went off the pill in July. The doctor said it could take several months to get pregnant, but it's now almost December and I'm still not pregnant. The doctor told me that's perfectly normal and not to panic, so I'm trying not to. I'm trying to just relax as we continue with the baby-making process, which is Pearce's favorite part of this. I love it too. We're still as attracted to each other as we were when we met. Pearce has continued to work out with his trainer at the gym and it shows. His muscles are even larger and more defined than last year. I love his body. He's my big, tall, muscular man and I can't seem to get enough of him.

Our anniversary was a little over a week ago. We went out for a nice dinner that night, but our real celebration is our trip. We're going back to Italy, only this time we're going to spend most of our time in that small village we liked so well. We decided not to go on our actual anniversary because it's so close to Thanksgiving and we wanted to spend the week of Thanksgiving with my parents, which we did. We arrived in Indiana last Monday and just got back today, which is Friday.

We're going back to Indiana for Christmas, since Pearce's parents want nothing to do with us. My parents are thrilled we'll be spending the holidays with them. Pearce gets along great with both my parents but especially my dad. They act like they're really father and son. We spent a week at my parents' house last summer and Pearce and my dad went golfing a few times and my dad took Pearce fishing, which Pearce had never done before.

"Did you pack a coat?" I ask Pearce. We're in the bedroom, packing our suitcases for Italy.

"I packed a light jacket," he says. "I don't want a big, bulky coat. It takes up too much space."

"Maybe I'll bring a lighter one too."

We leave for Italy on Sunday. I'm so excited about this trip. I've been looking forward to it for months. Two whole weeks of great food, friendly people, beautiful scenery, and lots of time with Pearce. It'll be another dream vacation.

Shelby's jealous. I talked to her last night. She really wants to go to Europe someday. Shelby's still dating Logan and they still live in different towns. She refuses to move in with him. I don't know why. They get along great and I know she loves him. She *did* move to a nicer apartment in a better part of town. I'm not sure how she affords it. She still only works two or three days a week.

The phone rings as I'm folding a t-shirt. I set the shirt down and go to the kitchen to get the phone.

"Hello?"

"Hi, honey. Are you all packed?" It's my mom.

"Almost. I just need to check the suitcase and make sure I have everything."

"What time do you leave on Sunday?"

"The flight leaves at noon, but we'll probably get to the airport at ten. What are you and Dad doing this weekend?"

"We might go see a movie. They say it might snow tonight, but I think it'll just be a dusting. Anyway, I don't want to take up your time. I know you need to pack. I just wanted to tell you to have a great trip."

"You're not calling tomorrow?"

"You'll be busy getting ready for the trip. I thought I'd just call tonight. When you're over there, be safe and keep your eye out for pick-pocketers."

I laugh. "Okay, Mom."

"I know you two will have a wonderful time. Oh, tell Pearce that Henry has something new to teach him when you two are back here for Christmas."

I smile at Pearce, who just walked by me. "What's Dad making him do now?"

She laughs. "He'll find out when he gets here. I love you, honey. Tell Pearce hi and that we love him."

"I will. Love you, Mom."

She hangs up and I put the phone down. I feel Pearce behind me, his arms around my waist. "Was that your mother?"

"Yes. She wanted to tell us to have a good trip." I turn to face him. "And she said to tell you hi and that they love you."

He smiles. "That was very nice of her to say."

He doesn't believe it. He thinks his own parents don't love him, so he can't imagine how mine could. It doesn't make sense to him.

"They do love you, Pearce. They're not just saying that."

He leans down and kisses me. The type of kiss that always leads to the bedroom.

"Pearce, I need to finish packing," I whisper as his lips trail down the side of my neck.

"You can finish tomorrow." His hands slide up my bare thighs and heat instantly fills my core. I took a shower earlier and threw on a t-shirt and panties and nothing else. Those panties are now on the floor and his hand is between my thighs, doing things that weaken my legs to the point that they can barely support me. I hold onto him, clasping the back of his neck as he kisses me.

"Bedroom," I whisper between kisses.

"Why not right here?" he whispers back.

"I don't want to do it in the kitchen."

"Let me finish what I started. Then we'll go."

"But..." My voice trails off as his hand continues its movements until he sends me over the edge, ripples of pleasure coursing through my body. They're still going when he lifts me up and takes me to the bedroom and lays me down on the bed. He shoves his jeans and boxers down, which was all he was wearing.

He lies over me and I gasp as he enters the already sensitive area, filling me completely.

"Pearce," I breathe out.

His mouth covers mine and he kisses me. Slow, sensual kisses that match the way he moves in and out of me, each powerful thrust intensifying the sensations building deep within my core. I crave the release as I feel it getting closer. He breaks from the kiss, both of us breathing hard as his movements get faster. And then I feel the tension finally let go, spiraling out of control, hitting every part of me and leaving my body reeling with the warm pleasurable aftereffects.

Pearce follows shortly after, then remains inside me, propped up on his forearms so all his weight isn't on me.

He's still out of breath as he kisses me. He looks into my eyes. "I love you."

"I love you too." I smile. "And I love what you do to me."

"Then I will do it again to you later tonight. And even more when we're in Italy."

"Mmm." I close my eyes, imagining it. "That sounds so good."

"Italy? Or the sex?"

I laugh. "Both. Although if the sex is like it was just now, then the sex."

"You liked that, huh?"

"I loved it. It was even better than normal."

"I didn't do anything differently."

"I guess it just gets better each time."

He rolls onto his back, taking me with him. "Let's just stay here all night."

"I need to finish packing for the trip."

"You're done. You don't need many clothes. I want you naked in bed the whole time." His hand goes behind my head and he brings my lips down to his and resumes those slow, sexy kisses.

He's right. I can finish packing tomorrow. I'd much rather be doing this.

CHAPTER TWENTY-SEVEN

PEARCE

Rachel and I slept in today. We were tired from having to get up so early for our flight back from Indiana yesterday. We spent Thanksgiving there. Beth made an excellent Thanksgiving dinner, even better than last year. And Henry and I had more father-son bonding time, watching football and playing darts at the local bar. My father would be furious if he knew I'd spent almost a week doing things with my father-in-law, which is ridiculous given that my father wants nothing to do with me.

I haven't spoken to my parents since the wedding. Rachel and I say hello to them when we see them at parties, but they pretend they don't know us. It's completely childish. If anything, *they're* the ones embarrassing our family when other people witness them snubbing us at parties.

People are finally starting to accept Rachel and me as a couple, but my parents refuse to, which makes them look bad. They need to move past this and stop acting like spoiled children who didn't get their way. I think my father is the one driving this behavior. Last October, I saw my mother at the symphony and she gave me a slight smile when she knew my father wasn't looking, so I think she's getting tired of this family feud. And I know she's upset that I didn't spend Thanksgiving with them and will not be there for Christmas.

Aside from my parents, the other parts of my life are going well. My job is interesting and challenging, yet it doesn't consume my life. My evenings and weekends are free to spend with Rachel.

I love our house and where we live. I have a great relationship with my in-laws. I have a great marriage. And I'm starting to feel better about the idea of being a father. I have to, because Rachel and I are now actively trying to have a baby. We've been trying for months. Nothing's happened yet, but the trying has definitely been enjoyable. We have sex all the time, sometimes several times a day.

Of course not everything in my life is good. I'm still a member of Dunamis. We've been having one meeting a month, but they've all been during the day so it's been easy to hide them from Rachel. The meetings have mostly been about our strategy for the next election. That's our focus right now, so my past three assignments have all been related to forging documents and covering up the bad behaviors of men we plan to get elected into office. I told Jack I was surprised I haven't been given a kill assignment for a while, but he said hardly anyone has. Everyone has been careful in their assignments so that innocents won't accidentally see or hear something they shouldn't. I hope it continues. That side of my life is much more tolerable when I'm not forced to harm people.

The other not-so-good part of my life is that I still have to participate in the high-society social scene. It's an obligation as both a member of Dunamis and as a Kensington, but it's not something I want to do. I used to go along with it without really thinking about it, but now I find it difficult. The formality. The fake smiles. Pretending to be interested in endless conversations with people you despise. I dread being around those people. Even though I'm just as wealthy as them, if not wealthier, I don't feel like I'm one of them anymore. I live such a different lifestyle now than I did a year ago that I'm starting to feel out of place at these events. Now I know how Rachel feels, having to go as an outsider. But she's much more comfortable with it now. She's come to know a lot of the women, so when we're at a party she has people to talk to other than just Martha, although she'd prefer to talk to Martha. Rachel and I are now good friends with Jack and Martha and we go out with them all the time. Even though they're much older than us, they've become our closest friends.

Overall, the past few months have been good. Almost normal. Like I'm living a regular life. I'm relieved and thrilled that things have gone so well, but I'm also worried about what lies ahead. I know bad things are coming. My life has been way too easy since the wedding last March. There's zero chance things will continue this way. I'm not trying to be negative. I'm simply being realistic.

I know I'll have to return to Kensington Chemical at some point. It could be in a few months or it could be years from now. I also get the feeling that my father is planning something. Some kind of revenge to get back at me. He's not someone who forgives and forgets.

As for Dunamis, I know I'm due for a bad assignment. I know a kill assignment will eventually come my way but I'm trying not to think about it. Then there's my punishment. Not knowing what it is, or when it will happen, causes me a great deal of stress. I try to hide it from Rachel, and just having her in my life helps take away some of that stress, but it's still there and it will never go away. Even when my punishment is over, I'll still have the stress of not being able to tell Rachel the truth about that side of my life. I'll always be burdened by that.

I hate lying to her. I don't want her knowing about that side of myself, but I also don't like that she doesn't. Because she'll never really know me until she knows that side is there. Jack keeps telling me that side isn't the real me. That it wouldn't be there if I wasn't a member of Dunamis. But I don't know if that's true. Maybe I really do have this dark side that would be there even if Dunamis didn't exist. Maybe I get that from my father.

"Pearce, do you want anything else?" Rachel takes my plate from the table. We just finished lunch.

"No, I'm done." I get up and clear the rest of the dishes and bring them to the sink where she's standing.

"We have ice cream if you want some for dessert."

I stand behind her and pull her into my chest. "I was thinking of a different kind of dessert."

"Again?" She turns her head so I can kiss her. "After last night, I thought you might be worn out."

"Not at all." I press up against her so she can feel what she does to me.

She smiles. "The dishes can wait. Let's go to the bedroom." She pushes me back, then races off to the bedroom.

I laugh. "I guess you're in a hurry."

The phone rings as I'm walking out of the kitchen.

"Let the answering machine get it," I hear her yell from the bedroom.

"I have to get it," I yell back. "It might be the travel agent calling about a change to our flight."

"Okay, but hurry up."

I smile. My wife loves sex as much as I do. God, I love her.

I pick up the phone. "Hello, this is Pearce."

"Mr. Kensington?" It's a man's voice but I don't recognize it.

"Yes, that's me."

"I have some bad news. This is the county sheriff's office in…" His words continue but I don't want to hear them. They're horrible, awful, devastating words. And they just keep coming.

"By the time the ambulance arrived it was too late," he says.

I collapse back against the kitchen wall, closing my eyes, rubbing my forehead, and trying to breathe.

This can't be happening. It can't be true.

"Pearce?" I hear Rachel's voice from the bedroom. "Who is it?"

Oh, God, I have to tell Rachel. I have to be the one to tell her this. How do I tell her this?

"I'll be right there," I yell back, covering the phone so the sheriff won't hear.

"I'm very sorry," he says. "I would've called Rachel myself, but I thought it would be better coming from you. We've never met, but Henry used to tell me all about you. He said you were the son he never had, but always wanted."

Tears flood my eyes and a few skim down my face.

"So you'll tell Rachel?" he asks.

"Yes." I'm so distraught I can barely get the word out.

"Tell her right away. Once the town finds out, she'll be getting a lot of calls and I want you to be the one to tell her."

"I will."

"Thank you. And again, please tell her I'm very sorry. They were good people. Taken far too soon." He pauses. "Call me if you need anything. Goodbye, Mr. Kensington."

I stand there with the phone in my hand, completely stunned. This is the first time I've ever lost people I truly cared about. Or loved. And I loved Beth and Henry. I really did. They were like parents to me. The type of parents I wish I'd had when I was growing up.

And now they're gone. I've never felt this kind of loss. It's deep. Gut-wrenching. Agonizing. And it's going to be a million times worse for Rachel.

I hear Rachel again. "Pearce, are you coming?"

"I'll be there in a second," I call back, trying to hide the emotion in my voice. I need to be strong for her. When I tell her this, she's going to break down, and she'll need me to be strong to help her get through it, not just now, but in the months ahead. Because she's going to be grieving for months over this. Maybe even longer.

I slowly walk to the bedroom. Rachel's lying in bed with the sheet covering her.

"I'm all ready for you," she says, a sexy smile on her face.

I look at her, not knowing what to say. How do you say something like this? What words do you use?

"Pearce." Her smile goes away and she sits up. "What's wrong?"

"There was an accident." Those weren't the words I meant to say. But I'm too shocked to think straight. I keep thinking this isn't real. There must be a mistake. But then I hear the sheriff's words in my head. *Slick roads...ditch...truck flipped.*

"What do you mean?" Rachel asks. "What accident?"

I remind myself to be strong. To pull myself together. I need to tell her. She needs to know.

297

I sit down next to her on the bed. "There was an accident. The roads were slick and..." I tell her the story, which is that it snowed last night in Rachel's hometown, and although it was just an inch of snow, it was enough to make the roads slick. This morning, Beth and Henry left to go to the grocery store but they never made it there. Instead they ended up in a ditch, their truck flipped upside down. It happened on a road that didn't get much traffic, and by the time they were found, it was too late. They were gone. The sheriff couldn't say for sure, but he assumed the truck hit a slick spot on the road, causing the accident. He said it was surprising because Henry was such a cautious driver and had driven in numerous snow and ice storms over the years and never had an accident. It raised suspicion in my mind when he said it, but then my grief overtook me and mind returned to the fact that they were gone.

"No, no, no." Rachel keeps saying the word, desperate for this not to be true. I hold her in my arms as she sobs uncontrollably. Then she shoves me back and runs to the bathroom.

"Rachel." I follow her in there and find her heaving into the toilet. I hold her hair back, then help her stand up and go to the sink. She rinses her mouth out, her whole body shaking, then she collapses in my arms and we sink down to the floor.

I hold her, rubbing her back. "I'm so sorry. I'm so very sorry."

She continues to sob, and my own tears return as I watch my wife suffer in agony over the news. Beth and Henry were the only family she had left. First she lost her sister, and now her parents are gone.

Rachel's face is against my chest and my tears drip down on her cheek. I was trying to be strong for her, trying to hide my tears, but she feels them and looks up at me.

She looks surprised that I'm crying, probably because she's never seen me do it. She reaches up and wipes the wetness from my cheek.

"I loved them too, Rachel."

She nods, her lip quivering, and then she breaks down again, sobbing as she clings to me.

The trip is canceled. Christmas is canceled. Our world has come to a screeching halt as we grieve this massive loss.

I knew bad things were coming. I just didn't know they would be this bad.

CHAPTER TWENTY-EIGHT
August 22nd

PEARCE

"Come on, sweetheart," I say as I stand next to her. "Just a little longer."

She squeezes my hand. "I can't do this anymore."

"You can do it. You're doing great. You're almost there."

I've been saying these same phrases over and over again for sixteen hours now. That's how long Rachel has been in labor. I knew labor could take a while but I hope it's not much longer. If it is, the doctor might do a C-section and Rachel doesn't want that. I don't either. That's major surgery and I'm already worried enough about a regular delivery and whatever complications could occur.

Rachel and I found out she was pregnant last January. The weeks leading up to that were spent dealing with the aftermath of the news we'd received late November. After we learned of Rachel's parents dying, we canceled our trip to Italy and flew to Indiana. We spent a couple weeks there, getting the funeral arranged, then dealing with the farm and the house and all their possessions.

The whole town pitched in to help. People assisted us with the funeral arrangements. They brought us food. They helped Rachel go through her parents' things and took care of boxing things up. Rachel's friends stopped by every day, missing work so they could check on her, offering to stay with her if she wanted to talk or just needed company. And everyone in town came to the funeral.

They had a meal ready afterward at the church, where people gathered and gave their condolences and support to Rachel.

I was in awe the entire two weeks as I watched this going on. I honestly didn't believe human beings were capable of being as kind and generous as the people in that town. When I used to hear that saying, 'he'd give you the shirt off his back' I thought it was a joke. Nobody would really do that. But the people in that tiny Indiana town would. They'd do anything to help their fellow neighbor.

Rachel inherited the farm and the house, but we decided not to sell it. It's the house she grew up in and she wasn't ready to let it go. So we found someone who wanted to rent it; a man from the next town over. He's in his thirties and married with two young children. He grew up farming with his father, so he'll be farming the land as well as living in the house. Rachel was happy that we found someone who would keep the farm going. We met the family and they seemed like good, hard-working people who would take excellent care of the house and the land.

When we got back to Connecticut, Rachel tried to get back to normal, but she couldn't. She was so sad and so depressed. Christmas was her family's favorite time of the year, so the fact that this happened during the holiday season made it even worse.

A few days before Christmas, she asked me to get a tree. I didn't think it was a good idea, but I got one anyway because she asked. I know nothing about Christmas trees so I ordered one and had it delivered, already decorated with lights. Rachel cried when she saw it, which I knew would happen. It just reminded her of her mom and all the years the two of them decorated the tree together. When I saw how upset it made her, I went to toss it out, but she stopped me, telling me her parents would be disappointed if she didn't have a tree at Christmas. So we kept the tree, but didn't put out any other decorations.

Christmas Day we stayed home and watched movies. Rachel didn't want presents, saying it would just remind her of opening presents with her parents, which is what we would've been doing if the accident hadn't happened. But I did give Rachel another ornament for the tree. A crystal angel that I bought months ago. Little did I know how much that angel would mean to her. She said it would always remind her of the year that God took her parents to be with her sister. Although that's not a good thing, Rachel, who always finds a silver lining, said that her parents and sister are reunited in heaven now, and that the ornament symbolizes the angel they sent down to watch over us now that they no longer can.

When Christmas was over I got rid of the tree, but before I could pack our two ornaments away, Rachel took the angel and set it on the fireplace mantel in the family room, saying she's going to leave it there year-round to watch over us. Then she took the other ornament I bought her the previous year, which she calls the Christmas star, and she had us make a wish. I don't know what Rachel wished for, but I wished for something good to happen to her that would take away her pain and make her feel happiness again.

My wish came true a week later, when we found out she was pregnant. The doctor said Rachel conceived at the end of November. Rachel and I both knew it was the night before her parents died.

Rachel was ecstatic when she learned of the pregnancy. She said it was a gift from God. He couldn't take her whole family and leave her with nothing, so he gave us this gift. The baby she so desperately wanted.

The pregnancy has been difficult, as the doctor predicted, but not as bad as we thought it would be. Rachel was on bed rest for the first four months, but was able to have limited activity up until the eighth month. Then she returned to bed rest, and now here we are. It's August 22nd and she's having the baby. Hopefully very soon.

We don't know if it's a boy or a girl. Rachel wanted it to be a surprise. But we already picked out names. Lauren Elizabeth if it's a girl, Elizabeth being Rachel's mother's name. And Garret Evans if it's a boy, Evans being Rachel's maiden name.

I'm hoping for a girl. If I have a daughter, she might have to marry one of the members someday, which is bad, but it's better than having to actually *be* a member, which would be the fate of my son. Unless the rules change. I still hold out hope that they will, and that my child's fate will be his or her own.

"She's ready," the doctor says to the nurses standing next to her. Then she looks up at Rachel. "Rachel, the baby's almost here so I'm going to need you to push when I tell you to, okay?"

She nods. "Yes."

"You can do this," I tell her. "You're almost done. And then we'll meet our baby."

She smiles weakly as she squeezes my hand. I've found that mentioning the baby helps Rachel more than anything else I tell her. She'll go through anything for this baby.

"Okay, Rachel," the doctor says, "it's time to push."

I remain at her side, and the pushing seems to go on forever. Then finally, the baby is born. We hear it crying.

"Boy or girl?" Rachel asks, smiling, as tears run down her cheeks.

Please be a girl. Please be a girl. I've been chanting this in my head all day.

"It's a boy." The doctor holds him up. "A healthy baby boy."

I should be happy right now, and I am, but I'm also terrified. A baby boy. Who will someday be a man and be forced to join Dunamis.

"Let me see him," Rachel says, reaching for him.

The nurse is wiping him off. I look back at Rachel and notice that her face is losing color and she's breathing faster.

I rub her arm. "Rachel? Are you okay?"

As the nurse goes to hand her the baby, Rachel passes out, her head and arms collapsing back.

The doctor bolts up and starts grabbing surgical tools and says something to the nurses but I couldn't hear what she said.

The nurse holding the baby races out of the room.

Machines are going off, beeping and making alarm sounds.

"What's happening?" I yell at the doctor, my eyes on Rachel who's still unconscious.

"Rachel." I brush the hair off her sweaty forehead. "Rachel, sweetheart, wake up."

"Get him out of here!" the doctor says. "Now!"

The nurse comes over to me and grabs my arm. "You need to leave. This is an emergency."

"No! I can't leave her!"

"Sir, you'll only make it worse. Let the doctor do her job."

The door to the room swings open and a whole team of doctors and nurses rushes in.

A male nurse replaces the female one and yanks harder on my arm. "Sir, you can't be in here."

There are people surrounding Rachel's bed and I can no longer see her. The male nurse practically drags me out of there, stopping when we reach the waiting room.

"What's happening?" I ask him. "No one will tell me anything."

"Your wife is losing a lot of blood. They're trying to stop the bleeding."

"And if they don't?"

"We'll give you an update as soon as we have one."

And then he takes off and goes back in the room.

What the hell just happened? The baby was born. Everything was fine. And then it all went to hell within seconds.

I walk down the hallway, nervously pacing the floor, my heart pounding, my hands fisted as anger overtakes me. How could they leave me out here without telling me anything? They need to tell me what's happening. Give me an update. Anything!

The nurse said Rachel is losing a lot of blood. People die from losing blood. What if she...? No. She can't die. She can't. She's my everything. My life. If *she* dies, *I* die. I was dead before I met her. She saved me. She brought me life. She can't die.

I'm not religious. I never pray. But right now I'm praying. I sit in a chair in the hall and close my eyes and think the words. *Please don't take her. You already took the rest of her family. Please don't take*

Rachel too. I'm begging you. Please don't take her from me. I am nothing without her. And I can't raise this child on my own. He needs her. He needs his mother. And I need her. Please don't take her from us.

I open my eyes when I hear a cart being wheeled down the hall. I can't see what's on it, but the person pushing it takes it into the room Rachel is in. I get up and hurry back down toward the room. I can't see inside it. I hear voices but I can't hear what they're saying.

I walk back to the waiting area. It's filled with new fathers and fathers-to-be, surrounded by their families. Parents, brothers, sisters, cousins. All those other men have people waiting with them. But not me. I have no one. Jack and Martha are on vacation in Europe. Rachel's parents are dead. And *my* parents want nothing to do with me. I'm sure they heard Rachel and I were having a baby. The way people gossip, my parents likely found out as soon as we started telling people. But they never called to say congratulations or to ask how Rachel was doing. We heard nothing. Not a single word.

So here I am. Alone. Waiting for news.

Rachel shouldn't be here. This hospital isn't good enough. She needs to be someplace better. She needs to be at the Clinic, where she'd be getting the best care in the world. But I can't take her there because she doesn't know it exists and she's not allowed to know. It's supposed to be a benefit of membership and yet I can't share that benefit with Rachel, which infuriates me. She's stuck getting care at a regular hospital with incompetent doctors and an idiotic staff that refuses to keep me informed of my wife's condition.

I continue to wait, staring at the door to the room she's in, not knowing if she's dead or alive.

Ten minutes later, Rachel's doctor walks out of the room.

I race over to her. "What is it? What happened? Is she okay?"

"She's stable."

I exhale the breath I feel like I've been holding since the moment I saw Rachel collapse.

"Let's talk privately," the doctor says.

305

I follow her down the hall to another room. It looks like a small private waiting room, with just a few chairs lined up on each side. Is this where they give people bad news? Is that why we're in here?

"What happened to her?" I ask the doctor.

She sits down and motions me to do the same. "Your wife was hemorrhaging, which is rare, but does occasionally happen after giving birth. But her case was more sudden and severe than I've seen in the past. Her blood pressure plummeted rapidly and became dangerously low."

"Low, meaning she could have died?"

"When the blood pressure drops that low, then yes, that can happen. But luckily, in her case, it didn't. We were able to get the bleeding under control and her blood pressure is returning to normal. We'll be keeping her here for a few days to make sure she's okay."

"Can I see her?"

"Not yet. The medical team is still in there with her and then we'll need to monitor her. You can wait in here if you'd like. I'll let you know when you can see her, but it may be a while." She gets up and opens the door, then looks back at me and smiles. "It looks like there's someone here to see you. Congratulations, Mr. Kensington."

She leaves and a nurse walks in, pushing a rolling bassinet. She sets the bassinet beside me and picks up a baby wrapped in a blue blanket with a blue cap on his head.

It suddenly hits me. That's MY baby! I haven't even seen him yet, other than a quick glance right after he was born.

The nurse holds him out to me. "He's all yours."

My arms remain at my sides. "Yes, um, I'm not quite sure how to hold him."

"You didn't go to the baby care classes?"

"I did, but that was a long time ago. And I held a doll, not a real baby."

She smiles. "Just cradle your arms, like I'm doing. And make sure to support his hand."

I nod. "Yes. I remember now. Support the head." I take him from her, feeling very nervous. He's so tiny. I'm afraid he'll slip right out of my arms.

"You're a natural," she says. "That's exactly how to hold him."

"He's very small."

"He's eight pounds, nine ounces. Twenty-one inches long. He's right within the normal range. He's a very healthy baby." She walks to the door. "I'll let you have some time with him. Congratulations, Mr. Kensington."

"Thank you."

The door closes and I'm left alone with this tiny infant. A baby boy. My son. Garret Evans Kensington.

I gaze down at his face and feel myself smiling. He's perfect. A beautiful, healthy baby boy.

His eyes are closed and he's softly breathing. What do I do? Should I talk to him?

I went to the baby classes with Rachel but I didn't really pay attention. The instructor went too fast and then people would interrupt her with questions, so I doubt I retained more than ten percent of whatever was said. And I didn't read the baby books. Rachel did. I didn't think I needed to read them. I assumed Rachel would just show me what to do.

But the doctor said Rachel will be in the hospital for days, which means I'll have to take the baby home. By myself! I can't do that! I can't care for a newborn by myself. And I can't hire a nanny. Doing so would upset Rachel. She's told me she doesn't want someone else taking care of our child. I don't either. I trust no one, and I definitely don't trust a stranger to take care of my infant. What if the person stole him, demanding money in exchange for his return? Or what if the nanny took him and disappeared? No. A nanny is not an option. I'll just have to figure this out myself.

I look down at the baby. "Hello, Garret. I'm your—" I stop when I see his eyes flutter open. He heard my voice and opened his eyes. I smile even wider, then hold him up and gently kiss his cheek. "I'm your father."

His eyes remain open. He has bright blue eyes that match his mother's. He's watching me, almost like he knows who I am. Rachel used to have me talk to her stomach. I thought it was silly, but perhaps he heard me. Maybe he recognizes my voice.

His eyes fall shut again, and as I hold him in my arms and look at him, I feel this overwhelming love. I wasn't sure how I'd feel when I saw him but I wasn't expecting this. This is overpowering. A love that fills my soul. A love that fuels an intense protectiveness. A commitment to give him the best life possible and to ensure that no harm ever comes to him.

"Garret." I run my finger over his cheek and his eyes open again. "I don't know how to be a father, but I promise you, I will do the very best that I can. And I will always protect you. I will never let them have you."

But what if I can't stop it? What if I can't get him out of the organization? What if the rules never change?

They have to change. I won't allow my son to become one of them. I won't allow him to know what I know, and see what I've seen. I won't let him develop a dark side and be forced to do bad things. I won't let him suffer the unending guilt that comes from taking a life. The guilt I feel every day.

No. I won't let that happen.

Garret is my son, but I will never let him become me.

www.ingramcontent.com/pod-product-compliance
Lightning Source LLC
Chambersburg PA
CBHW021314250626
47155CB00002B/528